THE AVON ROMANCE

Four years old and better than ever!

We're celebrating our fourth anniversary...and thanks to you, our loyal readers, "The Avon Romance" is stronger and more exciting than ever! You've been telling us what you're looking for in top-quality historical romance—and we've been delivering it, month after wonderful month.

Since 1982, Avon has been launching new writers of exceptional promise—writers to follow in the matchless tradition of such Avon superstars as Kathleen E. Woodiwiss, Johanna Lindsey, Shirlee Busbee and Laurie McBain. Distinguished by a ribbon motif on the front cover, these books were quickly discovered by romance readers everywhere and dubbed "the ribbon books."

Every month "The Avon Romance" has continued to deliver the best in historical romance. Sensual, fast-paced stories by new writers (and some favorite repeats like Linda Ladd!) guarantee reading *without* the predictable characters and plots of formula romances.

"The Avon Romance"—our promise of superior, unforgettable historical romance. Thanks for making us such a dazzling success!

Other Books in
THE AVON ROMANCE Series

BY LOVE ALONE *by Judith E. French*
MIDNIGHT DECEPTION *by Lindsey Hanks*
PASSION ROSE *by Mallory Burgess*
PASSION'S HONOR *by Diane Wicker Davis*
SHADOWS OF SPLENDOR *by Jillian Hunter*
SILVERSWEPT *by Linda Ladd*
WINDSTORM *by Katherine Sutcliffe*

Coming Soon

DEFY THE WIND *by Kate O'Donnell*
PROUD SURRENDER *by Karen Johns*

HEART'S POSSESSION

VERONICA GREGORY

AVON
PUBLISHERS OF BARD, CAMELOT, DISCUS AND FLARE BOOKS

AVON BOOKS
A division of
The Hearst Corporation
105 Madison Avenue
New York, New York 10016

Copyright © 1987 by Victoria Shakarjian
Published by arrangement with the author
Library of Congress Catalog Card Number: 86-92060
ISBN: 0-380-75330-8

First Avon Printing: July 1987

AVON TRADEMARK REG. U.S. PAT. OFF. AND IN OTHER COUNTRIES, MARCA
REGISTRADA. HECHO EN U.S.A.

Printed in the U.S.A.

K-R   10 9 8 7 6 5 4 3 2 1

Chapter 1

September, 1830

"Jessica! There you are. Your father and I have been looking all over for you."

Jessica noted the anxious expression on her mother's usually serene face and, picking up her pace, struggled with the unwieldy milk buckets, trying hard not to spill the creamy liquid. Chickens scurried out of her way, protesting loudly as she climbed the front steps, and she barely avoided tripping over one. She steeled herself against the urge to curse aloud. Her mother was constantly reprimanding her for using such language.

With her mother's assistance, and with great relief, she lowered the buckets to the porch. "Is something wrong? What can I do— Mama? Are you feeling all right?" Jessica was concerned by the distraught expression on her mother's face.

Sarah Blackwell collected herself and shook her head. She was a petite woman, but despite her fragile appearance, she had a strong will and commanded respect. Her long brown hair, coiled neatly about her head, matched the color of her eyes. Her beautiful smile transformed her plain face. Years of toiling on the farm had kept her figure

1

trim, and the inevitable apron was tied securely about her narrow waist. She looked affectionately up at her daughter and shook her head again, this time in exasperation.

"How many times must I remind you that you're a young lady now, Jess? You're eighteen years old today, but Lord help me, no one would guess that, seeing you in your present condition." She gestured at Jessica's usual dishabille. "Tsk, look at you—straw in your hair and clothes. No doubt you've been into some mischief with your brothers. Where are those six ruffians anyway? I haven't heard them about the house, and I'm always suspicious when it's so quiet."

Jessica shot her mother an innocent look and prayed Sarah wouldn't see the egg stains on the front of her blouse. She knew her mother would not be pleased to learn of the free-for-all in the hay barn initiated by her brothers.

"We weren't doing anything, just . . ." Jessica shrugged and flashed her mother a dazzling smile, her green eyes shining with suppressed laughter.

"Don't waste any of that charm on me, miss. I'm completely immune." Sarah smiled in spite of herself, then eyed her daughter's sunburned cheeks and sighed dramatically. "And you didn't wear your bonnet again. Whatever am I to do with you?"

"I'm sorry, Mama. I don't know what gets into me at times. Being a proper young lady can be so utterly dull."

"Proper young lady . . ." Sarah's eyes clouded once more, and her brows drew together thoughtfully. "How did you ever grow up so quickly, Dolly?" she asked rhetorically, using the pet name for her only daughter. "Anyway, get along into the house and wash up for breakfast. I'll see to the milk."

"But you said you were looking for me. Why?"

Sarah appeared uncomfortable for a moment. "We'll discuss it later, Jessica, I promise. Just get ready for breakfast."

Jessica walked around the side of the house to the kitchen door, wondering at her mother's strange behavior. Shrugging away her confusion, she carefully brushed as much hay and straw as she could out of her clothing and her tangled hair. She tiptoed into the house and up the narrow stairs to her room.

Being the only girl in the family did have some advantages. Although she had always wished for a sister as friend and confidante, it was a luxury indeed to have her own bedroom. Of late, her privacy was becoming more and more important to her, and although she loved her brothers dearly, their constant pranks and noisy chatter sometimes set her nerves on end.

She gratefully disrobed, happy to be rid of her itchy clothing. Her young figure, slim and toned, spoke of a life of hard work and exercise, and although she was rather tall for a woman, she had an abundance of natural grace. Her heart-shaped face was tinted golden by the sun, the high cheekbones unfashionably flushed with sunburn. Her soft pink lips seemed to be perpetually smiling.

She scrubbed her face with a damp cloth and dressed quickly. As always, she was starving. She pulled a brush through her gleaming auburn curls and hastily caught the thick mass in a ribbon.

"Jess!" Her father's voice thundered from below.

"Coming!" She fell back on her bed in a most unlady-like position as she struggled with her stockings and shoes. Then she was down the stairs in a flurry.

"Glad to see you could make it, lass," said Andrew Blackwell with a twinkle in his brown eyes. At forty-five he was still quite a handsome man, with a husky, solid build. Though his dark brown hair was was peppered with gray, it was as thick as ever. Jessica thought him most attractive.

She smiled a bit sheepishly and, taking her place next to her brother Robert, looked around the table with mock severity. Her brothers peered back at her innocently, and she smiled inwardly when she spied dried egg encrusting Robert's ear and straw adorning Timmy's unruly brown locks. Although the boys had ambushed her in the barn most unfairly, she had managed to leave her mark on them. She bent her head as her father said the blessing, and immediately upon its completion she leaned forward, fork in hand to spear the nearest biscuit.

Jessica caught her mother's fleeting look of concern at the boyish haste with which she attacked the food, and she sighed inwardly. If she had attempted to act the lady around her brothers, she surely would have starved to death by now.

The table was silent as everyone ate. Finally, as the meal drew to a close, Andy hesitantly voiced the question that was on everyone's mind. "When are we leaving for the harvest fair?"

The others looked hopefully at their father. Andrew leaned back in his chair and clasped his hands behind his neck, deliberately letting the tension mount.

"Your mother discovered earlier that you were all"—his look encompassed Jessica—"in the hay barn cavorting like a pack of excited mongrels." He shook his head. "Such behavior is no doubt the result of idle hands. Perhaps you need more chores to keep you occupied so that similar actions are not repeated." A groan went up from the table.

"Being the fair man I am, however, I will allow you all to repair the damage, and if you work quickly, and do a thorough job, we'll all be able to attend the fair."

At the cheer that arose, he laughed. Sarah and her husband shared a warm, amused glance. Jessica didn't miss their loving exchange and wondered idly if she would ever be as fortunate in love. Recently the subject seemed to take up a great deal of her thoughts. The gentry, of course, would have considered her almost a spinster at the age of eighteen, but Jessica was almost content to remain unaffected by men. After all, she had never even been kissed!

There *was* Beau Hastings, whom she had known all her life, but he was so shy, she was sure that by the time he summoned enough gumption to kiss her, she'd be an old maid. She often wondered how it would feel to be held by Beau. With his blond hair and light brown eyes, he was considered quite handsome, and Jessica knew most of the girls in the area fancied themselves in love with him. Her expression became dreamy as she imagined him holding her tenderly in his arms . . . She was prodded rudely out of her reverie by Robby's elbow digging into her ribs.

"You see, Alex," he explained to his twin brother, "there is life after death. Take Jess here for example." Her brothers cackled in glee at his teasing.

Jessica leveled a cool stare on her brother. "Since you seem so interested in the subject, how would you like to volunteer yourself"—she raised a fist in his face—"first-hand."

Her brothers snickered again, and Jessica began to help her mother clear the dishes from the table. Their energy refueled, the boys began to fidget on the bench. Joseph, the youngest at five years, leaned forward, and Edward started out of his dozing and turned to glare at Joey, who suddenly appeared fascinated with his plate.

Sarah glanced at her husband. "Andrew, would you please supervise the boys' work on the barn, and see that they do something properly for once?"

"Off you go, villains!" ordered Mr. Blackwell. Giving Sarah a martyred look, he followed the noisy crew out of the house.

The sun was climbing higher when Jessica and her mother finished the dishes and moved into the worn but comfortable parlor to wait for the boys. Jessica reached into her sewing bag with a grimace of distaste she carefully hid from her mother, and picked up the latest piece of botched embroidery on which she was working. She detested sewing, but for some reason her mother had always stressed its importance if she were to become a gracious lady. Actually, Jessica realized, her mother had been very careful to see that she was taught all of the feminine arts. She'd been given lessons on all sorts of subjects: dancing, social graces, feminine comportment, and even table manners. She had also been the recipient of a rather fancy education. While her brothers attended the local schoolhouse, she had a private tutor. Yet with all of this polishing, and to her mother's constant dismay, Jessica had staunchly remained unaffected. Only the threat of sending her to finishing school in Richmond had encouraged her to apply herself more conscientiously to her feminine curriculum.

She knew how cruel and uppity the gentry could be, and she had no desire to be subjected to such ridicule for two years of school. She enjoyed her scholastic studies much more, and on the rare occasions when she had gone to Williamsburg, she had gazed with undisguised envy at the young men who attended the College of William and Mary. Unfortunately, her efforts to better herself had only served to alienate her from the other farmers' daughters in the area. Sometimes she felt that she was balanced between two worlds, neither of which would accept her. Yet her brothers found her lessons in decorum a constant source of delight, and they often postured in front of her like some noble suitors come to woo the grand "Lady Jessica," as they had dubbed her.

Lady Jessica, indeed, she thought, looking down at her sloppy sewing. Why didn't she enjoy the kinds of activities suited for young women? She found them so confining, pointless, and dull. She sighed deeply and rose to sit next to her mother on the faded sofa.

"Mama," she began hesitantly, "I've been thinking a great deal about certain things of late, and . . . well"—she sighed again—"what is it like to be in love? I can tell when you look at Papa that you love him very much. How does it feel?"

Sarah put aside the sweater she was knitting and faced her daughter. "I was wondering when you would ask me that question. It seems like such a short time ago that you were a wee babe, unconcerned with such matters. Such a quiet little baby you were, with such big green eyes." Her own eyes grew misty with memories. "And now look at you, grown into a lovely young woman. Your father and I are very proud of you, Jess. But to answer your question, love is a dangerous emotion, daughter. At the same time, it's the most wondrous feeling of all. Because of it, there is laughter and life, and the world is filled with wonderful color and richness. Without it, there is no joy, no laughter, no meaning, merely existence."

Jessica watched raptly as her mother's face took on a radiant glow, and her voice softened to a whisper, as if she were sharing a great and magical secret. "Love can make your life a fantasy, when you find your own true beloved, or a wretched nightmare, when the love you feel for another is not returned. Sometimes you become so befuddled it's difficult to tell whether you're gloriously happy or utterly miserable, yet you wouldn't exchange your sorry state for anything on earth. He is your life, and you are his. If it is not mutual, it means naught."

"But, Mama, how do you know when you're in love?"

"Ah, Dolly, if you ask that question, then you're surely not in love," she answered quietly. "You know. You just know. It's like sweet music singing inside of you, getting stronger all the time. You'll know, Dolly."

"Do you think I'll ever fall in love? Do you think a man will ever fall in love with me? Despite all of my efforts, I know I'm still rather unpolished."

"You're a beautiful young lady, my Jess, inside and out. Someday I suspect you'll be quite a woman, but you must believe in yourself above all others. Confidence—that's the important ingredient which you lack, and I've a feeling that it will be very hard-won when it comes to you. You're so very eager to please, wanting everyone to like you, afraid that if they don't like you there must be something wrong with you. Can you understand what I'm saying?''

"I'm not sure I understand everything, but I know one thing—I love you. You're probably the finest mother a girl could ever hope for.''

Jessica brushed a soft kiss on her mother's cheek, and Sarah gathered her daughter in her arms, holding her tightly and smoothing her auburn tresses.

"You don't know how very much that means to me, Dolly.''

Later that morning, Jessica grabbed a light wool shawl and flew down the stairs, determined not to be the last one ready to go to the fair. She was surprised to find the huge kitchen empty, except for her mother and father seated together, drinking from steaming mugs of coffee. Usually they were busy with chores at this hour and the kitchen swarmed with activity. They looked up at her expectantly when she came to a short stop, her skirts flying.

"Is something wrong?'' she asked hesitantly.

"Nothing amiss, Dolly.'' Her mother moved over on the bench so that Jessica could sit between her parents. "Come sit here. Your father and I have something we must discuss with you. We've put it off much too long as it is.''

Puzzled by their unusual behavior, Jessica sat down hesitantly. She could have sworn her parents looked nervous. Her father placed a tender kiss on her cheek, while her mother reached for her hand.

"Today is your eighteenth birthday, Jessica,'' her father began. "First, let me wish you God's blessings and present you with a gift. Your mother and I have been saving it for you.''

He reached into his pocket and pulled out a ring. Sarah lifted Jessica's hand, and Andrew slipped the ring on her index finger. Her brows creasing, Jessica bent her head to take a closer look at this mysterious gift. The ring was made of gold with some sort of crest flanked by two small emeralds. It was undoubtedly a man's ring.

''Does this belong to you, Papa?''

Andrew drew in a long breath, but when he would have spoken, there was a loud crash, followed by an even louder ''Shush!'' The three people sitting at the kitchen table started to laugh. Andrew got up from the table and opened the side door. Five guilty faces greeted him, the shards of a broken pitcher at their feet.

''All right boys, what have you gotten into now?''

''Why, nothing at all, Pa. We were just . . . ah . . .''

''You were just eavesdropping on our conversation, and you boys were specifically told to leave your mother, Jess, and me some privacy. And where's Joseph? I can hardly believe he was left out of these shenanigans.''

Timothy reached behind a nearby table and, grabbing an available ear, drew the reluctant Joseph into view. He stood with the others, eyes downcast as Andrew sermonized on the value of privacy and respect for parents' wishes. He ended on a stirring note, mentioning the price of the pitcher they had overturned and the good judgment he was sure they would use when selecting a replacement at the fair. The boys grumbled loudly at this last comment, having already planned how they would spend the few pennies they had each saved. Joey's head hung even lower as his brothers all fixed resentful gazes in his direction.

Jessica hardly heard her father's diatribe. Her attention was focused on the strange gift her parents had given her. She was burning with curiosity to learn where it had come from, but when she looked up to ask her mother, she found that Sarah had moved away to wash the coffee mugs. She shrugged, supposing that the secret would have to keep until her parents were ready to talk to her again. Her father returned to the kitchen, an almost relieved expression on his face.

"I guess we'll have to finish our conversation after the fair. It's a beautiful day, and we don't want to waste it, do we? I'll just hitch up the mules." He pressed a kiss on Jessica's forehead and left the house.

Jessica followed her father outside and watched him hitching the mules up to the modest open landau that was too small to easily accommodate the large family. By the time her brothers came bounding out of the house, she was comfortably seated in the corner. Her mother followed more sedately, and the boys waited politely while she seated herself next to her daughter before squeezing in themselves.

As they started off, Jessica's thoughts turned inward again. What was love truly about? Did it make separating yourself from your beloved impossible? She wasn't sure she would like that feeling. It would certainly put her in a most vulnerable position.

She tried to settle back more comfortably against the frayed, worn seat of the landau, but it was impossible. What was wrong with her today? She had felt fine this morning, but now she was very impatient and nervous. Maybe it was because she was eighteen and unmarried. Most girls her age were already engaged, or married, or even mothers. But not her. Not Jessica Elizabeth Blackwell.

Actually, she realized, she didn't want to get married quite yet. She couldn't see marrying a man simply because it was time for her to settle down and have a family. She wanted to fall in love. Since her parents' marriage was obviously a love match, they were completely opposed to arranged marriages and had not pressured her into finding a sweetheart. She stared dully at the recently harvested fields as they rode by, wondering again at her restless mood.

But when they arrived at the fair, Jessica's spirits rose. After all, it was her birthday!

A kind of controlled pandemonium greeted them. Vendors had set up stalls, and merchants tried to lure customers to purchase their wares. Booths containing games of skill were lined up under the leafy awning of the black walnut trees. Farmers, their wives, and children were eagerly bustling about. Various spicy aromas rose into the shimmering, dusty haze.

As Jessica and her mother strolled amid the confusion, Joey came running up to her, his face already coated with dirt and sweat. "C'mon, Jessie, let's go to the game booths. You've got the best aim of all of us. Maybe you can win a prize."

He grabbed her arm and started to drag her away. Jessica cast a helpless look at her mother.

"Go ahead, Dolly," said Sarah, engrossed in the selection of fabric. "Don't worry about me, I've enough to keep me busy for a while."

Jessica let herself be whisked away to the entertainment booths, slowing only when several young ladies frowned in disapproval of her haste. Joey bounded off with the exuberance of a typical five-year-old.

Jessica glanced about, searching for the blond hair of Beau Hastings, and spotted him at the same game stalls that Joey ran to. She took a deep breath and, gathering as much dignity as she could muster, strolled casually over. She and Joey watched Beau attempt to throw brightly colored balls through wooden rings.

"Ah, you're better than him," Joey piped up.

Having thrown the last ball, Beau turned to see Jessica standing there demurely, wishing her brother to silence or to the nearest privy. Beau's eyes lit up with pleasure. His friends, however, stared in disbelief.

"Ah, she's just a girl," said one, "and everybody knows girls can't throw straight."

Beau ignored his friend. "Would you like to try, Jessica?"

"Well, I . . ." Jessica knew it wasn't proper for young ladies to participate in this kind of competition.

"Oh, c'mon, Jessie." Joey pressed a coin into her hand.

"Yes," said Beau. "Please try."

Jessica sighed deeply, knowing that for one more day she would have to put off being a proper lady. She almost groaned aloud when she saw the rest of her brothers making their way toward her. She staunchly ignored the crowd gathering behind her. Beau received five brightly colored balls from the boothkeeper and smiled encouragingly at Jessica. She grinned sheepishly and, standing back at the rough line drawn in the dirt, studied her target. Out of the corner of her eye, she noticed money changing hands. So, they were betting on this little game.

Beau handed her the first ball. Drawing back her arm, she let the ball loose, and it flew threw the ring with a satisfying *whoosh*. Her brothers and a few members of the crowd let out a cheer.

Beau handed her the second ball. Concentrating on the hoop, she threw it straight into the target hole. The third followed the second, and more money changed hands. By the time the fifth ball was soundly on its way into the hoop, her brothers were beside themselves cheering her victory and their increased wealth.

"Congratulations," Beau said sincerely. He handed her the lacy parasol she had won and reached out to shake her hand. "Where did you get such a keen aim?"

She was overwhelmed by his proximity and the touch of his warm, farm-callused hand holding hers. Could this possibly be the same naughty little boy who, along with her brothers, had always played pranks on her?

"I'm fairly accurate with my rifle. Perhaps—" Jessica was rudely interrupted by the loud voice of one of Beau's friends.

"C'mon Beau, let's find something to eat."

Jessica saw the flash of irritation in Beau's eyes as he reluctantly dropped her hand and moved away. "It was nice talking to you, Jessica." He stood undecided before her for several seconds, shifting his weight from one foot to the other. Finally, after taking a deep breath, he said, "Do you think your folks would mind too much if I came calling on you sometime?"

Jessica breathed in deeply herself. "No, I don't think they'd mind at all." She continued more softly, "Neither would I." Gazing up into his honest, youthful face, she felt her heart turn over.

"Beau, hurry up!"

Frowning, he pressed Jessica's hand warmly and turned away to follow his friends into the crowd. Jessica's gaze followed his retreating back. As her eyes swept over the crowd, she caught the stare of a large, hulking fellow with red hair, wearing a leather jerkin. His gaze was definitely not pleasant, and Jessica, disturbed, swung her eyes away from him—right into the stare of a well-dressed, elderly gentleman standing not more than ten feet away.

He was tall and held himself with assurance, as if he was very confident of himself and his lot in life. His thick dark brown hair was liberally peppered with gray, and his face was sternly lined with age. Yet his was a striking face, made more so by the bright green eyes that so thoroughly scrutinized her. He was very aristocratic and, Jessica thought fleetingly, very out of place at this common gathering. Something tugged at the back of her mind, for although she was positive she had never before seen the man, he somehow seemed familiar.

He continued to gape rudely, as if seeing a ghost, and she was thoroughly uncomfortable under his unrelenting stare. She fingered the new ring on her index finger, hoping the man would go away, but to her dismay, she saw him coming toward her, his eyes now on the strange ring on her finger. Jessica looked about for her brothers and saw them hurrying toward her, grinning broadly.

"Oh, Lady Jessica," crooned Edward, grabbing Andy's hand and getting down on bended knee, "however did you get such a keen aim, for I declare you have shot an arrow straight into my heart."

Andy slapped away Edward's hand. Putting his hand to his chest over his heart, he turned away coyly and patted his heart in a quick tattoo. "Oh, Beau, you bold devil you . . ."

Jessica stifled an urge to laugh and quickly brought the closed parasol down over Edward's head. "I dub thee Sir Jackass. Now please stand up and pretend that you have a brain. I can hardly wait until you are old enough to—"

Joey interrupted her, tugging hard on her skirts, and she saw to her relief that the elderly gentleman had disappeared into the crowd.

"You were great!" Joey was saying. "Now we have enough money to buy Ma a new pitcher, and some left over besides." He let out a loud whoop.

"You're all very welcome, and now if you'll excuse me, gentlemen, I'm off to find our mother, and don't worry that I'll be telling her that you all were gambling." The boys looked guilty for only a second, but she smiled brightly as she opened the parasol and strolled away leisurely, head held high, past a group of young women.

"My, my if it isn't Miss High and Mighty," one of them smirked to her friends.

Jessica recognized Priscilla Carswell's voice and realized belatedly that Priscilla was interested in Beau Hastings as well. Jessica lifted her chin a notch higher and kept walking. The last thing she wanted was to argue with that sharp-tongued vixen. She heard the girls tittering behind her as she stalked away.

It shouldn't bother me, she thought to herself but she had never had a real girl friend, and sometimes she'd so wanted to have someone to confide in. She looked over her shoulder at the giggling group and, not for the first time, felt completely shut out. She took a deep breath and turned around quickly—only to walk right into the older gentleman who had scrutinized her so thoroughly earlier.

"I say, I'm terribly sorry, young lady. Are you all right?" He grasped her hands lightly to steady her.

"Yes . . . yes sir, I'm fine, thank you. I'm afraid it is I who should apologize. I've been wandering in a daze."

"No need, my dear." He let go of her hands and glanced again at the ring on her finger. For a second she thought he might inquire about it, but instead he just stared at her with a half smile on his face, his green eyes bright and inquisitive.

"I should hope, however, that a lovely woman such as yourself isn't wandering about unattended. Surely your husband wouldn't approve."

"Husband? Me?" Caught off guard, Jessica blurted, "I'm not married."

Her remark seemed to delight the older gentleman, for his smile fairly beamed. "Not married, you say? Splendid." His voice lowered to a whisper, and Jessica strained to catch his words. "Then there's still a chance for the Montagus, and Nicholas should be delighted."

Jessica quirked a puzzled frown at the man. He certainly looked as though he was in possession of all his faculties, but what he said hardly made any sense at all.

"Sir, who—?"

"Never mind, young lady. We'll meet again, I'm sure." He glanced at her ring once more and, tipping his hat, strode briskly away.

Jessica followed the man with her eyes until he disappeared into the milling crowd. She looked down at the ring on her finger with a confused expression, consumed with curiosity. Why was that man so interested in it? Had he gone out of his way to bump into her? And who in the world were the Montagus and this Nicholas, and why would he be delighted with her? She craned her neck, attempting to locate the strange man, but could find no trace of him. She did see her mother, however, and made her way toward her.

"Jess, what do you think of this fabric for curtains in the parlor? Jess, are you listening?" Sarah saw the troubled look on her daughter's face. "What's the bother, child?"

"Something extraordinary just happened." While Jessica recounted the incident to her mother, an expression of alarm, which she was quick to conceal, flashed across Sarah's face.

"And you say he took particular interest in your ring?"

"Yes, that was the really strange part about it. I'm sure he made a point to look at it, and I thought he might ask me about it. What does it mean? I think you know."

"Let us forget the incident for now, Dolly. You don't see the gentleman about anywhere, and we've still got a good part of the day ahead of us. Why not enjoy the fair? Tonight we'll explain everything."

"But, Mama—" Jessica started to protest.

"No, Jessica, I'll not hear another word on the subject. Now, what do you think of this fabric?"

It was definitely a tired group that slowly made its way home from the fair at dusk. The swaying motion of the landau had lulled her brothers to sleep, but Jessica was fully alert and anxious to learn the history behind her new ring. She glanced at her mother. For the umpteenth time that day she had the impression that Sarah was nervous. Actually, she realized that both her parents had been acting rather strangely for the last month or so.

The mules finally turned into the short drive that led to the farmhouse, and Jessica was surprised to see a sleek covered phaeton in front of the gate, its driver holding the reins of a matched pair of magnificent bays. Someone was standing near the head of one of the horses, absently stroking the animal's well-muscled neck. She strained to see who it might be.

It seemed to Jessica that it took an inordinately long time for the mules to near the gate, and she kept willing the gentleman to show his face. Finally he turned, and Jessica gasped as she recognized the gentleman who had spoken to her at the fair.

Looking down at the ring on her finger, she had a strange feeling that the time for answers had finally come.

Chapter 2

Nicholas Carlyle leaned over his horse's neck and let the animal have its head. His handsome face, framed by thick black hair, held a determined expression as he concentrated on riding the spirited liver-chestnut stallion. He threw back his head and let out a burst of exuberant laughter. He didn't have a care in the world as he raced the huge stallion down the well-worn trail behind his plantation. But just then a white-tailed deer, startled by the pounding hooves, darted out into the trail, and the stallion, caught unawares, shied as he saw the creature, his forelegs pawing the air in fright.

Nicholas quickly drew in the reins and clamped his thighs around the heaving horse as he fought to stay in the saddle.

"Easy boy, easy Lancelot. Nothing to worry about. That's the lad."

Nicholas continued to talk softly to the high-strung thoroughbred until the animal's trembling ceased. He slapped him affectionately on the neck and continued his ride at a more sedate pace, having enjoyed the challenge of the incident immensely. Lancelot pranced a few yards and, at a sharp command from his master, gave out a resigned snort and settled into a walk.

The man on his back felt equally restive. Ten years ago he had left England and come to America to earn his fortune. Ten years of toiling to create a home had passed, ten years of taking the ramshackle plantation and turning it into a showplace. Ten years of practically signing himself into bondage to the estate. What did he truly have to show for his efforts? A fine home? Yes. Wealth and prosperity? Yes. He should have been content, but recently he had been feeling restless and bored with the pointless social engagements, the conservative life-styles of the elite planter class, the tedium of bookkeeping, the everyday routine.

There was no more challenge in his life, no excitement, but his discontent went deeper than that, and he'd be damned if he knew what was really troubling him.

Ten years of striving and struggling had changed him, turned him into a driven man, accustomed to getting his way. Gone were the days of his carefree youth of gambling, drinking, and wenching. He thought back on those days with a kind of sadness for the devil-may-care attitude that he had lost somewhere between London and America. At thirty and two years, he was still a young man, yet he felt much older than his contemporaries in London.

Yes, London, that was what had brought about his low humor. It had been a mistake to return to England on a recent business trip. It was the first time he had been back since leaving so long ago, and he had been anxious to personally find more lucrative markets for the cotton and other products he produced. The business end of his visit had been very successful, but the personal side of it had left him feeling disquieted.

Nothing and no one seemed to have changed but him, and after only two days in the company of friends whom ten years ago he had held in the highest esteem, he had been completely bored and wished only to return home, for his friends still gambled and drank as though their lives would continue in that happy fashion until the end of their days.

Much to his chagrin, he had discovered that home was no longer England. During the long, hard years of back-breaking toil, he had held on to his memories of England as a talisman of strength, vowing to return one day and buy back his family estate. America had charmed him, however—the rugged vitality of its various peoples, the freedom, the enthusiasm; and now he willingly let go of his dream, realizing its usefulness was at an end. He thought of his friends almost wistfully now, envying their carefree lives. The last ten years had taught him harsh lessons about life, about surviving droughts, monsoon rains, poor cotton harvests, and financial difficulties. But he had learned, and learned well.

Turning away from his mates, he had settled on another purpose in going back to England: the hope of finding a wife. There he had been disappointed as well. It seemed to him that the women were either milksop virgins, with a giggle for every occasion, or calculating adventuresses interested only in his bed or his money. He had despaired of ever finding a suitable wife to run his home and bear his children, and at this point he didn't bloody well care if he ever married at all.

"Women," he mused aloud. Was there a decent girl to be found anywhere? If there was, a little voice in his mind reminded him, she'd be well advised to stay away from him.

True, in his most honest moments he had to admit he wasn't an easy fellow to get to know. He had many friends, but no one really knew Nicholas Alexander Carlyle, no one except perhaps Titus. He wasn't even sure he knew what motivated his own actions on many occasions. He thought of how many of his acquaintances in Charleston would be surprised at his inner musings. To them he had always exhibited a self-confident and controlled demeanor. Perhaps that was why women considered him so unapproachable. He preferred it that way, liking to pursue rather than be pursued. And he was very selective.

The beautiful women with whom he had associated in the past had been vain, foolish creatures empty of compassion. He knew that their interest in him was purely mercenary; hence, he'd felt no remorse when the affairs had ended. Their passing left no emotional scars, only a growing cold void, a sense of unnamed loss, a recognition that something was missing.

Nicholas shook his head to clear his thoughts. Damn it, he knew very well what was missing from his life, but he preferred not to think of it. It was a fairy tale, a ghost from his past, something that silly poets wrote of.

Love, he thought contemptuously. Ha! He laughed out loud, startling his horse. What a dolt he was, a moonstruck lad out on a ride musing on the merits of love. An emotion far too dangerous to even think about. An emotion reserved for the pain of loss. An emotion long since written out of his vocabulary. He thought for a moment about his kind, good mother, Julia, and more fondly of his sister, Katherine, and the pain of their loss stabbed through him with fresh force. He remembered how, when he was young, his father had become more and more withdrawn after Julia's death, how the elder Carlyle had begun to drink and gamble, how he had invested his money irresponsibly, practically depriving Nicholas of his inheritance. Never, never would he allow any woman to affect him in such a manner.

And yet, he knew it was time for him to marry. He had worked hard to transform the run-down plantation into a home he could be proud of, and he wanted to pass that legacy on to a son. If only he didn't have to marry in order to have an heir! He laughed humorlessly to himself. Ah, well, there were times when even *he* could not get what he wanted. He supposed that one of the local girls would do as well as any English wench.

There were times when he regretted not pursuing Amanda

Cookes. She was quick, witty, and honest, but a scandal
had been attached to her name, and Nicholas, in his youth
and arrogance, had not wished to upset his precarious
social position, so he'd drawn away from her. What a fool
he had been, for now Amanda and her husband, Thaddeus
Windham, were close friends, and he enjoyed Amanda's
rather outrageous conversation immensely.

His thoughts turned toward another acclaimed beauty—
Charlotte Rosemond. A slow smile spread across his lips.
The girl flirted with him outrageously whenever he saw
her in Charleston, and even more scandalously at church.
He chuckled to himself. At least she had some spirit, and
he secretly admired her subtle skill in pursuing him.

He had called on her father many times in the past when
he needed advice. Charlotte had always seemed to be
hovering nearby, but as he was solely occupied in the
business of plantation management in those days, he had
hardly paid her the barest courtesy. The young woman had
remained undaunted in her attempt to attract his attention,
and recently it had been his pleasure to call on her many
times and to escort her about town as well, always chaper-
oned by the woman's mammy, of course. But Mammy
Harriet was easily subdued with whiskey. And although he
and Charlotte were not lovers, in the privacy of the drawing room or coach, Nicholas had found Charlotte's amo-
rous talents surprisingly sophisticated.

Perhaps he should consider courting her. She was a true
beauty, with her dark blond hair, cornflower-blue eyes,
and patrician features. Her father had quite a bit of good
farming land, and to make the prospect of marriage even
more sweet, Charlotte was an only child, hence the land
would someday fall to her and her fortunate husband.

Nicholas was momentarily disgusted by his thoughts.
He was no less mercenary than the rest of his mates in
London. "Damn!" he swore. "What am I thinking? I'm
no innocent, and if I'm not a complete fool, neither is
sweet Charlotte Rosemond. I'll talk to her father."

The woman was gracious and lovely, and although most of the exuberance and spontaneity had been polished out of her, making her a smooth, socially correct nonentity, he knew he would not be content with a gauche farmer's daughter. He was fond of Charlotte in his own way, and he was certain that she would make an exceptional wife. With that decided, Nicholas once more loosened up a bit on the reins and, urging his powerful mount over a fallen tree, continued along the trail at breakneck speed.

As he came within sight of his home, he coaxed his horse to a halt and regarded the mansion critically. Yes, it was a handsome home, whimsically named Providence by the previous owner. Who would have thought that it could have regained its former grandeur? Yet he could never have done it without Titus's help. He chuckled when he thought back upon their first meeting.

The first six months at Providence had been very lean indeed, and Nicholas often heartily cursed his folly in foolishly buying the dilapidated estate. But what was done was done, and although he had acted quickly and stupidly, he was determined to make the best of a bad situation. He had hired and fired three overseers, and although he deplored the practice, bought and sold as many as twenty-five slaves.

Nicholas was accustomed to having servants, but he had been unprepared for the brutal way in which the first overseer, a large, brawny man, had lavishly abused the slaves. At first Nicholas had ignored the plight of the blacks, accepting the overseer's explanation that such practices were common in the Carolinas. After all, whipping them was the only way to get anything out of the lazy devils. But one day, after he witnessed the man thrashing a poor woman almost to death, Nicholas's control had snapped, and he had heartily enjoyed grabbing the whip out of the man's hands and giving him a sound beating, his years of brawling in a variety of pubs standing him in good stead.

He had tended to the woman's injuries himself and

signed her papers of freedom. In those days the laws regarding the freeing of slaves were rather lax, the threat of the abolitionist movement barely felt. Astounded, the woman had clutched the papers to her ragged garments and praised him in a soft voice choked with emotion. The next two overseers had been as brutal as the first, and Nicholas had vowed then that, if he could avoid it, he would never own another slave. It was a difficult promise to maintain, for the whole economic structure of the Carolinas was built on slave labor.

Consequently, on his threadbare budget he was unable to hire any dependable house servants, and the result was that Providence's appearance continued to decline. In the six months he had owned the plantation, he had managed to clear only fifty acres of land, acquire two plow mules of dubious lineage, and deplete his inheritance far more than his father ever could have through his wild investment schemes.

Nicholas had reevaluated his position. He figured that with the money he had left he could barely afford seed, workers, and perhaps a cook. He made a face. His own cooking left much to be desired. If things didn't work out this time, he would be forced to sell Providence and return to England. He knew his failure would delight some if not all of his neighbors.

He shook his head. He had to be honest and admit that not everyone shared the common opinion of him. Some of the planters in the surrounding area had been very good to him, offering help and advice on more than one occasion, and he had gladly accepted their gentle hospitality. But many had come on supposed visits of good will to simply laugh at the youngster's bumbling efforts at plantation management. He sighed deeply. Come tomorrow, he would go to Charleston to find some help. But right now, he would fix himself something to eat.

Dusk was just beginning to settle over Providence when Nicholas had finished his meager dinner. He patted his

disgruntled stomach and tried hard not to think about all
the glorious meals it had once been his privilege to enjoy.
He had lost weight, yet he felt fitter than ever before. All
the hard work had hardened his frame, and despite his
weight loss, his clothes were becoming uncomfortably
snug.

He strolled through the dining room and into the empty
foyer. The pieces of furniture and other accessories he had
been able to bring from England had improved the appearance of the house, but the furnishings were far too meager
to fully enhance its aspect. Someday, he vowed, people
would gaze with admiration rather than ridicule upon these
marble floors and delicate plaster ceilings. He opened the
front door, reminding himself to fix its persistent squeak,
and walked out onto the wide porch to lean despondently
against one of the massive columns. It was hardly the
image he had first entertained in his mind—the grand,
wealthy gentleman planter standing proudly between two
columns.

What in the world could have possibly prompted a
spoiled aristocrat's son to leave the security of London and
journey to this godforsaken country? I must have been
mad, he thought despairingly. All my dreams of a better
life seem to be fading rapidly. He sighed, then spoke aloud
in frustration. "I fear the only thing that I've learned out
of this whole bloody experience is humility."

"Well den, suh, yo's learned a powerful lesson, if'n yo'
don't mind me sayin' so."

Nicholas whirled around at the sound of the soft, gruff
voice and was surprised to see a poorly garbed young
black man standing at the far end of the porch. He was
huge, at least six feet six inches tall. Though Nicholas
himself was only a few inches shorter than the man, while
Nicholas was lean and sinewy, the black man was bulky,
with brawny, muscular arms hanging from a threadbare
shirt stretched to the limit over a massive chest. Thighs as
strong and solid as tree trunks supported the giant easily as

he shifted his weight from one bare foot to the other. Not one strand of hair adorned his gleaming pate. He had a small gold hoop in his right ear.

"Who the devil are you?"

The man stepped forward confidently and nodded his head. The battered straw hat he twisted in his hands belied his easy manner. "De name's Titus. Jes' Titus. An' Ah comes 'round to see if'n yo' is lookin' fo' an oberseer to helps yo' manage yo' prope'ty."

Nicholas took an involuntary step backward as he regarded the apparition standing easily before him. "You look more like a bloody pirate to me."

The black man slapped his tattered hat on his knee and laughed loudly, showing amazingly white teeth. For the first time in months, Nicholas smiled.

"Law, Ah'se been called worse dan dat, Mistah Carlyle."

"How is it that you know my name, Titus?"

"Ah'se gonna be true with yo', suh. When Ah was in Charleston Ah heard yo' name bein' bandied 'bout. Seems like folks don't give much cotton to yo' gittin' dis place workin'. So Ah thinks to mahself, Titus, yo' needs a job bad, an' dat Mistah Carlyle needs an oberseer bad. So why don't yo' mosey down dat way, an' sees if'n yo' can help de man. So Ah'se here."

"Well, Titus, thank you very much for your offer, but I hadn't really thought of hiring someone like you."

"Yo' means a black man, Mistah Carlyle? Ah gots to admit, dere ain't no folks 'round 'bout here what gots a colored oberseer, but den lots of 'em have trouble with de ones dey gots."

Nicholas had to silently agree with the man, remembering his experiences vividly.

"Ah was thinkin' dat Ah gots mah pride too, an' Ah ain't gonna lie to yo', when Ah ses dat Ah could do a better job dan any white trash oberseer dat yo' is bound to hire. Ah's gots de know-how, an' Ah don't think yo'd do no wrong in givin' me a chance. Ah knows de business from front to back, an' Ah thinks we can make dis place turn a good profit outsid'n a year o' two. Ah knows Ah don't look like much now, but at least Ah is a free man, gots de papers to prove it, and Ah gots friends willin' to work fo' next to nothin' as long as dey ain't slaves. Dey be mo' free colored br'ers and sisters in dis town dan yo' can shake a stick at. Ah gots me a fine wife dat can take care o' yo' house, an' some small chilluns dat'll help clean an' sich, ah' some aunties dat are mighty fine cooks. On top o' dat . . ."

Nicholas put his hand up to halt the words coming almost desperately out of the black man's mouth.

"Titus, I've already made a fool of myself by buying this place. I'm all of two and twenty years old, and I feel as though three score should be added to that number. I need help badly, you're right, and I don't know a damn thing about running a plantation." Nicholas ran a weary hand through his tumbled locks and looked straight into the black man's honest face. "For the first time since I've been here, I think this place was aptly named Providence, for I believe Providence sent you here to me today." Nicholas held out his hand. "Whether win or lose, I'd deem it an honor to work with you."

A grin split the young black's face as Nicholas's hand was engulfed in the huge palm.

"Yo' ain't nevah gonna regret dis, suh, Ah promises yo' dat. Yessiree, we gonna make a good team, an' dis place is gonna shine like it nevah done befo'. Ah can't wait to tell de missus. Evah since we was freed when de old marster passed on, Ah'se seen some bad times. We been tryin' hard to find honest work, an' at de same time tryin' hard not to be sold back into slavery. Dis is de answer to our prayers. Yes suh!"

That was ten years ago, and Nicholas had never once regretted hiring the big black man. The first two years had been difficult, with Nicholas barely able to pay the men and women that Titus brought in droves, but gradually, working almost unceasingly, they had somehow managed to eke out a small profit by the end of the second year. After Nicholas had barely managed to secure a substantial loan, life had gotten much easier. Within five years he had paid back the loan, and with more profits coming in, he was able to invest his money into other lucrative ventures: the new steamer trade and textile factories.

As more planters moved out and sold their land he was able to annex almost fifteen hundred acres more. Most of it was devoted to cotton, but he still had healthy crops of rice, indigo, barley, and wheat. Most of the other planters had at first laughed at him, smirking behind his back at the way he carried on with all his "nigger friends." Nicholas ignored them and continued to flout convention by his continued trust in Titus and by his determination to own as few slaves as possible. The ones he did have, and they were few indeed, had the option of working to pay him back for their freedom. Consequently, his work force was chiefly black, but the men and women were "free colored," and so, they were proud to say, were their children.

For a small fee, they lived behind the big house in the old slave quarters, but unlike many in the area, the small cabins were neat and well kept. It seemed to be true that when people worked for themselves, they took pride in what they accomplished. Nicholas expected his employees to work hard, but he trusted the other blacks as he trusted Titus, and to the surprise of his fellow planters, there were few labor problems. Gradually, if almost grudgingly, Nicholas was accepted by the planters, and he found, much to his amazement, that many of them secretly admired him.

Nicholas shook his head, slowly coming back to the present. Life was certainly much better now, so why was he discontent? He shrugged and rode toward the big house. The stableboy, Aaron, ran forward to catch the reins that Nicholas threw to him as he dismounted.

"Did you have a nice ride, Marse Nick?"

"Very nice, Aaron. Lancelot's going to need some

walking.'' Nicholas ran a hand over the horse's chest.
"He's just a bit overheated.'' Nicholas loosened the girth
and slid the stirrups up. "Can you take care of that for
me?''

"Yes suh. He's a mighty fine hoss. Ah enjoys tendin' to
him.''

"Good, then I'll rest assured knowing he's in capable
hands.'' He slapped the horse on the neck and watched
smilingly as Aaron led the animal away.

"Yo' sho' does like dat hoss. Ah ain't nevah seen
nobody as fond o' dere hosses as yo' is.''

Nicholas jumped at the sound of the soft voice. "Titus!
Damn but you're quiet on those big feet!''

"An' yo' is loud on dem bitty ones yo' gots.''

"Agreed, but I thought you were out looking over that
newest small parcel of land.''

"Ah sho' nuf was. Ah thinks by Christmas we might be
able to clear a good bit of it.''

"Cotton?''

Titus shook his head. "Dat man what owned dem acres
took almos' eberythin' out o' de soil. Ain't nothin' gonna
grow dere fo' at least a year. We'll burn de brush dat
growed an' plant wheat first. Dere's gittin' a big demand
fo' grains lately.''

Nicholas nodded. "Then let's plant some barley as well.''

Titus agreed. "It's a good thing that yo' is goin' up to
Kentucky to buy some new mules. Dem critters we gots
now is gettin' powerful old and used.''

"I still think it's a long distance to travel for mules.''

"Yes suh, but dey ain't sendin' any down till de spring,
an' we needs dem mules now.''

Nicholas arched a black brow at Titus. "I thought the
sun had finally broiled through that shining dome of yours
the day you suggested I write to Richard Montagu.''

Titus pursed his lips, wearing the determined face that
Nicholas had come to dread. "Yo' knows we needs some
powerful strong mules now. Be a credit to yo' line. 'Sides,

yo' needs to git out fo' a spell. Yo' ain't seen Mistah Richard in a dog's age, an' Ah'm sho' he won't mind puttin' up with yo' uppity ways fo' a few days. 'Scuse me fo' sayin', but yo' been lookin' mighty peaked of late. Evah since yo' come back from London town, yo' long face an' short temper been gittin' eberyone jumpy as a coon on a hunt. Somethin' botherin' yo'?''

Nicholas opened his mouth to explain to his friend, shut it, and shook his head. ''You're right as usual, change of scenery will do me good. Montagu has some fine breeding stock, and I'm looking forward to picking up a good mare that'll breed well with Lancelot.'' Nicholas sighed, thinking of the journey ahead of him. ''I'll probably be leaving in a week or so, and you shouldn't expect me back for at least a month.''

''Yes suh. We need dem mules befo' it gits too cold.''

Nicholas eyes the man in exasperation. ''In other words, I should make provisions for my departure as soon as possible.''

''Yes suh. Have a nice trip.''

Nicholas waved the man off as he went into the house.

Chapter 3

"Mama, that's him. That's the man who stared at me at the fair. What do you suppose he wants?"

Sarah's cold hand fumbled for Jessica's and held tightly on to it. "Andrew, it must be . . . But I never thought he'd appear unannounced, or so quickly. What shall we do?" Jessica was alarmed at her mother's pale face and shaking voice.

"Calm yourself, Sarah, no need to fret," said Andrew. "I'll take care of this."

The driver tipped his hat politely to the Blackwells as their old landau pulled up next to the grandly appointed phaeton. The boys started to rouse from dozing.

"Might y'all be de Blackwell fambly?" asked the driver.

Andrew nodded his head curtly. "Who are you?"

The elderly gentleman stepped up next to the landau. He looked past Andrew to Jessica and executed a short bow. "I am Richard Montagu, and—"

At the sound of the man's name, Sarah let out a smothered gasp and grasped Jessica's hand more tightly. Jessica turned in alarm toward her mother.

"Andrew," said Sarah faintly, "I don't feel well at all. Please, may we go into the house?"

Andrew turned concerned eyes to his wife, then spoke directly to Mr. Montagu. "Please excuse us, sir. Perhaps we might meet at a later time." Richard nodded as Andrew continued to give orders. "Boys, get out of the carriage and give your mother some air."

They scrambled to do his bidding, all but Joseph, who began to cry at the sight of his mother's pale face. Jessica pressed his wet face against her shoulder.

Despite Sarah's protestations that she was capable of walking, Andrew lifted her tenderly from the landau while Timmy ran to open the gate and Alex fumbled with the latch on the front door. The other boys trailed behind protectively. Jessica turned with Joey in her arms to confront Richard Montagu.

"Mr. Montagu, apparently my mother has suffered a shock. Perhaps you can return at another time to discuss your business with my parents."

"I'm terribly sorry if my presence has caused you or your family any inconvenience, my dear. I shall be happy to meet with your parents at a later date. Please express my regret that this unfortunate incident occurred. I'm staying at the Edgmont Inn in Williamsburg. Do you know of it?"

"I've only heard of it, sir."

"Good lass. Then tell your parents that I anxiously await word from them."

"May I ask what your business concerns?"

"They'll know," was the enigmatic reply.

Richard Montagu stared at Jessica's face a moment longer as if memorizing her features, making Jessica very nervous. Finally when she thought she could bear his perusal no longer, he shook his head and stepped into his carriage. With a short whistle and a slap of the reins, the driver coaxed the smart team down the drive. Joey tightened his arms around Jessica's neck.

"Who is that man, Jessie?"

"I have no idea, honey, but I intend to find out."

She gently lowered Joseph to the ground and, taking his hand, rushed into the house, mounting the kitchen stairs two at a time. She raced down the narrow hallway to her parents' bedroom with Joey fast on her heels. Sarah was lying on the bed, and Andrew was sitting next to her, rubbing her cold hands between his warmer ones. The boys were gathered around her with anxious, worried faces.

"I'm telling you, Andrew. I'm perfectly fine. Please stop hovering over me as though I were some sort of invalid. I'm just sorry to give you all such a fright."

"What happened, Mama? Why did Mr. Montagu alarm you so?" Jessica couldn't help asking.

Sarah lifted her eyes to her husband. "I never thought this day would come, Andrew. After all, it has been eighteen years . . . I guess I just didn't want to think about it."

Andrew patted her hand consolingly. "There's no help for it now, Sarah. She must be told."

"Told what, Papa?" Jessica asked in confusion. "Mama? What's wrong?"

Sarah struggled to a sitting position. "Dolly, come sit by me. Your father and I have something we must tell you.

"About twenty years ago, Jessica, your father and I lived in New Orleans. We were newly wed, new to the area, and were looking to buy a parcel of land that we could farm and then someday, God willing, raise a family on. It was there that your father and I met Elizabeth Montagu and her husband, Jeremy. They were a young couple like Andrew and me, and just five years in America from England. Jeremy came from a wealthy family but had been cast out when he went against his parents' wishes to marry Elizabeth. You see, she was an orphan girl and not a member of the aristocratic set. Jeremy's parents considered her below their son's status, so they forbade the match. It was plain to see why Jeremy went against them and married her. She was such a beautiful girl, and so full of life, laughter, and enthusiasm in everything she did. Jeremy was smitten with her, and it was obvious that she fully adored him.

"After their clandestine wedding, they gathered what money they could and came to America. When I met them, their dress shop was doing a marvelous business, and they were prospering quite well. Jeremy, it seems, had a fine head for business and had invested their earnings wisely.

"Anyway, after we had known them for about two years, Jeremy and Elizabeth had a child. They absolutely doted on the baby. Andrew and I visited them often in their apartment over the shop, and our friendship deepened quickly. It was one of those very rare friendships that come once or twice in a life. Soon after the child was born, Jeremy received a letter from England telling him his parents had both been killed in a fire. I remember the day well." Sarah's eyes grew distant with the memories. "Poor Jeremy, he was devastated by the news, and especially since just the week before he had received a letter from his father pleading for a reconciliation.

"With the death of his father, Jeremy was now a wealthy man. The sizable family estate in England and all other accounts and assets were now passed on to him. Since Jeremy and Beth had prospered well on their own, the money really didn't mean all that much to them. They had all they needed in each other and their child, but they both missed England, and so decided to return there.

"About two weeks before they were due to leave, Jeremy, Elizabeth, and the baby barely escaped death when a fire mysteriously started in their dress shop in the wee hours of the morning. In the next few days, several more suspicious accidents took place, and Jeremy became convinced that someone was trying to murder him. Many members of his family could have profited from his death.

"He feared more for the lives of his wife and child than

for himself, and resolved to go off alone to track down those responsible. He never would have forgiven himself if something had happened to either the child or Beth because of his shortsightedness or refusal to take action against those who wanted him dead. But Elizabeth refused to leave him, and insisted on going along.'' Here Sarah sighed.

"They loved each other beyond anything else, Jess. You must understand that. They were afraid for their darling child, and so with heavy hearts they gave the baby into the care of their dearest friends, your father and I. We raised the little girl as one of our own.''

"No! You can't mean that—'' Jessica gasped and pulled away from Sarah in shock.

"Yes, Dolly,'' Sarah continued as gently as she knew how. "You are Jessica Elizabeth Montagu. The ring you wear is your father's, with the family crest emblazoned upon it.''

Green eyes wide, Jessica stared in disbelief at the only family she had ever known, as if seeing them for the first time. The boys returned her stunned perusal, then with a cry of pain, Jessica turned from the group and ran down the hallway, ignoring Sarah's pleading cry. She slammed her bedroom door behind her and flung herself on the bed, there to sob in abject misery.

With the utterance of one sentence, her whole life had changed. Nothing would ever be the same again. She looked down at the ring that symbolized her inner turmoil, pulled it from her finger, and threw it against the wall. She didn't know how long she lay there, her mind numb with the thoughts that swirled inside her head, but finally she felt herself drifting off into merciful oblivion.

When she awoke with a start, it was dark. She felt a warmth against her back and, twisting around, wasn't surprised to discover Joseph snuggled close against her. Whenever he was frightened or sad, he would often creep into her room for comfort. Tears rose anew as she stroked his curly locks. Although she tried hard not show it, he had always been her favorite. Now, as she looked down upon his sleeping form, she wondered how it was possible that he was no longer truly her brother.

Calmer now, she began to think about what her mother—no, her stepmother—had said. How tragic that she had never met her real parents. She wondered what they looked like, and with a start realized that she looked nothing like her adoptive parents in the least.

Did she resemble her mother or father? What were they like? Sarah had spoken highly of them, which meant they must have been fine people indeed. Of a sudden, Jessica felt their loss and wondered what had happened to them. Had they been murdered? Just the thought of it made her shudder as much from fear as from the chill in the air. There were too many unanswered questions churning in her mind. Careful not wake Joseph, she slipped off her bed and down the hall to her stepparents' room. She knocked softly on the open door.

"Is anyone awake?" she whispered. She stood uncertainly on the threshold, prepared to leave if they showed no signs of rousing. There came a creaking from the bed.

"Jess, is that you, child?" Her mother's voice was gravelly with sleep. "Wait just a minute."

There were more creakings as her mother searched for matches to light the whale-oil lamp on the bedside table. Finally a spark was struck and the lamp flamed. The light revealed Sarah looking very small in a flowing white nightgown. Jessica stood in the doorway, uncertain now of what she wanted to say. As always, Sarah came to her rescue.

"Let's go down to the kitchen and have a cup of tea." Sarah donned her robe and Jessica followed her down the narrow stairs to the kitchen.

Still silent, the women automatically went about the task of making tea and sat down feeling at a loss for words.

Finally Jessica looked up at her stepmother. "Why? Why didn't you tell me that I was not your true daughter? I think I had the right to know."

Sarah bit her lower lip and sighed. "We wanted very much to tell you, but we were afraid. At first, we waited and waited for Jeremy and Elizabeth to come back. Months went by. We moved out of the area, leaving word of our whereabouts with a trusted friend, and still we waited. It was a year, then two. We knew then, of course, that they would never return." Sarah brushed a few tears from her eyes. "When we moved from New Orleans and traveled to Williamsburg, we didn't think anyone would think to look for you here. Jeremy's parents had never known that you were born, and we wanted to keep the rest of the family ignorant regarding your whereabouts for as long as possible. We were afraid that if they knew you were alive, you would be in as much danger as your parents had been."

"Why should anyone want to hurt me? What do I have that anyone would want?"

"There's more to the story, Jessica. You see, when your parents left you in our care, they also left a will behind. Jeremy forwarded it to the family lawyer in England and left an exact copy with us. After a reasonable amount of time had passed, your father and I, assuming your parents to be dead, read the will. The provisions were quite explicit. They stated upon obtaining the age of eighteen, you were to inherit the family estate and everything else that was once your father's. The will went on to say, however, that if you were not married by your nineteenth birthday, the estate and all other holdings would be given to the same orphanage that had raised your mother."

For the second time that day, Jessica was stunned by Sarah's revelations. "I simply can't believe this is happening to me."

Sarah leaned across the table to hold Jessica's frozen hand. "Let me finish, Dolly. Your father and I think that the reason Jeremy insisted on your being married was because he wanted the family estate to have an heir as soon as possible. That, and perhaps he wanted to be assured that you were well taken care of, with a husband of your own choosing. Your father and I have kept you hidden these many years to protect you. We've never pressured you into marriage because we wanted to make sure you made a careful and wise decision. After all, whoever you decided to marry would become a rich man. We didn't want any fortune-hunting reprobates courting you. That was another reason for the secrecy regarding your heritage.''

"But how then do these murderous family relations know that I even exist? You said that my grandfather had no knowledge of my birth; consequently, his relatives must not know either.''

"Think, Jess. Your father's lawyer in England was told of your birth. When the will was read to the assembled relatives, they also became aware of your existence. Andrew has written to the lawyer several times reaffirming your continued good health, but he's never indicated where you have been residing all these years, until now.

"We wrote to Mr. Montagu and told him to come here." At Jessica's startled gasp, Sarah quickly went on. "We only told him where you were, and that you were safe. Your father loved Richard Montagu like a brother and yet was afraid that should you be raised by him, Richard, his wife and son, and you would all be in constant danger. Since no one knew us, Jeremy figured, correctly, that you would be safe with us until you were eighteen if anything happened to him and Elizabeth. Jeremy and Elizabeth both wanted you to live with your Cousin Richard thereafter, because with his connections you would have a better chance of finding a suitable husband. I only hope Mr. Montagu's intentions toward you are honorable and his memories and love for your father are as strong as Jeremy's were for him.''

"Husband?" Jessica grasped on to the word. "You mean I am to go away with this man so that he might

choose a husband for me?'' No wonder Richard Montagu
had been so overjoyed to discover that she was unmarried.
Jessica tried to jerk her hands away from her stepmother's
grasp, but Sarah held her fast.

"No, Dolly, you misunderstand. You know how we
feel about arranged marriages. Although we really have no
legal hold on you now, we will do everything in our power
to assure your happiness above all else. We wrote nothing
to Richard of marriage. We will meet this man. The choice
will be yours. If you do not like him, we would certainly
not force you to leave. How could you think it? Let me
remind you, Jessica, that you are a wealthy woman now.
No one can force you to do anything you do not wish to
do. But you see, your father and I were obligated by
Jeremy's wishes to send for Mr. Montagu. We had no
choice, and you deserve a better life than we could give
you.''

Sarah released Jessica's hand and sipped her tea. "Tomorrow, you and your father will go into town to talk to
Mr. Montagu.''

"Mama?" Jessica said the word hesitantly, but was
touched to see her mother smile for the first time that
evening.

"Yes, Dolly.''

"Is that why you were always so careful to see that I
was taught the ways and manners of a lady of quality?''

"Yes, Jessica. You were going to be a titled lady
someday, and I did not want you to be embarrassed or
disgraced by your upbringing.''

Jessica felt tears rising again to her eyes and thought
that only a selfish fool would be embarrassed by her
wonderful family. She quickly changed the subject. "Mama,
what did my parents look like?''

"It was a long time ago, but I remember them quite
vividly. But here, see for yourself.'' Sarah reached into
the pocket of her robe and pulled out a leather pouch. She
undid the thong and poured the contents onto the table.

Out came a beautifully filigreed gold cross with a small ruby in the center attached to a delicate gold chain. There was also a small gilt-framed miniature, which she handed to Jessica.

"These are your parents. This cross belonged to your mother. In the years I knew her, she never took it off. She gave it to me before she left. They had lost everything in the fire. 'I know it's not much, Sarah,' she said, 'but in case we don't come back, I want Jessica to have some small remembrance of me.' I can remember her words as if it was yesterday." Almost hesitantly Jessica looked down at the small portrait.

A handsome couple, she thought sadly. The man reminded her very much of Richard Montagu, but much younger. His hair was dark, his face lean and handsome. He looked very happy, and somehow Jessica had the impression that it was because of the lovely woman on his right. Although it was a tiny painting, Jessica could see quite clearly that she resembled her mother to an amazing degree. The same heart-shaped face and smiling lips looked back at her. The hair was the same auburn hue, but the eyes were not quite right. Jessica looked up at Sarah.

"Your father had the same color eyes that you have, Dolly, but as you can see, that is as far as the resemblance goes. You could be your mother's twin. Elizabeth was such a beautiful woman. You do her much credit."

Jessica stared in awe at the portrait. She felt tears fill her eyes and turned the portrait facedown on the table. She picked up the cross and fastened the chain around her neck. Somehow, it felt familiar. She felt badly now that she had thrown the ring away. She resolved to retrieve it and put it back on her finger.

Mother and daughter were silent for a moment, then Sarah spoke. "Jessica, there is one thing that I want you to know." She stared into the green eyes raised slowly to hers. "Even though Andrew and I are not your real parents, we've always loved you as one of our own. When

Jeremy and Elizabeth gave you up to us, it nearly broke their hearts. We pledged to take care of you because we loved them so, but as the years went on we were proud to call you our only daughter. Never, never forget that, Dolly. Your family loves you very much.''

"I know that, Mama. I wonder how my other family feels about me.''

"Tomorrow will come soon enough, and then you shall see.''

"But I don't want all of that property and money, Mr. Montagu,'' Jessica protested. "I didn't do anything to earn it. It doesn't seem right that I should inherit an English estate. I don't know anything about England, and I would never want to live there. I am an American. This is my home.''

Richard Montagu leaned forward to grasp Jessica's hands, a kindly light in his eyes. "I quite understand, my dear. I myself, though born in England, now consider Kentucky my home. There is no provision in Jeremy's will that states that you must live in the ancestral home. However, think on this, Jessica. Your father and mother risked their very lives because of the estate. Would you disgrace their memory by throwing it away as if it meant naught?''

"But I'm not married. I can't see just—''

"Now, Jessica, don't you even think about it. No one intends for you to marry the first available male just so you may inherit some wealth.'' Richard released her hands and leaned back in his chair, looking at Andrew. "This is all so sudden. A few weeks ago, I didn't even know where Jessica was, or if she was still alive.''

They were sitting in a private room in the hotel. At first conversation had been stilted, with Jessica unable to meet the inquisitive eyes of her newly acquired cousin, but gradually her curiosity had won over her timidity, and questions had tumbled from her mouth almost unceasingly. Richard Montagu now looked earnestly at Jessica. He urged her to leave Williamsburg and live with him at his home in Kentucky. Both Jessica and her father adamantly refused.

"Excuse me for being so blunt, Richard," said Andrew Blackwell, "but we must know each other better before we can allow you to take control of Jessica's future." He put a protective arm around his daughter.

"I understand your feelings, sir, especially considering your daughter's youth and beauty. If I had a child as lovely, I too would be more than reluctant to give her up to a perfect stranger. You've seen proof of who I am." He sat back, thinking aloud. "I must admit, I always wondered why the lawyers were so unwilling to settle Jeremy's estate. Most of the English cousins thought the eighteen-year trust ridiculous, since they obviously thought you dead, and I can tell you they've tried, without success, mind you, to break the will. I find it delightful, for I never cared for any of them. I must say that I was simply flabbergasted when I saw you at the fair, throwing balls, no less. I thought at first that your mother, Elizabeth, was somehow still alive and untouched by time."

"Mr. Montagu . . ."

"You know, Jessica, I am your cousin, and it would please me so if you would call me uncle or at least by my given name."

Jessica looked at the man helplessly. "Sir, I appreciate the compliment, but I hardly feel familiar enough to call you uncle. Please, I need some time. Everything has happened so quickly."

Andrew patted her clenched hands and turned to Richard to further discuss Jeremy's will. Jessica sat mutely during the remainder of the visit, afraid that if she tried to speak she would burst into tears. Finally her father stood up to shake Richard's hand.

"It was a pleasure to meet you, Richard, but I'm afraid we have to get back to the farm now. We've already taken up too much of your time."

"No trouble, I assure you. I do have one favor to ask, however. Do you think I could have a few words with Jessica alone?"

Her father glanced to her, eyes silently asking her approval. Jessica nodded, and he turned to leave the room.

Jessica looked up at her cousin. "Is there another deep, dark secret that I should know about, sir?"

Richard shook his head, chuckling, though his eyes were worried. "No, Jessica, I suppose all of the skeletons have been let out of the closet for now. What I have to discuss with you could not be said in front of your stepfather." He moved to stand behind her and continued with difficulty. "Jessica, this is a most distasteful thing I must say, but it must be said. I have some reason to suspect that your life might still be in danger."

Jessica gasped and half rose out of the chair. Richard pushed her down gently.

"Please, child, let me finish. Yesterday at the fair, I saw you staring at a rather oafish-looking fellow with red hair. When I went to call on you yesterday, I caught a quick glimpse of the same fellow lurking about in the shadow of the large oak just outside your barn. Of course, I could be mistaken as to his identity or intentions, but when something as precious as your life is involved, I can afford to be cautious. What I'm really trying to say in my own bumbling manner is that your adopted family could be placed in terrible danger by your continued presence in their home. I'm sure it is a burden that they would gladly accept and fight for, but . . ."

"I would no doubt be wise to disappear for a while," Jessica finished dully. She sighed. "Wouldn't you also be placing your family in danger by allying yourself with me?"

Richard Montagu took her hands in his. "Whereas I am a wealthy man, your father alas is not. I can buy you protection, and I must admit to a bit more cynicism than your parents possess. They suspect no one, and I suspect everyone. Jessica, I know you have had to accept many shocking facts lately, but this also is a reality which you can no longer escape.''

Jessica responded, ''Were I the suspicious sort, dear Uncle Richard, I would very well suspect you of attempting to spirit me away from my family, and thus stake a claim of your own in my fortune.''

''I'm sorry if you think that of me, though were the positions reversed, I'm sure I would have the same suspicions. However, I truly have only your best interests in my mind and heart. If you lived with my wife and me, just for a time, perhaps my fears would be proven groundless. After all, it has been eighteen years.'' Richard moved to a sideboard to pour himself a drink.

''I loved your father very much. He was my first cousin, but better than that, a good friend. When my parents died, I was but five years of age. My uncle, your grandfather, took me into his home and raised me as one of his own, so you see, Jessica, we two orphans have something in common.''

He rubbed his forehead. ''I understand your stepparents' situation better than you might think, for I have a son myself, and although it is no secret that we do not deal well with one another, I would not wish to give him up if asked to do so. I honestly think, however, that it would be in your best interest if you came with me.''

''Sir, I appreciate all that you have told me, and I will think carefully on everything you have said. You mentioned earlier that you wish to return to Kentucky by the week's end. I suggest that you continue with those plans without me. I cannot leave my family at this time. I need the security of my home for just a bit longer before I make any decisions at all. Can you understand that?''

Richard stared down into her tortured young face and smiled consolingly. ''Yes, Jessica, I can certainly understand that, but I shan't leave until I know you better. So, like it or not, you'll be seeing more of me. There's one more thing. If you don't mind, I'll have my lawyers start processing your inheritance. For the past eighteen years Jeremy made provisions in his will for a certain amount of money to go to the upkeep of the estate. You need not worry that you've been left with a decayed and moldy tomb, I assure you." He looked at Jessica. "Do you mind if I start these proceedings?"

Jessica sat uncomfortably. "Please talk to my father about that. If he agrees . . ." She took a deep breath and shook her head. "No, it is my responsibility and my decision. Yes, Mr. Montagu, please have your lawyers take care of it."

Richard stepped forward. "Jessica, I'm grateful that you have shown such trust in me. I also want you to know you will always have a home with my wife, Lucy, and me. Any time." He came to her slowly, arms outspread. "Now, will you humor an old man and at least give me a proper hug?" Jessica, grateful for Richard's understanding, went willingly into his arms. He squeezed her to him briefly and set her away with tears in his eyes.

"It was a delight to finally meet my dear Jeremy's lovely daughter. I'm glad to see that you at least have the Montagu green eyes. I wish we could have met sooner, for I would have considered it a privilege to raise you up as one of my own." He shook his head. "You've been denied so much, and I could have given it to you."

"On the contrary, sir," said Jessica, bristling at his words, "I feel my life has been full and good. My parents have been—"

"I did not mean to denigrate your family, my dear. Your parents are fine people, and it's obvious that you've been raised quite properly. Please forgive me if I am relieved, however, that you did not marry some local farmer. We can do much better than that."

"Much better . . . Sir, what exactly are you implying? Are you perhaps taking it upon yourself to find me a husband worthy of your standards?'' Then something suddenly occurred to Jessica. ''And who is this Nicholas that I heard you mention yesterday at the fair?''

Richard looked a bit chagrined at her outburst. ''So you heard me, eh? It's nothing, my dear. Nicholas is a dear friend of mine who will soon be on his way to visit me in Lexington. I'm sure he'd be pleased to meet you.'' Richard winked. ''He's a very handsome, proper gentleman, Jessica, and a bachelor as well. He lives on his own plantation in Charleston.'' He brought her hands up to his lips. ''Anyway, I've kept you long enough from your father. Until the next time, Jessica, God's blessings upon you, child.''

Jessica was quiet on the long ride home, and was relieved when her father did not attempt to engage her in conversation. Her mother anxiously awaited them by the gate, but Jessica couldn't bear the thought of answering her mother's questions.

''Papa? Do you think it would be all right if I went riding for a while?''

''Of course, my dear. I'll explain everything to your mother.''

Jessica ran into the barn. Her buckskin gelding turned sharply in his stall as he recognized her voice.

''Ivanhoe. At least *you* haven't changed at all.''

In the empty stall that served as the tack room, she found a pair of boy's riding breeches, a cotton shirt, and a chemise. Assuring herself that her brothers were not in hiding, she shucked off her clothes and slipped into the new outfit.

The trousers were old, soft, and comfortable—perfect for riding astride her horse. She had always hated riding sidesaddle, much to her mother's constant dismay.

She curried her horse long and leisurely, then vaulted lightly to his back and rode onto the trail that would eventually take her into a dense wood. She fully intended to spend the whole day away from the farmhouse.

When Jessica finally returned home, it was just a few hours before midnight. Although the moon was only half full, the night was clear enough that its light was sufficient to guide her easily. She dismounted and led her tired horse into the barn. Wearily she gave him a quick rubdown, then fed and watered him. She stood by his stall, watching him munch contentedly on his oats, and wished that she could feel as at ease with her life and surroundings.

Giving the horse one last hug, she walked out of the barn and firmly bolted the doors. She stood in front of the farmhouse and gazed up at the window of her room, surprised to see that the window was open and that a light flickered brightly inside. Strange; she remembered deliberately shutting the window before she left that morning. Someone must be waiting up for her, and she could guess who—Joseph. For a moment she thought she saw a ghostly shadow move in the bushes. She shook her head and stared again, then the acrid smell of smoke came to her nostrils. Smothering a cry of panic, Jessica flew into the house and up the stairs.

"Wake up! Everyone! Mama! Papa! Wake up. Fire!" she screamed. Sleepy heads popped out of doorways.

"What's all the ruckus?" Andrew called, as he pulled on his trousers.

Without answering, Jessica pulled open the door to her room. Black smoke came rolling out in huge waves, and she squinted against the searing fumes until her searching eyes spied her brother Joseph asleep on her bed, oblivious to the creeping flames. She screamed his name, intent upon jumping into the smoke-filled room, but, her arm was grabbed from behind and she was firmly pulled back into the hallway. She jerked away and turned to stare into her mother's horrified eyes.

"Whatever possessions you have can burn! Now get out of the house, so the men can put out the fire!"

''No! Joey's in there!''

Sarah's eyes went wide, and she began to shove past Jessica. Coughing from the fumes, Jessica firmly pushed her mother away and, closing her eyes to slits, ventured cautiously into the room. Sweat covered her body, and she completely disregarded her mother's cries begging Jessica to return. She bumped hard into her bureau, skinning her calf, and heard the sloshing sound. The ewer of water! She groped blindly for it atop her smoking bureau and, with a quick exclamation of triumph, poured the contents over her head and body.

The smoke was so thick she could barely see. The bed was beginning to smolder, and the flames from the curtains were creeping closer to her unconscious brother. Summoning one last breath, she dove blindly for the still figure and managed to grab a handful of his nightshirt. The flames licked greedily at her cotton shirt, but the water she had poured over herself kept them at bay for an instant before she gave a mighty tug and tumbled Joey's limp form into her arms. A scrap of burning sheet had wrapped around his leg, and she quickly tore it away, blistering her fingers and revealing his blackened and swollen flesh. Cuddling his body close to her, she quickly ran out of the room.

She collapsed in a heap with her precious charge a second before her brothers and father came storming up the stairs with buckets of water. Her mother, eyes streaming, took Joey from Jessica's arms and helped her to her feet. Jessica was coughing and choking almost uncontrollably from the smoke that clogged her lungs.

''Quickly,'' said Sarah. ''Get downstairs and outside. You're in no condition to help with the fire. Don't argue. I'll attend to your brother.'' Sarah held Joey close to her chest and hurried downstairs.

Jessica followed more slowly, blinking her tearing eyes, passing the line of boys who now formed a bucket brigade to douse the flames. Outside, her mother had Joey laid out on the ground, cradling his head in her lap. There was soot on his face, and his hair was singed. His leg was unnaturally red and puffed. Coughing the last of the smoke from her lungs, Jessica fairly flew to his side.

A sudden thought came to her, and she felt a chill crawl up her spine that had nothing to do with the coldness of the night air. She remembered the maliciously intent way a certain red-haired man had stared at her at the fair, and again heard Richard Montagu's voice speaking of a man lurking in the shadows of their barn. She could detect no movement near the barn now, but the hair at her nape seemed to bristle, and she was certain she felt hostile eyes upon her. Once, another fire had nearly killed her real parents and herself as well . . .

Sarah murmured words of heartfelt thanks, but Jessica felt undeserving of such praise for saving Joey. After all, if it hadn't been for her, none of this would ever have happened. The seed of a decision took root and grew more strongly by the second. From this moment on she knew her life would be changed. She just prayed that the fates would treat her kinder than they had treated her father, Jeremy.

"Are you sure this is what you want, Jessica?"

"Yes, Mama."

The Blackwell family was standing by the front gate, Richard Montagu waiting tactfully in his carriage while Jessica bid farewell to her family.

She knew her parents must be wondering at her sudden decision to leave Virginia and travel to Kentucky with her cousin, but Jessica was desperate to be away. She had been careful in the past few days to constantly scrutinize the farmyard, and had been horrified to catch fleeting glimpses of a hulking figure with red hair. She had told Richard Montagu of her discovery and had sworn him to silence. The last thing she wanted was to cause her family more concern. Every time she saw Joey's face, flushed and twisted with pain and fever from his badly burned leg, she felt doubly anxious to depart.

Richard's sincere kindness and concern for the boy had been the deciding factor in her abrupt decision to leave her home. Now, seeing tears gathering in her mother's eyes, Jessica spoke to her father with a falsely bright voice.

"Richard tells me he has a plantation on which he raises thoroughbred horses, so I suppose I shan't be bored in my new home."

Andrew smiled tightly. "You're sure you won't be taking Ivanhoe with you?"

"No, I don't think I'll be needing him." She leaned forward and quickly hugged her father. "Save him for when I return."

"He'll be here, Jess."

She took a deep breath, then turned to face her brothers. "You all behave while I'm gone, and help Mama with the dishes sometimes."

Alex stepped forward, rubbing his eyes. "Maybe."

Jessica gave them all a hug and a kiss, and for once they did not object.

"You tell Joey good-bye for me again, and tell him to get well, hear?"

They nodded solemnly, then Jessica went to her mother.

"Write to me?"

"I'm not much for letter writing, Dolly, but I promise I'll try." Sarah took a deep breath. "You'll probably be so busy with the Montagus that you'll have no time to think of us."

Jessica tightly embraced her mother. "Never," she promised. She stepped away and smiled brightly at the subdued group. "Well, I should be on my way. Richard has been patient enough."

"God bless you, daughter," whispered Sarah. Andrew moved to Sarah's side and slipped his arm around her.

"Be happy, Jessica," he said.

Jessica nodded sharply and climbed into the carriage.

Richard's driver closed the door behind her and hopped up to his post. With a soft jolt the carriage rolled smoothly forward. Jessica fought against the tears and tightness in her throat.

Suddenly she felt the warm touch of a hand, and she looked into green eyes of precisely the same shade as her own.

"You've done the right thing, child, and I'm very proud of you. It's what your father would have done."

Jessica took a long, shaky breath. "I hope so."

Chapter 4

Jessica drew in the lunge line on the horse she was exercising. The mare, named Diana after the Greek goddess of the moon, was an exquisite silvery gray with black points, and Jessica's favorite of the many magnificent thoroughbreds that Richard Montagu raised for profit. Richard had proclaimed the mare useless, for she had a temperamental streak that none of the grooms could train out of her. Jessica rubbed her abused posterior and had to admit that even now, after she had worked closely with the mare, Diana still had a bit of a temper. She respected the horse's continued efforts to defy her, however, thinking that she and Diana had a great deal in common, for neither of them had much interest in becoming civilized.

Jessica had lived with Richard and Lucy Montagu for nearly a month now, yet she felt no nearer to resolving her problems. Of one thing she was sure, however; she was not going back to Virginia until she was certain no harm would come to her family. She felt guilty enough about exposing the Montagus to danger, especially since they had been so sincerely considerate toward her. She was ashamed that she had once suspected Richard of ulterior motives in spiriting her away from Williamsburg. After living with the kind man and his gentle wife, she had to conclude that she had been terribly mistaken about him.

Shaking her head at her thoughts, she led the mare out of the paddock and into the large stable. One of the young apprentice grooms came forward, but she waved him away. He shrugged his shoulders, and Jessica knew that he must be wondering, along with all the other trainers, why his employer's cousin spent so much time in a stable, wore boy's britches, and insisted on attending to the mundane aspects of horsemanship. She was grateful that Richard allowed her unorthodox activity, despite Lucy's horror at her less than appropriate behavior.

Unfortunately Lucy had exacted retribution in her own way by striking a bargain with Jessica. In order to continue training Diana, Jessica was forced to sit with her aunt—for Lucy insisted that Jessica refer to Richard and Lucy as uncle and aunt—for four hours a day for lessons in feminine deportment. The lessons were torture, and the sight of her aunt's gentle features set in determined lines as she stood before a table aglitter with plates, silverware, and crystal stemware for one of her famous mock-meal lessons was beginning to cause Jessica to shake as if with palsy. She thought that if it ever came to the true test, she might just starve rather than reveal her inadequacy. Oh, she'd never fit in with the proper society in England, that was especially evident after the formal ball Richard had given in her honor just a few days ago.

Jessica closed her eyes and leaned her head against Diana's warm neck. Her nerves were still taut after that particularly unpleasant experience. Her aunt had completely taken her in hand and practically dressed Jessica herself, clucking over her until Jessica thought she would scream. When she had been presented to the assembled guests, she had barely avoided tripping down the stairs, and if not for her Uncle Richard's steadying arm, she just might have pitched headlong into the crowd. If she hadn't been so mortified, she might have found the situation hilarious. She had thought then that the worst had happened, and that the evening could only get better, but she had been wrong.

She had felt completely inept and out of place all evening. It seemed to her that the aristocratic set was arrogant and haughty, not given to warmth or genuine friendship. She couldn't rid herself of the impression that everyone seemed to be posturing instead of actually enjoying themselves, especially the young women. The way they primped and patted themselves, Jessica was reminded of the hens at her parents' farm. Yet she envied their graceful movements and their low, honey-smooth voices. Jessica had felt as though the walls in the room were closing tighter and tighter around her, imprisoning her in a hostile and unfamiliar world.

Diana nudged Jessica in the back, and she shook her thoughts away. What was wrong with her anyway? Anyone else would be overjoyed at suddenly acquiring as much wealth as she, but all she could think of was that learning of her heritage had disrupted her happy life. She also worried constantly about her youngest brother, wondering if his leg had healed properly. All the money in the world would little appease her if her brother had suffered because of it.

Jessica deliberately dismissed the subject and concentrated on rubbing down the mare and leading her into a large box stall. As she brushed against the wall, she heard the sound of rending cloth. Groaning impatiently, she jerked away the now torn tail of her shirt and inspected the damage. Someday she was going to have to do something about the long hooked nail that jutted out from Diana's stall. The grooms hung buckets from it, but it kept ruining Jessica's shirts.

Jessica wiped her grimy hands on her grimy trousers, and sighed in anticipation of a warm bath. Her clothes were filthy, her torn shirttails had come out of the waistband of her britches, and her hair was stuffed up into a boy's cap, short tendrils escaping down the back and sides of her neck. Her fingernails were coated with dried sweat and dust.

Wouldn't Aunt Lucy just swoon if she saw her now? She grinned at the image, and immediately reprimanded herself for such rudeness.

Outside, taking the path to the big house, she was surprised to see a lone rider cantering leisurely up the long, oak-bordered drive. She waited by the front steps to greet the stranger. Being Jessica, it didn't occur to her that she was hardly presentable to meet company.

The man sat easily in the saddle, and she admired the beautiful liver-chestnut stallion he rode. She looked closely at the rider but his face was shaded by a hat. He slowed his mount to a walk as he neared her, and upon his command, the horse came to a stop. The man leaned slightly forward to question her.

"Tell me, young man, is Mr. Richard Montagu in residence today?"

Jessica looked up at him in complete confusion until she realized he must think her a servant of some kind. Probably the stableboy! He had turned to stare at the house, and so missed her shocked expression. She looked down at herself and realized that the baggy shirt she wore over her dirty britches certainly gave no clue as to her sex. She stifled an enormous urge to laugh, but at the same time she was suddenly acutely embarrassed by her unsightly condition. Next to this masculine man Jessica very definitely felt dowdy, and she again felt the fears of her inadequacy close about her. Good Lord! She glanced around furtively, expecting to see Aunt Lucy descending upon her in horror with corset, satin pumps, and tea service in hand.

The gentleman was wearing a brown, brushed velvet frock coat in the redingote style that was unbuttoned to show a cream-colored waistcoat liberally piped with golden thread. Fawn-colored strap trousers fit snugly over his muscular thighs and shining black Wellingtons. She shuf-

fled uncomfortably as the man turned his attention to her.
She longed, just for the sheer audacity of it, to pull the hat
off her head and prop her thumbs under her armpits like
some cloddish yokel. With effort she mastered the impulse.

Perhaps she should play this charade to its logical conclusion until she could get into the house to bathe and
change. Disgruntled at how far her aunt had come in
civilizing her, she nodded dumbly at the man, pulling her
cap further down over her eyes and lowering her voice to a
rough drawl.

"Why, yes suh, Mistah Richard's home today. Might I
ask who's callin'?"

The man dismounted nimbly and handed the reins to
Jessica. Although she was considered tall for a woman,
she felt tiny next to his tall, lean frame. She took the reins,
noticing that the man's hands were much better manicured
than her own.

"I am Nicholas Carlyle, and this," he said, slapping his
horse affectionately on the neck, "is Lancelot. Please take
special care of him."

Jessica almost jerked in shock. Oh no, she thought. This
was the paragon of manhood that her uncle had been
constantly glorifying to her. How could she have forgotten
that Richard had been eager for the visit of "Lord Carlyle," as Jessica had dubbed him? She quickly gathered
her wits about her and, bobbing her head in a properly
subservient manner, covertly studied the man from the
screen of her thick lashes. She didn't know much about
men, but she had to admit he was as fine a specimen as
she had seen. She gestured with her thumb.

"Jes' go up to the big house. Peter'll announce ya."

The gentleman nodded. "Thank you, ah . . ."

"Jessie."

"Thank you, Jessie. My carriage should be arriving
shortly. Please see to it as well."

Reaching into his pocket, he pulled out a coin and
flipped it to her. Jessica caught it, bobbed again, and

hurried off with the man's horse, careful to assume a more bouncy, boyish stride.

In the stable she handed the reins and the money over to one of the grooms. Despite her faux pas, the humor of the situation struck her once more and, unable to control herself, she slid down the wall to the stable floor and burst into laughter, slapping her hat across her upraised knees.

"Nick, it's good to see you at last," Richard exclaimed. "I've been anxiously awaiting your visit. But tell me first, how is Theodore? There's no trouble, is there? He hasn't gotten into another of his famous duels with an outraged husband, has he?" Richard's normally soft voice was edged with sarcastic hardness, and his mouth curled down in distaste.

Nicholas shook his head, smiling at the man he had known all his life. "As far as I know, Dick, your son is fine. The last time I saw him he asked me for the name of my business agent. Perhaps he's decided to become respectable."

"I certainly hope so. I should hate to have to extricate him from another one of his indelicate predicaments."

Nicholas frowned at the almost disgusted and pained look that came into Richard's face when he spoke of his son. He found it very strange that the man who was more than willing to shower fatherly affection on him could not bear to do so for his only child. The fact that Richard had sent Theo to boarding school in Charleston at a very young age further puzzled him. In his own way, and because of the fondness Nicholas had for Richard, he always tried to keep an eye on Theodore, but he found the role of big brother singularly unrewarding.

It was hard for Nicholas to explain his feelings, but he reluctantly admitted he did not like Theodore. He felt that, at age two and twenty, Theo should have offered to take a hand in managing his father's estate, or to at least start earning money of his own, but he knew that Theo still received sizable amounts from his father every month. Nicholas also knew that Theodore frequently wasted Richard's hard-earned money in fancy gambling houses. Even the home that Theodore rented in a wealthy section of Charleston must have been difficult to afford on his allowance, generous though it was.

Well, thought Nicholas, he himself had once been a charming scoundrel, yet he had changed. Perhaps there was hope for Theodore as well.

He shook off his thoughts as Richard handed him a brandy and turned to pour one for himself. Nicholas gestured toward the stables. "I'm anxious to have a look at your bloods, Dick, and want to find a worthy mare to breed with Lance."

"I still can't believe you would journey all the way from the Carolinas to buy a mare . . . and some mules, I believe?" Richard raised his glass. "Ah youth, what energies they possess."

"Actually, Dick, I just needed to get away from the plantation for a short holiday. This last fortnight on the road has already done me a world of good. Anyway, how are you and Lucy getting along?"

"Fine, fine. The woman's a saint. And speaking of wives, has some young lady managed to get your ring on her finger yet?" Nicholas shook his head, and Richard went on carefully. "Marriage is a wonderful thing, lad. I would have suspected that a handsome chap like yourself would have tried it by now."

"I have a young lady tentatively in mind, but thought I'd wait until after this trip to secure the relationship."

"Gads, Nick, you make it sound like a bloody business arrangement!"

"Isn't that what marriage really is? The woman gains a household to run, and a man his heirs. And so-called stability."

Richard shook his head in genuine bemusement. "Ah, Nick, I can see you've little changed your view of women, but someday you'll meet a girl who'll bring you to your knees." Nicholas opened his mouth to protest, but Richard raised a hand. "Let's not argue about it and just agree to it as fact." He went on quickly before Nicholas could interrupt. "Speaking of women, I have some news. Tell me, Nick, do you remember my cousin Jeremy?"

"I was a lad when he married that girl, what was her name? Elizabeth. Yes, Elizabeth. I remember the incident only because my father and mother argued over it. Mama thought the marriage wonderfully romantic, but my father was quite scandalized. As you know, it was the chief source of gossip in the area for quite some time." He wrinkled his forehead in thought. "It all seems so long ago."

"Yes, yes. Well, Jeremy and Elizabeth had a daughter. We all thought her long gone, but just recently she has come into my care. A delightful child, although a bit unconventional."

"Child, you say? What twelve, thirteen?"

Richard chuckled. "When you get to be as old as I am, my boy, everyone under the age of thirty seems a child. No, the girl is just eighteen, and the very image of her mother. I'd like very much for you to meet her."

"I'd be delighted, sir, but tell me more about her. Her story must be fascinating."

Jessica managed to sneak through the back door and up the stairs to her room without disturbing the gentlemen in the drawing room. She asked one of the maids to draw water for a bath and slipped gratefully out of her filthy garments. With a sigh she lowered her bruised and aching body into the brass tub and leaned her head back against the high rim.

She leisurely soaped a long leg and frowned at the purple and blue bruise on her skin. No wonder Nicholas Carlyle had thought she was a boy. She was as bruised and scratched as any one of her brothers. A pang shot through

her as she thought of them. Did they miss her? Was Joey
fully recovered from his injuries? So far she had received
only one letter from her mother, and all seemed to be well,
but she knew Sarah would never tell her anything different.
Jessica still had nightmares of her brother aflame on the bed,
and she resolved to do anything to protect her family.
Anything.

After her bath, she towel-dried her wet hair and searched
through the colorful contents of her armoire for a suitable
gown in which to meet the fabled Mr. Carlyle.

She was still amazed at the amount of money her aunt
had spent on her wardrobe. Jessica had argued long and
hard with the woman over the costly garments, but Lucy
had remained stubborn. Jessica must have everything a
young lady of quality could need: boots, slippers, head-
dresses, silk stockings, ribbons, shawls of fine cashmere,
chemises of the finest batiste, starched white muslin petticoats; in fact, all manner of feminine frippery, and gowns
she'd never seen the likes of except in the more extravagant dress shops in Williamsburg. Everything was tailored
to her precise measurements and in the height of fashion.

"I intend to show you off to all of my friends, my
dear," Lucy had said. "Those proud mamas won't think
so highly of their plump darling daughters when they see
your slim grace."

Jessica finally selected a rose taffeta gown with enormous leg-of-mutton sleeves that were scratchy with rein-
forced horsehair and whalebone. The tightly fitted bodice
dipped daringly, and the full skirt swept the floor to cover
the matching slippers. Jessica slipped the gown carefully
over her head and settled it over her corseted waist and
elaborate petticoats.

She was still having trouble getting used to the corset.
Her aunt had been truly scandalized to learn that Jessica
had never worn one in her life. To pacify the woman—
after all, she had barely recovered from seeing Jessica in
trousers—she had reluctantly agreed to wear the horrible

thing. To her, it represented the strictures of the new society into which she was unwillingly placed. Many times after pulling it off, she had sent it sailing across the room with a well-placed kick.

As she was fumbling with the lace collar of her gown, there was a knock on the door, and the maid announced, "Mistah Richard would like yo' to come down to de drawin' room when yo' is ready. Dey's a gentleman he wants yo' to meet, and if yo' don't mind me sayin' so, a nigh handsome one at dat. Perhaps yo'd be wantin' me to dress yo' hair for de occasion."

Jessica turned shyly to the woman. "If you don't mind, Mary, I think a braided chignon would be fine."

Mary nodded and quickly and skillfully fashioned the chignon. Jessica slowly made her way down the stairs toward the sound of masculine voices. She took a deep breath, smoothed her skirts and, holding her head high, knocked boldly on the door.

Richard opened it and drew her into the room. "Come in, my dear, no need to knock. I'd like you to meet an old neighbor of mine from England. Jessica, this is Nicholas Carlyle. Nick, my cousin Jessica Montagu."

Jessica raised beautiful green eyes to him in timid greeting, praying fervently that he wouldn't recognize her as the grimy stableboy who had cared for his horse. She curtsied and graciously extended her hand. Nicholas bent low over it and straightened, still clasping her fingers.

"I'm delighted to make your acquaintance, Miss Montagu."

He raised her palm to his lips and gently kissed her wrist. Jessica quickly withdrew her hand, a puzzled look on her face. There was something threatening about being so close to his tall form.

"Please call me Jessica," she finally said. "After all, we would once have been neighbors of a sort."

As Jessica and Nicholas were introduced, Richard seemed to be studying them carefully. He bowed low and with a mischievous smile walked to the door. "I simply must see what is keeping your aunt. Jessica, do entertain our guest until I return."

Jessica cast pleading eyes at her uncle, but with a puckish grin he left the room. Jessica turned back to Nicholas and realized that he had been gazing at her with rapt appreciation. She was genuinely irritated by his perusal, and wary. He looked very much the socially correct and confident aristocratic gentleman, and to Jessica he symbolized everything that was painful and alien to her. She raised her chin a notch and held out her arm, indicating a tapestry-covered settee, determined not to let him see her weakness.

"Please make yourself comfortable, Mr. Carlyle. May I freshen your drink?"

Nicholas raised an eyebrow at her crisp tone. Her displeasure with him was obvious and, oddly enough, he found it wonderfully refreshing. Although he had no desire for more brandy, he nodded and held up his glass so that she would be forced to come fetch it. His lips quirked at her expression. She was not happy. Her skirts rustled as she glided toward him to take the glass, and the fragrance of spring lilacs drifted with her.

"Thank you, Jessica. And you must call me Nick, as everyone else does."

She nodded curtly and turned to splash more brandy in the balloon snifter, clumsily spilling some onto the table. She cursed inwardly, his eyes upon her making her skin prickle with goose bumps. Why was she acting like a nervous simpleton? But his polish and poise made her feel even more inept than usual, and he as too sure of himself, too superiorly complacent, like all the other "gentlemen" she had met.

As she handed the glass to Nicholas, he wrapped his fingers briefly around hers. At his warm touch, Jessica again felt a strange jolt, similar to what she had experienced when he had kissed her hand. She moved quickly away from the settee, rubbing her fingers, and sat opposite the man. Since conversation seemed to be required, Jessica spoke first.

"So tell me, how long have you known my cousin?"

Nicholas sat easily across from her, his legs outstretched and crossed casually at the ankles. Jessica sat with her back ramrod straight and her hands clasped primly in her lap. To her, the half smile on his lips suggested that he knew she was nervous and found it amusing. Jessica was not pleased. Finally he deigned to answer her question.

"Before I moved from England, your cousin and I lived on neighboring estates. We've been keeping in touch for years."

A very evasive answer, Jessica thought, but then she didn't care in the least about the man or his past. She wished desperately for Richard's return and couldn't fathom his motive in leaving her alone with Mr. Carlyle and his roving eyes. Of a sudden she missed her parents dreadfully. She never would have been put into such a position in their home. Suddenly Nicholas's deep voice interrupted her thoughts.

"Richard briefly explained the circumstances that brought you here. How do you like living in Kentucky?"

Jessica almost started out of her seat. "What? Oh . . . Kentucky. It's beautiful here. I enjoy being around the horses."

"Ah, yes. Richard mentioned that you are an accomplished rider."

"Yes, I enjoy riding, but also all the other aspects of equitation; everything from training to grooming."

He raised an eyebrow at her reply. "I've never met a woman yet who would willingly dirty her hands to curry a horse."

"But that's part of the fun. I get much satisfaction in training my mare on the line, although sometimes she does not acquiesce to my commands, and it is more than my hands that become dirty." When Nicholas's eyebrows shot up again, she realized it might not be proper to admit her unorthodox activities. But she was eager to impress him with her expertise. Well, she would not apologize.

"You have chosen some very hard work for yourself," he said. "Few women have the stamina or strength for such activities. I would think that riding sidesaddle would do nothing to strengthen the legs, and—"

"Yes, I agree," Jessica interrupted enthusiastically. "That is precisely why I ride astride. I find that—"

"Oh?"

You mean, oh no, Jessica thought to herself, mentally adding another faux pas to her growing list.

"I don't believe I have ever met a 'lady' who rides astride." His pale, silvery eyes crinkled in amusement.

Jessica felt her face heating up. She wasn't sure whether Mr. Carlyle was teasing her, but she was not about to take any abuse from a starched gentleman who probably never dirtied his own fine hands. She was ready to make a heated reply, but he must have noticed her discomfort, for he spoke hastily.

"I meant no offense, Jessica. I am simply amazed to discover that a beautiful young lady such as yourself is such a revolutionary at heart."

"Revolutionary? I am no such thing," she said. To herself she added, and neither am I beautiful, nor a lady. Aloud she said, "I must admit I am known to be quite stubborn when it comes to something that I feel strongly about."

Nicholas smiled at the honest, unaffected way she had stated her feelings. He was liking her more every minute. Charlotte Rosemond no doubt would have said something like, "But, Nick darling, you know how very naughty I can be when I don't get my way, and you know that I must always have my way if you are to keep me happy." His smile widened, for he could almost hear her petulant voice in his ear.

Misunderstanding his smile and the cause, Jessica felt

that he was somehow making sport of her. She was used to being teased by her brothers, but somehow this was different, and she once again straightened her back and stared frostily at him.

They were interrupted by a shriek as Lucy flew into the room, followed by Richard. Nicholas quickly rose to his feet.

"Nick, you're here at last! How are you, dear? My word, Richard, I believe he's even more handsome now than he was the last time he came to visit. I simply cannot believe you've managed to remain a bachelor."

Ignoring Nicholas's pained smile and Jessica's lifted eyebrows, Lucy threw her arms wide and Nicholas accepted her hearty embrace. He leaned down and kissed Lucy's soft cheek.

"How are you, Lucy? Dick's been treating you well, I see."

"Yes, yes, as always. I see you've met the newest addition to our family."

"Yes, indeed I have," he said, gazing warmly at Jessica.

Jessica pointedly turned away. Nicholas raised an eyebrow and continued to gaze upon the lovely profile. Out of the corner of his eye he saw Richard and Lucy exchange glances. Lucy nodded slightly, as if silently giving her approval to some scheme. Now, what were those two planning?

Chapter 5

Jessica suffered Nicholas's presence through dinner, and the strictures of polite society that his company imposed upon her solidified her dislike of the man. She could hardly take a bite without feeling his eyes upon her. Good Lord, weren't there any other women in the Carolinas? Finally, the meal mercifully concluded without mishap, despite the formidable array of china and silverware, and as soon as she thought it graciously possible, she excused herself, pleading a headache.

Free, she thought as she left the dining room. But instead of going to her room, she quietly let herself out the front door and, walking down the steps, enjoyed the beauty of the evening.

It was a cold, crisp night, colder by far than any October night in Williamsburg. A bright crescent moon glowed defiantly from behind loose, ghostly clouds that flitted in wispy swirls across its surface. The silhouettes of the creaking tree limbs were etched sharply against the starlit night sky. A fresh breeze ruffled the crisp taffeta of her gown as she silently made her way to the stable. All was quiet except for the faint rustling of the wind and the distant call of a barn owl. Jessica breathed in deeply, feeling a strange mood of longing wash over her. But longing for what? Beneath the overwhelming grandeur of the sky she suddenly felt infinitesimally insignificant.

Shivering in her thin gown, she pushed her melancholy thoughts away. After struggling with the stable doors, she finally managed to undo the bolt and step inside. The heat of the horses made the air significantly less frigid, and the horsey smells of hay, liniment, and leather soothed her strained nerves. She fumbled on a shelf for matches and a lamp, and finally managed to produce a light. Sighing in relief, she made her way to Diana's stall, stepping carefully away from the long, hooked nail in the wall. She unbolted the top half of the door to see the mare contentedly muching hay. At the sound of Jessica's voice, Diana lifted her head and leaned over the stall door.

"Looking for a treat, I'll wager."

Diana butted her nose against Jessica's raised hand and sniffed up and down the bodice of her dress. When no apple was offered, she snorted loudly and continued eating hay. Jessica smiled sadly at this pointed rejection, unable to shake her strange mood. Some very important realization was dancing just beyond her grasp. Her brow furrowed in concentration. What was it?

For a long time she let the sight of the horse soothe her troubled thoughts, but suddenly she became aware that someone was opening the barn door.

She whirled in surprise and held the lamp higher, dismayed to see Nicholas's tall frame silhouetted in the doorway. Irritated at this interruption of her solitude, she cursed silently and, bracing herself to meet the man, hung the lamp on a convenient hook on the wall.

"Jessica?" He came to stand next to her. "What in the world are you doing in the stable? I thought you weren't feeling well."

"I'm not," she answered shortly. "However, I might ask you the same question."

"I'm here at Richard's invitation. I've come to purchase a mare for my stallion, and I asked Dick if I might take a quick look at his brood mares." He cast an appraising eye over Diana. "You have a good eye for horseflesh," he said, indicating the horse. "Her conformation looks perfect, legs sound and unbowed, hooves nicely rounded and not too long, back straight. Richard told me you've done a wonderful job gentling the mare in the short time you've spent with her. Since I know now you're an obvious expert, perhaps you can show me the other mares as well."

Jessica cursed her fate. She was not in the mood to be charitable, especially since the man might decide to take Diana away from her. "This is hardly proper, sir, as we are unchaperoned. However, if you still wish a tour tomorrow, I would be more than happy to oblige you. Until then, I wish you a pleasant good evening."

She turned sharply and almost cursed aloud when she felt her skirt catch and tear. That stupid nail! She grabbed frantically at her dress, trying to free herself from the long nail, but she only succeeded in worsening her situation. Nicholas began to smile at her obvious distress and moved closer to assist her.

"Here, Jessica, you're only making it worse. Let me see to it."

The mere thought of his touch made her pulse leap. Wishing only to be away from him, she gave a mighty tug at the hampering material. Suddenly the entire nail came away from the wall, and she completely lost her footing. Instead of leaving Nicholas in a dignified huff as she had intended, she was falling into an unladylike sprawl.

But in the next moment strong arms reached out and pulled her against a hard chest. For a second Jessica gratefully clutched the lapels of Nicholas's frock coat. She looked up into his face to voice her thanks and saw his pale gray eyes staring down at her wonderingly. Unbidden, her melancholy mood of longing returned in a rush, and a painful ache caught at her chest. Somewhere in the background she heard the stamping of the horses in their stalls and the creaking of the timbers above her head, but those sounds seemed unreal and far away. More real were the features of Nicholas's face, the clean scent of his cologne, and the texture of his fine black hair. She stared, fascinated, at the full, firm lips that were coming slowly toward her.

Nicholas was shaken at the intensity of her gaze. By the soft light of the lantern he could see that her cheeks were flushed, and when he tightened his hold around her slender body, he could have sworn that she shivered. Her lips had parted with her rapid breathing, so close and so full that their temptation proved too much for him. He bowed his head slightly, all the while staring into her widening green eyes, his mouth eager to taste what she seemed to be offering him.

Suddenly he felt a sharp kick to his shin. The pain released him from the enchantment she had woven around him. Cursing, he released the now struggling girl and watched in amused frustration as she ran away from him and out the stable door. Rubbing his abused shin, he leaned down to pick up the twisted nail. He unhooked the lamp and limped toward the door, musing on the unpredictability of women.

Jessica was awake early the next morning. She dressed in her boyish garb and, grabbing her cap, quietly made her way down the stairs and out of the house.

The last person she wanted to see was Mr. Nicholas Carlyle. Something had happened to her last night in his arms, and she never wanted it to happen again. She had enough to worry about without having to dissect her roiling emotions.

She sneaked into the stable and, much to Diana's dismay, forced a cold bit into the mare's mouth. Half dragging the reluctant steed out of the barn, she grabbed a handful of mane and vaulted onto the mare's back. She reined the horse sharply away from the house and followed the well-worn trail past the fenced fields and out to a small copse of trees about three miles from the house. There, a natural spring had formed a small, clear pool. The place was strangely alluring, and Jessica was often drawn to its serenity when she wanted to be alone.

She slid off Diana's back. It was a crisp, cold morning, though the sun was shining brightly through the remaining leaves on the swaying tree limbs. Jessica loosely wrapped the reins of Diana's bridle around a low-hanging tree limb and patted the horse affectionately. The carpet of brown leaves made a warm, comfortable resting place and, giving in to the temptation, Jessica lay down on her stomach, her head with its small cap pillowed in the crook of her arm. She had hardly slept last night, disturbed by the incident in the stable, and felt her eyes drooping heavily.

Gradually Jessica became aware that someone was shaking her. She opened her eyes with a gasp and stared up into Nicholas's concerned expression. Finding the object of her tormented emotions so close at hand, Jessica rolled away from him and scrambled to her feet. She put a shaking hand to her forehead, and her precariously balanced cap needed no further urging to tumble from her head. Her hair fell thickly around her face and past her waist. She backed away from Nicholas as he stepped forward in concern. She noticed fleetingly that he was dressed in a riding outfit every bit as superb as the one he'd worn the day before.

"Are you all right, Jessica?" he asked. "I caught a glimpse of Diana between the trees, apparently riderless and untethered. When I saw you on the ground, I thought you might have been thrown."

Quickly regaining her composure, she lifted her nose in the air. "I am never thrown from my horse."

He ignored her haughty remark, yet continued to thoroughly scrutinize her state of dress. A smile lifted his mouth. "Jessie," he murmured. "No, I suppose you are never thrown from your horse. You possess such versatile talents."

"What exactly do you mean?"

"Only that it must be difficult to schedule time for all of your duties."

"If you insist on baiting me, I believe I'll just be on my way."

"Yes, I'm sure there are some stalls in the barn that need mucking out, or perhaps some saddles that need to be soaped?"

Jessica's smile was tight as she realized he had recognized her as the stableboy who had greeted him the day before. "You are quite right. And since I am so very dedicated to my duties, you must excuse me. I wouldn't want to degrade you with my lowly presence."

"Of course, it wouldn't do for me to be seen with you. After all, we are unchaperoned."

Jessica bit her lip, refusing to reply to his deliberate teasing. She was completely unaware of the charming picture she presented, with her hair loose and flowing, and some of the buttons on her shirt undone, showing the lacy chemise beneath.

"When Richard told me you were a bit unconventional, I could hardly believe him. You put on such a convincing show last evening of the demure young lady. The bit about having a headache was especially well done."

"Yes, wasn't it. I pride myself on my acting abilities."

"Indeed. You're doing it right now, aren't you?"

"Of course."

"I'm afraid you've not perfected your technique, my dear, because I can tell you'd dearly like to kick me again."

"Really, Mr. Carlyle. Tell me, what else am I thinking?"

He smiled. "You're thinking that you truly would have enjoyed having me kiss you last night."

"And do you enjoy kissing stableboys?"

"Not usually, but in your case I could make an exception."

Jessica inclined her head in his direction. "I'm honored, sir. However, if you ever attempt to take liberties again, I'll be forced to bruise more than your shin."

Nicholas bowed mockingly. "I look forward to the moment with anticipation, for I'm sure your sweet kiss would be well worth any thrashing you could give me."

Jessica groaned in exasperation. She folded her arms across her chest, unconsciously pushing her bosom up to the limits of her chemise, and beat a rapid tattoo on the ground with her foot. She shot a quick glance at Nicholas and, following his unswerving gaze, glanced down at her open shirt. Oh, good Lord! With a muffled shriek she turned her back on him and with fumbling fingers quickly buttoned the shirt. She stooped to pick up her cap and, unceremoniously twisting her hair into a knot, stuffed the thick mass up into the cap. Without a backward glance she untied Diana's reins from where Nicholas had resecured them and jumped lightly onto the mare's back.

She urged the horse to a gallop, seeking to put as much distance between herself and Nicholas Carlyle as she could, and uttered a short, unladylike curse as her cap flew from her head. Seething, she only gradually became aware that Nicholas was calmly riding alongside her. She slowed her mount to a walk and, stiffening her back, turned to vent her frustration.

"Sir, I do not recall having asked you to join me on this ride, so if you please, I bid you stop this ceaseless hounding."

Nicholas continued to ride beside her unperturbed, admiring the way her long legs gripped the sides of the mare without seeming effort. Her thighs showed strong muscles under the britches, the calves rounded and firm, and her small, booted heels lightly touched the horse's belly, toes sharply pointed outward.

"Mr. Carlyle, do your ears function, or is that ability limited only to your wandering eyeballs?"

His mouth quivering with suppressed mirth, he nodded politely, not fully trusting himself to speak. He seemed to be utterly enjoying himself.

Jessica, however, was not and felt so foolish that, had a bolt of lightning come from the sky to roast her person, it would have surely provided relief. For the first time she felt acutely embarrassed about donning britches. For some reason, this irritating man made her feel more and more childishly gauche every time she was unfortunate enough to encounter him. Her mother certainly would have moaned with shame to see Jessica dressed like a plowboy riding bareback on a horse in the company of a gentleman. Her face flushed to the roots of her hair at the thought, and she wanted to scream her frustration. Equally strong was the urge to stick out her tongue at the man and make a rude noise. She glanced over at him and noticed he rode easily next to her, wrapped, it seemed, in his own thoughts, looking ever so polished and regal.

"Even smells polished," she muttered crossly to herself.

"What was that, Jessica? I'm afraid my wandering eyeballs were not allowing my ears to hear your remark."

She shifted her gaze to straight ahead, her face growing hotter. To her dismay, she felt frustrated tears beginning to prick her eyes. Taking a deep breath, she furtively wiped at the telltale moisture. The sooner Mr. Carlyle finished his business with her cousin and returned to the Carolinas, the better she would feel.

How could she ever face Richard and Lucy after this faux pas? Using the wrong spoon was one thing, but this—this was certainly an engraved invitation to more of Aunt Lucy's endless lessons. Or perhaps they'd put her on display at another ball. She swallowed her pride and turned to the man beside her, speaking quickly and earnestly.

"Mr. Carlyle, the Montagus have endeavored long and hard this past month to make me feel at home. I am not wont to reward their efforts with complete disrespect. Please, it would mean so much if you could let me return to the stable alone. If they see me with you like this—if anyone sees me like this—it will cause nothing but trouble.''

Nicholas leaned forward in the saddle as if seriously pondering the situation. Jessica held her breath until finally he sat back and nodded slightly.

''I can see your point, Jessica, and I will be more than happy to oblige you; however, there will be a price.''

Unwillingly, Jessica remembered the lamplight shining softly on his face and the tremulous, confusing emotions that had arisen in her when she thought he might kiss her. She swallowed heavily and raised round green eyes to him.

''Yes?''

''Don't look so stricken, little stableboy. It is a small bribe, I assure you. You offered last night to give me a tour of the stables. I now hold you to that promise. Agreed?''

Jessica sighed in relief and turned the full charm of her smile upon him. Bright lights danced in her green eyes, and the sun reflected brilliantly off the red highlights of her wildly tousled hair.

''Certainly, sir, it is a small bribe at that.''

She extended her hand to seal the bargain, and he took it gently and raised it to his lips. She pulled her hand out of his grasp. At her outraged expression, he laughed aloud and wheeled his horse about, coaxing the stallion into a leisurely canter. She watched as he rode away, hating him all over again, yet unable to help noticing what a handsome man he was. She sighed. This afternoon was going to be the longest of her life.

Nicholas followed a well-marked trail that he assumed circled widely back to the house. He was actually glad of the respite from Jessica's overwhelming presence. The girl had no idea how unconsciously alluring she was despite her coltish manner, and for the first time in his life he felt himself becoming thoroughly enthralled with a virtual stranger. When he was near her, it required great effort to affect the light, teasing tone that riled her so thoroughly. He sighed, remembering her brilliant smile, dancing green eyes, luxurious hair, and the way her boyish shirt had gaped from the curves of her very womanly bosom.

He chuckled to himself. It was so unlike him to be attracted to an innocent. Charlotte was more in keeping with his tastes—pampered, worldly, poised, beautiful. Yet for the first time he realized that, for all Charlotte's beauty—and he had to admit that she was more beautiful than Jessica in the classic sense—he had never truly enjoyed being with her. Her conversation was limited, her chatter almost grating, and her apparent innocence calculating. She was not at all like Jessica, who was completely honest and unaffected.

Yes, Jessica was innocent, but with an intriguing style of innocence, not the giggling schoolgirl kind. Hers was an earthy, unrehearsed variety far different from the role of false sophistication she had played the evening before. Nicholas had to admit he found her interesting, unconventional, and a challenge. Certainly she didn't like him.

He smiled widely. No, she didn't like him at all. What a refreshing thought. She couldn't even bring herself to call him by his given name.

He recalled the feel of her soft yet firm body in his arms, the lamplight shining in golden waves over her flushed cheeks, and his eyes grew wistful. She was a challenge, indeed. With her, he thought, he would never be bored. Bruised perhaps, but never bored.

As he neared the stable he slowed his horse and warily handed his reins to the stableboy. This time he was sure the servant *was* a boy. Richard came out on the porch steps to greet him.

"Egads, you're up early, Nick."

"When you work on a plantation, rising early becomes a fact of life."

"Well, come in for a bite of breakfast then. Jessica is

still abed, although I find that strange since she's usually an early riser.''

Nicholas stifled a smile and followed the older man into the dining room. He was surprised to see only two place settings on the mahogany table.

''Where's Lucy?''

''Oh, she had some matters to attend to, and I wanted to speak with you alone, my boy. Please have a seat.''

Curious, Nicholas dropped into a chair. A servant put a plate of tempting food before him and poured dark, rich coffee into his cup.

''What is it you want to discuss, Dick?'' Nicholas asked. ''Does it have anything to do with the gray mare I was interested in purchasing?''

''Might be a double bargain at that,'' Richard muttered. ''Nick, this is a matter of much delicacy,'' he hastened to explain, ''and I approach you with it most hesitantly. If you find what I am about to say unacceptable, it will go no further than this room.''

Nicholas raised an interested eyebrow and watched in amusement as Richard flustered about for a moment before he caught Nicholas's gaze with a steely look of his own.

''I should like very much for you to propose marriage to my cousin Jessica.''

Nicholas abruptly sat forward as he choked on a mouthful of coffee. Richard pounded him soundly on the back as he sputtered and wheezed. Finally Nicholas straightened up and wiped his mouth with his napkin.

''Good God, man, have you lost your mind? Why in the name of heaven would I want to marry Jessica?'' Unbidden, a brief image of her lovely smile and sparkling eyes flashed in his mind.

''I can give you several good reasons, Nicholas, one being that the girl needs to marry quickly in order to keep her inheritance—an inheritance that would profit you both. I explained all that yesterday. My first concern is for the girl. There are certain parties, unknown as yet, who would very much like to see Jessica kept from what is rightfully hers. Just before she came away with me from Williamsburg, she barely escaped death—jumped into a burning room to save her brother. She's a brave girl, and she'd do any man credit as his wife. Lucy and I are afraid that we will be unable to protect her for much longer. She needs a man.''

"That may be so, Dick, but why do you think I am that man? I hardly know the girl.''

"Yes, yes, quite right. I know that you are interested in another young woman, and I can understand where your loyalties might stand." Richard sighed heavily. "I trust you, Nick. I've known you ever since you came into this world, and there's no one to whom I'd rather see the girl wed. You're a man of honor and principle, and not many like that are left. You've wealth of your own, hence I have no fear that you would rob Jessica of her inheritance." A sly look came over his face. "And I know for a fact that you are strongly attracted to the girl, despite her rather aloof behavior last night.''

"Let us assume that what you have said is true," Nicholas replied after a thoughtful silence. "What makes you so certain Jessica would even consider marriage to me? As far as I can tell, she's not fond of me, although I can't for the life of me understand what I've done to set her against me.''

Richard regarded him enigmatically and spoke with confidence. "If you want her as your wife, Nicholas, she'll marry you.''

"How can you be so sure?''

Richard shook his head. "Call it a gut feeling. If you agree to marry her, Lucy will approach the girl with your proposal." He stood up, and Nicholas rose to his feet as well. "Well, my boy, I'd be honored to have you in the family, but of course the decision is yours. I'll let you think it over. I wouldn't have come to you so soon with this outrageous proposition, but you will be leaving us shortly, and I thought the sooner the better." Richard picked up his pipe from the table, prepared to quit the room.

"Dick, just one moment. You said that Jessica would have to marry to retain her inheritance, correct?" Richard nodded. Again an image of Jessica's face lingered in Nicholas's mind. "You would dangle Jessica's inheritance before my eyes as bait to ensure that I marry the girl. Why is it so important to you? If I am not mistaken, you told me last night that she has almost a year to marry."

Richard shifted uncomfortably and continued with difficulty, "Jeremy and I were very close. I loved him as a brother. I have to admit I am disappointed that he didn't consider me the logical choice to raise his daughter, but instead gave her over to a farmer and his wife. Jessica has been the one to suffer for it. She has been deprived of the kind of upbringing that was her right as a Montagu. Now I have the chance to right this wrong. She is entitled to all that her father intended for her, and I mean to see she has it. I fear for the girl, and can only suspect—without proof, mind you—that whoever murdered her parents is still lurking about.

"I know that I have no right to pass the burden of her protection on to you, but you see, as soon as she is married, the murderers will have no way to lay hold of her wealth. It will be hers completely, as it should have been Jeremy's. I'll not let anything happen to her, Nick. She's too innocent to be involved in such dangerous intrigue."

Nicholas nodded, convinced of the man's sincerity. Richard continued. "But I don't want you to marry the girl out of pity for her. She's a fine woman: decent, honest, and intelligent. You would be proud of her, Nick."

"I have known her for only a day, but I sense that what you say is true—though she does have a temper and is not the innocent angel you paint her to be." He recounted their meeting in the stable the night before, to Richard's amused delight.

"So she kicked you, eh? Ha, I knew I liked the girl."

"Yes, and I have quite a nasty bruise to prove it."

Richard laughed all the harder. "Well, at least she's no simpering ninny, and I'd hate to see all that spirit wasted on another man who might not appreciate it as you would."

Nicholas's brows drew down in concentration. For some reason the idea of Jessica married to someone else was definitely distasteful to him. More than that, it was almost unthinkable. Jessica was certainly not his responsibility, but for some strange reason he suddenly wanted her to be, a thought that utterly amazed him. Nicholas was not by nature an impetuous man, far from it; he was most deliberate in everything he did. So he was astounded by the sudden, overwhelming urge that pressured him to quickly accept Richard Montagu's offer.

He knew there were practical reasons why Jessica would make an even better match than Charlotte. After all, Jessica would bear title to estates neighboring his own ancestral home, and she looked strong enough to bear him several fine children. And yet, the image of her huge green eyes staring longingly up into his in the glow of lamplight eclipsed his more sound reasoning, and the feel of her tall, firm body in his arms lingered enchantingly. Of a sudden he stepped forward and extended his hand to Richard.

Richard smiled widely as the two men shook hands, sealing the engagement. Nicholas himself couldn't suppress a grin. He had come to Kentucky with the intention of buying several mules. Now, it seemed, he would come away with a wife.

"He wants me to *what!?*"

"Hush, my dear, he might hear you." Aunt Lucy's faded blue eyes roamed over the rows of books in the Montagus' library.

"I hope he does hear me. How can you even suggest that I marry that—that—that— There are no words to do justice to the way I feel about him."

"Calm down, Jessica, you're working yourself into apoplexy. You needn't marry Nicholas if you find the idea utterly distasteful. Only listen to reason." Lucy grabbed Jessica's arm and forced her into a chair. Even through the red haze of her rage, Jessica was surprised by the strength of the petite older woman. She sat down ungracefully with her arms crossed, her mouth tightened in a mutinous line. "Are you listening, dear . . . Jessica?"

"Yes, damn it all!"

"Good heavens, I'll have none of that language in my home, do you understand?"

"Yes, aunt." Jessica lowered her head, meekly contrite.

"That's better. The very idea! Now that you're calm, I want to explain why I think marriage to Nicholas would be very wise."

Jessica stared up at the large oil portrait of her parents that hugn over the mantel and spoke rhetorically to the smiling couple. "This cannot be happening. I cannot believe that this is happening. Wake up, Jessica, you're having a nightmare. Your aunt is insane, and you're having a nightmare."

"Jessica, darling, do stop babbling. You must see reason. Nicholas can offer you security. He's wealthy, so you know he doesn't care a fig about your money, and you do need to marry to keep your inheritance. Your uncle and I are old, and we don't know how much longer we'll be able to protect you."

Jessica turned away from the tormenting words. She was so confused; she needed the comfort of her mother's wisdom. Then her aunt's insistent voice brought her head up with a start.

"Your uncle tells me he has received a letter from your stepfather." Jessica dreaded the words to come. "I know I shouldn't tell you this. Your uncle would be most displeased if he knew, but it's the only thing I can think of that will make you see reason. You stepfather intends to come after you. He believes any danger to you is past now. Jessica dear, think. If you are married when he arrives there will be no need to place your family in danger again. I'm sorry to have to say these things to you, my dove, but . . ." Lucy's voice trailed off into a whisper as she looked at Jessica's face, which had turned white with shock.

She rose woodenly to her feet. "Yes, aunt, I can see your reasoning. You have given me much to think about. I'll let you know of my decision tonight. Right now, I promised Nicholas that I would give him a tour of the stable."

With drooping shoulders, Jessica slowly left the library. She closed the door quietly behind her and continued up to her room. She did, indeed, have much to think about.

"I'm not going to cry, I'm not, I'm not," she repeated over and over. "Many women marry for reasons other than love. Why should I be any different?"

A fleeting image of her father sitting on the bed holding Sarah's hand and staring tenderly down at his wife's pale face cauterized her mind. She knew her mother would never have allowed her to enter a loveless marriage, no matter what the cause. Maybe she could just run away. She laughed humorlessly to herself. Run away where? England, to her unwanted, unfamiliar estate? Anyway, unless she married, she would have no money, no way of supporting herself.

She just couldn't do it. Nicholas Carlyle thoroughly intimidated her. And how could she possibly consider marriage to a stranger? Unbidden, the image of his handsome face leaning down to kiss her in the glow of the lamplight sprang into her thoughts. It was quickly followed by the vision of Joey sleeping amid leaping flames. She gasped aloud. Oh, God, no. What was she going to do?

The only answer that repeatedly battered against her aching head was the one from which she constantly sought to escape.

Selfish fool, she thought. You're acting childishly. So far you've managed to get through eighteen years of your life without the grand emotion of love. You can safely manage to survive the remaining years without it. Perhaps, given time, you'll even learn to love this stranger, this Nicholas Carlyle. After all, you said you would do anything to ensure your family's safety. Now it is time to live up to your promise.

Sitting on the floor in front of the cold fireplace, she sought to bolster her courage until she heard the delicate chimes of the mantel clock ring twelve times. She rose slowly, her muscles cramped, and wearily dressed in a fashionable smoke-gray riding habit. She went down the stairs, crossed the foyer, and glided toward the door that the butler held open for her.

"Peter, do you perhaps know where Mr. Carlyle might be? I offered to take him on a tour of the grounds."

"Why, yes, miss. He's gone to the stable. I overheard him tellin' Mistah Richard that his horse threw a shoe this mornin'."

"Oh, that's nice," she said in distraction, and ignored the strange look Peter gave her.

The sky was beginning to darken with ominous gray clouds, and a chill breeze had sprung up from the west. Jessica pulled her fur-lined pelisse more closely about her shoulders as she started the short stroll down to the stable. How in the world was she going to face Nicholas?

As she reached the stable she squelched a nervous laugh that might have led to hysteria. Pausing uncertainly in the doorway, she heard the distinct sound of a hammer and anvil. Nicholas, holding Lancelot's forehoof firmly in his gloved hand, was looking over his shoulder at the blacksmith.

"Doesn't seem to be any damage to the frog," he said. "Thank you for taking care of it for me so quickly."

The blacksmith nodded, and Nicholas stood back, carefully watching the man fit the shoe. Jessica cleared her throat, and Nicholas looked up. He smiled at the sight of her in the pearl-gray cashmere pelisse. Dainty, feminine gray boots peeped out from under her stylish habit.

"I did promise you a tour," she said. "Are you still interested?"

Nicholas nodded as he grabbed his redingnote and quickly slipped into it. Her manner was so solemn and subdued that he could only assume that Lucy had approached her with his proposal. He searched her beautiful face for some clue as to her answer, but could read nothing in her dull green eyes. He took her elbow and led her out the back door next to a large shed where Richard kept his farming equipment.

"Jessica?"

She looked up into his gray eyes—gray like the clouds, gray like her mood—and knew what he wanted her to say. She would have given anything not to have to speak the words.

"It seems I shall marry you," she said quietly.

Nicholas let out a slow breath, surprised to realize he had been holding it, suddenly aware of an overwhelming sense of relief. Staring down at her, he saw only the top of her bowed head.

"Dick said you would agree to my proposal." He put his thumb under her chin and forced her to meet his eyes. "Why?"

"I'm sure Richard told you that I must marry to keep my inheritance. Isn't it obvious why I would marry you?"

"You do not necessarily need to marry *me* in order to hold your estates in England. Why did you agree?"

She pushed his hand away wearily and moved to lean against the shed. "Does it really matter?" Then a thought occurred to her that had somehow escaped her mind before. She looked up at him. "You asked me why I agreed to your proposal, but I can turn the same question upon you. Why do you want to marry me?"

"Does it really matter, Jessica?" he said, turning her

previous words against her. "Suffice to say that I find you an attractive woman and our arrangement can be mutually beneficial. Aside from that, you're unique and pose quite a challenge to me."

"A challenge? How so?" Her brows drew down in a puzzled frown.

"You dislike me."

"And so because I dislike you, you immediately propose marriage. That is precisely the sort of answer one might expect from either a madman or a fool. Which might you be?"

He smiled sheepishly. "And what of you, Jessica? After all, you agreed to marry this demented, idiotic soul."

"I can always change my mind, sir. We are not yet married."

Nicholas moved closer to where she stood. The wind whipped her hair about her cold cheeks, and he reached up to sweep the tangled curls away from her face, a face that seemed to be drained of color. He smiled gently.

"You should be wearing a hat." His hand moved to cup her chin, and he stroked her lower lip with the ball of his thumb. "Don't be sad, Jessica. I promise I'll be good to you." He leaned down, intent upon pressing a soft kiss to her trembling mouth, but felt her hands push forcefully against his chest.

"I told you, I'm not your wife yet, and I don't remember giving you permission to touch me," she stated coldly.

Nicholas forced a tight smile and stepped slowly away from her rigid form, his hands held palms outward at his shoulders. He shook his head slowly, and the smile slipped a little wider as he sensed the open defiance in her stance. He dropped his hands to his sides.

"You're right, of course. I apologize. But you do have such a kissable mouth. I find myself wondering if I shall ever be given permission to taste it." Jessica turned away in a huff as he continued, "I suppose I should count myself fortunate that you didn't kick me again."

A strangled sound met his ears. Nicholas chuckled. "In any case, my dear, ours promises to be a very interesting marriage."

Sarah reread Jessica's letter for the third time. She looked up quickly when the sound of creaking floorboards alerted her to Andrew's presence in the kitchen.

"Are they all asleep?" she whispered.

Andrew nodded and sat down next to her at the table. "Yes, finally."

"How's Joseph?"

"Fine, just fine, Sarah. I think he feels better now that he's back in his old room with Alex and Robert."

"Thank God, Andrew. I never thought he would get well. If the doctor had had to amputate that leg, I just don't know what we would have done."

"It doesn't matter now, love. The way you nursed him night and day, I don't think he had any choice but to get well. Poor lad, he's been through a lot."

"As have we all." Sarah sighed. "And now there's this letter."

"I know you've been upset about it all day."

"Jessica sent this letter weeks ago. My God, Andrew, she's probably married by now. Married! Can you believe it?" Sarah jumped up from her seat, and Andrew grabbed her hand to pull her down next to him again.

"Don't worry, so, Sarah. I'm sure she's fine."

"I don't know, Andrew. I just don't know. Something is not right here."

"Sarah, I think you're being too suspicious."

"Suspicious? Andrew, our daughter has been gone such a short time, and already she has managed to find the perfect husband." She frowned. "The way she describes him, one would think he has descended from the gods."

"Don't you remember how it was to fall in love for the first time?"

"Of course," she snapped. "I'm not that old!"

Andrew laughed. "Nor was I suggesting that you are, my love. Believe me, I share your concern, but we must trust that Jessica is mature enough to make her own decisions. It is her life to lead, not ours."

Sarah slumped against him, leaning her head on her husband's shoulder. "I know. You're right. It's just that I don't trust this Carlyle fellow. His association with Richard Montagu is suspect enough, but this part about his having once owned the land next to Jessica's properties. . ." She shook her head. "It just seems too convenient. You know how gullible Jessica can sometimes be. If this man is as accomplished a gentleman as she describes him, then he would fine it an easy task to manipulate her into falling in love with him just so he could wheedle his way into her inheritance."

"Come now, Sarah. Jessica is not such a fool as to be taken in by polish and poise. She's an intelligent girl. Have faith in our teachings and in the way we raised her. Besides, Jessica said the man is very wealthy."

"I just cannot help worrying about her. Her letters are much too cheerful. And look here." She pointed to one particular paragraph. "What's this all about? 'Now that I will soon be married, Papa, I have saved you the trouble of journeying all the way to Lexington. I hope, however, that someday you and the rest of the family will visit me in the Carolinas.' Did you ever write her to say we were going to Kentucky?"

Andrew shrugged. "No, I didn't, but maybe she became confused and thought we might go to Kentucky for the wedding. Who can tell? Sarah"—he pulled his wife into his arms—"Sarah, what is really bothering you?"

She leaned her head against his chest. "I don't know, Andrew. It's just an uneasy feeling. If only I could see her and hold her in my arms. Then I would know whether my fears are of my own making."

"Does it mean all that much to you?"

"We haven't even met this man she married. And why

did she not invite us to the ceremony?'' She put up a hand in anticipation of her husband's reply. "And no, it is not that fact that has me distraught. I'm not angry that she neglected to tell us about the wedding in ample time to ensure our attendance. It almost seems as though she wanted to be safely married before she let on about it. It's just not like her to behave that way.''

"Perhaps she did not want us to feel obligated to make the long journey.''

"Ridiculous! She knows I would travel twice as far to see her happily wed. There is something not right here, Andrew, mark my words. I just know it, and here I stand, too far away to know for certain.''

"Sarah, if you continue in this manner, you will soon have me equally worried. Let us give her some more time to adjust to her new life and her husband. I don't think it would be right for us to interrupt what should be a private time for both of them. Please, Sarah. It is hard for me, too, to digest this news of her marriage, but we must give her time.''

Sarah sighed raggedly. "All right, Andrew, but just a bit more time.'' Looking down at the letter, she prayed that all was well with her only daughter.

Chapter 6

"Jessica, please try to eat your dinner, my dear. Unless it is your desire to look emaciated by the time we arrive in Charleston."

"What?" Jessica practically started out of her seat.

She and her new husband had been on the road for about a week now, and the tedium of travel had sapped Jessica's energy. She was certain that even her bones were sore from bouncing up and down all day long.

"I'm not hungry. It's difficult to acquire an appetite when all I do is sit in the carriage all day."

"Don't tell me you're going to become a complaining wife already," Nicholas said teasingly.

Jessica looked up defensively. "I truly did not mean to nag at you. I am just unused to such enforced inactivity."

"Ah, yes, with your stable duties and whatnot. I'm sure you kept yourself very busy in Kentucky."

Jessica lowered her eyes, refusing to react to his baiting. Instead she spoke quietly. "You're never going to let me forget about that, are you?"

"Not when it bothers you so much." Nicholas's smile was only slightly exaggerated.

Jessica looked up at him in exasperation. "You're a frightful tease, do you know that?"

"It is something I've managed to excel at since meeting you."

"And may I say that you do it quite well," she replied tartly.

"Thank you. I am happy to accept any compliment from you, and I believe that was the first and only."

Jessica felt her face growing hot at his slow smile. His eyes seemed to caress her features fondly before he leaned across the small table and gently took her hand in his. Instinctively Jessica pulled away from his grasp and sat further back in her chair. For a tense moment his silvery-gray eyes seemed to bore into her skull, but finally he sighed shortly and withdrew his fingers, smiling in bemusement.

"Surely, my dear wife, we are well enough acquainted so that I might at least hold your hand," he said dryly.

"Of course . . . it's just that . . ." Flustered, she sought an explanation but could not find the proper words.

His smile softened. "Please don't feel you must explain yourself to me."

"No, you are right, but I . . ."

Her voice dwindled to an embarrassed whisper as she became painfully aware of what Nicholas was implying. It had been six weeks since she had met him and two weeks since the wedding, yet their marriage had not been consummated. Jessica knew instinctively that since she had so soundly refused Nicholas's kisses from the beginning, he was waiting for her to make the first overtures in that direction. And for the life of her, she had no idea how to proceed.

He must have seen the confused expression on her face, for he reached across the table again and firmly took her hand. This time she did not protest.

"I'm sorry if I upset you, Jessica."

"No, not at all. It's just that I don't know . . . I mean I've never . . ." Her face flushed again. "Oh God, I don't know what I mean."

He squeezed her fingers and smiled warmly. "I think I understand."

She released a shaky sigh.

He let go of her hand and, laughing, sat up in his chair. "I'm glad that is settled. Now, please humor me and at least eat something. I wouldn't want anyone to think I was starving you, and I dislike skinny women."

"But you like Aunt Lucy." She put a bite of potato into her mouth and chewed unenthusiastically.

"That one! If there ever was a formidable mother-in-law, it is she. I still don't know how you baffled her grand plans for our wedding."

"That was simple. I told her that if she wanted to attend our wedding, she would have to do as I requested, or I would run away." Jessica smiled in memory of Lucy's dramatic reaction to being thwarted.

"And . . ."

"And, after I revived her from a dead faint, she began to realize that I could be as stubborn as she."

"I, too, am already realizing that fact."

"Pardon me, but I adamantly refused to be displayed at my own wedding in front of strangers. My goodness, I think she had in mind to invite the whole state of Kentucky. I know it's late to ask, but I hope you don't mind that I deterred her."

"Not at all, my dear. I am not too fond of pomp myself, and our simple ceremony was more to my liking, although I hope you won't insist on staying in hiding when we arrive in Charleston. I'd like very much to show you off to my friends."

Jessica practically blanched at the thought. What would they think of "Lord Carlyle" and his common wife? What had she gotten herself into with this hasty marriage? His voice interrupted her dire thoughts.

"Jessica, it's late, and we must be on the road early tomorrow. Have you finished your dinner, or would you like more time to massacre your potato?"

Jessica abruptly dropped her fork and, shaking her head, pushed herself wearily away from the table. Her husband came around to offer his arm.

"With your permission?"

"As always," she said a bit sarcastically.

They left the common room and went up the stairs. Nicholas opened the door to her room, and she preceded him inside. She lit the bedside lamp and stood rather awkwardly holding it. She always hated saying good-night, for somehow it made her feel very guilty to watch him turn away and go to his own room. She tensed as he stepped close to her and reached out to toy with one of the thick curls lying over her shoulder. He spoke softly and slowly.

"Is there anything I can get for you before you go to sleep?" He leaned closer to her. "Anything at all?"

A little flustered by the strange feelings his nearness evoked, Jessica turned away to set the lamp down, but could still feel him caressing her hair. She twisted her hands together and then, realizing what she was doing, dropped them to her sides.

"No, I don't want anything right now." She sighed deeply, then suddenly turned to look straight into his eyes, giving voice to a fear that had haunted her since the beginning of their marriage. "I don't know if I can learn to live in your world."

Nicholas looked surprised for a moment at her honest, heartfelt statement and then spoke softly, feeling lost in the depths of her wide green eyes.

"You can do whatever you wish, Jessica." He drew his fingers through her red-brown tresses. "I think you'll be well able to live in anyone's world, even mine. I suspect you'll be a breath of fresh air in the stuffy, complacent atmosphere in Charleston, and don't worry that I'll desert you, for I shan't. We rebels must stay together, mustn't we?''

She lowered her gaze to stare at his polished boots. "I appreciate all you have already done for me. I am very grateful.'' She felt her chin being lifted and met his intense stare.

"I would like much more than your gratitude, Jessica.''

"You've been very patient, and I . . . I . . .''

He put his fingers to her lips. "Say no more. I understand more than you think I do.'' He walked to the door connecting his room to hers. "Good night, Jessica.''

She watched his broad-shouldered frame duck through the doorway and heard the latch click quietly behind him. She thought about what he had said. In a few days she would be among strangers again. Would she ever feel at home at his plantation, Providence? Even more pressing were the doubts she had about herself and her abilities to live in a genteel world. She ached to express her worst anxieties to someone, but she didn't know to whom she could turn.

Nicholas seemed willing to listen, but he still intimidated her, and it took all the control and wit she could muster to casually banter with him. She knew that soon she would have to submit to him, and she was surprised that the prospect didn't seem as unpleasant as it once had. Yet she was amazed that he did not force the issue. She reminded herself that she was only his wife by convenience. Perhaps he didn't care for her strongly enough to demand intimacy between them. Why else would he be so kind and understanding? Perhaps he just saw her as a frightened child who needed guidance. She snorted—his child-bride.

The weeks before the wedding should have been a time during which to become acquainted, yet, chiefly due to her stubborn reticence and fear of an unknown future, she had learned practically nothing of her husband-to-be. The many horseback rides they had taken together—with her in proper attire for once, and shadowed by a groom—had been strained and silent. Nicholas, of course, had been the perfect gentleman. She cursed her shyness in retrospect, but knew she could not change the past. She was more than a little amazed that Nicholas had even gone through with the wedding, considering the almost beetle-brained way she had behaved toward him. But then he wasn't marrying her for love, so she supposed he didn't care in the least that his future wife showed a marked inclination toward mental deficiency.

How she wanted him to think of her as a desirable woman! The strange feelings she experienced when she looked at him were growing stronger, and yet she didn't quite know what to do about them.

She was such a ninny. Why didn't she just present herself to him and have the act behind her? She was certain that the waiting was the worst of it. She looked toward the door. It was so close, and he was just on the other side. She took a tentative step forward and stopped. Oh Lord, she didn't even know what it was that she was supposed to do. She sighed and began to change into a lacy nightgown.

Tonight, she promised herself, she was not going to cry.

Nicholas lay on his back with his hands clasped behind his neck, his thoughts on the young woman who was his wife. How much longer could he keep from kissing her into submission? When would his control finally snap?

Maybe he had been unwise to marry the girl. She seemed so lost and forlorn, as if all her happiness had abruptly ended the day she had agreed to become his wife. It was hard for him to admit, but he was at a loss as to how to overcome her reticence, especially since his strong desire for her body kept his mind in constant turmoil. It was no wonder that he spent so much time riding beside the carriage on Lancelot and not in it. It seemed to him that she preferred solitude to his company, so he patiently continued to bide his time. But by now he thought he had shown more than enough patience with the girl.

He could certainly understand her homesickness for her family in Virginia. He could certainly respect her fear, pain, and the awkwardness of being an innocent married to a stranger. But why was she so damned skittish? Women! Was losing their virginity such an all-fired mystic ritual?

If only she wasn't so beautiful, then maybe it wouldn't be such a considerable struggle to stay away from her during their journey home. Just last night he had slipped into her room while she was asleep and gazed at her face. Even in the dim firelight, he had seen the dried tears on her cheeks. So he had maintained his distance, hoping that in time she would come to him.

He would accept nothing less than a willing and eager partner. He was completely opposed to forcing himself on any maid, let alone his wife. How long would it take for her to reach out to him? Groaning at the ache in his body, he hoped it would be soon.

Jessica came awake slowly when she heard a strange scraping noise at the foot of her bed, followed by a high-pitched squeak. She bolted upright, holding the bed-covers to her chin. The scratching became louder, and with trembling fingers she reached for the lamp and managed to light it. Holding it up, she heard a scurrying noise and saw a large, furry rodent scuttle out from under the bed and scamper across the floor.

Jessica clapped a hand to her mouth to prevent a rising scream from escaping. Being raised on a farm, she was afraid of few creatures, but rats absolutely terrified her. She glanced longingly at her husband's closed door. Earlier this evening it had seemed too near; suddenly it felt too far away. One thing was certain, however; she was not going to spend to rest of the night in this room with a rat! The mere thought made her shudder in disgust.

Carefully she placed the lamp on the table, leaned low over the side of the bed, and lifted the quilt from where it had slid onto the floor. More scratching noises made her bolt back in alarm.

"Don't panic, don't panic," she whispered, hoping the sound of her voice would calm her nerves. Then, taking a deep breath, she lowered her feet to the floor. There were more scrapings, and she jerked her feet up again. Oh Lord, after all she had been through the last few months, it was galling to be trapped in her bed by a rat.

She tightened her hands into fists and closed her eyes. The only solution was to make a mad dash for her husband's room. All right, she was ready. Summoning every ounce of courage, she bolted from the bed and ran across the cold floor. Perhaps it was her imagination, but she could almost hear something scuttling after her. She fumbled with the latch on the door as the scratching grew louder, and almost screamed when the door seemed to stick.

Finally the latch lifted, and she burst into Nicholas's room. Not pausing to think, she bounded onto his bed. His body jerked under the blankets at her rude interruption of his sleep.

"What the devil . . . ?" Instinctively he lashed out with his fists, and Jessica barely avoided having her nose adjusted.

"It's me, Jessica," she whispered frantically.

The thrashing stopped, and he sat up under the covers. "Good Lord, what's the matter?" he asked, noticing the pinched look of fear on her face. "You're pale and shaking, and your eyes look like twin moons."

Jessica pointed a trembling finger toward the door. "It's in there waiting for me. It might have even followed me out."

"What in the world are you talking about? Is someone in your room?" He started to push back the covers, a concerned expression on his face, but Jessica's words stopped him.

"A rat. A big, furry, ugly, hairy, disgusting rat, with big teeth and sharp, filthy claws, and . . ."

Nicholas's shoulders began to shake.

"It's not funny, I tell you! It could have bitten me, and there's no telling what disease I would have died from."

"Good Lord, Jessica if I had known that this fear of rats would have catapulted you into my bed, I would have put one in your room long ago."

"It's not in the least amusing. I hate rats. They're foul, repulsive creatures."

"I know. With big teeth, and sharp claws and beady little eyes."

"I never said beady little eyes." Although Jessica looked at him spitefully, she was still shaking inside.

Nicholas smiled and, relenting, leaned forward to take her in his arms. "It's all right now. I'm sure you scared the poor thing away."

Jessica sighed in relief and began to relax. Nicholas was stroking her hair comfortingly, and she smelled the pleasant musky scent of his body. For the first time she realized that her head was pressed up against his naked chest. She could only assume that the rest of him was naked as well. His lips moved against her hair.

"All right now?"

"Yes. Thank you."

She felt his lips move down to press a soft kiss against her temple. "Are you sure?"

"No . . . I mean, yes."

This time his breath was warm in her ear. "Which is it, Jessica, yes . . ."

She felt strange shivers when his teeth tugged at the lobe of her ear, and her heart nearly jumped out of her chest when his lips moved down to her throat.

". . . or no?"

She knew he was speaking of something entirely different from her fear a moment earlier. He slid his hands to her shoulders and pushed her away so that she was forced to look into his eyes. A strong, primitive emotion rose up in her at the sight of his handsome face and his broad, naked chest, and the feeling frightened her even more than the rat had. Something flickered in and out of Nicholas's eyes as he stared down at her face, framed by her wildly mussed hair. His eyes narrowed as they slid lower to the curves revealed by her flimsy gown. Jessica swallowed with effort as his hands began to stroke up and down her arms.

"I . . . ah . . . I'm tired now."

He smiled meaningfully. "Do you want to go back to your room?"

Jessica glanced toward the door. If ever she was caught between the devil and the deep blue sea, this was it.

"No," she said.

"Do you want to stay with me, then?"

"No."

He leaned forward to kiss the tip of her nose. "Are you sure?"

She sighed. "No."

"Then why don't you stay?" Of a sudden his hand moved very deliberately lower, and slowly his fingers moved over the peak of one breast.

Jessica's breath seemed to catch in her throat, and a strange tingling began at the juncture of her thighs. Completely confused by these sudden feelings, she pushed away from her husband and scrambled off his bed. Nicholas closed his eyes for a moment, seeming to fight with himself, and released his breath slowly. He stared at her for a moment in frustration, then looked behind her at the light streaming in from her room. Suddenly he pointed.

"Look, there's something behind you!"

Jessica screamed and in one leap was back in his bed, clutching his chest. His arms went around her, and she could feel his shoulders shaking. Angrily she shook him off and crawled back to the foot of his bed.

"You tricked me!"

Nicholas laughed. "It did get you back into my bed."

"Well, if you were a gentleman, you would offer to sleep in *my* room tonight."

"My dear wife, if I were anything less than a gentleman, there would have been no question of separate beds on this or any other night."

Jessica's cheeks flamed scarlet as he raised her chin, forcing her to see the naked desire in his eyes. "I don't know what you want from me," she murmured.

"Oh, I think you know more than you're willing to admit. I can feel your body trembling with the same passion that is making me ache from wanting you."

"But we hardly know each other. What about caring and friendship and . . . ?"

Nicholas shook his head. "No, Jessica. What I want from you tonight has very little to do with any of those tender emotions."

"Well, I don't think I could ever be intimate with a man unless I was first in love with him."

"You don't know what you're talking about. It's past time you learned a few things about the feelings that can be very easily aroused between men and women."

"I don't need you to tutor me. I've been tutored to death about everything from how to pour tea to which fork to use when I eat artichokes, and I loathe artichokes."

"Fine, just fine! Then there is nothing I can teach you. There is nothing you do not know."

"Correct!"

"Well then, if you will avert your tender, virgin eyes, I am going to get out of this bed, and like the damn fool gentleman I am, I will go into your room and there spend a miserable night!"

"Good!"

Jessica turned her head away and closed her eyes as he threw back the covers and stalked across the room. He stopped, and she could hear his angry footfalls coming toward her.

"Did you forget something?"

"You are sitting on my robe."

He practically flipped her off the bed as he yanked the robe out from under her.

"Thank you," he said sarcastically. Then she heard a weary sigh. "You know, you could be sending me to certain death in there, if your furry friend is still about."

"I'll weep at your funeral."

He gave a stifled curse, then added more softly, "Jessica, you need not keep your eyes closed. I am wearing my robe."

She opened one eye cautiously, and when she saw he was telling the truth, opened the other as well. He was standing with legs braced and arms akimbo. His hair was tossed and sticking up in the back. Somehow he didn't appear quite as intimidating as he had earlier.

"Are all you farm girls so blasted provincial?" he asked.

"Only when we want to be."

His hands dropped to his sides. "I'm leaving now. Lord knows I've been patient enough. Be warned, Jessica, that I will not always be so in the future." Giving her a warning glare, he turned on his heel and strode from the room, closing the door firmly behind him.

It was just like him to have the last word, Jessica thought resentfully as she crawled to the head of the bed and quickly pulled the covers over her. They were still warm from his body and smelled of his cologne. She wrapped her arms around his pillow and smiled. He really wasn't such a bad fellow, and she had to admit that she had deliberately provoked him.

Her smile disappeared. Sometimes, like when he kissed her, he made her feel so strange, so unlike herself. If only she knew how he really felt about her. Perhaps, as he had stated, his interest was purely physical. Her mouth drew down in an unhappy frown. She wanted more than that from him. Her brow wrinkled. Could it be that she was beginning to actually like him? No, that would never do, she thought as she drifted off to sleep. It would only give him something more to tease her about.

Chapter 7

The cold wind and rain made it a night that invited people to stay behind thick doors, preferably seated comfortably next to a crackling fire. Had Nicholas any choice, that is precisely where he would have been at that moment, and as the carriage bounced and slid along the muddy road, he heartily cursed the broken wheel that had delayed their arrival at Providence. With obvious malice the November storm had even provided a rare display of thunder and lightning to add to the discomfort of the weary travelers. It was well past midnight now, and by Nicholas's ciphering, Providence was another good hour away.

With arms folded, he stared at Jessica huddled in the corner of the seat opposite him. Although she shivered from the cold, the light from the wall sconces, their flames swaying with the rhythm of the coach, confirmed that she was deeply asleep. Releasing an exasperated sigh, he unfastened his heavily lined cloak and draped it carefully over her, then lifted her unresisting body onto his lap. She smiled fleetingly in her sleep and burrowed more comfortably in his lap, her hand coming to rest on his thigh. Nicholas inhaled sharply at the sensations she aroused, fighting to gain control of his emotions. Idiot, he silently rebuked himself.

Except for the night on which the rodent had sent her scurrying into his bed five days ago, this was the closest he had come to the stubborn girl. He looked down at her face, innocent and touchingly lovely in slumber, and a feeling almost like pain shot through him. Even in her sleep, however, there was a disturbed frown marring her countenance. He stroked her hair gently, marveling at the soft, silky texture, unashamedly enjoying these peaceful moments alone with her without the ever-present tension between them.

There was a muffled thump on the top of the carriage, and Nicholas heard Isaac's voice above the din of the storm outside. "Two miles to go, Marse Nick."

He sighed in relief. They would be at Providence sooner than he had anticipated. It would be good to get home. He laughed humorlessly to himself. Two months ago he had been anxious to get away, and now he was just as anxious to return. He looked down at Jessica's relaxed face and reluctantly bent to awaken her.

"Jessica? Jessica, wake up."

"In a moment, Papa, I'll be down," she mumbled as she stirred slightly.

Nicholas smiled softly and tried again, this time shaking her shoulder gently. "Jessica, we're almost home."

Her eyes blinked open, and she lay for a moment unsure of her surroundings. She felt so warm and comfortable just now, the blanket over her body exuding a familiar and stirring scent. Why did the voice keep insisting that she wake up? She hugged her pillow more closely to her, and suddenly realized that it was no pillow she held. She tripped into full awareness and bolted upright out of Nicholas's arms, regarding him in embarrassment.

"I'm terribly sorry." She noticed the cloak wrapped around her and smiled timidly. "Thank you."

Nicholas smiled warmly back into her flushed face as

she handed him the garment. He leaned forward and rewrapped the cloak around her. "The pleasure was mine, I assure you."

Jessica pulled aside the heavy curtains and looked out the window, but she could see no sign of a house. She turned to Nicholas in confusion.

"I thought you said that we were almost there."

"We've still a little ways to travel. Don't worry, you'll soon be able to go back to sleep."

Jessica clutched her hands in her lap and wondered in whose bed she would sleep. She leaned against the leather seat and, under the amused stare of her husband, attempted to straighten her hair and brush the creases out of her traveling outfit.

"No need to primp, Jessica. The servants are no doubt all abed at this hour. I'm not so harsh an employer that I demand that they put off their rest so that they may await my pleasure."

"Employer?" she said coldly. "You mean master, don't you? I've heard that all the plantations in the Carolinas use Negro slave labor, and although I must admit that Virginia's tobacco farms are not much better, I find the practice intolerable."

"So do I, my dear. That is why the only slaves I own, and they are very few at that, receive some credit for their labors, and thus have the option of working to buy their freedom."

"Oh."

Why did he always have the last word? She clasped her hands tightly in her lap and, adopting the restrained attitude that had bolstered her during the past few weeks, refrained from further comment during the remainder of the ride. She was relieved that she didn't have to meet the servants right away. After all, what would they think of her, an inexperienced farm girl who knew nothing about being the mistress of a large plantation? She imagined the introductions.

Yes, I met Nicholas in Kentucky. He went to buy some mules but came away with me instead. Jessica put her hand to her mouth to mask a nervous chuckle behind a wide yawn.

The speed of the carriage began to slacken, and she leaned forward to catch the first glimpse of her new home. In the gloom of the storm it was hard to see the big house clearly, but between flashes of lightning, she could barely make out stately Ionic columns and wide wings jutting off a central structure. It was, indeed, a splendid mansion, and she was more than a bit awed by the thought of being the mistress of such a home. How could she possibly manage such an imposing plantation house?

Glancing at Nicholas she was surprised to see him watching her with an anxious gleam in his eyes. Curiously enough, she was reminded of the way Joey sometimes looked at her when he desperately wanted her approval. She couldn't resist a smile and lightly squeezed Nicholas's hand.

"It's a lovely home. You must be very proud."

He leaned back in his seat and nodded. "It took a lot of work to make Providence as you see it now, but I think the effort was well worth it." He took her hand warmly.

Isaac came to open the door and unfold the step. Nicholas popped on his beaver hat, jumped nimbly out, and turned to hold his arms out to Jessica.

"I can manage myself, I assure you."

"I have no doubt of that, my dear. But as you can plainly see, the ground is very wet and your slippers will not protect you from the cold, so please allow me to do this small husbandly service for you."

Jessica gritted her teeth, feeling outmaneuvered, and allowed herself to be swept into his arms. She tried not to notice how her pulse jumped at his touch, or how raindrops caught on his thick, curling eyelashes, or how easily he held her against his rock-hard body. He climbed up the steps and released her legs, almost reluctantly it seemed.

She felt herself sliding down the length of him and moved quickly away, feeling again that strange, jolting sensation speeding through her body.

He opened the door and gestured her in ahead of him. She entered an enormous foyer with polished marble floors. Nicholas quickly lit a lamp and held it high so she could see more of the interior. By the flickering flame and occasional flashes of lightning, she was able to make out a beautifully curved staircase that wound up to the second story. An immense crystal chandelier, tinkling slightly with the vibrations of the booming thunder, hung from a delicate white plaster ceiling. Nicholas spoke with pride. "Welcome to Providence, Mrs. Carlyle."

After she had changed into her nightgown and robe, Jessica drifted over to the French doors in her new bedroom. The rain and wind swirled together in a frenzied dance, and she turned quickly away, drawing the heavy velvet curtains over the raging turbulence. She belted her rich burgundy robe more closely and drew near the lively blaze that Nicholas had kindled in the fireplace. Memories of the events of the past few months sped through her mind, and it seemed she abruptly came out of a daze. Now that she was firmly ensconced in her husband's home, she suddenly realized the enormity of what she had done.

"Married," she whispered in renewed astonishment. "Married to a man I hardly know." The thought still amazed her, and her emotions felt as chaotic as the storm raging outside.

Jessica sank to the gold-swirled white marble in front of the fireplace. She drew her knees to her chest and wound her arms tightly around her legs, resting her chin on her raised knees and contemplating the cheery blaze and her virgin state.

Now that she was in her husband's home, would her grace period come to an end? He seemed content to wait for her to make the decision, but lately—especially since the incident with the rat—she had sensed he was becoming impatient. More than once she had looked up to find his pale gray gaze running assessingly over her person. She shivered. The barely repressed emotion in his eyes gave her little ease, and yet curiously she felt a part of herself responding to him.

She let out a disgusted sigh. She should have given him her damned virginity and put the act behind her. But it was so difficult. She had been brought up to believe that love was always the most important reason for intimacy to occur between two people. Oh, maybe that old-fashioned precept was just another foolish ideal. Why couldn't she just give in to him? At least then she wouldn't feel so guilty at having denied him his husbandly rights, especially when he had been so patient with her. She hadn't expected to find that kind of compassion from someone of his social stature, for she still had the unfortunate habit of equating wealth with snobbery and callousness. As far she knew, neither of those nasty attributes applied to her husband. On the contrary, aside from his tendency to tease her mercilessly, he had been an absolute gentleman.

She smiled wryly. If only she knew more about what went on in a "gentleman's" head. To her, it seemed impossible that a man—and such a handsome one at that—would simply marry a woman because he decided it was time to marry, or because she represented a challenge. What was his true motive? Although these arranged, love-less marriages were still common, the custom rankled her. And yet, in some strange way, she already felt bound to him.

The fire was beginning to feel uncomfortably warm on her face, and she moved away from its penetrating heat toward the tester bed where she leaned her head against one of the delicately wrought rosewood posts.

If only Nicholas had spent more time with her during the tedious days of travel, but he had often ridden on horseback while she'd been confined to the carriage, and they'd conversed very little. She had covertly watched him, increasingly amazed that such a handsome, sophisticated man had chosen her for a wife. The strange pulling sensations inside her were growing stronger every day, and she knew that those confusing feelings, more than anything else, kept her away from him. That and the fact that she was terrified she would ultimately embarrass herself when she finally went to bed with him.

Again and again she cursed her inexperience. If only the mere sight of him did not rattle her so, if only she could retain some semblance of poise when she was with him! She blushed every time she recalled the way she had scrambled onto his bed that one night with a complete lack of decorum. Would she ever be the kind of lady he would be proud to call his wife?

Looking down, she frowned at the plain gold band encircling her finger. How she had dreamed of proudly bearing the proof of her husband's commitment of love, but to her this band only represented his stamp of ownership.

A creaking door alerted Jessica to someone's presence in the room. Her wide green eyes met eyes of cool, silvery gray.

"You look beautiful, Jessica," Nicholas said warmly as he strolled into the bedroom from his connecting suite.

Fleetingly she noticed that he was casually dressed in a white shirt, gray trousers, and white stockings. Again his powerful masculinity took her breath away. As he firmly shut the door behind him, her old fears of inadequacy rose up anew. Unconsciously clutching her robe closer to her throat, she moved nervously toward the fireplace. Nicholas released an impatient sigh.

"My God, Jessica, don't look like such a scared rabbit," he said in an irritated voice. "Judging from your expression, it would appear you expect me to leap onto you at any moment and have my way with you, like some deranged Bluebeard. I am not such a cad—much to your relief, I'm sure. I simply came to bid you pleasant dreams and inquire after your needs. Is there anything you require?''

"You mean you don't intend to . . .'' Jessica's face flushed crimson. "I mean, you . . .''

"Aren't going to ravish you?'' he supplied helpfully. "Another time perhaps. At the moment, I'm thoroughly exhausted and wish only to find my bed.'' A hint of humor lit his eyes.

"Surely you didn't think I would sweep into your room like some dark, wretched fiend and force you to consummate our marriage regardless of your feelings. Or mine, for that matter. Jessica, my innocent, romantic wife, I hope you harbor no illusions about our agreement.'' At Jessica's puzzled look he elaborated.

"In your innocence, don't believe that I have fallen madly in love with you, my dear, and seek to woo you with tender words and gentlemanly courtesies. Ours, madam, is what is candidly referred to as a marriage of convenience. I require a wife to bear me sons. You need a husband to protect you and your estate. All parties benefit quite nicely, wouldn't you agree?''

His insulting remarks banished her fear and replaced it with searing anger. The weeks of waiting had taken their toll on her already frayed nerves, and she needed only this small excuse to vent her frustration.

"Yes, all parties benefit nicely,'' she spat. "You, however, left out one very important factor, m'lord.''

"What could that be? Oh, surely you aren't referring to love again? In my experience, love is an emotion reserved for either hopeless romantics or manipulative opportunists.''

"Then, m'lord, you have a very cynical view of life and are ignorant of one of life's greatest treasures. You—''

"Will you teach me then, Jessica?'' he interrupted. "You are an authority on so many subjects. Will you lead these cynical feet down that sacred path?'' When her eyes became hard with spite, he added, "Ah, just as I thought, you will not condescend to share your precious knowledge.''

At his words some of the fight went out of Jessica, and her shoulders drooped. "You mock me unkindly, Nicholas." she said in a soft, tired voice.

"And you honor me, Jessica. Do you know that this is the first time you have spoken my given name? Even in the coach and the dining rooms of the inns we visited you sat across from me with downcast eyes and silent tongue. Have you perhaps become afraid of me since our wedding?" He reached down to rub his shin. "You certainly did not appear so beforehand. Believe me, madam, I am not an ogre." He walked slowly to where she stood and looked down at her. "But neither am I a saint."

The soft sweet smell of spring lilacs filled his head, and he inhaled deeply of her scent, thinking how aptly it suited her. Somehow, with her fresh, unaffected personality, Jessica seemed to represent the embodiment of spring, and he felt a twinge of regret that he himself had lost that youth and freshness.

What a lovely creature she is, he thought. Tall and slender, with thick auburn hair and a beautifully smooth and golden complexion.

He lifted her chin so his gaze could roam unhindered over her pristine beauty. Her nose was delicately boned, her pink lips soft and full. The color of her green eyes reminded him of new leaves in spring, the long, thick brown lashes a vivid contrast. He could only wonder at what her bulky robe concealed and was doubly frustrated that she was so unwilling to satisfy his curiosity. Once more he focused his gaze on Jessica's lovely features. Her eyes were clear and curious now, and he realized that she was examining him with equal intensity.

"You are very beautiful, my wife. I find myself a fortunate man."

Jessica stared up into his warm gaze and timidly examined his features. He was the kind of man she had often dreamed about. He was taller than she by at least six inches. His hair was raven black, thick, and curled loosely about his face in careless waves. His nose was narrow and finely boned with just a little bit of a bump in the middle to mar its perfection. His silvery-gray eyes seemed almost black in the firelight and his face was sharply chiseled, with lean cheeks and a square jawline. He had a cleft chin, and his lips were full and firm. As she looked up dreamily into his handsome face, she felt a strange tingling again and surprised herself by wondering what it would be like to kiss his mouth.

Gradually Jessica realized that Nicholas's arms had gone tightly around her. She caught her breath, her warm expression turning to one of alarm. Judging from the longing in his eyes, she could sense he wanted more than the innocent kiss she was willing to give. She tried to bow her head, but her chin was still caught in his firm grip. She closed her eyes tightly, her heart pounding wildly in her chest.

"Jessica, for God's sake, look at me."

Eyes still shut, she shook her head. He gave her a small, tight squeeze, and reluctantly she opened her eyes. His gray ones searched her face wonderingly, and he moved his hand from her chin to smooth her hair from her face.

"Would you deny me a simple kiss, my wife?" he asked in a soft whisper. "It's really such a tiny thing to ask."

Jessica's heart fluttered uncertainly within her. She had no right to refuse his request, but it was all she could do to cease her trembling.

"I've almost never been kissed before. I really don't know how to . . ." she whispered.

Nicholas smiled at her candid reply and put his fingers to her lips. "How much the better that your husband be the one to initiate you."

Jessica's eyes widened. Instinctively she knew that a single kiss would not dampen his desire, yet still he had not spoken of love. She was mortified to feel tears squeezing out from under her tightly closed lids and sliding down her now pale cheeks. She felt the warm, soft touch of Nicholas's lips on her eyelids. He continued down to dry the tears from her cheeks, then very gently kissed her forehead and temples, and moved further down to her lips. Jessica stiffened in his arms, her hands clutching her robe.

"Don't be afraid, Jessica," he whispered.

She forced herself to look up at him.

"I'm not afraid. It would take more than your kiss to do that. But I've a feeling that you've something else in mind, and I'll not be forced. Nicholas, I hardly know you, and although you are my husband, if you force me against my will, it will be no better than rape, and I promise to hate you for the rest of my life."

For the life of her, that was not what she had intended to say! She knew her words sounded ridiculously melodramatic, but she was simply unable to accede to him.

"How do you know that making love to me would be such a loathsome experience?" Slowly he ran his hand down the sleeve of her robe, caressing the soft velvet. "Who can tell, sweet Jessica. You might even enjoy yourself."

His hands moved to her shoulders, and she took a deep breath as the fire died in his eyes and was replaced by a cold, bitter look.

"In any case, dear wife, I don't need your consent. You are mine, Jessica. I own you body and soul. If I choose to exercise my husbandly rights, there is nothing you can do to stop me. I can easily overcome your struggles, and I will take what I want regardless of your tender sensibilities. As far as your hatred is concerned"—he shrugged—"I consider it an idle threat on your part. I do not have to love you to find pleasure in your body, though it would prove troublesome to be forced to fight you at every turn. Neither do I intend to wait much longer. Do you understand me? I will not tolerate disobedience of any kind, from anyone. You are no exception." He stepped away and

raised an eyebrow at the sight of her face, which was
flushed with rage.

"You cannot order me about like the lowliest of your
servants," she exclaimed. "I have feelings and a mind of
my own, and I choose not to be dictated to. I don't need
you. I don't love you. I don't want you. How dare you
preach your 'law' to me as if it were a commandment from
God Himself. I loathe your petty tactics and will not be
forced into anything that I find distasteful."

She threw her head back, her hair reflecting the firelight
like a living flame and her darkened eyes shooting defiance at him. From his shocked reaction, Jessica could only
assume that he had expected her to meekly consent to his
directives.

He surprised her again by bursting into hearty laughter,
his whole body shaking with mirth.

"Perfect," he cried, clapping his hands together. "Bravo,
my dear. That was quite well done; very impressive. Since
the wedding you have been such a quiet little mouse of a
girl, I'm pleased to see that your spirit has returned.
But"—his laughter disappeared as quickly as it had come,
and he grasped her tightly by the shoulders—"spirited or
not, I will not tolerate your blatant disrespect."

He locked his arms tightly about her and pulled her
close just before lowering his mouth to hers. Jessica's eyes
widened when she felt his warm, moist lips plunder hers.
This was hardly the kind of kiss she had imagined! She
closed her eyes tightly and pushed hard against his chest
but only succeeded in tearing open his heavy silk shirt to
reveal the muscular chest beneath. She pushed even harder
against him, straining away from his harsh invasion, her
arms aching with the effort. A short muted sound issued
from the back of his throat.

Then the pressure from his mouth was suddenly gone,
and Jessica met his angry, frustrated gaze. He muttered a
soft curse under his breath and tightened his hold on her,
one arm around her waist, the other behind her head. His

head dipped down once more, and Jessica pressed her lips together, expecting to feel his hard mouth against her own. This time, however, the kiss was soft, tender, tentative. As a confusing whirl of emotions rose up within her, she almost gasped, and the pressure of his kiss deepened persuasively, his open mouth moving slowly over her own.

They were pressed so closely together that Jessica could feel the heat of his desire against her body. His hand wandered down to her buttocks, and he pressed her lightly against him while his lips, still soft, placed tiny, tender kisses on her mouth.

With something close to shock, Jessica realized that she was no longer struggling in his embrace, but instead lying complacently in his arms, her head thrown back, her eyes closed, her lips parted, her breathing rapid. The pressure of his hard manhood against her caused a strange but pleasurable tingling in her loins. His open mouth returned to take hers, and she felt his tongue enter between her slackened lips. She opened her mouth slightly when she felt his kiss deepen.

What is he doing to me, and why am I letting him? she thought breathlessly. Somehow this must be wrong. He didn't love her; he didn't care for her or know anything about her. Yet she was wildly aroused by his persistent caresses.

Her arms moved haltingly up and around his broad back. In her present rattled state it mattered little that she barely knew this man, or even that he was her husband. He was here and he was deliberately arousing feelings in her that she had never thought possible. The taste, the touch, the feel of him as a man against her were all deeply pleasurable. A deep, instinctive need had begun to grow in her, and now it spread throughout her body. She lost some of her shyness and raised herself to her toes to more intimately feel him against her, opening her mouth and returning his kisses. His hand moved caressingly along her back, and a small moan escaped her lips as she felt his palm slide over her breast, the material of her nightgown silky smooth against her flesh. Shamelessly she pressed more closely.

Then abruptly he pulled away. In frustration Jessica unconsciously leaned toward him, wanting him back in her arms. He grabbed her roughly by the shoulders and shook her until she opened heavily lidded eyes.

"You see, Jessica," he said quietly, "you do need me, and you do want me, although your innocence prevents you from completely understanding your feelings."

She shook her head dazedly.

"Soon, very soon, you'll discover just how powerful your feelings are." He dropped his arms abruptly from her shoulders and turned away. "Good night, my wife." She watched in disbelief as he strolled casually to the connecting door and closed it behind him.

Jessica stared after him as the desire he had kindled in her body slowly ebbed. She slumped into a chair near the fireplace and covered her scarlet face with shaking hands, thoroughly overwhelmed by the feelings that had exploded in her out of nowhere, and equally confused by them. How could she have pressed herself so intimately against this stranger? And now he was furious with her, why she wasn't sure. All she knew for certain was that her simple arranged marriage had become far more complicated than she'd ever anticipated.

Chapter 8

Nicholas stood just beyond Jessica's door, his arm braced against the wall for support. It had taken every ounce of his willpower to walk casually out of her arms. Taking a few deep breaths, he looked at her door longingly and ran his fingers through his dark hair. My God, he thought, how was it possible for him to lose control of both his temper and his body over such a young slip of a girl? He was thoroughly disgusted with his weakness and bullying tactics, but at the same time he couldn't forget the sensations she aroused in him. Damn her! Why did she have to be so alluring yet so dead set against him?

He told himself for the thousandth time that he would not force himself on her, or on any other woman, and it frightened him to realize how close he had been to doing just that to his virgin wife. Oddly enough, now that the incident was past, his first instinct was to get away from her. Any woman who could rattle his emotions as easily and unknowingly as she did must be avoided at all costs. What the devil was wrong with him? He was not exactly inexperienced in such matters, so why did she have such an effect on him?

Perhaps the strain of the last few weeks was wearing on him more than he realized. It wasn't every day that a man took on the responsibility of a wife. Or perhaps he had simply been without a woman for too long. Nevertheless, he was still chagrined by his response to Jessica, and by the ridiculously pompous speech he had made to her.

He smiled slightly. Good Lord, for a moment he had almost sounded like his father. He could well remember the many conflicting orders and blustering commands from that gentleman. Nicholas had been expected to meekly kowtow to his father's irrational demands without argument. And now he had demanded the same of Jessica.

No wonder she had turned on him in anger.

Nevertheless, he had to admit he admired her spirited reply, and he vowed to be more patient with her, although he didn't know how that would be possible without locking himself away in a monastery.

He could hear her moving about her room. As he pictured her graceful form tending the fire and preparing for bed, overwhelming desire rose up in him again, and before his saner half could argue, he found himself turning the door handle and staring into her shocked green eyes. She had removed her robe, and the sheer nightgown she wore served only to present him a view of the more tantalizing curves of her woman's body. It was difficult to remember that she was an untouched maiden.

"Jessica . . . I find myself unable to bid you goodnight," Nicholas said with disconcerting honesty. "This marriage of ours has begun quite strangely, yet I have no wish for us to be at odds with one another." He gestured toward the windows. "The night is cold, and colder still when spent alone. Perhaps, if you are willing," he said with great difficulty, "we might seek to combine our warmth under one blanket. I'll not touch you if that is what you desire."

Jessica stole a fleeting glimpse at the doorway behind him. Was he teasing her? She glanced at him briefly. His expression was quite sincere, which gave her despairing spirit hope. What would it be like to lie in his arms, the arms of a stranger? The idea tickled the back of her mind, and the fact that he would defer to her wishes bound her more willing to his proposition.

Unbidden, she remembered the warmth of him pressed against her, awakening her to the feel of his man's body. She wished very much to be held that way again, and he had promised only to lie beside her. She walked to him and lightly placed a hesitant hand on his arm. Her lips curved in a shy, soft smile.

"Perhaps we should start over again," she said.

Nicholas let out a long breath, dazzled against his will by her captivating smile. Her pale cream-colored gown was like a gauzy cloud floating around her slender form, leaving her limbs exposed to his warming stare. Her unbound hair flowed over her breasts and down to her hips, and he longed to push the tresses aside to better view her charms. Abruptly he chided his wayward emotions into order. Taking her cold hand from his arm, he clasped it warmly.

Silently longing for a heavy, warm robe to shield her from the cold and her husband's gaze, Jessica reluctantly allowed him to hold her hand. He squeezed it lightly and led her through the door connecting their suites. A fire burned brightly on the hearth, illuminating the rich surroundings, but she had no time to gaze at their beauty, for Nicholas was taking her other hand and leading her to the large four-poster bed that occupied a great portion of the chamber.

"Would you care for some wine? I have a fine Madeira, or perhaps some sherry."

"Yes, anything."

As he moved to fetch the wine, Jessica looked down at her hands held tightly against her stomach. She could count on the fingers of one hand the times she'd sipped wine, but she'd heard that spirits sometimes calmed one's nerves. She looked curiously at Nicholas as he poured amber liquid from a crystal decanter. What had caused this change in attitude on his part, and why had she responded so quickly to his suggestion?

Regardless of his avowed cynicism regarding love and marriage, was it possible that he cared for her in some way? She remembered the way he had so considerately wrapped his cloak around her in the coach, and the night he had slept in her bed when she had been so frightened of the rat. Although she knew little of marriage, she felt deep within her that marriage must begin with friendship and respect. Desire would be fleeting at best without the stronger emotion of love behind it. Would she someday learn to love him?

He said he wanted sons. Perhaps he meant for her to conceive as soon as possible. That would explain some things. What was he thinking? Lord, she knew so little of men and their needs and motives. Such questions churned unanswered in her mind as Jessica raised puzzled eyes to him and accepted the glass of wine he offered. She took a small sip to steady her nerves.

"Thank you. It's quite good."

She noticed that he chose to pour himself a generous snifter of brandy. Feeling chilled in her sheer nightgown, Jessica was drawn to the crackling fire. She was naively unaware of the slow, admiring smile that curved on Nicholas's face when the light from the fire illuminated her shapely curves. He took another sip of brandy and joined her.

"Are you tired?" he whispered close to her ear, his warm breath tickling her. His hand came up to stroke the length of her long, thick hair. "You have beautiful hair."

"My mother had the same color hair as I—my real mother, that is. The only family I've ever known is in Virginia." The thought of her lost family made her throat tighten, and she looked away from him.

"You love them very much, don't you?"

The most she could manage was a nod. She felt his arms go lightly around her waist. Resting his chin on her head, he silently contemplated the fire. Jessica closed her eyes, feeling a pleasant sense of security at the enveloping closeness of his tall body. Emboldened by his gentle touch, she asked a question that had long been on her mind.

"Do you perhaps have any family here?" She felt his body stiffen and wondered if maybe she should have contained her curiosity.

"My parents are dead," he finally said. He straightened and took a deep swallow from his glass.

"I'm sorry. We have one thing in common then."

"Yes." Nicholas tossed off the rest of his drink. Taking her glass from her fingers, he set both glasses on a table. "Perhaps we can discover other similarities as well."

Once again Jessica felt nervous as he led her to the bed and invitingly folded down the covers.

"Make yourself comfortable, and I'll join you in a moment."

"Couldn't we just talk for a while?" she asked, grabbing his hand. She risked a quick glance at his body. He was so long and big, surely she would be crushed by his weight.

"As you wish, Jessica." He sat on the edge of the bed and pulled her down next to him. "What is it that you want to know about me?"

"Well, Nicholas . . ."

"You may call me Nick if you wish."

"Well . . . Nicholas." She ignored his smile. "Since I know nothing of you at all, I suppose I would welcome anything you might tell me." Her voice was small in the silence of the room. She looked around her at the grand appointments. "You said you were born in England. How did you come here?"

Smiling, he reached to take the hand clenched tightly in her lap and absently toyed with her slender fingers. "I came to this country ten years ago. Would you like to hear the story behind this house?" She nodded enthusiastically.

"This estate once belonged to a wealthy though assuredly eccentric old Philadelphian named Garland Jefferies, who caught a passing fancy for the South and the seemingly idyllic lives of the planters. He bought the land and, sparing no expense, built this home."

Jessica noted the pride in his voice as he spoke of the estate.

"You'll see how it looks tomorrow in the light of day, but massive live oak, willow, cypress, tulip, and Carolina pine surround the house, affording shade in the summer and protection from wind and rain, during the winter months. The cobbled drive is lined with dogwood and magnolia trees. They're lovely in the spring, as are the gardens." He sighed.

"But it wasn't always this beautiful, was it?" Jessica asked. "Once you mentioned something about the estate requiring a lot of work and that somebody else named it Providence."

He smiled. "So you do on occasion pay attention to what I say. Yes, you're right. Jefferies is the one who whimsically named this estate Providence. Here he planned to settle down and spend the rest of his days raising horses and cotton, and most probably consuming large quantities of mint juleps."

"What ever happened to Mr. Jefferies?"

"After only two years, mismanagement, coupled with Jefferies's rather lackadaisical attitude toward hard labor, forced the old man to sell. I assume he retired back to Philadelphia and is living a comfortable life there."

"So that's what you meant about the estate needing a lot of hard work."

"Yes, it was almost decayed by the time I arrived here."

"Why did you buy it?"

Nicholas gave a snort of laughter. "I've wondered the

same thing myself many times. There was something very majestic, albeit faded, about the place. I suppose I couldn't resist its charm. I don't regret buying it."

"Surely you have adapted well to America. Your English accent is much diminished." Jessica changed the subject, hoping to discover something of a more personal nature. "Why did you leave London if it was your home?"

His fingers tightened quickly over hers, and she wondered what caused his reaction. "Let me just say that I grew tired of society there and wanted to start a new life."

He finished the statement curtly and volunteered no more information. Again Jessica was curious, but did not feel bold enough to press him. Had he perhaps left an unhappy love affair behind him? She tried a different approach.

"Do you have brothers or sisters perhaps?"

A fleeting look of pain flashed across his eyes, so brief that she thought she might have imagined it.

"I had a sister once."

He sighed deeply, and Jessica could see that his sister's memory was very dear to him indeed. Hoping to lighten the mood, he smiled down at her with a hint of mischief in his eyes. "She used to call me Sir Lancelot because I was always dreaming epic, heroic adventures of rescuing the fair Lady Gwenhwyvar from the clutches of fiery dragons. Kate would sneak into my father's wardrobe to find articles with which she could fashion costumes worthy of King Arthur's court. More than once I brandished an umbrella in lieu of Excalibur. And more than once did I feel the sting of the same umbrella upon my buttocks after hopelessly ruining it beyond repair. I learned quickly that umbrellas make slow swords but are devilishly effective weapons in the chastisement of mischievous boys."

Jessica could hardly imagine him as a little boy, but his narrative touched her heart. As she began to see him more and more as a human being, rather than a paragon, she felt herself relaxing.

"You must have been a naughty little boy indeed to have earned a thrashing from your father."

Nicholas's jaw hardened, then he shook his head and continued more easily, "Fortunately, my father was fond of Katherine, and she often intervened on my behalf."

"You must have loved your sister very much. She sounds like a very special person."

Nicholas grunted. From his expression Jessica could tell that he regretted talking so openly of his past.

"Enough of me and my misspent youth. Jessica, what of you? Tell me about your adopted family."

"There's nothing much to tell, really, except that they are the finest family anyone could ever ask for. Including myself, there are seven of us—six boys and I. We were always getting into some kind of trouble. I sincerely miss their rowdy humor. I was always more of a rascal than was proper."

"After seeing you with dirty face and grimy britches, I can certainly believe that, though, seeing you as you are now, I find it difficult to imagine you in such childish pursuits."

"You simply do not know me well enough, Nicholas."

"That, my dear wife, is something I intend to remedy shortly." He brushed her hair away from her neck, and she felt his warm breath on her throat a moment before his lips followed. "Don't you agree that we should get to know each other better?"

"Yes, certainly, Nicholas, but . . ."

Her voice dwindled to a whisper as again she felt the unfamiliar sensations his lips aroused.

"Jessica, I believe we've talked enough for one night. I'm beginning to feel quite tired. Now be a good girl and pull down the covers and get comfortable. I'll join you in a moment."

Before she could protest he put two fingers to her lips and rose to his feet. Left with no alternative, she slipped down into the massive bed and brought the blankets up to her chin. Nicholas had crossed to his wardrobe and began to undress. She quickly averted her gaze, her cheeks blushing furiously as she caught a brief glimpse of broad shoulders and muscular arms. Never in her life had she seen an entirely naked man. She regarded the aspect with increasing awe and a great deal of trepidation. Suddenly remembering the night she had blundered into his bed, she recalled that Nicholas didn't wear a nightshirt. She allowed herself a small peek in his direction and was mortified to see his tall, naked form silhouetted in the firelight.

Surely her gauzy nightgown would not insulate her from his body. She turned on her side away from him, praying for confidence.

The bed dipped as he settled next to her. What would he do next? She must have been mad to agree to his proposition. She turned her head in his direction and found him reclining on fluffed pillows, the blankets drawn up to his waist, regarding her with a tender expression.

"Are you comfortable?"

She turned her back to him once again. "Yes . . . yes, I'm fine thank you."

"You can hardly be comfortable the way you have pulled yourself together in a tight little ball." He touched her hand. "Why, you're freezing. Come, you're cold. Would you mind very much if I held you? You will feel warmer, my love."

The endearment slipped from his lips quite naturally, and Jessica was surprised at her pleased reaction to it. He took her silence as agreement and slid his warm body closer to her much colder and stiffer one. She was intensely aware of his unclad form pressed lightly against her. His pleasant musky scent mingling with the odor of brandy aroused all her senses. For a while he lightly stroked her hair. Then his voice came to her in a hesitant whisper.

"Jessica, did Lucy talk to you at all of your wedding night?"

Heated blushes spread over her body, and she replied through stiff lips, wishing desperately that she could vanish in a puff of smoke.

"There was no need, sir. I lived on a farm, remember? I've seen the cats . . ." Her voice dwindled off to a mortified squeak. The bed begin to shake and, turning to face Nicholas, she was surprised to see him lying on his back with a pillow over his face. Obviously he was laughing. Jessica sat up in a huff.

"I hardly see cause for amusement, Nicholas. You asked me a question, and I answered you. Whatever do you find so humorous?"

He peeked out from under the pillow. "Forgive me, my dear, it's just that I've never quite compared lovemaking between two people to the antics of a pair of barn cats with their heat up. I'm sorry. I wasn't laughing at you, you know."

He began to stroke her hair again, and she relaxed until she felt his hands moving softly up and down her back and over her buttocks. She jerked against him in shock.

"I'm sorry, my love," he whispered against her hair. "I did not intend to startle you, but I'm afraid you make me forget my good intentions." Not allowing a response, he moved his hands familiarly down her back again, then up along her arms. "You really can't blame me for longing to touch you, Jessica. You're a very lovely woman."

His hands continued their gentle coercion as they moved lightly over the material of her gown. Jessica lost the last vestiges of her chill. She meant to insist that Nicholas stop his persistent caresses, but felt foolish since he was doing nothing to warrant her refusal. He is my husband, she kept telling herself.

Nicholas's searching fingers wound themselves in her auburn hair and pushed the heavy mass aside as his lips sought the tender flesh at the nape of her neck. He placed a single kiss there, then massaged her shoulders gently and almost casually moved a hand over her breast. Jessica sucked in her breath as he lightly stroked her hardening nipples with his thumb. The sheer cloth of her nightgown slid sensuously across her achingly sensitive skin.

"Nicholas . . ." she began, but he cut her short by pressing his body boldly against her. Clearly her mere presence beside him in the huge bed would not be enough to satisfy him. She knew now that she'd been purposely manipulated into this impossible situation, and the seduction was full proof of her suspicions. She made an involuntary movement of flight.

"Hush, Jessica, relax. I swear I'll not hurt you," she heard him saying. She was temporarily relieved of his hot body against hers, until she felt his hand on her shoulder, gently pulling her down on the pillows.

"Nicholas, I think you're seducing me," she accused him softly.

"Is that what you think, my darling?" he replied with a wry smile.

Leaning forward, he lightly tasted her lips and ran a hand over her breast to her narrow waist. "I think you may be right, dear wife. I am finding it increasingly impossible to lie beside such beauty as yours and not long to touch and make love to you." He lowered warm, parted lips to her mouth in a deep, soft kiss. "You're lovely. So sweet and untouched. I want you more than I can say."

Jessica's heart hammered in her chest until she thought Nicholas would surely hear its frantic beat. Never had she dreamed that it would be so wildly exciting to have a man's hands on her, caressing her, arousing her. Surely her husband must have had many lovers to have gained such expertise, while she felt extremely inept and inexperienced. What was she supposed to do? she thought frantically as she felt him unfastening her gown and slipping it from her shoulders. Part of her trembled in a mixture of fear and anticipation of his lovemaking, and another saner part of her mind reminded her that this was her marriage, and what was happening without love was somehow not right.

"Nicholas," she began in a trembling voice, but he ignored her protest and continued his caresses, his lips gliding hotly over her flesh. His mouth moved lower to her shoulders and then lower still to the swell of her breasts. His tongue circled one pink crest and gently sucked the erect nipple into his mouth.

Jessica gasped and tried to focus on something else, to stop her reeling world, but the feelings he evoked with his mouth and hands were driving her beyond all rational thought. His experienced fingers continued to stroke her body with a butterfly's touch. After an eternity he lifted his mouth from her breast and moved his caressing lips to her neck. A light fragrance of lilacs softly rose from her silky tresses and he breathed deeply of the heady aroma.

"You smell as fresh as springtime, Jessica."

His breath was warm in her ear as his tongue explored the lobe, traveling the ridges and valleys while his hands wandered again to her breasts. His lips moved again to capture hers, and it seemed to Jessica that he kissed her endlessly, teaching her with his mouth and tongue how to respond to his lips. She reached up to caress his dark hair, trailing her fingers through the thick mass, and sweetly opened her mouth to him to timidly experiment with her own tongue. His hands seemed to roam even more demandingly over her body, and the combined effect of his caresses and the feeling of his hot, taut manhood against her thigh was almost more than she could bear.

As she felt him rise above her, she opened heavy lids to stare dazedly at his handsome face, his gray eyes dark with passion, his hair curling around his lean face. He smiled slowly.

"Still frightened, my love?"

Unable to speak, she shook her head. Already the unmistakable urgings of her body were demanding release, and the small voice that had shouted "Wrong" was only a dim memory.

"Do you want, me, Jessica?"

"Yes," she whispered.

His smile widened at her words, and she could clearly see her own passioned-darkened eyes reflected in his. Capturing his stare, she felt Nicholas's hand glide once more down the velvet smoothness of her skin, caressing the firm, flat stomach and moving deliberately lower between her thighs.

Although she doubted her continued ability to deny him anything, she momentarily clenched her legs against his questing hand.

"Let me, Jessica . . . let me," he said in a hoarse voice and pressed his lips against her waiting mouth. He groaned, and his mouth slanted against hers, his tongue delving deeply. Trembling, she relaxed her limbs and opened them to his gentle fingers. As he gently stroked the sensitive flesh there, incredible sensations spiraled out along her limbs at his touch, until Jessica knew she could bear it no longer. Unconsciously she arched her back, desiring to be closer to him.

"Open your eyes, love. Look at me," came his breathless command. Her chest heaving, she obeyed. The sensations he evoked were building steadily, painfully, craving release. Her arms moved up to lock around his neck, pulling him on top of her. Abruptly he ceased his caresses and moved his hands up to her hips, her waist, her shoulders, finally to hold her flushed face.

Their burning gazes met and held. He was right. She needed him, needed something. His lips lowered to hers once again, and she hesitated but a second before eagerly opening her mouth to his searching tongue. His kiss was so soft, so gentle, so deep, Jessica wanted it to go on forever. His warm, moist body was like a secure blanket enveloping her, his manhood lying rigidly between her thighs.

Of a sudden she felt a strong urge to know his man's body as well as he knew hers. Her hand moved boldly down between them to hold him, and at his sharp intake of breath, she felt encouraged to further explore him.

She pushed him to her side and closed her eyes, wanting only her sense of touch to guide her. Jessica haltingly moved her hands over her husband's body, from his hard stomach and well-muscled chest to the steel-thewed arms. How different was the texture of his skin from the coarse, curly hair on his chest.

Her innocent touch seemed to excite him, and Jessica continued to sate her curiosity, her hands gliding eagerly. Suddenly he caught her wrists in a steel grip and pulled them slowly over her head. Puzzled, she looked up into his almost savage gaze.

"Have I done something wrong?" she questioned hesitantly, moving invitingly beneath him, opening her legs. He drew her arms higher over her whirling head and she closed her eyes, crying out softly as he sank down to cover her, filling her ever so gently and slowly.

She bit her lip as he pressed deep where no man had ever been, hiding her face against his shoulder, her arms tightening spasmodically around his broad back. His tiny, tender kisses covered her like drops of molten rain on a hot day.

"You're mine now, Jess, all mine," he cried in a hoarse whisper as he moved slowly against her. At the sight of her glorious hair spread over the pillow and her green, liquid eyes spilling over with trust, a strange emotion bubbled up inside him. She was so innocent, her passion so wholesome and unrehearsed. He wanted to stay deep within her softness. A tremendous tenderness . . . and something else much stronger . . . welled up inside him. But it slipped away as she arched her back and moved under him.

"Please . . ." she whispered. Painfully controlling his desire, Nicholas purposely moved against her, allowing her passions to build, guiding her gently in the ways of love. He wanted this first time to have a special place in her heart. She moaned softly, clinging to him, and barely heard his urgent whisper.

"Wrap you legs around me, Jessica."

She complied and felt sensations beyond anything she had ever experienced before. Using his lips, hands, and body, he was driving her toward an unknown fulfillment. She lost her hold on reality, didn't even care that this man whom she had mistrusted and disliked was now the center of her universe. As the feelings built to an unbearable crescendo, she gazed at Nicholas with overwhelming ecstasy at the sight of his warm, handsome features.

Nicholas continued his carefully controlled movements against her supple form, and she cried out as the full splendor of his lovemaking burst within her. Unable to control himself any longer, he pushed deep within her as she rose to meet every hard thrust of his body, and he found his pleasure as well. It was wondrous, and more wondrous still because they shared the moment together.

So this is what it's like, Jessica thought wildly. This is what it means to love a man.

Gradually their heartbeats slowed. Jessica opened her eyes and stared in awe at her husband's face. His eyes were closed, but a satisfied smile hovered lazily on his firm lips. Gently she traced those lips with trembling fingers. He kissed her fingertips and pressed her palm against his lips. She slid her hand across his cheek and leaned forward to place a shy kiss on his mouth. His arms tightened around her possessively as he rolled to his back, and she settled herself more comfortably against him, laying her head on his shoulder, an arm across his chest.

The dying fire threw muted shadows across Nicholas's body, and she felt herself completely unable to keep her eyes from him. He was tall and lean, with firmly rippled muscles ranging the length of his long legs and smoothly bulging arms. Amazed at her boldness, she scrutinized his form more closely. His chest was wide and superbly developed with a mat of curling, crisp dark hair that tapered down to a flat, firm stomach and lean hips. She blushed involuntarily as she gazed at his flaccid manhood resting atop dark, coarse hair. If a man's body could be beautiful, his certainly was. Her eyes softened with pride.

Jessica was as puzzled by her deep feelings for this man as she was content to lie in his embrace. What did she really know about him? Why had she allowed herself to be taken? She had vowed to never willingly give herself to any man unless she was in love. Yet she had been most willing without once thinking of love. What did she know about love and loving? The memory of her mother's voice whispered in her ear: *You'll know Dolly. You'll just know.*

Her body jerked in shock. Could she have possibly fallen in love with Nicholas without knowing it? A sweet, painful ache constricted her chest. Oh Lord, how could it have happened?

And then an ugly thought came to her and brought on a rush of fear.

Perhaps now that he had claimed her, he would no longer be interested in her as his wife. After all, he had once said she was a challenge. Now the challenge had been met and conquered. Would he now cast her away?

Jessica realized how vulnerable she was and recalled her birthday, when she had dismissed the idea of ever making herself vulnerable to a man. What a fool she had been— and still was. The splendor of their lovemaking dimmed somewhat, and she longed for Nicholas's reassurance.

"Nicholas?" she questioned softly, fearing that he had drifted off to sleep.

When there was no response she sighed wearily and slipped quietly from the bed, taking care not to wake him. She was about to smooth the covers over her sleeping husband when he rolled over and threw an arm out, searching for her. When he didn't find her next to him he sat up abruptly. His eyes finally settled on her naked form.

"You fell asleep," she explained. "I was just about to cover us against the chill."

"I thought you had left me. I thought I had dreamed the

whole thing.'' His eyes caressed her fondly. ''I'm relieved to discover I'm wrong.''

He did look rather relieved, Jessica thought in surprise. ''Come to bed, my love.''

Under her husband's warming gaze, Jessica got into bed. He pulled the covers over them both and lay back, drawing her now chilled body close against him.

Nicholas considered his feeling of panic when he had thought Jessica was gone. Now that she was back he felt complete, though the feeling did little to content him. He had to admit that he had never experienced as much pleasure as he had with his untried wife. Jessica had truly surprised him with her honest warmth and passion, and it pleased him immeasurably to know that he had been the first.

He looked down at the dark head on his shoulder and stroked her tangled curls. He felt so right, so . . . clean. Yes, that was the word. Clean. She was honest, wholesome, and untouched by the cynicism and debaucheries of the sophisticated, fashionable set with whom he had too long associated. He had been given a wife far better than he deserved.

She must have felt his gaze on her for she turned sleepy green eyes to him. Was he falling in love with her? He dismissed the notion as ridiculous. He was beyond such nonsense. But when her eyes glowed more warmly in response to his caresses, his heartbeat quickened.

''Thank you,'' she said simply and without guile, then closed heavy eyes and, curling her arm about his neck, drifted off to sleep.

Nicholas gazed at her for a long time with confused emotions before he, too, was able to fall asleep.

Chapter 9

When Jessica awoke the following morning, she was surprised to meet her husband's warm gaze. He lay on his side, propped up on an elbow, staring down at her with a gentle, pleased smile on his face.

"Good morning, my love," he said softly.

Jessica felt unaccountably shy as she returned his perusal. "How long have you been staring at me?"

"Long enough to come to the conclusion that I must have been blind to mistake you for a lad when first we met." She smiled up at him, and he leaned down to bestow a lingering kiss upon her lips, his hand moving to caress her face. Jessica once again felt the strange tremors that his touch evoked. Feeling very uncertain about her newly discovered emotions, she sat up abruptly. Quickly she slipped her nightgown over her head and made her way to the fireplace.

"It's c-cold in here," she said, stirring the embers. She stamped her feet and hugged herself against the chill. The lazy smile that hovered around her husband's lips did little to add to her comfort.

"If you will allow me, Jessica, I can think of many ways to warm your sweet, delicious body."

Jessica blushed furiously. Her body tingled at the thought of what those eyes promised, and she was amazed at the rush of love and desire that left her aching to go to him. Annoyed and confused by her feelings, she backed closer to the fireplace, her thighs almost touching the mesh screen, and forced a smile that did not quite reach her eyes.

"No, thank you, the fire will do sufficiently."

"Pity," he murmured, pursing his lips and moving his clasped hands to the top of his head.

Amused, Jessica relaxed her grip on the poker. Nicholas reminded her of a petulant little boy whose favorite toy had been denied him.

"Come, Nicholas, get out of bed. I am anxious to see the rest of the house—and I'm starving."

"Of course, my dear, how boorish of me. I shall have Alcey bring us some breakfast. I'm sure that she will be pleased and surprised to meet you." At Jessica's puzzled look he elaborated, "I gave explicit instructions to Isaac and the other grooms not to tell a soul that I had wed. I preferred our first morning together not be interrupted by curious servants." He smiled crookedly. "Actually, I'm surprised Titus hasn't been pounding the door down to see me." He gave her a thorough, lecherous perusal. "I am not usually abed at this late hour."

At her flush of embarrassment he sighed. "Jessica, please fetch your robe and slippers. I expect to see you leap into the fireplace to get warm at any moment."

On her way back to his room, after doing as he'd bid, she stood unnoticed in the doorway, silently observing him. He had gotten out of bed and now stood before a long window, his arms over his head and his back arched. Her eyes became smoky as she admired the way the sunlight streamed through the crystalline panes, accenting his tall, lean, muscular build. He turned from the window and was slipping into a pair of trousers when he became aware of her presence.

"Please come in, Jessica. You needn't stand so timidly in the doorway."

Fastening his pants, he strode over to where she stood and lowered his head to whisper in her ear. "You were truly enchanting last night, my Lady Gwenhwyvar." His hands tightened around her waist, and he pulled her closely against his thighs. Jessica closed trembling eyelids as sweet sensations rose within her.

Abruptly there was a loud knock on the door. She gave a frightened squeak, and Nicholas reluctantly released her. A huge black man burst into the room, and Jessica moved closer to her husband, frightened by this towering apparition. Behind him stood a beautiful, slender black woman, who entered blithely, momentarily unaware of Jessica's presence. The woman's smile of welcome froze on her face when she finally caught sight of Jessica.

"Law, Titus, we gone an' done did it dis time." She looked hesitantly at Nicholas. " 'Scuse us, Marse Nick, we didn't know yo' was entertainin'."

Nicholas smiled hugely at the uncomfortable pair and, reaching behind his back, pulled forward a pale and embarrassed Jessica.

"Jessica, I'd like to introduce you to two very good friends of mine. Titus is my overseer, and his wife, Alcey, is housekeeper. Titus, Alcey, I'd like you to meet Jessica Montagu Carlyle—my wife."

The two stood openmouthed with shock. Titus was the first to recover. He stepped forward, a wide grin splitting his face, and bobbed his head several times.

"It sho' is a pleasure to meet yo', Miz Carlyle." He turned to his wife. "Hear dat, Alcey? Marse Nick has done gone an' got hisself married. Who-ee, Ah nevah would have believed it!"

Now Alcey stepped forward beside her hulking husband and smiled warmly at Jessica.

"Yes suh, it sho' is nice to meet you', Miz Carlyle."
She looked Jessica over from top to bottom. "Law, ain't
yo' a purty young thing. Marse Nick, yo' sho' done good
fo' yo'self marryin' dis gal, yes suh. Ah still can't believe
it. Yo' only been gone two months, an' here yo' comes
back with a missus. No wondah dat fool Isaac looked like
de cat what done swallowed de canary dis mornin'."

Jessica smiled timidly. "Please, Alcey, Titus, you must
call call me Jessica. Mrs. Carlyle sounds much too formal
to suit my tastes."

Titus stood nodding and smiling until his wife's elbow
connected with his ribs. "We gots some chores to tend to,
but we jes' wanted to welcome yo' home. If'n yo' gots a
mind to, Miz Jessica, Ah can give yo' a tour of de house
later on."

Jessica looked up at Nicholas, who nodded. "That would
be wonderful, Alcey, thank you," she said.

Once more Alcey's elbow prodded Titus into awareness.
He turned to Nicholas. "Dem mules yo' sent back a while
ago is doin' jes' fine. We started clearin' back behind de
creek while yo' was gone. De work goin' much faster
now."

Nicholas nodded, pleased. "I'll be out directly to see
how you have fared."

As soon as Titus and Alcey left the room, Jessica
visibly relaxed.

"I was so afraid of meeting anyone," she admitted. "I
was certain they wouldn't like me."

"Nonsense, Jessica. You must have more confidence in
yourself." Nicholas glanced at the clock atop the mantel
and sighed. "I suppose now that the whole household is
aware of your presence, we might as well get dressed.
Everyone will no doubt be anxious to meet you." He
smiled slowly. "But before you're taken away from me, I
should like a proper good-morning kiss."

Sometime later, Jessica walked foggily into her room

and wondered at her feelings for Nicholas. Last night seemed like a dream. Had that possessed woman really been she? It seemed incomprehensible that she could have acted in such an uninhibited fashion, that she had clung to him while the unbelievable feelings washed over her. How could she have lost all control? Did she truly love him? What a dangerous man he was! Suddenly she felt almost frightened of him. Would he always hold such power over her? Would he always seem such a stranger to her?

"Confidence," she whispered aloud. "You must have more confidence in yourself, Jessica."

Sometimes she felt like such a simpleton. Last night was ample proof of her naivete—the way she had tumbled so innocently into her husband's bed. Of course, he had intended from the beginning to make love to her. What did she expect, that they would hold hands under the blankets, and he would pat her chastely on the head and go to sleep? She sniffed. He said she had posed a challenge to him. Yes, she was about as challenging as an eager harlot.

She focused her gaze and determined to put the matter aside until she could think more clearly. She moved around her new room and concentrated on admiring its beauty.

The most lovely feature was the Persian carpet of light blues, taupe, cream, and gold that lay upon the gleaming light oak floor. Two exquisite bleached rosewood Louis XV armchairs, with violin backs and padded armrests, upholstered in moiré ecru taffeta were placed before the fireplace. A bleached walnut Queen Anne tallboy stood against the wall opposite the tester bed next to a superb armoire. One section of the room had been partitioned off into a washing and dressing area. Nearby was a Queen Anne dressing glass above a walnut kneehole dressing table. Two bedside commodes and the William and Mary secretaire-bookcase completed the elegant furnishings.

The plaster ceiling was high and embellished with delicately intricate designs. Jessica was rather in awe of the room, especially when she compared it to her small cubicle in Virginia. With a catch in her throat, she thought of how much her mother would have admired the room. Perhaps someday she would be able to show it to her. She heard a knock on the door and swallowed deeply.

"Yes, who is it?"

"It's Alcey, Miz Jessica." Brushing at her eyes, Jessica hurried to the door to let the woman in. "Ah was wonderin' if'n yo' might like a bath befo' yo' has yo' breakfast."

"Thank you, Alcey. That would be nice." The woman nodded but seemed hesitant to leave. Jessica gave a small laugh. "Is there anything in particular you'd like to know about me, Alcey?"

"No, chile, Ah guess not. Seein' as Marse Nick is so taken with yo', that's all de proof Ah needs. Must have been love at first sight, 'cause Ah knows dat marse ain't one to give up bein' a bachelor fo' no ordinary woman. From what Ah can see yo' ain't ordinary. No suh." She smiled kindly. "Yo' bath and breakfast will be up shortly, an' Ah'll have someone unpack yo' things. If'n yo' needs help with yo' dress, my daughter, Ella Mae, will be happy to oblige."

"Thank you, Alcey, thank you very much."

The black woman left the room, and Jessica drifted over to open a traveling chest to find a dress to wear. So Alcey thought Nicholas was in love with her. Jessica wished it was so, but she knew differently. She might not know much about her husband, but she was well aware of his views regarding love. She sighed deeply and selected the first gown she saw, a dress of midnight-blue velvet liberally embellished with white lace.

After Jessica's bath, Ella Mae, a delightful girl no more than fifteen years of age, helped her into her gown. She combed out Jessica's hair and piled the curls high on her head, leaving a few to cascade down her shoulders. Jessica admired the girl's handiwork in the mirror above her dressing table and thanked her graciously.

"Mammy's waiting fo' yo' downstairs in de drawin' room to show yo' 'round, Miz Jessica."

After Jessica finished her tour of the house with its many sitting rooms, dining halls, and guest chambers; and after she'd met all the aunties in the cookhouse and surveyed the surrounding grounds, she felt absolutely overwhelmed by the grandeur and tasteful beauty of her new home. She was amazed that her husband had chosen all of the elegant furnishings himself. He was truly a man of many talents, and she felt her heart swelling with pride in his accomplishments.

It was midafternoon when Alcey completed the tour, and Jessica decided to go riding to fill her empty time. She changed into her modified riding habit, unable to suppress a grin when she thought back to Lucy's reaction to it. Jessica had toiled long and hard carefully splitting the voluminous skirt and matching petticoat in two. The modified design allowed her to ride astride comfortably.

Still smiling, she braided her hair and pinned it securely on top of her head, thinking that it shouldn't be too difficult to find a bridle path. When she found the stable, the stableboy came to greet her.

"Yo' must be Marse Nick's new wife." He bobbed his head. "My name's Aaron. Glad to meet yo.' "

"Nice to meet you too, Aaron. I was wondering if you might saddle Diana for me? She's the gray mare that Mr. Carlyle brought with him from Kentucky."

The boy shuffled his feet in embarrassment. "I'd sho' be happy to, missus, 'ceptin' we ain't got no sidesaddles here. Nevah had need of 'em befo'."

Jessica smiled at his discomfort and leaned forward to whisper confidentially. "Just between you and me, Aaron, I can't abide the thought of riding sidesaddle, so just saddle Diana up as you would, and I'll be off."

The boy smiled hugely and went about readying the mare. He led her out of the barn and gave Jessica a leg up.

She leaned down from her mount, adjusting stirrups meant for much longer legs, and casually questioned the boy.

"Do you happen to know where Mr. Carlyle might be?"

"Yes'm." He pointed to a wide trail that went into the trees. "Follow dis trail out 'bout two miles till yo' comes to a stream. Dere's a small wood bridge dat goes ober it. Follow dat an' yo'll see a trail dat goes into de woods. Up a ways, yo'll see where dere's some land bein' cleared. Dat's where marse said he'd be."

She smiled her thanks and set the mare on the trail, gazing in awe at the lofty Carolina pines swaying in the chill autumn breeze. The thick carpet of pine needles muffled the sound of Diana's hooves, and the air had a fresh, pine-tinged fragrance after the previous night's storm. Jessica breathed deeply and coaxed Diana into a slow trot. Finally she found the small bridge of which Aaron had spoken. But Diana suddenly became skittish as Jessica urged her across the bridge, and the mare backed up fearfully, unwilling to step upon the wooden structure, her eyes wide, her nostrils flared. Jessica leaned forward in the saddle and applied more pressure with her lower leg, but Diana tossed her head and sidled away, fighting the bit and Jessica's commands.

Once again she pressed the horse forward, but Diana threw her head and refused to cross. Jessica's brows drew downward in a frown. She reached up to break a stiff limb off a nearby tree to use as a crop.

Suddenly the stillness of the air was shattered by the loud retort of a pistol, and Jessica saw the limb she was reaching for explode into a thousand splinters. She screamed as Diana reared, fighting to keep her seat. Escape was uppermost in her mind as she tightened her hold on the reins and wheeled Diana away from the bridge. No wonder Diana had acted so skittish. Someone had tried to kill her! As the full horror swept over her, she urged the mare quickly away. But first she risked a brief glance behind her and saw a man wearing a blue coat and riding a large dark horse quickly disappear into the trees, holding a smoking weapon. A beaver hat obscured his face.

She must get back to the stable. Through the frenzy of her flight, she gradually became aware of hoofbeats pounding behind her. Terror mounting, she looked over her shoulder. The blue-clad rider was fast approaching! Stifling a scream, her heart hammering in fear, she leaned further over Diana's neck and urged the mare to a breakneck pace, the trees whipping by her in a blur. Diana seemed to sense her mistress's fear and raced even faster, her dainty hooves sending clods of mud flying behind her. But with a sinking heart Jessica heard the hoofbeats behind her getting louder, and she knew the man would soon be upon her. In desperation she sent the laboring mare off the trail and into the trees, hoping to slow the man down. Dry branches clawed her habit, and the pungent scent of pine and fear were thick in her nostrils, yet she held steady to her course.

Diana, quick and strong, dodged the trees easily with Jessica giving only minimal commands. After what seemed an eternity, she finally slowed the horse, bowing her head to listen for following hoofbeats and hearing none over her rasping breath and the frantic pounding of her heart. She pulled Diana to a halt, then looked up. Her heart lurched once against her chest, then seemed to cease its thumping as she saw the large horse standing directly before her, the blue-clad rider on his back.

Unable to stop herself, she screamed again as she realized she had been outmaneuvered. She stared down at her trembling white-knuckled hands clutching the reins. Should she dismount or rear Diana up into her pursuer's mount? Silently and efficiently the man in the blue coat and beaver hat moved quickly to crowd Diana against a large tree and reached to pull the reins from Jessica's suddenly stiff fingers. Her breath a rattle in her throat, she made a sudden decision. Raising her leg, she kicked Diana hard, and the mare jumped aside into the man's horse.

In an instant she had dismounted. Fear giving her strength, she took off into the trees, cursing the stifling habit that seemed to drag her down with every step. She heard the man's angry shout and realized with a sinking feeling that he was riding up behind her. Tears blinded her as she heard him jump to the ground, and her soul cried out in horror as she felt his arms go around her thighs and drag her to the pine-covered earth. Immediately her fist came around swinging and smartly connected with something solid. Her eyes tightly closed, she thrashed wildly, her opponent unable to still her flailing limbs. Suddenly her arms were caught in a viselike grip and pulled roughly to either side of her head while her body was pinned spread-eagle under a rock-hard body.

"What in the name of God did you think you were doing, you little fool?" he barked. "Bloody hell! It is entirely possible that you've broken my jaw!"

Jessica's eyes flew wide at the first sounds of Nicholas's enraged voice. He released her wrists and sat up on top of her to gingerly test his jaw. Jessica was so happy to see him that she moved to wrap her arms around his anger-stiff form, sobbing out her relief. His body softened, and he put his arms around her, dragging them both to a more comfortable sitting position. Gradually she grew calmer, and looked tearily into his eyes.

"Thank God it is you, Nicholas. I've never been so frightened in all my life," she managed to say. At his puzzled expression, she went on, watching his face go whiter with every word. "Someone tried to shoot me, Nicholas—over by the bridge. I thought he was the one chasing me, not you."

"I heard the gunshot and went to investigate," he explained. "When I saw you and Diana racing up the trail, I didn't know what to think. I called out to you, but you didn't hear me."

"Believe me, Nicholas the only thing I could hear was my heart practically leaping out of my chest."

His arms tightened around her, and he rocked her comfortingly. "When you charged off into the trees like some avenging madwoman, I was so angry. I thought you were playing some sort of game with me. You didn't know that this trail forks around these trees, did you? I kept straight on the trail and so was able to head you off."

Jessica sniffed tearfully, trying to regain her composure. "I'll bear that in mind the next time someone tries to shoot me."

"I would be lying if I said I wasn't furious when you drove your damned horse into me and took off into the woods on foot, but I can see your reasons now."

As he spoke against her hair, soothing her fears, a sobering thought stiffened Jessica's spine. A brief image of her assailant flashed in her mind, and it occurred to her that he was wearing the same color coat and the same hat as her husband, and the horse—the horse had been liver-chestnut in color. She straightened abruptly and got quickly to her feet, brushing pine needles and mud from her habit. Nicholas jumped to his feet as well but regarded her in puzzlement.

"What the devil is the matter now?"

Forcing herself to be calm, Jessica spoke quietly. "I'm fine now. I don't like to be mollycoddled, that's all."

She walked determinedly back to grab Diana's reins. Leading the mare to a fallen tree to mount, she stepped into the stirrup and swung astride onto the saddle. Nicholas mounted Lancelot and spoke ruefully. "I should have purchased a sidesaddle while we were in Lexington."

Jessica guided the mare back onto the trail. "There was no need for you to do that, Nicholas. I don't ever intend to ride sidesaddle, so you'd just be wasting your money. I think I've compromised enough by wearing this ridiculous riding habit."

Riding beside her, he smiled at the fast recovery she had

made from her fright. Again he found himself admiring her spirit and, unbidden, the echo of Richard Montagu's words rang in his ears. *You could be proud of her, Nick,* he had said.

"Even though you must surely have been scared out of your wits, I noticed that you kept your seat very well on the mare. You're a fine equestrienne, my dear."

"My, Nicholas," she couldn't help taunting as suspicion ran high in her mind, "you sound almost disappointed that I didn't fall and break my neck. Or is that what you intended by giving chase?"

"Good grief, Jessica. Don't be ridiculous."

Glancing at his puzzled frown, she decided she must have been mistaken about her suspicions. Surely Nicholas would have no reason to scare her. She *was* being ridiculous. The strain of all she had gone through lately was taking its toll on her overwrought nerves.

"I'm sorry, Nicholas. My nerves are still all aquiver. It's not every day that someone tries to blow my brains out, you know."

He stared at her with wide eyes for a moment and shook his head. "Well, at least you haven't lost your sense of humor, my dear. But we must find out who was responsible." His hands tightened on the reins, and his eyes grew cold. "I will not have you threatened this way. Until the scum is found, I do not want you to ride out unattended. Agreed?"

As much as Jessica disliked this stricture on her freedom, the scare convinced her that she should not go out alone. Slowly she nodded.

It was a silent ride back to the house, both Nicholas and Jessica were wrapped in their separate thoughts. When they arrived at the stable, Nicholas quickly dismounted and came to help Jessica down, but she calmly urged Diana away from him and dismounted herself.

"I told you, I don't like to be mollycoddled," she said.

"I've been riding all my life, and I assure you I am well able to dismount without assistance."

Nicholas bowed low in response to her crisp tone, but after Aaron had led the horses away, he took her forcefully by the elbow and led her up the lane to the house. They had walked only a short distance when suddenly she felt herself being swept up into his embrace, his arms going to her back to press her hard against him. Startled, Jessica looked up into his face.

Before she could speak, he put his fingers to her lips and quickly replaced them with his mouth, softly, tenderly. To her utter dismay, Jessica found her body reacting instantly to his kiss, and she pressed herself more closely against him. When he felt her body relax in his arms, he released her with an odd half smile on his face. "Jessica, my wife, it seems that I have grown fond of you, and the thought of your life being threatened by anyone or anything . . ." He shrugged, his gray eyes staring down at her intently. "I promise I'll let nothing happen to you." he smiled at her rather dazed expression and gently swept some loose hair from her face, picking out a few stray pine needles as well. "You still refuse to wear a hat, I see."

She smiled softly into his eyes and reached up to smooth his cheek. "If you will recall, the last time I wore one it blew off my head."

"Ah yes, you were running away from me. I feel suddenly fortunate that I did not allow you to get very far."

Still he smiled down into her eyes, and Jessica felt suddenly happier than she had been in months. Nicholas grabbed her hand, whirling her around.

"I have an idea. Next week I must go into town to take care of some business regarding your inheritance, among other things. You shall go with me."

Jessica raised a defiant eyebrow and, dropping his hand, faced him, arms akimbo. "Are you asking or ordering me, m'lord?"

Nicholas took off his hat and swept it before him in a low bow, speaking humbly. "I beg your pardon, m'lady. Please forgive my unpardonable audacity and allow me to rephrase my request. Would you care to accompany me on my outing? I leave the choice entirely up to you."

A small smile dimpled Jessica's mouth. "For some reason, Nicholas, I grow a bit leery when you phrase your requests in such a manner. I seem to recall that just last evening I was given a choice that happened to be no choice at all."

Nicholas looked affronted. "Surely, madam, I am innocent of any such duplicity. I am offended that you should question my honor on so delicate a subject." His eyes grew soft. "Can you honestly say that the outcome was not to your liking?"

Jessica met his gaze steadily, ignoring his question. "I should like very much to accompany you to Charleston."

His smile deepened. "Then we're in complete agreement?"

"Yes."

Nicholas put his hat on his chest and lifted his gaze to the heavens. "Another precedent in our relationship."

Jessica laughed at his foolery as he took her hand, and they once more proceeded up the lane. A fine carriage was parked in front of the house. Seeing it, Nicholas groaned out loud.

"Whatever is the matter, Nicholas? Have you taken ill of a sudden?"

He dropped her arm and rubbed his forehead with his fingers, drawing his hand down the rest of his face to leave it clapped over his mouth for a brief moment. He turned to face Jessica and took her hands in his, speaking earnestly.

"Jessica, there is something I should have told you, but . . ." He let the sentence drop and shrugged his shoulders. "There was a young lady whose company I was keeping before I met you—a Miss Charlotte Rosemond."

Jessica's eyebrows shot up, and she glanced toward the

carriage. A sick feeling rose in her chest as she thought of the inevitable meeting, but she resolved not to let Nicholas see her weakness. For once, she determined to be confident and brazen it out. Nicholas, seeing her gaze stray to the carriage, nodded.

"Yes, that is most certainly her father's carriage, and I am almost certain that she is in attendance."

When once again he turned to Jessica with an explanation, he was surprised to see a devilish grin spreading across her face.

"You seem to have gotten yourself into a quandary, Nicholas," she teased. "Although I've known you for only a short time, I assume that if you plied the young lady with as much persuasion as you did me last evening, she is no doubt awaiting you with open arms—either that or she would like very much to do severe damage to your person. I will be very interested to see how you extricate yourself from this delicate situation."

Nicholas frowned darkly into her impish eyes. "Have I ever told you that you are an evil witch?"

"Not often enough, I would imagine."

Jessica smiled prettily into his frowning face and, head held high, preceded him into the house with a queenly air.

"Where are they, Josh?" Nicholas asked the butler.

Pursing his lips, the man inclined his head toward the drawing room. Sighing, Nicholas turned to Jessica. "Are you quite recovered from your fright? You needn't meet the Rosemonds if you don't feel up to it. Or perhaps you would like to change out of your riding attire."

The idea was tempting, for Jessica was sure she looked absolutely disastrous. However, if she did not meet the woman now, there was no telling how long her shaky confidence and fraying composure would last. Jessica shook her head.

Nicholas led the way to the drawing room and, bowing once more, opened the door for her. Jessica swept before him gracefully, all the while shaking inside. Nicholas came to stand beside her, and Jessica turned to face their guests.

Mr. James Rosemond was a trifle portly, with puffy face and sagging jowls, yet the twinkle in his eyes hinted at a merry disposition. Almost hesitantly, Jessica turned her gaze on the young lady. Instantly she regretted her decision not to freshen herself after her ride. Charlotte was undoubtedly the most lovely woman she had ever seen. For a few seconds she stared in awe of the woman's striking beauty.

Charlotte appeared to be about five years Jessica's senior, her maturity adding to her air of sophistication. Her dark blond hair was burnished to a high sheen and woven in a fashionable coiffure away from the small, delicate, aristocratic features of her oval face. She was small-boned and petite, making Jessica feel exceedingly clumsy and large. Her soft blue eyes darted back and forth between Jessica and Nicholas, and Jessica again wished she had taken Nicholas's advice and fled like a coward up to her room. Instead, she straightened her shoulders. Nicholas stepped forward smoothly.

"Good afternoon, Charlotte, James." The pair nodded their greetings. Nicholas took Jessica's hand and drew her forward.

Charlotte cleared her throat softly. "Is this a relation from Kentucky, Nicholas? I had no idea you had family there."

At the sound of the woman's smooth, cultured voice, Jessica felt extremely lacking. Surely she herself must sound like a crow in comparison. Nicholas shook his head. Mr. Rosemond remained silent.

"Charlotte, James, I'd like to introduce you to my wife, Jessica."

Charlotte's eyes grew wide and, with a small gasp, she put an immaculately manicured, dainty white hand to her chest and dropped quickly into a chair. Jessica hid her own trembling hands in the folds of her riding habit. Smothering a small smile, James recovered quickly from his shock and stepped forward. Jessica had no choice but to offer her hand.

"It's a pleasure to make your acquaintance, Madam Carlyle."

With her eyes on Charlotte's recumbent form, Jessica murmured the appropriate words. "Please, you must call me by my given name."

Jessica raised her eyes to her husband's face and felt her heart wrench at the look of compassion he was directing toward Charlotte. He seemed to have entirely forgotten her own existence. Finally Jessica went haltingly toward the stunned woman and offered her hand in friendship.

"How do you do, Miss Rosemond?"

A cold, brittle look came into those cornflower-blue eyes. Pointedly ignoring Jessica's hand, she rose haughtily from her chair.

"My, Nicholas, I had no idea that you had gone to the back hills of Kentucky to find a wife. You told me you were going to fetch some mules."

Her eyes ran insultingly over Jessica's rather bedraggled figure, carrying the implication home. Jessica straightened at the snide insult, her eyes beginning to glow greenly. Nicholas stepped forward and took Jessica's hand.

"Jessica is the cousin of a good friend there, a Mr. Montagu, who breeds thoroughbreds."

Charlotte sniffed and then wrinkled her pert, delicate nose in disgust. "Ah yes, that is quite evident."

Her hands slowly curling into fists, Jessica tried desperately to keep tight control of her temper.

Mr. Rosemond spoke hastily. "Are you talking of Richard Montagu? Yes, his stables are well known, and quite exceptional." He glanced at his daughter's face and spoke quickly. "But I can see that we are intruding. Joshua told us that you arrived only last night. I shall return at your convenience at a later time to discuss business."

He reached out his hand and Nicholas clasped it warmly.

"Thank you, James. Next week I must go into the city to call on Mr. Darby, my lawyer, so perhaps we can meet before then." He turned to Charlotte, but she averted her face and spoke to her father.

"Come, Papa, we mustn't take up any more of the newlyweds' precious time."

She nodded coldly to Nicholas, still pointedly ignoring Jessica, then took her father's arm and practically dragged the gentleman out of the drawing room. Nicholas watched them go, an amused expression on his handsome face. As he heard their carriage rumble away, he turned to Jessica and was surprised by her expression of silent thoughtfulness.

Jessica was confused. Why, if Nicholas had been keeping company with Charlotte, would he have suddenly decided to marry her instead? It was obvious that Charlotte had been very shaken to hear of Nicholas's marriage. Her reaction suggested that she thought she had a prior strong claim on him. What was going on here? Was Nicholas all he appeared to be, or was there something she didn't know about him? She raised suspicion-filled eyes to meet her husband's concerned expression.

"I'm terribly sorry about the way Charlotte behaved toward you, my love. She tends to act the spoiled child when she feels it will gain her sympathy."

Jessica turned away from him to stare into the fire and spoke very slowly. "She's very lovely, Nicholas. Exquisite, actually."

At the dull sound of her voice, Nicholas ached to go to her and hold her in his arms, but suddenly he remembered her feelings about being pampered. With an effort he crossed his arms in front of him and shrugged.

"Yes, I suppose she is attractive, but I certainly find you more so. Charlotte's beauty is patently superficial, and I find you are a much more intelligent and lively companion."

Jessica glanced sharply at him, almost certain he was making sport of her. Finally she made a brief remark about changing her attire and swept past him and up to her room.

She shut the door behind her and slowly lowered herself to the bed.

For a brief moment today she had been almost certain that Nicholas cared for her. He had seemed genuinely angry when she told him of her near escape at the bridge. Had he been acting? Did he still have feelings for Charlotte? Were the inducements of Jessica's property the only reasons he had married her? Perhaps now she was only an inconvenience of which he would rather be rid. It was an overwhelming coincidence that both the man with the gun and Nicholas had been similarly garbed and riding the same color horse.

Now that she could look at the situation a bit more objectively, she began to suspect that she had been all kinds of a fool to agree to this marriage. But with everyone pushing her toward that end, and with the added strain of her fear for her family, she had fallen easily into the trap. Was it possible that her cousin and Nicholas had planned the marriage from the beginning? After all, Richard had been showering Nicholas with glowing praise long before she had even met him. Idiot! she berated herself. How could she have been so stupid?

It followed easily that Nicholas had not wished for her to meet Miss Rosemond. Perhaps as they walked from the stable he had seen the carriage and swept her up into his arms to fool her into believing that he cared for her. Her thoughts whirled in a confusing flurry as she recalled the way Nicholas had pursued her, seduced her, and acted the tender, loving husband. Could it have all been a lie—a deliberate lie to get his hands on her estates, estates that so conveniently bordered those of his ancestral home? How could she discover whether her suspicions were valid?

She had come to know Nicholas as a man. At the memory of the night before, an ache started deep within her. He had desired her. Even in her inexperience she knew that as fact. But desire was so different from love. Could she ever make him love her?

She started to laugh, but at the same time tears poured unchecked from her eyes. How amusing. Could she have possibly fallen in love with a man who wanted only her money? How marvelously theatrical! If only she knew him better, then she might determine whether her suspicions were groundless. But he was still a relative stranger. He could have been sincere when he told her he thought her more beautiful than Charlotte. Or was that too a lie to fool her into a false sense of security?

She thought back to the incident at the bridge. She wasn't absolutely certain that it had not been Nicholas with the gun this afternoon. Somehow, without arousing his suspicions, she must find out. Until then, until she knew all the facts, she would not, could not, be intimate with Nicholas. She must keep her defenses raised at all times.

But it would be so difficult, knowing what she did now of her feelings for him.

Chapter 10

Charlotte Rosemond sat huffily in the corner of the luxurious coach that her father had recently purchased for her. Her chaperone, Mammy Harriet, was comfortably slouched in the seat opposite, snoring blissfully, happily ignorant of the steady, bitter diatribe that Charlotte was delivering to Theodore Montagu. That gentleman was becoming rather bored with Charlotte's petulance, but he was certain she didn't suspect he felt that way. His handsome face with its healthy, ruddy complexion and crop of wavy blond hair nodded at steady intervals during Charlotte's scathing attack on Jessica, and his deep blue eyes seemed attentive to her every gesture. His full, wide lips were smiling ever so slightly, and he flexed strong, stocky muscles as he stretched his arms over his head before once more focusing his attention on Charlotte's petulant expression.

Charlotte Rosemond was not happy. No one had ever gotten the better of her, or taken what she claimed for her own, until both Nicholas Carlyle and his childlike wife had succeeded in doing so. After her anger had finally run its course, she abruptly fell silent and looked up distractedly at her companion, smiling tightly when he squeezed her hand.

"I can't understand why you are so upset over the matter, Char," he said. "If, as you say, you no longer care for Nick, why do you persist in this martyred female charade? It's quite boring."

"Oh, Theo," she said, pulling her hand from his grasp, "what do you know about it? I've known Nicholas practically since he came to Charleston. I was a child at the time, of course, but I honestly thought that someday, when I got older, he would ask me to marry him. It seemed only logical. He's wealthy and handsome, and I know my father would be overjoyed to have him in the family." Her expression grew puzzled. "Sometimes I have the impression that Papa prefers Nicholas's company to mine." She shook her head.

"Anyway, the match would be so perfect, don't you see? I would be the envy of my friends in Charleston, and I should live at Providence." Her lovely eyes narrowed. "Perfect. If only Nicholas wasn't so familiar with his servants." She wrinkled her nose in disgust. "He allows them far too much freedom. It demeans him and can only cause more trouble." She pouted prettily and went on when Theo would have interrupted her.

"Why, the humiliation of his marriage is unbearable. Now I'm the laughingstock of all my friends."

Theo smiled. "Come now, Char, are you trying to make me jealous by expounding on Carlyle's many divine attributes? You know how I feel about you."

Charlotte turned to Theodore and smiled softly. "I can hardly believe your confession, Theo. Why, Jessica is your cousin. Surely your sympathies must lie with her. How can I believe your sincerity?"

He gazed deeply into her eyes. "I've stayed away from you all of these years because of Carlyle. It was no secret that you had, shall we say, plans for him. Now that he is no longer available, forgive me if I am overjoyed and want to waste no time in getting to know you better.'' Theo shot Charlotte a disarming smile. "Why, I didn't even know I had a cousin until my mother wrote to me just a few weeks ago. I haven't even met the girl. What can I do to convince you?"

Charlotte sat in exquisite repose as she pondered his words, tapping her pursed lips with a well-tended forefinger. An idea occurred to her, and a slow smile crept to her lips.

"I want to humiliate Nicholas the way he humiliated me today. I want that girl he married to despise him. If you can help me do this, Theo, then perhaps I will believe your sincerity."

Theo glanced warily at the snoring form of Mammy Harriet, but Charlotte waved a careless hand. "Oh, don't worry about Mammy. Even if she could hear what we were discussing, she'd never be disloyal to me. Not if she values her black hide."

She looked expectantly up into Theo's handsome face and caressingly slipped her hand under the lapel of his frock coat. "Will you do that for me, darling?"

Theo smiled down into her sultry gaze. "When do you want the deed done, my dear?"

Charlotte toyed with the buttons of his waistcoat and leaned close to whisper in his ear. "Next week. He's going to visit his lawyer in the city. The same one with whom you have dealings. Do you think you can arrange something by then?"

Theodore Montagu smiled and nodded. With a satisfied grin Charlotte leaned back against the plush upholstery and rudely prodded Mammy Harriet awake with the pointed toe of her boot. Nearly starting out of her seat, Mammy rubbed her ample flesh, keeping her eyes meekly lowered.

They rode back to the Rosemonds' plantation in silence. Theodore leaned lazily back in his seat, but his mind was working fast. Here was the chance he'd been searching for. Charlotte could help immeasurably to further his plans, and those plans had to move quickly. Things were becoming decidedly unpleasant with his creditors, and the sooner this business with Jessica was finished, the sooner his problems would be solved. The money he had received from his father last month had barely covered his rent. He knew the plantation was not as lucrative a business as it had once been, but he was still irritated that his father could not see fit to give him a tolerable allowance. But then, he and his father were well known to have different views regarding money, as well as everything else.

Thank goodness he could depend on his sweet, kind-hearted mother. If not for the funds Lucy had sent the might have had to alter the flamboyant life-style that only he knew was a complete ruse. Charleston's community thought him an independently wealthy young man who was sunny in temperament and mild in disposition. A very pleasant young man with an unfortunate tendency to gamble a bit too heavily. No one suspected how wrong that impression truly was, or how obsessed he was with changing his financial situation.

Only one obstacle kept him from achieving his goal, and that obstacle would soon be removed. It wouldn't be much longer before all his financial worries were behind him. His mother's chatty letters had been full of useful information about his newly acquired cousin. In fact, there was one little thing his mother had mentioned in passing that he could use against his cousin very soon.

He rubbed a hand across his cheek. Lucy had described Jessica as a very beautiful woman. With any luck, that beauty would follow her to her grave.

After her unfortunate meeting with Charlotte Rosemond, Jessica bathed and spent the remainder of the afternoon in her room with a rare translation of Voltaire's *Candide*, which she had been delighted to find in the secretaire. So engrossed was she in the novel that she was startled when Ella Mae knocked on the door and announced that dinner would soon be served. Jessica's stomach knotted at the thought of food, and she wondered if she could possibly invent an excuse to keep to her room.

She squared her shoulders. No, she would not give Nicholas the satisfaction of seeing her cringe cowardly in the safety of her room. She slapped the book closed with determination.

Ella Mae helped her to don a modest gown of violet de Parme damask and rolled her hair into a sedate chignon. After giving herself a last-minute appraisal, Jessica slowly descended the stairs.

Nicholas stood before the drawing room fireplace quietly contemplating the blaze. At the sight of his regal evening attire, Jessica's heart lurched painfully. Lord, please get me through this evening, she prayed to herself.

Nicholas turned toward her and a broad smile lit his face. "Jessica, you look lovely."

He bent low to press a kiss on her lips, but with a mumbled comment about dinner, Jessica deftly eluded him, her composure slipping a bit at his proximity. A baffled smile appeared briefly on his face as he bowed shortly and swept his hand in front of him. Jessica gave a tight smile and sailed into the dining room.

She was relieved to see that the mahogany table was long and that their places were set far apart at either end. Alcey hastily served the meal, and although the food was tempting, Jessica only toyed with it and gave minimal replies to Nicholas's attempts at conversation.

"Jessica, are you not hungry again?" He gestured at her full plate. "Hazel has prepared this quail with juniper berries beautifully, and the vegetable potage you left untouched was excellent."

"I'm afraid my appetite has deserted me, Nicholas."

"You disappoint me, Jessica, for Richard told me you had a most remarkable appetite for a woman. So far I have seen little evidence of it."

"I am simply not hungry today."

"I hope your lack of appetite is not the result of what happened earlier today in the woods."

"No, I feel fully recovered."

"Very well. Can I tempt you with dessert then? Hazel said you mentioned today that apple pan dowdy is your favorite, and I'm sure you'll agree that no one prepares it better. Promise to take at least a bite. You're still much too thin."

A servant placed the ramekin of rum-laced apples topped with crisp bread rounds in front of her. The wonderful aroma revived her appetite, and she thoroughly devoured the dessert. Nicholas laughed at her obvious delight in the dish.

"So I see that desserts are your preference."

"I never considered myself especially fond of sweets— although once"—she leaned forward in whispered confidence—"my father brought home some chocolates." She closed her eyes and, licking her lips, smiled at the memory. "They were wonderfully delicious."

Nicholas chuckled. "And so now your secret is out, Jessica. All I need do to keep you happy is to buy you chocolates."

Jessica's eyes clouded for a moment, then she shrugged and nodded. He leaned forward and spoke in a conspiratorial voice. "I know of a delicious confectionery in Charleston. Perhaps next week we'll purchase some chocolates for you."

He smiled as her eyes lit up involuntarily and, wiping his lips with a napkin, rose to help her from her seat. Seeking to escape his touch, Jessica pushed herself abruptly away from the table, clumsily upsetting her chair. He bent to retrieve it, looking at her in exasperation.

"Jessica, what the devil is the matter with you? I expect to see you jump out of your skin at any moment. Aren't you feeling well, or are you, indeed, still upset over what happened this afternoon?"

"Yes, I suppose that must be what's bothering me,

Nicholas. I'm afraid I'm not going to be good company this evening. I think I'll just retire to my room early and go to sleep. If you'll excuse me.'' She turned to leave the room.

"Very well, you may as well rest.'' His brows drew together in concern as he spoke to her retreating back. "I'll come up later to see to your comfort.''

Jessica whirled around at his words. "Oh, no,'' she said breathlessly. Forcing herself to calm down, she said more quietly, "No, that will not be necessary. Ella Mae will assist me.'' Drawing herself up she looked straight into Nicholas's eyes across the room, her gaze unwavering. "I should like very much to rest undisturbed.'' The words were spoken very softly, but she could tell that Nicholas was well aware of the strength and meaning behind them. Without giving him an opportunity to reply, she turned sharply and left the room.

Nicholas remained watching as she hurried out of sight, at a loss to explain her strange mood. He shook his head and credited it to her scare earlier that day. Settling himself in the drawing room with a brandy, he sat thinking about who might have been responsible for the shooting.

Toward the back of the house he heard Alcey and Titus laughing uproariously over some jest. Feeling lonely, he gazed longingly toward Jessica's room. Then realizing that he must look like some lovelorn adolescent, he angrily slammed his glass down on a table.

"To hell with her,'' he said out loud and stomped angrily up to his bedroom, pointedly ignoring the closed door between their two suites.

Jessica was sitting in her robe before the fire, idly brushing her hair when she heard his angry footfalls on the stairs. What was bothering him? She hoped it had nothing to do with her. She drifted over to the closed door between their rooms and listened for other signs of agitation. She heard a drawer slam shut and then a loud thud followed by a sharp curse. Without thinking she jerked the door open and rushed into Nicholas's room.

Nicholas was standing near the tallboy bent over at the waist and balanced on one stockinged foot, the other foot held in his hands. A large brass figurine rolled to a stand-still on the carpet next to him. His face reddened as, trying to conceal her concern, Jessica stepped toward him.

"Nicholas, are you all right?"

He jerked up in surprise, wincing as he put weight on his foot. "What the devil do you want?"

She took a step backward at his sharp tone. "Well, I heard something fall, and I thought that you had . . ." She pointed to his foot. "Look, you're bleeding." Completely forgetting her earlier promise to keep him at a distance, she rushed over and bent down to see to his injury.

He grabbed her tightly by the shoulders and hauled her to her feet. "I can take care of it myself. I don't need your mothering."

"Don't be ridiculous, I can help you."

"I don't want your help." He limped away from her to the washbasin.

"Nicholas, don't be so stubborn." She followed doggedly on his heels. "Do you think I've never seen blood before? Believe me, with six brothers, injuries are a daily occurrence." She propped her hands on her hips. "Admit it, you're just miffed because I caught you looking like a demented stork."

Nicholas leaned his head back and closed his eyes. "Please go away."

"At least let me look at it before you bleed all over the carpet."

"Jessica . . ."

Ignoring him, she unceremoniously pushed him into a nearby chair. "Now let me see it."

"Jessica, I am beginning to lose my patience, so if you would please just—"

"Be quiet. You're acting like a spoiled child." She held

out a cupped hand with authority. "Now give me your foot."

Nicholas released a disgusted sigh, but extended his leg.

"Thank you," she said calmly.

She bent over the wounded member and gently began to peel down his stocking. Nicholas leaned forward, trying to see around her head, but instead found himself more interested in the soft perfume that rose from her unbound hair and the shapely outline of her body under the velvet robe.

"I'm afraid you'll live," she said quietly, completely absorbed in her work. "Although your toenail will not be as fortunate. It doesn't look at all well, and I think there's a probability that you may lose it. That brass weight must have hit hard. How did it fall off the tallboy?"

When he didn't respond, she turned to look at him, and her eyes locked on his intense gray gaze. "It must have been very . . ."

He buried his hands in her hair and gently pulled her face up to his. Then his lips were moving slowly over hers. Jessica responded instantly to his kiss, ignoring the strange, incoherent buzzing in her head. His hands left her hair, and she felt herself being grasped firmly under the arms and hauled onto his lap. Then his arms were around her, holding her close. As his kisses continued, the buzzing became more distinct, and of a sudden it came to her that she had vowed to avoid him.

Before she had time to dismiss her better judgment, she put her hands on his chest and pushed away, sliding her feet to the floor. Looking everywhere but at him, she said, "Well, I can see that you're fine now. The best thing would be to enjoy some undisturbed sleep." She shot him a quick glance. He was sitting in the chair with a thunderous expression on his face. She wet her lips. "I'll go to my room now." She spun on her heel, anxious to be away from him.

"Jessica!"

His voice brought her to an abrupt standstill. Still, she

refused to yield to him. "Good night, Nicholas," she said quietly, without turning around, and slipped into her room.

She sighed in relief as she shut the door and listened for any sound of approaching footsteps. There were none. Strangely enough, some part of her was disappointed when she climbed into bed alone.

Nicholas sat furiously in his room, trying in vain to fathom his wife's female mind. More than anything he wanted to march across the room, tear open that damned door, and finish what he had started. He could still feel her sweet lips moving over his and her supple body cradled in his arms. He closed his eyes, fighting for control, determined not to force himself on her. Having experienced her willing response, he would accept nothing less.

But what had caused the abrupt change in her today? No answers came to him, but he was certain of one thing. He would not touch her again and feel the sting of her rejection. I'd sooner cut off my hands, he thought.

He looked down at his foot, which had begun to throb spitefully, and almost welcomed the distraction.

A new strain developed between Jessica and Nicholas during the first few days in Providence. As always, he was polite and gentlemanly, but the warmth that she knew he possessed was gone. Even worse, he had stopped teasing her, and she sorely missed his bantering. As the week drew to a close, she began to reevaluate her feelings and admitted that perhaps she had overreacted regarding both Charlotte and the mysterious gunman. She sighed, pushing away her confused thoughts as Ella Mae brushed out her hair one evening.

"Anythin' else yo' needs, Miz Jessica?"

Jessica started out of her reverie. "No, thank you, Ella Mae. You go on to bed."

"Yes, 'm."

Sighing heavily at the unappealing prospect of spending

another night alone, Jessica decided to write to her mother. She pulled down the writing surface of the desk, her thoughts caught up in what she would reveal about her new life. Shrugging, she looked down and stifled a scream.

A dead rat lay next to the inkwell.

Instinctively she jumped back, upsetting her chair, and raised a hand to her pounding heart. Good God, where had *that* come from? Unwillingly her gaze traveled to Nicholas's room . . .

A knock sounded on the door between their rooms. Gathering all her courage, she snapped shut the secretaire. Repressing a shudder, she breathed deeply and fought to gain some semblance of poise.

"One moment, please." She opened the door. Nicholas stood there casually dressed in trousers and an unbuttoned shirt.

"May I come in?" Jessica gestured him in with her hand. "I thought I would inform you that on the morrow we can be expecting guests, and as mistress of this home, you will, of course, be expected to . . ." He peered at her more closely. "Jessica, are you ill? Your face is very pale."

Had he come to her room to gauge her reaction to his trick, or was his timing strictly a coincidence? Abruptly she made up her mind to trust him. What other choice did she have?

"Nicholas, come with me." She walked to the secretaire and pointed at the closed desktop. "Pull that down, please."

He did as she requested, and Jessica closely watched his face. His start of surprise seemed genuine, as did his dark frown.

"When did you discover this thing?"

"Just a moment ago, right before you knocked on my door." She regarded him carefully. "Have you any idea how it came to be in my room?"

He shook his head, and it seemed to Jessica he was deep in thought. "I've never seen a rat in this house. I can't understand it.'' Then his head snapped up at the implication of her words, and his eyes bored into hers. "Surely you don't think I am responsible?"

" 'If I had known that this fear of rats would have catapulted you into my bed, I would have put one in your room long ago.' I believe those were your exact words.''

Nicholas stiffened in anger. "Believe me, madam, I am not so desperate for your companionship that I would stoop to such despicable methods to gain your company in my bed. Nevertheless, you will no doubt continue to believe what you will." He drew a handkerchief from his trouser pocket and picked the rat up by the tail. "I merely wanted to inform you that we will be expecting two guests tomorrow for dinner—Amanda Windham and her brother Daniel Cookes. You will see to it."

"Of course." Jessica nodded tightly.

"Very well. Good night."

She watched as he strode stiffly from the room, looking quite ridiculous as he held the swaying rat well away from him. Perhaps she had been wrong to accuse him. Certainly his anger had not been feigned. Feeling a certain sense of relief, she climbed into bed, determined to make amends on the morrow.

Jessica regarded her reflection critically in the full-length mirror. The topaz taffeta gown she wore was lovely, one of the few that Lucy had allowed her to select herself.

"Marse was right to tell yo' to wear dat dress tonight, Miz Jessie. Yo' is beautiful."

"Do you really think so, Ella Mae?" Jessica's worried expression was reflected back at her.

"Yes'm. Don't yo' worry none."

Jessica gave the girl a grateful smile. "Well, if you say it is so, it must be true. Thank you for all your help."

"Yo' sho' is welcome."

Jessica turned back to the mirror after the girl had gone, hoping she wouldn't disgrace either herself or her husband this evening. She had made an effort to be especially pleasant to Nicholas today, and perhaps sensing her remorse, he had behaved less stiffly toward her. There was still a certain tension between them, but of a different sort. Perhaps, thought Jessica, if all went well tonight, that also might be alleviated. She smiled at the thought and turned as she heard a knock on the door between their rooms.

"You look beautiful," she blurted when she saw him dressed formally for the evening.

Nicholas smiled and shook his head. "Your ingenuousness never fails to amaze me."

Jessica winced. "Was I being unsophisticated again?"

"Not at all. But you must promise not to stare at Amanda and her brother Daniel like a country girl in awe of her betters, or I shall pinch you."

Jessica stiffened at his remark, then realized that he was teasing her. "I promise not to prop my thumbs under my armpits, if that makes you feel more comfortable, or make use of the brass spittoon in the foyer."

"Very generous of you."

"Thank you." She inclined her head primly.

"Now you, madam, look very beautiful this evening, but there is something missing."

"Missing?" she said in dismay. "I'm sure I am wearing all the proper garments under my gown."

Nicholas laughed. "My dear, you are utterly priceless, but I was speaking of this." He pulled a flat black box from the pocket of his waistcoat.

"A gift?" She stared at the box in confusion.

"Aren't you going to take it? I haven't met a woman yet who didn't like presents."

"But I . . . haven't done anything to deserve . . ."

"Fine. If you don't want it, I'll take it away."

"Oh, no, wait a moment. I never said a thing about not wanting it." She glanced coquettishly into his eyes. "May I?"

Holding her hand palm upward, he dropped the box into it.

Jessica's face took on an expression of girlish wonder when she lifted the lid, and her gasp of disbelief was in no way contrived.

"This is for me?" She lifted out the strand of sparkling yellow diamonds, dazzled by their brilliance. "This?"

"Of course." He reached into another pocket. "And these as well."

"More?" She shook her head. "This is too much already."

"Certainly not." He opened the other box himself and, tossing it away, held up the matching earrings for her approval. "Is it not traditional for a bridegroom to shower gifts upon his new wife?"

"But Diana was as fine a gift as any woman could ask for. I'm embarrassed now that I never properly thanked you for her. You must have thought I wanted more." Jessica's face flamed bright in mortification.

"Nonsense, Jessica. When are you going to realize that I am a wealthy man and can afford such things for you? All you need do is ask."

"Ask for such"—she looked at the necklace draped over her palm—"things?" She shook her head. "No, I couldn't, but thank you. Thank you. I've never owned such beautiful jewelry before." Her voice was hushed, and unbidden tears rose to her eyes.

Nicholas was touched by her reaction and almost reached out to take her in his arms but remembered the vow he had made about not touching her. With effort he crossed his arms in front of him. He did not wish to spoil the moment by risking her rejection.

"No tears, Jessica, please." He could not stop himself from reaching out with a finger and wiping the moisture from her cheeks. He handed her a handkerchief.

"Thank you. I'm terribly sorry. You must think me a ninny." She mopped at the tears and wiped her nose.

"Not at all. I think you quite adorable. Now please turn around so that I might fasten this necklace on you."

She held her breath as she felt his warm fingers on her neck. His hands slid to her shoulders, then dropped away.

"Here are the earrings, my dear," Nicholas said in an oddly strained voice. "Why don't you try them on?"

"Thank you." She took them from him and, fastening them as she walked, moved to stand in front of the mirror. She stared at the glittering stones around her throat in awe.

"Nicholas, I really don't know what to say. To merely thank you doesn't seem adequate for such extravagant gifts." She took his hand. "I'll treasure them always." She stared up into his silvery eyes and smiled tentatively. He looked down at her in complete helplessness for a moment, then cleared his throat.

"You are very welcome, Jessica," he said rather curtly. "Now, if you will excuse me, I must see to a few things before dinner."

Jessica watched in puzzlement as he left the room. What had she done wrong now? She fingered the stones around her neck. Why had she complicated her already complicated life by falling in love with a unfathomable man?

As she shook off her thoughts, she heard voices downstairs in the foyer. Their guests had arrived. Her heart began to pound in panic, and she scolded herself severely. There was no reason why she should be intimidated by Nicholas's friends. Giving herself one more quick appraisal, she squared her shoulders and left the room.

"Madam Carlyle, you don't know how happy I am to meet you at last! Why, you're lovely, contrary to what I have heard, and I am honored to be among the first to have a look at the mysterious woman whom all of Charleston is talking about."

Jessica quirked a puzzled grin at the strange comment as she was introduced to Amanda Windham.

"Oh, don't mind my sister," said Daniel Cookes. "She's

famous for speaking the first thing that comes into her scattered mind. You should count yourself fortunate, for she is usually much more outrageous." He raised an amused eyebrow at his older sister, who shot him a disgusted look.

"If that is true, Daniel dear, then it is less than charitable of you to mention my failing to others. Now, please be silent." Amanda turned to Jessica and offered her hand. "I am quite well known for my shocking lack of tact. My husband, Thaddeus, is forever scolding me."

"No offense taken, Madam Windham," Jessica said as she took Amanda's hand. "But why in the world would anyone think me mysterious?"

Amanda shot a quick look at Nicholas, who was regarding her fondly and shaking his head. "Never you mind. I'll explain it all to you after dinner when we're well away from these—" she seemed to search for the right word— "men. And none of this Madam Windham formality. You and I shall be good friends, so you must call me by my given name."

"May I return the compliment?" asked Jessica.

"Of course."

"Now that we have dispensed with the formalities, may we all go into dinner?" asked Nicholas.

Joshua held open the door to the drawing room, and Amanda, with Jessica firmly in tow, led the way. Jessica surprised herself by thoroughly enjoying dinner. The conversation remained light, and she joined easily in the ceaseless bantering. She found Amanda's candor wonderfully refreshing and hoped that perhaps she might have found her first female friend.

Amanda was almost as tall as Jessica, but she possessed a more delicate, willowy frame. She looked to be about thirty years old. Her hair was very dark brown, almost black, and her brown eyes sparkled with good humor. Her face gained beauty from her animated expression.

Daniel Cookes was quite different from his sister, being a bit more reserved, yet he possessed a dry wit that Jessica found delightful. He was just a few inches taller than his sister, with the same dark brown hair and eyes. The resemblance between brother and sister was most striking when they smiled.

After dinner, Daniel apologized to the ladies and begged a few minutes alone with Nicholas to discuss business.

"It's just as well," said Amanda, turning to Jessica. "It will give us a chance to become better acquainted."

Jessica smiled. "I'd like that."

"I really am very happy you're here, Jessica."

"Yes, but I don't understand . . ."

"I hope you won't be offended by my honesty, but I'm very fond of Nicholas." She put up her hand. "No, not the way you might think. It's true that I once had, shall we say, devilishly feminine designs on your handsome husband, but Miss Rosemond put a stop to that—and nearly ruined my reputation in the process."

Jessica stiffened in her seat. "Charlotte? What did she do to you?"

"You wouldn't want me to repeat that old yarn."

"Yes, please, I'd like very much to hear it."

"It happened so long ago, suffice to say that Charlotte deliberately manipulated me into a situation with a man that to all outward appearances looked most indelicate. I was almost ousted from polite society, and I'm sure Nicholas, who was so desperate in those days to fit into our tight little group, avoided me because of it—as did every other eligible male."

"Why, how terrible for you."

"You're very sweet. Yes, it was unbearable for quite some time, but as you can see, it was all for the best, for I married Thaddeus, and a better man I'll never find. A pity he is away on business. I'd like so much for you to meet him."

Jessica thought how fortunate Amanda was to have a husband who returned her love.

"But enough of that," Amanda continued. "The reason

I spoke of it at all was to let you know how happy I am that you, and not Charlotte, married Nicholas. It is absolutely delicious to see her set back on her arrogant little heels.''

"She's so lovely, though. I've never seen anyone more beautiful.'' All of Jessica's fears of inadequacy returned in a rush as she pictured Charlotte's face.

"Oh, pooh!" said Amanda. "She's a shrewish, evil woman who has had designs on your husband ever since he came to Charleston. Now she's just in a rage because Nicholas chose you instead.''

"Instead?''

"Heavens, how indelicate of me. Thaddeus is right. My wagging tongue will be the end of me someday.''

Jessica leaned forward and clasped Amanda's arm. "What did you mean? Please tell me, it's very important.''

"Jessica, it's nothing really, only gossip and rumor. I spoke quite out of turn.''

"Please.''

"It's really nothing, and since you are the one married to Nicholas . . .'' She sighed and relented at Jessica's pleading eyes. "Oh, very well. There was just a rumor going about, and probably completely unfounded—I don't know how these things get started—that Nicholas was about to propose marriage to Charlotte. Charlotte most probably started the rumor herself.''

Jessica sat back on the sofa. "I see,'' she said softly.

"Good Lord, Jessica, don't look so stricken. Nicholas kept company with many beautiful women, but he chose you. That is what you must remember.''

"Yes, he did choose me, didn't he?'' But for what reasons? she thought to herself. She forced a bright expression to her face. "I've been most remiss as a hostess. Would you care for some tea, perhaps?''

"Why, yes, that would be nice.'' Amanda looked carefully at Jessica's face. "Jessica, if what I said has upset you, please don't give it a thought. I am older than you, and I suppose I view things differently. It's obvious that Nicholas cares for you, I could plainly see it at dinner. You've nothing to fear from Charlotte, believe me. She is nothing.''

Jessica regarded her friend gratefully. ''Thank you. Now let me find Alcey and see to our tea.''

She went out into the hallway, looking for Josh, but he was not at his usual post. As she continued toward the library, she noticed the doors were open. She stopped as she heard her name being spoken and couldn't resist listening to the conversation.

''. . . Jessica is very lovely, Nick, but I don't find that surprising.''

''I've found that there is much more to Jessica than just her beauty.''

''And what do you mean by that mysterious remark?''

''Come now, Dan, you know I am not that indiscreet.''

''Indeed not. In fact, you are so discreet that I've often wondered at the sultry gazes I've seen you receive from a number of lovely, shall we say, 'ladies' who frequent the more exclusive clubs in our city.''

Nicholas laughed. ''That's all in the past now, Dan. I'm a married man.''

''I see. However . . .''

''Miz Jessica?''

Jessica started guiltily at the sound of Alcey's voice and spoke loudly.

''Oh, Alcey, there you are. I was looking for you. Do you think you could bring some tea to the drawing room?''

Alcey shot her a puzzled glance. ''Why, yes'm. Ah'll brew some right away.'' Giving Jessica one last look, she turned and, shaking her head, went about her duty.

The rest of the evening with Amanda and Daniel passed in a fog for Jessica. She was deeply disturbed about what she had learned regarding her husband and his past affiliations with both Charlotte and other women. Her feeling of distrust returned in a rush, and again she thought that perhaps she had been wise to keep Nicholas at a distance.

She played her role of hostess perfectly, however, and gained some small pleasure in the fact that she had managed not to disgrace herself. Pleading fatigue, she excused herself soon after their guests had gone, ignoring Nicholas's frown. Tomorrow they would be going to Charleston, and she would need all her inner resources to endure spending an entire day alone with him.

Chapter 11

The ride to the city proved delightful, and the nearer they got to their destination, the lighter Jessica's mood became. She was amazed at the beauty of the surrounding countryside, and the wealth concealed behind the elaborate wrought-iron gates that they passed. She listened raptly as Nicholas pointed out landmarks and described the estates they rode by. Against her better judgment, she found herself relaxing in his company and thoroughly enjoying his ready wit.

By the time they reached the city, they were getting along quite companionably. Nicholas directed Isaac to drive to a quiet side street, and the carriage finally pulled up across the lane from a small, neat brick building.

"Jessica, this is where my business agent and lawyer, Mr. Lawrence Darby, has his office. He will proceed in the matter of settling your estate. I must speak with him for just a few moments and give him the papers that Richard's lawyer passed on to me. Would you like to join me?"

"You won't be long?"

"Only a few moments, my love."

She smiled at the endearment. "I'd just as soon wait for you in the carriage then."

Nicholas nodded. "You'll be safe with Isaac here. Just be sure to stay in the carriage." He jumped down, and after crossing the street, proceeded into the office.

Jessica leaned against the velvet seat to await her husband's return and wondered about her suspicions of him. On a beautiful day like today they seemed so unfounded. It had been a wonderful morning, and she had enjoyed their long trip.

The minutes ticked by, and gradually she began to feel chilled in the damp air, despite the warming pans at her feet and her fur-lined pelisse with matching muff. She looked out of the window, trying in vain to catch a quick glimpse of her husband. Where was he, and what was taking him so long? Finally she rapped her knuckles lightly at the top of the coach ceiling.

"Isaac, I'm going to see what has become of Mr. Carlyle."

"Does yo' wants me to hasten him out, missus? I'd be mo' dan happy to."

"No, that won't be necessary. I'm becoming chilled to the bone, and I need to get warm."

Isaac jumped down from his perch, opened the door for her, and folded down the step. Jessica flashed him a happy smile and proceeded across the narrow street, staring at the windows of the brick building, hoping to catch a glimpse of her husband.

Suddenly she froze in midstride in the middle of the street. There was Nicholas silhouetted in the window—standing in the loving embrace of Miss Charlotte Rosemond!

Charlotte's arms were clasped firmly around his neck and she curved her slender body wantonly into his. Her lips were parted and firmly attached to those of Jessica's husband. A gasp of pain was wrenched from her stiffened lips, and a great heaviness fell upon her heart, ruthlessly smothering the sunny feeling that had been there one

moment before. Tears blurred her vision, and she did not
see Nicholas take the woman by the arms and angrily push
her away. Only gradually through a sea of pain did it come
to her anguished mind that someone was urgently screaming her name.

Dully she looked in Isaac's direction and saw him gesturing wildly up the street. He ran from around the horses,
and she turned in the direction he indicated. As if in a
trance, she saw an angry team of runaway horses bearing
down on her at a full gallop.

Curiously she felt no fear. The world seemed to slow in
small degrees until she felt everything was moving in a
gentle, soft rhythm. The ground shook under her booted
feet, and a detached part of her mind saw the horses
coming toward her, their muscles bunched, their harnesses
flapping wildly, steam rising from their flared and quivering nostrils. Vaguely she realized that Isaac's face was
etched in terror.

At the sound of the uncontrolled team and Isaac's hoarse
voice calling Jessica's name, Nicholas whirled away from
Charlotte's smirking face and pressed his hands against the
windowpane. He stared into the street in disbelieving
horror. An icy cold hand gripped his heart as he saw
Jessica standing so quietly in front of the team.

"Jessica!" he screamed helplessly. No God, not again,
he thought as the faces of his mother and sister flashed
before him.

Unable to move, having somehow lost the will to fight
against her heart's defeat, Jessica closed her eyes and
waited. It came as an almost unwelcome interruption when
she felt her arm being practically jerked from its socket
and strong arms pulling her violently away from the runaway
team and certain death.

The world sped up to its proper pace as Jessica hit the
ground in the arms of her unknown rescuer. She struggled
to a half-reclining position and stared up into the bluest
eyes she'd ever seen. The gentleman smiled a raffish grin

and laughed aloud at her stunned expression. His hat had tumbled from his head, and his thick, wavy blond hair was violently tossed.

"What? No thanks, beautiful lady? I believe I have just saved you from a dire fate, and according to the Oriental mode of thought, that means I am now responsible for your life to the end of my days." He jumped to his feet and with a flourish helped Jessica to her shaking legs. Her knees buckled under her, and she collapsed weakly against the man's chest. His arms went around her, not unreluctantly, and she clung to him for support. Vaguely she heard a commotion behind her, and the sound of Nicholas's shaking voice came to her ears.

"Thank the Lord you're safe!" Nicholas had burst out of the lawyer's office like a madman, and now he grabbed his wife from the arms of her rescuer, clasping her as tightly as if he was afraid she might disappear.

He spoke softly against her hair. "Jessica, Jessica, I promised I'd never let anything happen to you. Oh, Lord, how could I have been so unwary?"

She raised her unfocused gaze to his, and he kissed her warmly on the mouth, then once more held her trembling body close to his.

Nicholas's concern was very convincing, but Jessica couldn't rid herself of the feeling that her near death had been no accident. He straightened, then turned to her rescuer, keeping a possessive arm around her shoulders. For a moment the gentleman looked shocked, then his face split into a wide grin.

"Damn, wouldn't you know that you'd be lucky enough to be married to the lovely Jessica, Nicholas. You seem to be much too fortunate of late." Theodore Montagu picked up his hat and executed a courtly bow. "I am delighted to make your acquaintance, Jessica, although certainly not under these circumstances."

Jessica hardly heard the stranger's words. She looked in confusion into Nicholas's blatantly concerned face, vividly remembering his embrace of Charlotte Rosemond, which she'd witnessed just a moment before. Her eyes filled with accusation and betrayal, shakily she turned to the blue-eyed gentleman, Nicholas's steadying arm still around her.

"You seem to know who I am, but I am sure that we have never met. Sir, I don't know how I can thank you for what you did today. Your courageous act speaks for itself. May I ask your name?"

Theo bowed again. "Why, I am your cousin, Theodore Montagu, and thanks are certainly not necessary."

Jessica experienced a second shock. "Montagu? You are Richard and Lucy's son?"

"None other."

Jessica fell mute as she digested this last bit of information, her thoughts still swirling giddily.

"My wife is modest with her praise, Theo," Nicholas observed. "I don't know how I can repay you for risking your own life to save her. This is hardly the sort of family reunion I had in mind."

Nicholas gestured Isaac over and began to bark out orders. "Isaac, I want you to recover that team and find out who the devil it belongs to. Use the carriage. Jessica and I will find a hired livery. Scour the city if you must, but get some answers!" His eyes became hard. "I'd dearly love to join you, but I'll not leave Mrs. Carlyle unattended. Understood? Do anything you think necessary to find out who owns that damned team—and fetch me a pistol."

Isaac nodded. He handed Nicholas a gun, then leaped onto the seat and with a sharp slap of the reins set off with a vengeance. Nicholas stared after the man for a long moment, his fists clenched in impotent rage. He seemed to control himself with an effort, then turned back to the very quiet Mr. Montagu.

"Lord, Theo, I don't know what good fortune brought you here today, but whatever it was, I am certainly grateful. Is there anything I can do to repay you?"

Theo shook his head and smiled grimly, "Nothing at all, Nick. I can see that you have more important concerns at the moment. It was, indeed, fortunate that I had business with Mr. Darby today, and my reward is seeing my cousin unharmed. I hope you find the fool who let those horses loose."

Nicholas nodded his agreement and looked down into the stricken face of his wife, touching her pale cheeks with a gentle hand. Her body shivered uncontrollably in reaction, and he bent close to her in concern.

"Are you all right, Jessica?"

Desperately she hoped he had not been a party to the seemingly careless accident that had just occurred. He put on such a convincing show of concern. Of a sudden the scene replayed itself in her mind, and she gasped as the full horror of the incident washed over her anew.

"Jessica?"

Nicholas's voice was insistent, and she felt his arm tighten around her. Her shivering increased.

"Nicholas, I don't feel well at all. I'd like to lie down please." She closed her eyes, blotting out the sight of him, and Nicholas led her carefully across the street to a waiting livery.

Watching them, Theodore Montagu smiled before his gaze shifted across the street into the gleaming cycs of Charlotte Rosemond.

Hours later, Jessica awoke suddenly, surprised to find herself comfortably snuggled in a warm bed. She sat up with a start and immediately regretted doing so as her head began to throb painfully. As she raised her hands to her head, she felt the bed dip next to her.

"Are you feeling better, Jess?"

Her husband regarded her with a tender expression as he eased her back against the pillows. Her eyes went wide as she realized that she was wearing only her briefest chemise, and she sank back under the covers, watching him

warily. He pressed a cool cloth over her throbbing forehead and caressed her cheek with feather-light strokes,
almost as if he couldn't get enough of touching her. How
could he look at her with that oh-so-loving expression
when she knew he was practicing a cruel game of deceit
behind her back? Did he have no scruples whatsoever?
How could she be in love with a barbarian who made a
mockery of honest, decent feelings?

Jessica moaned softly, as much from her inner turmoil
as from the pain in her head. I love you, her brain silently
screamed at him. How could you do this to me? Staring up
at him, her eyes gradually filled with great tears of hurt.

Nicholas bent down to tenderly wipe away the teardrops
and thinking that she needed comfort, softly kissed her
trembling mouth, again realizing painfully that he had
almost lost her forever. For an instant her supple lips
parted under his, and he buried his hands in the silken
strands of her hair, aching to draw her closer to him.

Oh Lord, oh Lord, Jessica thought, does he know what
he's doing to me? Or is this merely another part of his
plan? The gentle kiss seared through to her innermost
need, and she ached for him to continue his deep and
tender caresses, her suspicions be damned. But the tormenting images of the man on horseback with the smoking
gun, the dead rat, and Nicholas clasped in another woman's arms would not fade. With a smothered cry she
shakily pushed him away.

"Please, Nicholas, I'm still feeling a bit unstable after
all. Could you please get me some water?" She sat up
more slowly this time and looked around in confusion.
"Where are we?"

He came to her with the full tumbler and slipped an arm
behind her back as she drain the contents thirstily. "We're
still in the city, at the King's Inn, my love. You fell asleep
in the carriage on our way here."

"Of course." Then she remembered the trauma of her

accident and, turning her head away from him, asked, "Did you find out anything about those horses?"

Nicholas stood tensely before the fire, feet braced and hands clasped behind his back. He turned sharply to face her, his eyes filled with anger.

"Yes, but it will do us no good. The horses were stolen only this morning, and there are few clues as to who the thief was." He grasped the back of a chair in a white-knuckled grip. "But I promise you, Jessica, I'll find out who is behind all of this, and then we'll see how the coward reacts when faced with a man, not a frightened woman." The murderous fire in his eyes died and was replaced with concern for her. "Are you feeling better now? I've ordered us some dinner if you're hungry." He indicated a covered tray before the fire. "You should eat something to regain your strength."

Jessica shook her head, puzzled by his solicitous manner. Something was terribly wrong. Why did he act as though he sincerely cared for her when she knew that now to be false? If only she could think undisturbed. His gray eyes were full of a strange emotion she had never seen before.

Then, as though giving in to an undeniable force, he bent down, and his mouth was suddenly moving against her lips, poignantly telling her of feelings that were completely at variance with what she had seen that day.

Weakly she pushed against his chest, seeking escape from his tender kisses. He raised his eyes to hers, and she thought she must be imagining the hurt and frustration that flickered momentarily in their depths. "Nicholas, I'm feeling very thirsty again. Could you please get me some more water?"

When he returned, he stood gazing down at her, looking for all the world like a man lost. Against her better judgment Jessica felt her heart go out to him.

Finally he said in a tight voice, "Is there anything else you require?"

"Yes . . . privacy."

Nicholas paused in the act of handing her the glass of water, his polite smile freezing on his face. He straightened in a jerky movement and roughly set the glass on a bedside table. "Very well, Jessica. I shall leave, but I shan't go far. I'll be downstairs in the taproom in case you need me." Jessica sighed in relief.

As he shut the door firmly behind him finally able to relax. She lay quietly under the covers for a few moments, then realized with a start that it was already dark outside. How long had she been asleep? She put a shaking hand to her head and heartily cursed her wayward emotions. Her first inclination was to flee from her husband, but something was just not right in this deadly tangle.

Fact one, someone had tried to kill her that night in Virginia when her room was set ablaze. She hadn't even known Nicholas then, so how could he have been responsible? Unless he and Richard had planned the whole thing . . . Suddenly she remembered Richard's voice saying that she wasn't expected to marry the first available male who came along, but damned if that wasn't just what she had done. In fact, he had expounded on Nicholas's qualities so often that Jessica felt sure he had been scheming for the marriage from the beginning. Why had he been so anxious for her to marry Nicholas? Because they knew each other well, and the properties she owned were quite an attractive inducement.

Perhaps after they disposed of her, they would split the profits, and Nicholas would live happily ever after with Miss Rosemond. But Nicholas was already wealthy. Why did he need her money? Maybe it wasn't the money. Maybe it was the properties themselves, properties that bordered those of his ancestral home.

What a muddled mess!

Fact two, someone who could very well have been Nicholas had tried to shoot her last week. Fact three, someone who knew very well that she was afraid of rats had deliberately put one in her desk. Fact four, she had seen Nicholas in the embrace of his former fiancé, and fact five, she was quite sure that someone had set those horses loose to run her down. Was Richard somehow involved, or had Nicholas engineered the whole plan?

Her mind refused to believe the damning evidence against her husband. True, she did not know him well, but she felt deep in her heart that he was honestly distressed at these repeated attempts on her life. No one could act that well . . . or could he?

One thing was certain. If not for Theodore Montagu, she would be dead right now. She shuddered at the thought.

Downstairs in the taproom Nicholas was industriously applying himself to the serious business of getting drunk. Tending a pint-sized mug of ale, he sat at the oak bar where he could closely watch the goings-on, assured that no one would do further harm to his wife. Two hours, and nine or so tankards later, he began to work up a healthy anger toward the woman he was so set on protecting.

The inconsistent witch, he grumbled to himself. One minute she turned her smile on him, and the next she pushed him away. He wasn't accustomed to being rejected by women, and he certainly would not tolerate such behavior, from his wife.

Damn her! he thought, and slammed his empty tankard down on the bar. Several patrons started out of their drunken reveries and looked hazily in his direction, shaking their heads and mumbling in their cups. The barkeep filled his mug and wandered away, muttering sourly. Nicholas stared at the full tankard in surprise and happily bent to the task of draining its contents.

Why the hell should I care what she does? he thought morosely. She's just a woman. Use her and forget her. "Damn right!" he muttered out loud.

What was her game? He was not fool enough to think she had not enjoyed herself when they'd made love. His

eyes narrowed. The passionate minx, she'd enjoyed every
bit of it. Just the thought of how it had been between them
sent hot blood rushing through his veins, and he shifted
uncomfortably on the stool. Goddamn virgin wife, how
could she deny him so easily when he so burned to possess
her again? He lifted the mug to his lips and realized that it
was empty. Cursing, he slammed it down and called to the
barkeep. The man strolled over in his good time and
leaned an elbow on the bar.

"What's yer pleasure, mate?"

Nicholas gazed blearily into the man's rough features.
"Whiskey!" he practically shouted.

The man moved off to get the requested spirits, shaking
his head. He returned shortly and placed a brown bottle
and a glass in front of Nicholas's red-eyed gaze. He
gestured to the bottle.

"Need some help pourin'?"

"I think not," Nicholas said testily as he threw some
coins onto the bar. Disdaining the short glass, he grabbed
the bottle by its neck and stalked over to one of the less
conspicuous tables in a darkened corner. "Impudent sod,"
he mumbled to himself. His thoughts settled once again on
his wife.

"Now there's impudence aplenty," he muttered out
loud. "Woman's got more nerve than ever I gave her
credit for."

He took a long pull of the whiskey, and his eyes flew
open as the liquid burned a path to his gut. He held the
bottle away from him and peered reverently at the label.
"Christ, that's bad," he mumbled.

His thoughts turned to Jessica once more, and he remembered cradling her sleeping body in his arms on the
carriage ride to the inn. She had looked so still and life-
less. More piercingly real was the horror that had swept
through his every nerve when he had seen her standing in
the street before the runaway team. He shook his head
groggily, the thought of never again gazing into her spring-

green eyes or kissing her soft, warm lips suddenly sobering him. But he made no confession to himself regarding his feelings for her.

Stupid fool, he thought.

His concern had been wasted on the little chit. Obviously she wanted nothing to do with him. For some reason, her rejection cut him to the quick, and he struggled for a reason why she would turn so completely against him. His head shot up suddenly, and he dragged a hand through his tumbled hair. Perhaps she had seen Charlotte Rosemond's unwanted kiss. It had surprised him beyond belief when the brazen woman had suddenly declared her undying love and thrust herself into his arms. Could Jessica have seen and mistaken his action?

He pounded his fist on the table, nearly upsetting the whiskey. Of course, he thought to himself. From where she'd been standing in the street, she could easily have seen Charlotte's unwanted attentions. Perhaps she was jealous. He smiled slightly at the thought. If she was upset about the incident, that must mean she was not as indifferent toward him as she pretended to be. Once he explained to her that Charlotte held no appeal for him, she was certain to change her mind about him.

Getting stiffly to his feet, Nicholas tucked the bottle under his arm, giving it a fond pat. After visiting the privy behind the inn and washing away the foul taste of whiskey that lingered in his mouth, he managed to negotiate the stairs with marginal difficulty and walked purposefully to his room. He turned the doorknob and fell unceremoniously into the room. Through sheer luck he was able to keep hold of the bottle without spilling a drop, and he carefully placed it on a table, ignoring Jessica's exclamation of surprise as she bolted upright in the bed. She struggled to light the bedside lamp.

"Nicholas, what in the world are you doing?" As he came closer to her, alcoholic fumes reached out like a tangible force. "Good God, you're foxed!"

She stared in dismay as he strode to the foot of the bed and leaned negligently against the bedpost. "You certainly are observant, my dear. However, rest assured that I am coherent enough to discuss some important matters with you, wife."

Jessica peered uncertainly into his face. "What are you babbling about? I hardly think you are in any condition to discuss anything, and I do hope you are not in the habit of drinking yourself semistuporous."

"Not at all, but I can see that you need proof of my temperance."

Nicholas knew that the conversation was not heading in the direction he intended, but contrary to his previous statement, the alcohol had served to loosen his inhibitions. At the sight of Jessica's lovely body in the thin shift, his rational thoughts slid out of his mind. Instead, before Jessica could react, he covered her body with his and efficiently captured her wrists in a forceful grasp.

"Nicholas, what are you doing? Leave off!"

Jessica was furious. The besotted swine, drinking up his courage so he could fall upon her like a sex-starved madman! Twisting violently, she squirmed out from underneath him. Nicholas reached out a hand to hold her but caught only a handful of her chemise. Jessica pulled away even more furiously, and as the fabric tore, Nicholas found himself holding an empty shift. He rolled off of the bed and coming heavily to his feet, continued to purposefully stalk her. Prepared to do battle, she stood her ground, breasts heaving and auburn hair wildly mussed.

"You take one step toward me, Nicholas Carlyle, and I swear, I'll kick you right in the cobs!"

Nicholas stopped dead in his tracks. Unconsciously he reached down a hand to protect his manhood, regarding her with reddened eyes. "You wouldn't dare, witch. In case you have forgotten, I am your husband, and you have no right to refuse me."

"You're a reeling sot, and I have every right to keep myself from your lecherous hands."

"Ah, but even Sir Lancelot was beset with madness at the thought of possessing the fair Lady Gwenhwyvar." He came closer a half step, whispering, "You are mine, Jessica."

She would have retreated further, but she realized that her back was already to the wall. "To hell with your Lady Gwenhwyvar, and to hell with you! Listen well, Nicholas Carlyle, for if you put one hand on me, I shall soundly savage your manhood."

His eyes wandered slowly over her slim figure. "Damn me if you haven't already done so."

But he had heard enough of her threats. The drunken haze was fast lifting from his mind as he saw the delicious, naked splendor of his wife's body. He moved forward to capture her in his arms, and Jessica drew back her leg and kicked with all her might. Fortunately for Nicholas, he stumbled on a fold in the rug and her kick missed its mark by a narrow margin. Jessica was thrown off balance as her foot swung in midair. Nicholas miraculously regained his equilibrium, and took the opportunity to pick her up and throw her on the bed. He followed her body down, laughing like a swashbuckling pirate king.

"Get off, damn you! Get off!"

He held both of her wrists in one hand and stilled the movement of her thrashing legs with his body. In the firelight his eyes glittered like pieces of smoked glass, and Jessica shivered at the unfulfilled longing she saw in his gaze.

"Damn me, will you, Jessica? Yes, damn me for a fool because I have become enchanted by you. And if I am to burn in hell, I would do so gladly just to have your warm, sweet body in my arms, to feel your soft kisses against my mouth."

His words seeped through Jessica's body like darkly aged red wine, and she fought against their paralyzing effect. Had she not just that afternoon seen him in the arms of another woman? The thought gave her renewed strength against him.

"No! I'll not be taken by the likes of you!"

Holding her arms above her head, Nicholas lowered his mouth to hers, seeking to stifle her angry words. With the touch of his warm, moist mouth against her lips, Jessica's body jerked in shock, and a thrill of pleasure tingled all the way up to her clenched fingers. He continued to kiss her passionately, his tongue sliding silkily past her parted lips. Groaning, Nicholas released her wrists. Placing his hands under her taut buttocks, he pulled her more intimately against him. One hand moved lightly against her supple skin to the warm flesh of her breast, where he softly stroked the peak with the ball of his thumb. Jessica's senses began to whirl alarmingly at the strangely tender fierceness of his ardor. She could feel his manhood against her thigh, rigid with desire, and closed her eyes in shame, wanting him, wanting him so much.

"No," she whispered. "No."

Nicholas lifted his mouth from hers and murmured thickly against her reddened lips, "Never say no to me Jessica. Say yes." He kissed her again, tangling his hands in her hair, pressing her softly against his hard form. His mouth moved from her trembling lips to her throat, branding her with his touch, and lower still to her breasts, where he lazily circled a nipple with his tongue, his eyes dark with passion.

"Say yes," he repeated huskily.

Jessica squeezed her eyes tightly shut against this unfair invasion of her senses. Vividly she remembered the intoxicating rhythm of his lovemaking, the gentle touch of his caresses, the pleasure he so freely gave to her. Then she thought of how Charlotte had probably enjoyed the same thunderous feelings he awoke in her. Loveless marriage or no, did his vow mean nothing? Her eyes flew open. "No!" she strangled out. With renewed strength she pushed him from her and leaped from the bed. "No, I said no! Never with force."

Lying on his back, he looked up at her desirable body shining beautifully in the firelight—wanting her beyond anything else, yet all too aware that her mind was set implacably against him. He found his control, disgusted beyond words that he had broken the promise not to touch her, and rose to his feet.

"Then, damn you, enjoy your lonely bed tonight!" Picking up the bottle of whiskey, he went to the door and slammed it forcefully behind him.

Chapter 12

Jessica stared suspiciously at the door long after its reverberations had ceased. Gradually her anger began to ebb, and her disappointment grew. What? Disappointed because she hadn't been forcefully seduced by a raving tosspot?

You must admit, Jessica, my girl, that the man has an exceptional flair for the dramatic, she thought. That exit was magnificent.

Wearily she ran a hand through her hair and, locating her trunk, shuffled through the contents in search of a hairbrush and nightgown. She donned the gown and moved to sit in a comfortable chair before the fire, brushing her long tresses, and wondering where her husband had gone. Thinking back on the incident that had just taken place, she couldn't help smiling. Lord, but it was marvelous to have the last word for a change.

She finished with a few last strokes of the brush and rose hesitantly from the chair. Should she bolt the door before she retired for the night? In view of the recent attempts on her life, she was inclined to do so, but she was also reluctant to shut Nicholas out of his room. For a moment she felt a stab of guilt, then she hardened her heart. He was probably finding solace in Charlotte's arms right at this moment, and branding his evil wife the villain. In a determined movement she slid the heavy bolt to the wall. As an added precaution, she tucked a sturdy branch from the woodbox and the pistol Nicholas had forgotten under her pillow, and drifted off into an uneasy slumber.

Nicholas did not go far. Aside from the fact that his legs probably wouldn't have carried him to the inn's door, he was coherent enough to remember that he had sworn to protect his wife, despite his own murderous thoughts concerning her. He sat down at the same darkened table in the taproom and propped his feet on the sturdy oak, preparing to settle there for the night. Resolutely he pushed away the bottle of whiskey. His thoughts were clear now, and he was angry—angry at himself for acting like a fool over a woman, and angry at her for somehow bringing out this bloody weakness in him.

Jessica had rejected him, and he had gotten drunk. Perhaps he was, indeed, his father's son, for he could remember his father behaving in a like manner many times when he had been thwarted or angry. Nicholas closed his eyes and leaned his head against the chair. The last thing he wanted to be was just like his damned father.

Theodore Montagu slipped quietly out of the same taproom and hurried to the waiting carriage. Before the driver could assist him, he swung open the door himself and jumped in. He smiled into the eyes of the other occupant.

"Well?"

Theo settled himself more comfortably before answering the impatient question.

"Everything is going just as we planned. From all appearances, Mr. Carlyle will be spending the night alone in the taproom." He laughed aloud. "It was almost too easy—faking the rescue, the bogus embrace, everything."

"Don't become overconfident, boy. We've still a long way to go before the end of this charade."

Theo looked out of the window, still smiling. "Yes, I suppose you're right, but I have every faith in you and your ingenious mind. What happens next?"

"It's all very simple. I want you to call on the Rosemond girl and paint a detailed picture of Nicholas's ejection from Jessica's bedroom. No doubt she will be thrilled by your success and consider you her devoted slave. Then we can easily use her for the grand finale, which will turn Jessica away from Nicholas forever. I can almost pity Jessica, but then, she won't have long to bemoan her fate." A gruff laugh followed. "By the way, did you reward that sorry lout we employed to steal the horses?"

"Yes. Pity he won't be able to enjoy the money." Theo reached into his pocket and drew forth a large gold coin, which he flipped lazily in the air. "Poor fellow, it's a shame he never learned how to swim, although he gave it a gallant effort to the last."

His companion chuckled as Theo leaned forward with a question of his own. "What is the situation with the Blackwells? Are they still in Williamsburg? I have a feeling they could ruin everything we've planned thus far."

"No need to worry about them. They pose no threat to us." The other occupant of the carriage lifted an indolent hand. "There's nothing to fear from a farmer, his wife, and six children. My man sent me a message to say that they are completely unaware of any wrongdoing concerning their daughter, so don't worry about them. They are my problem. Yours is Charlotte and convincing her to be an unknowing participant in Jessica's, shall we say, premature demise. But until Charlotte is our pawn, you know what to do regarding Jessica."

Theo nodded and, striking a gallant pose, spoke heroically. "St. George to the rescue."

Their mocking laughter mingled as the carriage rumbled away into the swirling fog.

*   *   *

Jessica awoke the next morning with a start, and only gradually became aware that someone was pounding on the door. Yesterday's events caught up with her in a rush, and she had a strong desire to pull the covers over her head and hide for the rest of her life. But she pushed the tempting thought away and inched cautiously toward the door.

"Who is it?" She held her breath until she heard an infuriated groan.

"Who the devil do you think it is?"

Sighing in relief, she unbolted the door and stepped back as Nicholas burst into the room. His clothing was rumpled and his black hair disheveled.

"Where have you been all night?" she demanded suspiciously.

"That, my dear, is none of your blasted business, since you were the one who sent me from my own bed." He held up a hand to silence her denial. "Enough. I've had quite enough of arguing with you. I've ordered a bath for myself, and then I have some business to attend to. You will stay in this room or under the watchful eye of the innkeeper's wife in the common room until I am finished with my business. Do you understand?"

Jessica stepped forward in dismay. "Do you mean to say you intend to leave me here alone all day, while you are free to wander about at your leisure?"

"My, my, aren't we astute today?" Nicholas shot her a mocking look, lifting a black, sarcastic eyebrow. "That is precisely what I mean. I have neither the time nor patience to escort you about the city, and since you seem to find trouble whenever you roam freely about, I insist that you stay here alone behind bolted doors."

"And you expect me to meekly concede to your commands?"

"My dear, if I expected that, you surely would not have spent the night alone. However, in this instance it is for your own protection that I insist you stay here, for I cannot take you with me.'' Jessica opened her mouth to protest, but Nicholas silenced her. ''Now, I won't hear another word. You have sorely tested my temper, and if you persist in arguing with me, I will lift that nightgown from the body you are so set on protecting and paddle your bare backside.''

Her shriek was muffled by his silencing hand over her mouth, which remained until Jessica nodded her acquiescence. He removed his hand and addressed her like an undisciplined child. ''Now, isn't it easier when you agree with me?''

Turning in a huff, Jessica presented her back to him refusing to acknowledge his presence even when his bath arrived. The chambermaid gave Jessica a puzzled frown as she retrieved the tray of untouched food left from the night before and stoked the fire. Jessica's gaze remained fixed on the rekindled blaze as the maid left the room, and she heard Nicholas stepping into the tub. She fumed inwardly, wishing childishly that she could drown him. Finally his voice drifted pleasantly to her.

''Jessica, fetch me a towel, won't you. The maid left them on the bed.''

Her brows shot up at the request. After all he had said to her, he expected her to wait on him like some doting wife? She crossed her arms in front of her.

''I'm sure you can manage very well without my help,'' she said tightly.

The water swished in the tub as Nicholas sat up. ''I did not make an idle request, Jessica. Either retrieve the towel or face the consequences. I assure you they will not be pleasant.''

Her jaw clenched in anger, Jessica bounded off the chair and grabbed the towel. She turned around, intending to fling it at him, but something about the way his square jaw was set made her change her mind. Summoning up a honeysweet smile, she sidled shyly up to the tub and presented him with the towel. Bending low, she saw his eyes stray unwillingly toward her bosom.

"Perhaps my master would like me to scrub his royal back for him as well?"

"Perhaps my mistress would like me to pull her into the water with me?" Jessica straightened abruptly as he continued. "Don't play games with me, Jessica. As you can plainly see, I am not in a jesting mood. So unless you intend to make use of this water, I suggest you dress for breakfast. I've no time to delay."

When he began to rise from the concealing suds, Jessica quickly turned her back. Seeing his wet, naked body would only more acutely remind her that, despite her deliberately belligerent behavior, she ached for his tenderness.

Quickly she slipped behind the dressing screen and donned a light blue cotton gown. She fumbled a bit impatiently with the lace around the collar and was giving a last adjustment to the ruffle when Nicholas stepped in front of the screen. He was dressed casually in buff-colored riding trousers, a matching waistcoat, and a double-breasted brown frock coat. White collar tabs peeked out over a light brown silk muffler. He gave an exasperated sigh as he gazed at her half-dressed state.

"What in the world are you doing back here? Do you intend to be all day about it?"

Jessica drew herself haughtily up, her unfastened gown gaping from behind. "Good Lord, but you're an absolute irritant today! Please excuse me if I seem to dawdle, but considering the ridiculous amount of clothing a lady is required to wear under her gown, I think I have done admirably."

After giving a hurried glance at his timepiece, he grabbed her by the arm and whirled her around. "I bow to your greater knowledge of the facts, but come, before we are delayed any longer, allow me to fasten you."

Jessica bowed her head as his fingers began their ascent to the ruffled collar, which he pulled roughly into place.

Momentarily his hands lingered at the nape of her neck, and then they were snatched away. He turned her around more gently, regarding her startling green eyes, soft lips, and golden complexion. Jessica met his gaze and was only too aware, despite her suspicions, of how painfully she was attracted to him. Despite his treachery, it was difficult to keep her anger alive when he stared down at her with that soft, wistful expression in his eyes. Anger was the only defense she had against him.

"Didn't you say you were in a hurry, Mr. Carlyle?"

The soft look in his eyes instantly evaporated. Nodding curtly, he preceded her to the door.

After ordering a hearty breakfast, which Jessica only picked at, Nicholas offered to escort her back to their room. But she adamantly refused. "I'd rather sit here, in the taproom for a while, if you don't mind. There are many patrons about and no drunkards, so you needn't worry that I'll be molested. I brought a book with me. I'll read while you're away."

"Very well." With a deep sigh, Nicholas threw up his hands in surrender. "I'll speak to the innkeeper's wife again. She can watch you. But I want you to promise me you won't leave this inn." He grabbed her hand tightly and gave it a sharp shake. "Promise me, Jessica."

Looking up into his earnest gray eyes, she felt again their irresistible pull and nodded reluctantly.

"I promise I won't do anything foolish, but that's all I'll say." He opened his mouth to protest, but she raised a hand. "Do not badger me, Nicholas. I promise I won't find any trouble while you are gone. That will have to suffice."

"Very well. I'll probably be back by four, no later than five o'clock."

After a quick word with an obese woman who Jessica assumed to be the innkeeper's wife, he set his hat on his head, leaned down to press a quick kiss on her lips, and strode from the inn. Jessica touched her lips where his mouth had been and smiled sadly. He had such a nice firm mouth. She pouted as he disappeared behind the stout door. Here she was, in the marvelous city of Charleston, trapped in an inn, while he was doing God knows what—probably meeting his mistress or attending one of those fancy clubs she had heard Daniel Cookes mention.

Sighing in disgust, she concentrated on reading *Candide*. After a time she became aware of someone standing over her and raised her eyes quickly. Had Nicholas returned? But no, to her surprise she found Theodore Montagu standing before her.

He wasn't as tall as Nicholas, or as lean, but his face was quite handsome. His impossibly blue eyes were his most striking feature—that and his undeniably merry smile. He swept off his beaver hat and bowed before her, favoring her with that charming grin.

"Excuse my intrusion, Jessica, but I must confess that yesterday I overheard your husband telling the driver to take you both to this inn. I was quite concerned for you, and so made it my business to check on you today."

Jessica couldn't resist a smile, but out of the corner of her eye she saw the innkeeper's wife heading determinedly in her direction. The woman put her meaty hands on massive hips. "Here now, young man. What business do ya have with the lady?"

Theo turned innocent blue eyes to the woman and smiled charmingly, but before he could reply, Jessica interrupted. "Why, Mrs. . . . ." She waited for an introduction.

"Mrs. Ames, Mrs. Luella Ames."

Jessica smiled. "Mrs. Ames, there's no need for you to be concerned. This is my cousin, Mr. Theodore Montagu. Didn't my husband mention that he was coming to call on me? Why, I've been waiting for him all this time."

Giving Theo a disbelieving look, the woman nodded grumpily and, heaving her massive bulk around, made her way to the back of the common room, the wooden planks squeaking in protest under her ponderous footfalls. Jessica pulled out an empty chair, and Theo sank into it. He leaned forward and regarded her with amused eyes.

"Why did you tell the enchanting Mrs. Ames that I was coming to call on you?" he asked, apparently delighted with her game.

"After what happened yesterday, Nicholas was reluctant to leave me unattended, so bade the woman look after me. I was hoping that if Mrs. Ames thought that our meeting was prearranged, she would leave us alone."

"Pardon me for being so blunt then, Jessica, but why didn't your husband take you along with him? Surely he didn't expect you to sit alone all day with only your fears to keep you company, especially after what almost happened yesterday?"

Jessica turned away, hiding her concern. Of course she'd been wondering the very same thing. Where was Nicholas going that he couldn't take her with him? How lacking in concern and sensitivity he'd been!

"I'm sorry, Mr. Montagu . . ."

He clasped her hand warmly. "Please, Jessica, you must call me Theo. We can't have such formality between cousins now, can we?"

She smiled and nodded. "No, I suppose not. And I would return the favor if you were not already so forward as to be calling me by my given name."

Laughing, he shook her hand. "Agreed," he said. "Now, if I'm not mistaken, sitting in a dark taproom is not an ideal entertainment for such a lively lady. I look forward to getting to know you better and plying you with questions regarding my parents. My carriage is outside, and since I happen to be unoccupied today, it would be my pleasure to take you on a tour of the city."

The offer was extremely tempting, but, remembering her promise to Nicholas, Jessica felt obliged to decline, though with a spark of mischief in her eyes.

"I don't think my husband would approve of my being

escorted about by a rather forward and handsome fellow such as yourself, even though you are my cousin.''

His eyes lit up at her compliment, and he spoke quickly. "But who could offer you more protection than your dear cuz, the man who saved your life only yesterday?''

Jessica laughed in spite of herself. "You make a very convincing argument for yourself, but nevertheless, I beg to decline.''

Theo looked crestfallen. "Jessica, I am crushed by your refusal. However, perhaps when Nick returns from his affairs he will take you out in my stead.''

His tone made the suggestion sound dubious at best, and at the mention of Nicholas and his affairs, Jessica was tempted to do something utterly childish and rebellious. Why should she sit alone when there was someone gentlemanly enough to offer her his company and protection? She stood up with determination.

"Upon reconsideration, I find your offer too tempting to refuse, Theo. If you are sure that it will not interfere with any plans you might have made, I would be delighted to tour the city with you.''

A wide grin split his face. "Splendid! I promise to act only as your protective slave.'' He presented his elbow with aplomb. "Cousin?''

Laughing gaily, Jessica took his arm, and they left the inn. Theo gestured to his driver, who attentively helped Jessica into the carriage. Theo climbed in behind her and took the seat opposite. He leaned forward, his eyes sparkling in excitement.

"Now then, Jessica, where would you like to go first? I leave the choice entirely up to you.''

"The battery,'' she answered immediately. "I've longed to see it. It will be wonderful to get some fresh air and go for a stroll there.''

"The battery it is then, dear cousin.''

Theo spoke briefly to the driver, and the carriage moved

off into the street. Theo sat quietly studying Jessica's face as she stared out the window with unabashed enthusiasm.

"You know, Jessica, you look remarkably like your mother. Except for the color of your eyes, the resemblance is extraordinary."

"Did you perhaps know my parents?" she asked, startled from her rapt contemplation of the shops and passersby.

Theo shook his head. "No, I was but a baby when they once came to Kentucky to visit my father. I vividly remember the portrait, however."

"Yes, the portrait that hangs over the mantel in your father's library. The artist captured their characters admirably in that work. It is easy to see, just by looking at them, how young and hopeful they were, and how very much in love."

"Ah, so you are a romantic, are you, Jessica?"

"A hopeless romantic, I'm afraid." She smiled sheepishly. "How embarrassing for you to have found me out so quickly."

She thought of Nicholas, and her smile slowly faded. Theo noticed it immediately and rapidly changed the subject.

"Tell me of my parents. I assume they are well."

"Yes, yes, they are both healthy. How long has it been since you last saw them?"

"Almost a year now. I never liked Kentucky very much; I prefer the mild climate in the Carolinas."

Jessica smiled mischievously. "I have a feeling it is not only the climate you prefer here. There seems to be an abundance of lovely young ladies in this fair city."

For a moment Jessica wondered at the hard look that entered his eyes, then his cheerful demeanor returned.

"But none more lovely than you, dear cousin."

Chapter 13

Nicholas spent an exhausting day trying in vain to track the thief responsible for stealing the horses that had almost killed his wife. He and Isaac visited practically every dingy waterfront saloon in search of clues, but by the end of the day they were no closer to finding any helpful information. When Nicholas consulted his timepiece, it was getting on the hour of five o'clock.

Isaac pulled his weary team to a halt in front of a particularly tawdry saloon sagging on its precarious foundation. Shutters hung askew at odd angles, and the white-wash was faded to a dull gray broken by intermittent streaks of yellow where the less than elite patrons had relieved themselves. Several horses, swaybacked and drooping with age, were tied to the leaning hitching posts in front of the warped steps.

Sighing in disgust, Nicholas hopped out of the carriage and spoke resolutely to Isaac. "This is the last one today, Isaac, and God be praised."

The servant cast a wary expression toward the building and rolled his eyes upward. Sounds of breaking glass and flying furniture could clearly be heard over the loud din of a screaming woman and laughing men. Seeing his master's determined face, he sighed heavily and whispered a quick prayer.

"Ah wish Brer Titus could be with us on dis one. Dem big fists o' his would make short work o' dis here white trash."

Nicholas silently echoed the man's sentiments. Titus was good company with which to meet disaster, and more than once he and Nicholas had put mischief to rout. Shrugging the thought away, Nicholas patted the pocket of his waistcoat and, assured that his pistol was still safely there, turned to Isaac. Isaac affectionately patted the double-barreled shotgun he was carrying and nodded slowly.

The two began to ascend the rickety steps when a dark form was suddenly catapulted headfirst through the door. The unfortunate object hit the porch nose first and slid down the steps still riding on his face. Nicholas stepped nimbly aside as the man landed in a crumpled heap near the back legs of a chestnut nag. The gelding stared dully at the man's recumbent form, indolently lifted its tangled tail, and swished dust onto the man's face.

A disheveled woman in a ripped green gown appeared in the doorway and stared admiringly at Nicholas before spewing a well-aimed stream of tobacco juice at the unconscious man's back. When the deluge failed to revive him, she sniffed derisively and turned in a huff, giving Nicholas one last appraising glance before returning to the noisy crowd inside. Nicholas's curiosity got the better of him, and he called out a loud greeting.

"Good day, madam." He gestured at the unconscious man. "Would you perhaps like me to fetch the sheriff and have this man arrested, or is it simply a personal matter?"

In an unmistakably English accent the woman gladly gave vent to her ill-concealed wrath.

"'At bloody toad's been guzzlin' gin all day—said a mate o' 'is wud be gettin' paid fer stealin' some 'orses an' wud cover 'is expenses. Since I'm th' barmaid what gave 'im th' whiskey, it's me 'oo'll be 'avin ter pay fer 'is drinks.'' She shifted the wad of tobacco she was chewing and spat with remarkable accuracy into a brass spittoon three feet away.

Nicholas's pulse leaped with the mention of stolen horses. "What happened to the man with the money, then?'' he asked.

The woman narrowed her eyes contemptuously. " 'Oo are ya anyway, an' why're ya so in'trested, gov? From me own experience, I've found 'at nobody does nothin' fer nobody 'less there's somethin' in it fer 'imself.''

Nicholas executed a short bow and smiled charmingly into the woman's suspicious brown eyes. "My name is Nicholas Carlyle, and I am investigating the matter of some stolen horses.''

Reaching into the pocket of his frock coat, he pulled out his purse and drew forth a few shining coins. The woman's eyes lit up.

"Now what would you be willing to tell me for, say, two of these gold pieces here?''

She came down the steps in a rush, and Nicholas almost recoiled at the smell of grease, sweat, ale, and powerful perfume. She smiled coyly up at him and held out her dirty hand. Gesturing Isaac back, Nicholas placed one of the gold coins in her hand. Holding the other one palm up in his hand, he slowly curled his fingers around it.

The woman frowned. " 'At there be Ned McInerny. 'E's got a mate, Charlie MacKensie, 'oo did a job yesterdee mornin'—stole some 'orses fer a tidy price. We all knew about it.'' Once more she settled a baleful stare at Mr. McInerny. " 'At's why I was so anxious ter serve 'at bleedin' slob.'' She looked hopefully at Nicholas, but still he held the coin tightly in his hand.

"And . . . ?''

The woman sighed. "An' Charlie made a very nasty appearance in th' bay just a while ago, if ya know what I mean. I just 'eard about it, an' when I tried ter collect from Ned 'ere, it so 'appened that 'e didn't 'ave a bleedin' cent ter 'is name. The bloody sod! I shoulda known never ter trust no Irishman. I'd like ter throttle 'im all over again!''

Nicholas frowned at the unfortunate fate of Mr. Charles MacKensie. ''For whom did Mr. MacKensie steal the horses?''

The woman shook her head, her straggly locks bouncing limply. ''I dunno. Charlie said it were a real secret—that if 'e said anythin' ter anyone 'e wudn't get paid—an it's no bleedin' wonder since we 'eard 'em 'orses almost ran down a lady in th' street.''

''Damn!'' Nicholas swore heartily, slamming his fist in his hand, and at the woman's fearful expression turned back to her with a consoling smile. ''Thank you very much for your help, Miss . . . ?''

''Florence Winters, but everyone 'ereabouts calls me Flo.''

''Thank you, Flo.''

He handed her the coin, and she smiled happily, her harsh features turning almost pretty beneath the dirt and grime. Nicholas smiled sadly, thinking the woman obviously had a hard life.

''Tell me, Flo, how much gin did Mr. McInerny here drink today?''

Flo told him the amount, and he once more reached into his purse and brought out two silver pieces. ''Here,'' he said, handing her the money. ''This will more than cover his expenses. The rest is for you.''

Her brown eyes widened as she stared slack-jawed into Nicholas's face. ''Thank ya, Mr. Carlyle. Thank ya very much, an' if I 'ear anything more 'bout them 'orses, you'll be the first ter know.''

Nicholas's eyebrow lifted in amusement as she secured the money in a ragged purse at the top of her frayed chemise. On impulse she leaned forward and gave Nicholas a long, bone-crushing embrace, then very soundly kissed him on the lips. She gave Ned one last withering look, winked hugely in Nicholas's direction, and hurried back into the rowdy atmosphere of the saloon.

Nicholas stared into Isaac's round eyes and wrinkled his nose at the lingering scent of the woman's perfume. Sighing deeply, he walked over to the unconscious form of Ned McInerny and pushed him onto his back, then attempted without success to rouse him. Spying a horse trough half filled with brackish water, he gestured to Isaac, and between the two of them they managed to drag the man's dead weight over to the trough. Nicholas grabbed Ned roughly by the hair and plunged his head into the murky water.

Sputtering weakly, Ned abruptly came out of his stupor and flailed about, seeking escape from the hand that repeatedly dunked his head into the foul water. Finally Nicholas drew him gasping from his bath and released him. Ned sank slowly to the dusty street, hanging his head in his hands and moaning. He noticed Nicholas's well-polished boots and, squinting, lifted his reddened gaze up the length of his tall body. His eyes came in contact with the black bore of the pistol leveled at his head.

"Good afternoon, Mr. McInerny," Nicholas said pleasantly. "Allow me to introduce myself. My name is Nicholas Carlyle, and this"—he indicated Isaac, who also looked down the sights of his own weapon—"is my driver, Isaac."

Ned jerked upright, and his eyes crossed a second before he fell, sprawling backward in the dust. Sighing in disgust, Nicholas filled a filthy bucket with water from the trough and threw the contents into Ned's face. The man was as drunk as a boiled owl, and if he himself had been half as intoxicated last night as this sot was now, he could hardly blame Jessica for fighting him off. Perhaps, he thought reluctantly, he owed her an apology.

Ned rose groggily, and Nicholas reached down to grab the man's ragged coat collar and jerk him to his knees. "Listen here, mate, you pass out once more and I'll put this pistol to your head and discharge it through your bloody ear. Do you understand?''

Mouth hanging slack with bloated jowls quivering, Ned nodded vigorously, and Nicholas released his hold on the man. "Good. Now I want some answers. Yesterday my wife was almost killed by a team of runaway horses, horses that it so conveniently happens were stolen by a friend of yours." Nicholas was gratified to see the man swallow hard.

"Hones', mate, I 'ad nothin' to do wif it. Charlie's the mon you want, but 'e's dead—found washed up in the bay.''

"So I've heard, but what I want you to tell me is who paid him to steal those horses.''

Ned's eyes became very large, and Nicholas hoped that the man's fear would prompt his memory. He nodded to Isaac, who drew back the heavy hammers on the shotgun. Ned seemed to quickly sober up as he looked pleadingly up into the hard gray eyes before him, but Nicholas allowed no pity to show in his face.

"I swear to ya, Mr. Carlyle, sir. I don't know 'oo 'e did the deed far. 'E wouldn't tell, 'cause 'e was afraid 'e wouldn't be paid far the job. I swear on me mum's grave, I don't know 'oo it was.''

Huge tears began to pour from the man's eyes, and with an exclamation of mingled compassion and disgust, Nicholas thrust the drunk away from him.

"Very well, Ned my friend. I believe you. However, if I find out that you've lied to me, I will come back and find you. Understand?''

Ned looked to Isaac, who still had the gun aimed in his direction, and nodded readily. "I swear, I ain't alyin' to ya!''

Nicholas smiled coldly at the man. "Just remember what I've said to you, Ned, and you just might live out the remainder of your miserable life.''

Nicholas viciously kicked the crusted bucket aside as he

walked away. "Come on, Isaac, we're late, and there's one more short stop we must make." He turned to grasp the black man's shoulder briefly. "And, Isaac, thanks for your help. I know playing the villain is not your forte, but nonetheless, you performed admirably."

Isaac clasped Nicholas's hand heartily. As they continued to the carriage, he said, "Yo' sho' is right dere, marse, but Ah ain't nevah seen no man asceered as dat poor white trash. We almos' plumb sceered 'im sober. Yes suh."

Laughing, Isaac climbed to his seat and coaxed the tired horses down the littered street, away from the docks and in the direction of the inn.

At the King's Inn Jessica was beside herself with worry. Theo had brought her back to the inn at about three o'clock and, reluctant to lose his pleasant company, she had invited him to dine with her and Nicholas this evening. Theo had been delighted to accept the invitation and had promised to return to the inn promptly at eight o'clock. Since then she had paced the small room, unable to find any interest in her book. Her pride and passions were raging furiously. Finally her passions won the day, and she ordered a bath and prepared herself carefully for her husband's return, going so far as to have a chambermaid dress her hair.

She chose her gown carefully, settling at last on a low-cut, off-the-shoulder gown of forest-green velvet. Charlotte or no Charlotte, Nicholas was her husband, God help her, and regardless of his suspected infidelity she was unwilling to give him up without a struggle.

She had thought long and hard of her suspicions of Nicholas in the attempts on her life. It just didn't make sense that he would so callously desire her death. Of the little she knew of his mettle, she had strong doubts that he would have anything to do with something as cold-blooded as murder. The fact that his servants seemed to worship him spoke very well of his character.

By half past five she was becoming anxious, and by half past six she was nearly frantic with worry. Nicholas was always prompt, and she was concerned that something might have happened to him. She paced the room in agitation until she heard footsteps coming toward her door. The handle was tried, and then a knock sounded. She sighed in relief and threw the door open. Nicholas stood on the threshold carrying a large flat box with a red ribbon tied around it. His clothing was again rumpled and ill-used. Her nose twitched, and her eyes hardened into twin green stones when she smelled the unmistakable odors of sweat and strong perfume. What a fool she had been to worry over his delay!

Nicholas's eyes grew warm at the lovely picture that greeted him. Delicate ivory lace rose temptingly with her labored breathing, and he viewed her for a delightful moment before lifting his gaze to her flushed and angry face. He stiffened immediately and sighed inwardly. What was wrong now?

As she took in his disheveled appearance, Jessica was beyond reason. She remembered the conversation she had heard between Nicholas and Daniel Cookes, and with the evidence presented before her, it took only a modicum of intelligence to deduce where her husband had spent the day. Because she had been so worried about him, she became more angry still.

"Where have you been all day," she raged, "or couldn't you bear to tear yourself away from your mistress's welcoming arms?"

Nicholas strode angrily into the room, throwing the box carelessly at the foot of the bed, and closed the door sharply before the full import of her speech brought his head up with a snap.

"Sweet Jesus, I've only just stepped in the door and

already you've set your claws into my skin! What the devil are you babbling about now?''

Jessica stood, arms akimbo, her bosom practically overflowing the bounds of her décolletage. "You know very well what I'm talking about, or do you intend to lie straight to my face?''

Nicholas's brows drew sharply downward at this defamation of his character. He'd be damned if he would defend himself like a meek, browbeaten husband to this cocky wench, regardless of the tempting picture she presented with her eyes brightly lit with anger and her bosom pressed against the confines of her gown.

"I told you, I was out on business, and that's precisely where I have been. It falls to your simple mind whether you choose to believe me.''

With short, jerky movements he began to undo the muffler about his neck. Jessica strode over to him, her anger lending her strength, and whirled him around. She stamped her foot in outrage.

"How can you stand there and plead your innocence when I saw you just yesterday in the embrace of your ladylove?''

His eyebrows shot up with this revelation. So, as he had suspected, she had seen Charlotte's unwelcome advance.

Jessica stepped back in triumph, a smug expression on her face. "You see, you cannot deny what happened yesterday.''

"My God! Your farmgirl mentality is showing through the thin veneer of sophistication that you attempt to affect. Do you honestly think me stupid enough to invite you to Charleston if I was planning a liaison with my mistress? Good God, at least credit me with a bit more intelligence than that. I was out today,'' he said clearly, enunciating every word, "looking for the person responsible for stealing the horses that almost killed you.''

Jessica was caught up short at his words. How could he so blatantly lie to her? "How commendable that you would attempt to find the fiend. He must not have been very difficult to subdue, since the only thing strong about him appears to have been his perfume.''

"What are you talking about?"

"You see? You cannot deny it." Her eyes sparkled furiously through distraught tears. "I know ours is a marriage of convenience, but what of your vows? Did they mean nothing to you?"

Relenting at last in the face of her tears, and remembering Florence Winters's cheap scent. Nicholas drew a handkerchief from his trouser pocket and moved to comfort her. "Here now, Jess, don't cry. The truth of the matter is—"

But Jessica backed away from him, wiping the back of her hand across her face. "Don't come near me. I don't want your damned pity or your version of the truth. I don't want anything from you."

Nicholas's face hardened again, his eyes freezing into bleak chips of ice. "That has been quite evident of late, my dear, but why then have you gone to so much trouble to dress yourself so elaborately?"

"My cousin Theodore called on me today. He was concerned about my welfare and helped me pleasantly pass the afternoon. He even offered to take me on a tour of the city."

Nicholas found the thought of Jessica in another man's company deeply unsettling, but he had no intention of admitting the fact. "And did you go with him?" he asked with seeming indifference.

Hurt and angered by his unconcern, Jessica turned to the mirror to repair her appearance. "Does it matter, Nicholas? After all, if you can enjoy Charlotte's company, why shouldn't I go on a tour of the city with Theo?"

Nicholas experienced a strong urge to throttle her. How dare she bait him this way, the little witch? Ignoring all reason, he walked up behind her and whirled her around, keeping a light hold on her arm.

"Did you go out alone with Mr. Montagu?"

Jessica stared up into hard gray eyes livid with suppressed rage and tilted her chin up in defiance. "Yes, yes I did go with him, and I very much enjoyed myself. I even invited him to join us for supper."

Nicholas stared down into her rebellious face for a very long time, his cold eyes practically boring through her skull. Slowly Jessica began to feel very uncomfortable as her anger ebbed, and she realized anew just how much a stranger Nicholas really was to her. The pleasant, attentive, sometimes tender man she had known recently vanished before her eyes and was replaced by a cold, angry tyrant who could be calculatingly violent, perhaps even capable of murder.

The power of his barely controlled emotions frightened her. Involuntarily she attempted to back away from his menacing form, but he tightened his hold on her arm. She had the terrifying conviction that he wanted to strike her, and she closed her eyes, her face tensing for the blow.

Nicholas continued to stare down at her, overwhelmed at the powerful emotions that lay hold of him. He was incensed that she would so openly disregard his authority by leaving the inn when she had promised not to go out. He was more deeply hurt because she had enjoyed the company of another man, whom she had gone behind his back to meet.

He had never been fond of Theodore, dismissing him as an undisciplined rake who lived on his charm and little else. Now he felt that dislike hardening into hatred.

Looking down at Jessica, he saw her eyes close as though to blot out his violent assault. The thought brought him abruptly to his senses. His eyes narrowed as he viewed her apparel, his gaze straying to the low-cut bodice. Finally he spoke in a quiet, deadly voice, childishly wanting to hurt her as she had hurt him.

"So that is the cause for your elaborate coiffure and immodest décolletage, eh? I had no idea that you were so fickle, Jessica. Here I was under the misguided impression that you were a loyal and innocent young woman. My, my, what a little actress you are.''

Jessica's fear evaporated. She felt like screaming with rage at his handsome face, but she would not give him the satisfaction of seeing her react to his ugly words. Instead she spoke through clenched teeth.

''Nicholas, you tempt me sorely to tell you precisely what I think of your character, but as my mother had endeavored long and hard to teach me the manners of a lady of quality, I shall refrain from such a graphic description.''

''I had no idea that you possessed any womanly qualities at all, my dear. Or perhaps now that I have initiated you into the more intimate aspects of marriage, you would rather practice your newly learned skills on men other than your husband. I suppose I shall have to get you with child very quickly.''

Jessica's hand flew up to slap his face, but he caught her wrist easily and clamped her arm tightly against her side. They were standing toe to toe, their faces barely a hand's breadth apart, Jessica trembling with impotent rage at his careless, cutting words. That he would so easily degrade what to her had been a magically wonderful and beautiful coming together, shattered her girlish innocence. In that instant, she grew up.

She spoke very softly, yet every word was more bitter than the last. ''I hate you. You don't know how much I regret ever having married you. Damn me for a fool! I should never have left Kentucky and put myself in your despicable hands, and I should rather die right now than know that I might carry your child.''

Nicholas winced at her words and released her wrists to grasp her tightly by the soft flesh of her upper arms. For the first time in his life, he felt a powerful urge to strike a woman, yet could not bring himself to use violence against his wife. Instead, using another, more destructive weapon, he spoke softly and clearly to her.

"Yes, I can see that this marriage was a mistake, and since it's obvious that our dislike is mutual, I will be only too happy to take myself out of your life. We will have our little supper with Mr. Montagu, and come the morrow we will return to Providence. You will see little of me after that, my dear. There are many amusements of which I can easily avail myself. I don't need you to find enjoyment."

He flung her forcefully to the bed, where she fell in an untidy jumble of petticoats and crushed green velvet. He stood staring down at her, his expression unreadable as Jessica glared her defiance. Uttering a short, crude expletive, he turned sharply from her.

"I shall reserve a private dining room for our supper," he said coldly. "I'm sure Mr. Montagu will enjoy having you to feast his eyes upon tonight. Do try to tidy yourself, however. We wouldn't want Theodore to find fault with your appearance."

The door slammed shut, and Jessica slowly gathered her skirts around her and sat up, dragging herself to lean against the bed's high headboard. She had never considered herself to be a weepy female, but that too seemed to have changed since Nicholas's entrance into her life. She turned over and lay full length on the bed. Careful to stifle her sobs lest he return prematurely, she buried her flushed face in the coolness of her pillow and cried long and hard, feeling as miserable as she ever had in her whole life.

Why had she goaded him into saying those hateful things? She had practically accused him of adultery the moment he entered the room, and all because of her uncontrollable jealousy. If she had any confidence at all in herself, she could easily have won Nicholas away from Charlotte or any other woman, but instead she had acted a madwoman, spouting her suspicious conjectures like an adolescent schoolgirl caught in the throes of her first romance. What a fool she was. Surely Nicholas hated her now, and she had too much pride to apologize to him after the terrible, degrading words he had hurled at her.

Through bleary eyes she spied the forgotten box at the foot of the bed. She untied the ribbon and lifted the lid.

Chocolates. Dark chocolates nestled in crinkly gold and silver paper. Jessica's eyes widened at the sight of so many different kinds in one box. Slowly she replaced the lid, and fresh tears sprang to her eyes.

"Oh, Nicholas," she whispered.

It must be near eight o'clock. Theo would soon be there, and she dreaded the evening to come. How would she ever sit through supper? Breathing deeply, she moved to the mirror and applied a damp cloth to her flushed and puffy face. Staring back at the face that seemed to have just now gained new maturity, she shrugged.

"Your growing up was long overdue anyway, Jessica."

Chapter 14

Jessica looked up casually from the book she was reading, her eyes vacantly scanning the room lined from ceiling to floor with cloth- and leather-bound books. She loved the comfortable snugness of this room, with its dark wood-paneled walls and leather chairs. Her eyes fell upon the lazily ticking brass clock on a nearby table and, noting the hour, she quickly set her book down. Earlier that morning she had promised Theodore she would go riding with him, and she was looking forward to the outing.

Startling Jessica out of her lethargy that night when the three of them had dined together at the King's Inn in Charleston, Nicholas had stunned her by inviting Theo for a visit to the plantation. Theo had mentioned he was having some refurbishing done at his townhouse in the city and that everything was in a state of perpetual confusion. It was then that Nicholas had graciously extended the offer to visit, a sarcastic inflection in his deep voice. He had stared across the table into Jessica's shocked expression and lifted his wineglass in a mocking salute.

Theo had been more than happy to accept the invitation and had proven to be delightful company this last week, especially considering Nicholas's withdrawn behavior of late. It seemed that as quickly as she and her cousin became fast friends, she and Nicholas became strangers once more.

With Theo she spent long hours talking about their families and their likes and dislikes. Theo had suggested they take walks, and Jessica had been relieved to escape the oppressive atmosphere of the house. She was glad that Theo monopolized her company, for aside from her cousin, no one else seemed interested in her.

Theo always sensed when she was upset about something. A few days ago they had been in the library, and Jessica had been telling him what it was like to be raised on a farm. Speaking of her family, she had felt a bit homesick, but Theo had immediately joked her out of her gray mood. They had been laughing together quite uproariously, Jessica holding on to the sleeve of Theo's frock coat, when Nicholas had paused in the doorway. They had stopped laughing immediately.

"Come in and join us, Nick," Theo had invited, "Jessica has some wonderful stories about Virginia."

To Jessica, it had seemed that Nicholas regarded her like some foreign object he was disgusted to discover in his soup.

"No thank you, Theodore. I have work to do."

He had made it sound as if he was the only person engaged in any productive enterprise. Giving them one last damning glare, he had turned on his heel and left them. Theodore had made a comic face of pompous affront at Nicholas's retreating back, and Jessica had been unable to contain her laughter. She was certain Nicholas had heard her, she hoped he hadn't thought she was laughing at him. She still loved him dearly, but was hurt by his behavior.

Ever since their heated argument at the inn, Nicholas had treated her with cold tolerance. She saw him only at dinner, yet she might as well be a superfluous article of furniture for all the attention he showed her even then.

Her anger had long since evaporated, replaced by stubborn pride. How dare he act as if he had somehow been wronged, when in fact it was she who had been a witness to his philandering? With every passing day he was becoming more and more aloof, and she was at a loss to deal with this withdrawn stranger.

Hoping to relieve some of the tension at dinner the night before, Theo had jokingly asked Jessica why she had married such a gloomy bear of a man. She had shrugged and made a flippant remark about wishing she had known Theodore sooner. Nicholas had stiffened at her comment and soon excused himself from their company, saying he had to see to a small problem of Alcey's.

"What is the matter with Alcey?" Jessica had asked, concerned, for she had become very fond of the black woman.

"Such concern, madam? No need to trouble yourself, although I'm sure you would not in any case. Alcey thinks she heard some snakes in the kitchen adjoining the dining room."

"Snakes?" Theo was surprised. "At this time of the year? Why don't you have one of the servants attend to it, Nick?"

"Everything that goes on in this house is my business, and I am very observant," he had replied, staring at Jessica meaningfully. "Aside from that, I wouldn't want to see anyone injured." He had nodded curtly in their direction and left the room.

"Fancy that," Theo had said musingly. "Snakes in December."

Now Jessica realized that the week with Theo was nearly over, and somewhere deep inside, she was a bit put off that Nicholas didn't seem to mind that she and Theo spent so much time together. But she pushed the feeling even deeper and refused to be disturbed by the way he had dismissed her from his life.

Each night she had tossed in her bed, feeling more

lonely and unfulfilled than the previous night. Often she had heard Nicholas moving about in his room and wanted desperately to go to him and set things right between them. Just remembering the one night she had lain with such passion in his arms, and knowing she was now not welcome there, brought on a deep melancholy.

More than once she had thrown back the covers and moved with determination to the door separating their two suites. But at the last moment she had always stood undecided. Why should she make the first effort at reconciliation? It was all too obvious that he wanted nothing to do with her. So she held her tongue.

Now she put the book away and left the library, deep in thought, quickly climbing the curving staircase to the second story. She was halfway to the top when she paused to look down and came in direct contact with Nicholas's unwavering stare. He stood in a relaxed stance, one hand resting on the polished bannister, one booted foot on the first step, a half smile on his lips as he lazily watched her.

She drew herself erect, prepared for some scathing comment, and was surprised to see the brief glimpse of an unreadable emotion in his eyes. Could it have been longing? If so, he quickly disguised it, and instead began slowly, almost reluctantly, to climb the stairs. Jessica stood immobilized, watching him come toward her, the soft, deep burgundy carpet muffling his deliberate footsteps. He reached the step where she was standing, and she lowered her gaze to his polished boots, painfully aware of his nearness, deeply aroused by his fresh, spicy cologne.

Don't be a fool, she thought to herself. Look him in the eyes. Don't play the timid female. Remember, Jessica, confidence.

She raised her eyes and stared up into his gaze. He reached out slowly and twirled one of her reddish-brown curls around his finger.

"Where are you going in such a hurry, and in so thoughtful a mood, madam?"

Jessica was confused by his teasing manner. Unwilling to see the return of the black scowl he wore so often these days, she purposely neglected mentioning her ride with Theo and hid her shaken composure.

"Was I looking thoughtful, sir? Why, I assumed, according to you that is, that I hadn't the brains for anything as sophisticated as thought."

His eyes crinkled at the corners in appreciation of her quick reply as he smiled down at her, refusing to be annoyed. "Did I say such a thing?"

He unwound her hair from his finger and gathered the heavy mass from around her shoulders, sweeping it behind her back and lightly caressing her neck.

"My, you do have a remarkable memory—among other things." A pained expression filled his eyes, as if some memory disturbed him.

"Oh?" Jessica was surprised. "What else about me do you consider remarkable?"

She held her breath as his gaze grew warm once more, and he smiled, putting a hand on her shoulder, intent on leaning forward to whisper in her ear. Suddenly Theo's loud voice interrupted the intimacy of the moment.

"Oh, there you are Jessica. Are you ready for our ride?"

Nicholas's hand tightened briefly on her shoulder before he straightened with a jerk and stared accusingly into her face, the hardness returning to his eyes. He turned to look down at Theo's embarrassed expression. Her cousin coughed uncomfortably.

"I'm terribly sorry. Did I interrupt something?"

Nicholas raised a sardonic eyebrow and shook his head. "Not at all. Jessica was just on her way to change into her riding clothes, I believe."

Silently damning Theo for his unwelcome interruption, Jessica nodded. Assuring Theo that she would be ready shortly, she quickly fled up the stairs to her room.

She took off her dress and petticoat, leaving on her chemise, and pulled out her riding habit, then stooped to find her boots. Usually they were near the front of the armoire, but not this time. She reached into a dark corner, fumbling in search of them, and touched something that moved. With a gasp she drew back her hand.

An ominous hissing sound sent a shudder through her frame. She saw the coiled, copper-red snake marked with dark bands a second before it flew forward, attaching its fangs to the flesh of her upper arm. Jessica screamed in anguish as pain lanced down her arm in agonizing waves. She grabbed hold of the snake's swaying body and threw it away from her instants before Nicholas burst into the room. The snake's thick body fell to the carpet and coiled venomously to strike again. With a shouted curse Nicholas grabbed a poker from near the fireplace and brought it down on the snake's body, crushing the triangular head with one mighty blow. The tail twitched momentarily and then was still.

He rushed to Jessica's side. She was on her hands and knees, her hair falling over her face. The green eyes she raised to him were full of pain and confusion. The two tiny puncture wounds on her arm were dripping blood and fast becoming red and inflamed.

His face savage with distress, Nicholas picked her up and placed her gently on the bed. He fumbled impatiently with the ties of his silk cravat.

"Don't worry, Jessica. You'll be fine. I know what to do."

She spoke softly, her eyes filled with fear and accusation. "I'm sure you do," she said.

Ignoring her strange remark, he finally freed the cravat from around his neck and twisted it tightly around her upper arm, just above the wound. With stiff fingers he smoothed the tangled hair from her face, and she closed her eyes, unable to bear his false look of concern.

"Jessica? Jessica? Look at me please, my love."

She winced and opened her eyes, a queer little smile on her lips. "Why should I look? So you may have the last laugh? Congratulations, Nicholas.'' She laughed weakly. ''Strange how these animals are forever finding their way into my rooms at the most appropriate moments, don't you think?''

Nicholas' lips tightened as he dropped her hand. She turned her head wearily as he charged through the door connecting their rooms. How could all of these accidents possibly be happening to her? She swallowed thickly, almost tasting the bitter venom in her body.

The coward, she thought. He's left me here to die.

But barely ten seconds passed before he rushed back into the room carrying a pocket knife. Jessica lifted her head and tried with difficulty to focus her gaze. Everything was becoming so blurred. Was that really a knife she was in Nicholas's hand? Her thoughts were so muddled.

She gave a little cry as her arm throbbed in renewed pain and leaned her head back on the pillow, chuckling weakly. What did it matter? ''A knife, Nicholas?'' She spoke sarcastically, her words slurred, little caring if she provoked him. ''Isn't that rather like beating a dead horse? Surely you're not going to stab me to put me out of my misery. Very considerate of you, but why don't you just let the poison take me? I assure you, I'll suffer more that way.''

''Jessica, my love, you don't know what you're saying. I'm not going to let you . . .''

Jessica heard a loud gasp from the vicinity of the open doorway, then running footsteps. ''Marse! Ah was down in de hallway when me an' Josh heard a scream. What's goin' on? What yo' doin' with dat knife?''

Alcey, thought Jessica in relief. He surely wouldn't stab her if Alcey was there to witness the deed.

''Jessica's been bitten by one of those damned copperheads we found in the house yesterday.''

''Oh, lawsy me, how'd dat varmint git in here?''

Jessica was fast fading from consciousness. Their anxious voices became an incoherent rumble of sound. She

felt her arm being pulled away from her body where she
had cradled it protectively against her. She screamed involuntarily. Oh Lord, hadn't he caused her pain enough?
Mercifully the blackness began to expand inward, spreading over her anguish in soothing waves. Then there was
nothing.

Nicholas looked down at Jessica's unconscious face.
"Dear God," he prayed. "Don't let her die."

He held her arm over the bowl that Alcey held out and
made a shallow slit into the flesh surrounding the puncture
wounds. Blood spurted over her arm and into the basin.
He put his mouth to the wound and began to suck fiercely,
drawing the poison from the arm and spitting into the
basin. He repeated the action again and again until finally
Alcey's voice interrupted him. "Ah think dat's nuf, marse.
Yo' gonna drain away her strength if'n yo' takes anymo'
outta her. Yo' go an' wash yo' mouth real good to git de
pizen out."

"No." Nicholas shook his head emphatically. "I've got
to stay with her."

He reached up to slightly loosen the tourniquet, but
Alcey was determined. "Now what good yo' gonna do dat
chile if'n yo' falls over sick yo'self? Now git along an' do
like Ah tells yo'."

Before he could move, Titus burst through the open
doorway, practically filling the space with his massive
bulk. He saw the dead snake on the carpet and Jessica's
bloody arm. His face froze in horror.

"Lawsy, Ah'll git down to de cabin. Old Br'er Thomas,
he make de best snakebite poultice dat evah dere was.
Don't yo' fret none, marse. We ain't gonna let anythin'
happen to de missus."

Nicholas wearily nodded his thanks. Soon he heard
Titus yell something to Josh, followed by the loud slam of
the front door.

Half an hour later, Jessica's arm had been securely

bandaged with the healing poultice thickly applied to the wound. Alcey had stripped Jessica of her chemise and dressed her in a warm, flannel nightgown. Her body was bathed in sweat, and she thrashed from side to side, her lips moving constantly. Alcey, Titus, and Nicholas stared with concern at her pale cheeks.

Finally Nicholas said, "Alcey, Titus; please leave us now. I'd like to be alone with her." They nodded in unison and turned to leave the room, Alcey leaning heavily against her husband, his brawny arm around her slender shoulders.

"Ah'll be 'round if'n yo' needs anythin', marse.'"

Nicholas nodded, not taking his eyes from Jessica's features. Suddenly he looked up at Titus, blatant fear in his gray eyes.

"Titus . . . I . . ."

"Ah knows." Titus smiled softly. "But don't yo' give up hope. An ailin' body can tell, so don't yo' go givin' her no reasons fo' slippin' away. She ain't leavin' us yet, marse. Ah gots me a good feelin'." Softly he shut the door behind him.

Nicholas wet a cloth in a basin of cool water and applied it to Jessica's heated forehead. Suddenly he imagined he was fifteen years old again, looking down into the wide gray eyes of his eighteen-year-old sister, Katherine, his hands holding a damp cloth over her fevered forehead. Her thin face was etched with suffering and pain, and her once glorious black hair was snarled and dull. Her body seemed shrunken and withered under the blanket. Nicholas closed his eyes, letting the memory have its way.

"Don't look so sad, Nickie. You still have Papa, and despite what you think, he does love you." Her dry, skeletal hand fumbled to grasp his weakly.

"Papa hates me, Kate. You know that. You're the only one I have left." He stared at her with wide, frightened eyes as her gaze became unfocused. *"Kate? Kate?"*

She sighed, her breath a rattle in her chest, and looked vaguely up at him.

"I'm still here, Nickie. Don't you worry." She gasped for breath with an effort. "You must have more patience with Papa. He was not always the way he is now. You . . . you were very young, but when Mama was alive he was so much better . . ." She closed her eyes and coughed weakly. Nicholas clutched her hand harder. She opened her eyes, the gray light in them fading. "Nickie? Are you there?"

"Yes, Kate." He held the frail hand to his chest. "Please don't leave. When Mama died, you said you would always stay with me. I love you. I love you, Kate. Please stay."

She gripped his shirt with failing strength. "And I love you, Sir Lancelot. Please don't hate me . . . for dying . . ." She closed her eyes, and her hand grew limp in Nicholas's grasp. He stared down into her pale face, the expression peaceful at last.

"Kate! Kate! Don't go! Kate!" He flung his arms over her and buried his head in her chest, sobbing wildly. His Kate. His wonderful Kate. She was gone.

Nicholas came slowly back to the present, the specters of the past softly fading. He swallowed heavily, remembering. His thrice-damned drunkard of a father hadn't even been at Kate's bedside during her final hours. He had closeted himself at his club, steeped in self-pity and alcohol.

Nicholas blinked and shook his head sharply, staring down at Jessica's face. Jessica was the same age his sister had been when she died. That was seventeen years ago, the last time he had told anyone of his love. Since then he had protected his heart against the ravages of love's loss, or so he had thought.

All at once Jessica cried out incoherently in her troubled sleep, and he spoke soothingly to her, stroking her cheek with gentle fingers. How had this thoroughly unsophisti-

cated, earthy imp of a child crept past all his carefully
erected defenses? Finally he admitted to himself what he
had known since the beginning.

"I love you, Jessica. I love you. I told you once that I
would let nothing happen to you. Please forgive me."

He knew she was much too deep in the throes of her
illness to hear him. Her lips continued to move involuntarily, and his brow furrowed in concentration as he tried to
decipher her muddled ramblings, but to no avail. Suddenly
her arm flew out, knocking the basin of water to the oak
floor. It fell with a crash and splintered into a thousand
glittering shards of porcelain.

"Joey!" she screamed. "My God, he's in my room!
It's so hot." She thrashed about, pushing the blankets
away from her. Then she began to cry. "Don't die, Joey.
My fault. My fault." Nicholas leaned forward to soothe
her, grasping her hands in his. After a while she quieted
and was still, so still that Nicholas became concerned.

The hours ticked slowly by. Alcey came and went, her
faced lined with worry. She left a tray of food, but it
remained untouched. Nicholas continued to sponge Jessica's
body with cool water, endlessly stroking her heated flesh
and wringing out the cloth, as the venom-induced fever
intensified. The darkness of the night settled softly about
him, yet he didn't bother to light a lamp as he stayed true
to his lonely vigil.

All the time his thoughts churned. Why had Jessica looked at
him with such fear while he held the knife? He cursed
vehemently, blaming himself for the incident. He and
Titus had found three large snakes in the kitchen. Obviously there must have been one more that they'd missed,
one that had somehow found its way to Jessica's room.

He renewed his prayers for her safe deliverance from the
poisons that gripped her body. The fever must soon break.
No one could withstand so high a temperature for so long
without its leaving some permanent damage, and he didn't
dare think of the consequences to an unborn child, should

Jessica be pregnant. He continued to sponge her body methodically. The mantel clock chimed three o'clock. As if on cue, Jessica began to speak once more.

"I'll marry him, this 'Lord Carlyle.' Such a gentleman. I'll no doubt disgrace myself, but Richard said Papa would come after me. My fault." Her eyes flew open, and she stared at Nicholas in horror, sitting up and gripping his shoulders. "He was chasing me on the trail. My God, I thought he'd kill me. I saw him kissing her in the window, and then the horses came." She closed her eyes, falling weakly back onto the bed, and tears wet her cheeks. "I hate him for what he's done to me. My life is ruined."

Nicholas stroked her hands, his throat tightening at her words. "Hush, Jessica. Be calm. You must be strong. You must get well. Get well for me. Please." He bowed his head and grasped her hands, squeezing them tightly. When he looked up, her eyes were open again, and she smiled her brilliant, lovely smile, showing a different side of the delirium.

"Nicholas, you're here. You stayed."

She reached up to kiss him, and he took her into his arms, pressing his lips gently against her mouth, which parted eagerly for him. Suddenly he jerked away in pain as he felt her teeth sink into his lower lip. She sat up, her eyes glowing with hate, and her voice lowered to a husky growl.

"I'm not going to die! I wouldn't give you the satisfaction!"

Her eyes closed abruptly, and her body went limp once more, dropping to the bed like a marionette whose strings had been severed.

Nicholas massaged his lower lip with his thumb. My God, had the snake in her room been deliberate? Like the horses, the gunshot, and even the rat? He looked down at her once more. No one was going to hurt her again, he vowed to himself. No one. But who was responsible for all of these "accidents"? Who? He racked his brain, but could recall no shred of evidence that might point to the guilty party.

Now she hated him, though he knew she had not always felt that way. If only he could win her back. If only it wasn't too late. Was it only a few weeks ago that he had held her willingly in his arms? Damn Theodore Montagu to hell! Couldn't Jessica see the man for what he was, a smooth-talking bastard?

He would never let her go, and no one would take her from him. Somehow he'd find a way to make her love him. Somehow.

Jessica began to mutter once more, and he leaned forward to hold her hand. She would survive. She must.

Chapter 15

"I know we are doing the right thing, Andrew." Sarah leaned past her husband to put a few cooking utensils in the wagon that would be the Blackwells' home for the next few weeks. "Well, that's the last of it."

"I only wish you and the boys would stay somewhere safe, perhaps with the Hastings family."

"Andrew, I would be frantic with worry without you, and it would be weeks before I received word from you in South Carolina. I'm certain I would expire from a nervous condition by then."

"But, Sarah . . ."

"All I can think of is Jeremy and Elizabeth. They left their daughter behind and never saw her again. No, Andrew." Sarah adamantly shook her head. "Our family will not be separated."

"All right, my dear. I never could say no to you, and you know I'm as set on going to Charleston as you are. I wish I had listened to you sooner. Your intuition has yet to be proven wrong."

"It is more than intuition this time, Andrew. The tone

of Jessica's letters has become steadily less cheerful. She hasn't said anything directly, but I gathered that she and her husband have separate beds. Don't you find that strange for a newly married couple? And I don't like this business of her finding the dead rat in her desk. You know how terrified she is of rats.''

''I know, I know. We've talked of nothing else.''

''She keeps writing that she wants us to visit, that she is homesick for the farm and her brothers. It just doesn't make sense. If she was in love, the last thing she would want to see would be this ugly mob. Andrew, I know there's something wrong. I can feel it as sure as I see you standing there.''

''Sarah, I'm convinced.''

''And that worries me too. I know how logical you are. If you're worried about Jessica, then there *must* be something wrong.''

''We'll soon find out. We'll see her for ourselves, and then we'll know.''

''My Dolly.'' Sarah sighed shakily. ''If anything has happened to her because we allowed her to go away with Richard Montagu, I'd never forgive myself.''

Jessica opened her eyes and blinked them hard several times, trying in vain to focus her gaze on the ceiling, which seemed to swim before her straining eyes. Try as she might, she wasn't able to marshal her whirling senses into control. Her mouth felt thick and her eyes crusty, as if someone had shoveled sand into them.

Where in the world was she? She tried to sit up and was amazed by the wave of nausea and dizziness that accompanied her ill-advised movement. She raised a hand to her forehead and sank back down beneath the warm quilt. She was never ill; in fact, she was one of the most unfashionably healthy women she knew, never suffering from an attack of vapors or other delicate feminine ailments. What was wrong with her? Her eyes flew wide as suddenly the reason for her infirmity came rushing back.

She groaned involuntarily and jerked her arm up in alarm, staring at the neat white bandage wrapped securely around it. She squeezed the flesh experimentally and winced. The wound was still tender. Her brow furrowed in painful concentration as she tried to recall the events that had led up to the present.

She remembered looking for her boots in the armoire, and reaching back into the corner. Then suddenly . . . She shuddered at the mental image of the coiled snake, its fangs dripping venom as it struck swiftly at her unprotected flesh. Then Nicholas had been there with a knife, but Alcey had come to save her.

I must get away from here, she thought wildly. As long as I am in his house, I am in danger of being killed.

But where could she go? Certainly not Virginia. She would not involve her family in anything remotely dangerous. Where else? A vague image of her inherited estate in England, as both Richard and Nicholas had described it, wavered hazily in her thoughts. England? Was that far away enough for safety, or would Nicholas follow her even there?

At least she was alive. Although her body felt bruised and beaten, she was deliriously alive. Moving slowly so as not to disturb her pounding head, she levered herself into a sitting position and with a gasp recognized Nicholas's tall form arranged uncomfortably in a small chair near her bedside.

How innocent he looked lying there, a wave of his thick black hair dangling over his forehead, his face boyish in repose. He looked so tired and ill-kempt, she almost reached out to touch him, but she squelched the feeling of tenderness. Sweet Jesus! After all he had done to her, how could she feel tender toward him? Was there no end to the effrontery of this disease called love?

He did look rather badly though. His face seemed gaunt,

his hair wildly disheveled, his clothing rumpled. She humphed silently to herself. For once, she hoped she presented a better appearance than he. She glanced again at his haggard features. At least several days' growth of beard covered his face.

She stifled a gasp. How long had she been unconscious?

Perhaps sensing her movement, Nicholas began to rouse. Not wishing to be near him, Jessica unwisely swung her legs over the side of the high bed. As her feet touched the floor, her legs collapsed under her. Her head began to spin alarmingly, and she crumpled to the carpet in an untidy pile of flannel nightgown and snarled auburn hair.

She heard a gasp and rapid footsteps. Then strong arms were drawing her upward, and she was being held against a hard chest, one muscled arm around her waist, the other folding down the blankets.

Jessica closed her eyes in despair. Even now his mere touch sent warm quivers of pleasure up her spine. The room dipped and swayed as she was placed in her warm bed, the covers immediately pulled up to her chin. Looking up, she saw Nicholas standing over her with such an intensely loving, tender look in his eyes that she was momentarily shaken. His expression quickly changed to one of surprise when he realized she was conscious.

"Jessica, thank God you're awake at last. I feared I had lost you forever."

Jessica frowned. What the devil was his game this time, with this mock show of devotion? Were there no depths to which he wouldn't sink? Perhaps he assumed that, because of the fever, she would not remember his treachery. Very well, she would play his game.

"What happened?" she murmured.

He sat down on the bed and took her hand. She flinched and pulled it from his grasp. Hurt flickered in his gaze.

"Don't you remember?"

"Remember?"

"The snake."

"I remember you said you had to help Alcey find some snakes that had somehow gotten into the house."

That she could so calmly lie in bed next to the man who had betrayed her, broken her heart, and attempted her demise several times astounded her, but for some reason she felt no fear of him. Perhaps she was truly insane.

"Perhaps it's just as well that you don't remember," he said. "You were bitten by a copperhead."

Jessica pretended alarm. "Copperhead?"

"Yes. Fortunately I heard you scream and was able to kill it before it could strike you again."

"Thank you." Jessica found it difficult to say the words.

"I thank God I was there to help." He looked at her with the most peculiar expression, then he sighed, changing the subject. "Alcey and Titus will be happy to see that you have recovered. They've become quite attached to you and were frantic with worry."

Nicholas, too, must be worried, she decided—now that she had miraculously survived her ordeal. He continued to stare down at her with a tender expression that made her nervous.

"What are you staring at?" she snapped in irritation, vexed with this continued false show of affection. What a consummate actor he was. He had truly missed his calling for a life on stage, she thought waspishly.

Nicholas shrugged away her apparent ill humor. "You cannot blame me for filling my eyes with the sight of your healthy features. After listening to your mumbled ravings for two days now, it's a pleasure to hear coherent speech, no matter how typically caustic, spill from your lips."

Jessica rolled her eyes. What drivel. It was enough to make her retch, and her queasy stomach needed no prompting. Then she became aware of the import of his speech.

"Two days? You mean to say I have been sick with fever for two days?" Nicholas nodded. "And I have been speaking in delirium? God help me. I can only imagine the tales with which I regaled you."

Nicholas chuckled, delighted that her mind seemed to show no ill effects from the fever. "Yes, there were quite a number of amusing incidents you recalled from your childhood. They involved rotten tomatoes, a harum-scarum ride through the moonlit woods with a sheet over your head, chicken eggs, a horse called Ivanhoe, and an ambush in the hayloft. You seem to have been quite the little hellion."

Jessica whimpered as if sorely wounded. Now she was lost. She had no secrets from him and would be forever damned. Nicholas continued a little more soberly.

"You also mentioned a fellow named Beau and were in a dilemma over which skirt you would wear when he came to call on you."

"Beau," Jessica whispered longingly, wishing for the simple times he represented—times now lost to her. "It all seems so long ago."

Nicholas's voice cracked when he spoke. "Were you in love with this fellow Beau?"

Jessica gave a bittersweet smile, aware of Nicholas's power over her and chosing her words carefully. "Beau was a good friend when I was a little girl. As we got older, he grew into a handsome young man, solidly built, kind, gentle, and naive in the way I once was." She laughed softly, humorlessly. "I fear I have outgrown him, and although at one time I would have liked very much for him to court me . . ." She shrugged. "There's another girl who will make him much happier than I ever could. She's a spoiled thing, but I suppose decent despite her airs. Beau is a simple farmer. I envy him."

Nicholas looked down into her shuttered face and defeated his almost undeniable urge to take her in his arms and kiss her, so happy was he to see that she had broken out of the fever seemingly unscathed. He imagined her slender body curving into his, her firm young breasts pressed against him, her soft lips open under his.

He rose quickly from the bed. He could not stand

another rejection from her now, especially since he had discovered his love for her.

"I imagine I've worn out my welcome," he said. "You must be tired and hungry. I'll have Alcey bring up a tray after a while. Until then I want you to rest." His hands clenched into fists, and he spoke tightly. "Theo has been beside himself since your accident and has been very anxious to see you."

Jessica's face lit with a smile. "Theo? He's still here? Please, I'd like to see him right away."

Nicholas abruptly turned away. "Very well. I'll send for him." Picking one last glance at her eager face, he mumbled a sharp curse under his breath, and left the room.

"Jessica, I'm so glad to see you are well at last." Theodore sat next to the bed, gently holding her hand.

"Thank you, Theo. I'm sorry we never had the chance to take our ride."

"Do you know that I waited for over an hour for you to appear at the stable? I would probably still be there if I hadn't seen Titus flying out of the house screaming for a certain Br'er Thomas and snakebite poultice."

"Yes, I must remember to thank Br'er Thomas. He saved my life."

"Jessica, I've grown so fond of you. I don't know what I would have done if something had happened to you."

"I suppose Nicholas would have been an even wealthier man, eh?"

Theo's lips curled in distaste, and he looked as though he desperately wanted to say something to her, but shook his head. "Yes, it was opportune that Nick was there to save you. I wonder how that snake got into your armoire?"

"I've been wondering that myself. It seems awfully strange, doesn't it?"

"Jessica, you don't think it was deliberate, do you?"

"Of course not, Theo. I simply have a vivid imagination." So far, she had kept her suspicions regarding her husband to herself, and she wanted to keep it that way for just a while longer. She unsuccessfully stifled a wide yawn.

"How rude of me!" Theo exclaimed. "I can see that you are tired. But I was so concerned, and Nicholas would hardly speak to me. I'm surprised he even allowed me to visit you." Still holding her hand, he pressed a soft kiss on her cheek.

"Thank you for your concern, cousin."

"Pardon me."

Theo and Jessica turned to stare at Nicholas silhouetted in the doorway, holding a tray of food. "I passed Alcey on the stairs with this tray and thought I would deliver it myself. But I can see you are otherwise occupied."

Jessica's face stiffened at his thinly veiled insult. She indicated the bedside table with a sweep of her hand. "Please place the tray there. I am quite famished." She yawned again. "Now, if you gentlemen will excuse me, I'd like some privacy."

Nicholas dropped the tray with a loud clatter and indicated that Theodore should precede him out of the room. The door shut firmly behind him, and just as firmly, Jessica knew in that instant what she had to do.

Cautiously she pulled back the covers and slid her feet to the floor. She felt dizzy for a moment, but by breathing deeply she managed to stop the whirling in her head. She walked slowly to the secretaire, dragging a small chair behind her, and she gratefully slumped into it. She pulled down the writing surface, put her elbows on the desktop, and hung her aching head in her hands. She sighed deeply. Best to have this unpleasant act behind her, she thought, and reached for some paper and a bottle of ink. Again thoughts of England swirled in her head, but she temporarily pushed them away and closed her eyes, carefully gathering her thoughts. Only then did she begin to write.

A week of slow convalescence dragged by for Jessica.

In all that time she didn't once see her husband. She learned from Alcey that Nicholas had been solely responsible for her recovery. It was he who had sucked the venom out of her arm, he who had soothed her delirium, he who had refused to leave her side.

At first the news puzzled her. Then she realized that when Alcey had burst into the room, Nicholas had had no other recourse but to use the knife to help her. As for his devoted ministrations, no doubt he wanted no one else to sit beside her should she speak some words in her delirium that might implicate him in the "accidents."

Still, she couldn't understand why he had allowed her to survive at all. It would have been a small thing to do away with her then, helpless as she was. She shivered at the thought. How could anyone be so evil, yet attract her so strongly? Sometimes when she looked out her window, she saw his tall form striding from the house to the stable. Her heart caught at just the sight of him, and her longing made her weak. How could she still love him?

How she wished she could speak to her mother about her warring love and suspicion, but she hadn't received a letter from her parents in over two weeks. She had turned for solace to Theo who had proven to be a good friend.

Amanda had also come to visit her. Amanda's visit had thoroughly cheered her lagging spirits, and because of Amanda's exuberant energy, Jessica now planned to escape the house today and take her long-postponed ride with Theodore.

Feeling like a thief, for she knew Alcey would never let her out of the house if she was aware of what Jessica planned to do, she silently made her way down the stairs. There was no one in sight, and she breathed a sigh of relief as she slipped out of the house, knowing that Theo would already be at the stable.

The wind whipped her habit around her legs, and it looked as if a storm was brewing. Maybe she and Theo shouldn't go out after all. But Aaron had saddled Diana when Jessica arrived at the stable, and Theo was already mounted on a fine bay gelding.

"It looks like it's going to storm, Theo. Perhaps we had better wait a few hours before we go riding." Theo looked distressed at her pronouncement and, remembering how thoughtful he had been the last two weeks, she sighed and relented. "Well, maybe we'll take a short ride then."

Aaron frowned darkly as he helped Jessica to mount. "Dese winter storms can be almo' as mean as dem summer squalls, Miz Jessie. Yo' sho' yo' feelin' good nuf to go out?"

"Don't worry, Aaron. We'll be all right, I'm sure. At the slightest hint of rain, we'll turn around, and I promise we won't go far."

Aaron made a final adjustment to the chin strap on Diana's bridle, frowned at Theo, and stepped back, not missing the glare the man shot at him. Jessica nodded to her escort and, guiding their horses toward the trail, they rode sedately away from the stable.

After going just a short way, Jessica was glad she had decided in favor of the ride. The cool air was wonderfully invigorating, and Theo's bright company lifted her spirits immediately. She turned to him shyly during a rare stretch of silence.

"Theo, I want you to know that I've truly appreciated your companionship these past weeks. You're a good friend."

He turned suddenly serious eyes upon her and smiled tightly. "I, too, have enjoyed our time together, Jessica. I never dreamed you could be such intelligent and amusing company."

Jessica looked puzzled at his strange remark, and he hastened to add, "It's only that when I first met you that day you were so silent and shaken. To be quite honest, I thought you a silly, stupid girl to stand in the street just waiting, it seemed, to be run down."

"I suppose I was in a bit of a shock." Once again Theo surprised her with his compassionate gaze.

"Yes, I can imagine. It must certainly be shocking to see your husband in the arms of another woman."

Jessica jerked upright in the saddle and tightened the reins to force Diana to a halt. "What are you talking about?"

"I saw them in the window that day, just as you did. You looked so lost standing there, and afterward, when I pulled you out of harm's way, you were like a piece of stiff wood in my arms."

Jessica turned her head away. It was one thing to know of her husband's indiscretion but quite another when a friend knew of them as well.

"So you knew all along, and yet you never said a word."

"I am not the only one who knows about Charlotte and your husband, Jessica."

She closed her eyes tightly for a brief instant. "What do you mean?"

"I do not like to be the one to carry tales, but you must know that I have very deep feelings for you and I hate to see you wasting yourself on a scoundrel."

"Go on."

"Jessica, it's no secret in Charleston that your husband and Charlotte have been lovers for quite some time. Nicholas wanted to marry her, but she refused, saying he hadn't wealth enough—although I must admit his is one of the most successful plantations in these hard times. Apparently Charlotte has changed her mind. But I'm afraid her rejection hurt his pride. That's when he went to Kentucky."

Jessica slumped wearily in the saddle. So that's why he had married her. Hysterical laughter threatened to escape her lips. It all made sense now. She took up Diana's reins and, sharply kicking the mare, galloped madly down the trail, needing to put as much distance between herself and Nicholas as possible.

More and more it seemed he was trying to kill her.

Perhaps he and Richard Montagu had planned the entire marriage scheme. Perhaps Nicholas had hired that red-haired brute to start the fire. Perhaps it had been him on the trail that day with the gun. And he must have put the rat and snake in her room. Perhaps he'd intended that she see the embrace in the window, just in time for those horses to run her down. Then Nicholas and Charlotte would have had her wealth and the rest of their lives together.

But there was something missing, something that didn't quite fit into place. Despite the growing evidence, she just couldn't believe Nicholas was trying to kill her.

Nicholas was sitting at his study desk looking over some accounts when he heard a crisp knock on the door. "Come in, Josh."

The black man ushered the stableboy Aaron into the room. The boy appeared ill at ease, and Nicholas came around to the front of his desk, smiling encouragingly.

"What brings you into the house, Aaron?"

The boy seemed reluctant to speak, and Josh nudged him with an elbow. "Go on, boy. Tell marse what yo' done tol' me."

"M-marse, Miz Jessie done gone out ridin' in dis bad weather. She say she come back soon if'n it got worse, but she ain't come back yet, an' I'se afraid fo' her."

Nicholas's voice was sharp with concern. "How long ago was this, Aaron?"

"Not long, not even an hour."

"Why did you wait so long to tell me? I'm surprised you wouldn't be more worried, letting her go out on her own, and so soon after her illness."

Aaron looked down at his scuffed boots. "Well, she didn't go out alone, marse."

"And with whom did she go riding then?"

"Mistah Theodore."

Nicholas's jaw clenched, and his hands curled into tight

fists. He spoke very softly. "I see. Thank you for telling me, Aaron. You did the right thing. Now please find Titus and saddle up two horses for us. I can see that a bad storm is coming, and we're going to have to go after Mrs. Carlyle."

Josh quickly ushered Aaron out of the room. Nicholas stood staring out the window for a moment watching the thrashing trees. He was tempted to let Jessica carry on her rendezvous with Theo. But an image of her face flushed with fever rose up in his mind. With a vicious curse he left the room and violently slammed the door behind him.

Jessica raced on beneath the turbulently swaying Carolina pines, feeling the sting of the cold air and her own salty tears against her cheeks. Damn! Damn! Was anyone as much a fool as she? How would she ever learn the truth about her husband? She couldn't simply confront Nicholas with her suspicions. Whether guilty or innocent, he was sure to deny her accusations.

Hysterical laughter threatened again, and with an effort she suppressed it. The light mist of a drizzle clung wetly to her face, but still she rode on, heedless of the cold and her heavy wet cloak.

Theo gave a self-satisfied smirk as he rode just behind Jessica's flying figure. He regretted nothing that he had said to the woman. In a way, however, it was a pity, for she was quite beautiful and, had circumstances been different, he would have enjoyed wooing her away from her husband. But she had to pay the price for depriving him of what should have been his all along.

He urged his horse to a faster pace and with some difficulty managed to catch up to her as she left the woods behind and rode out into a fallow field.

The sky was gray, the earth a dull brown. The trees swayed with the fury of the approaching storm, and the two figures fleeing wildly on horseback seemed to blend with the turbulence that surrounded them.

At last Theo reached out to grasp Diana's reins from Jessica's stiff fingers. He slowed the horses to a walk and moved to grab Jessica by the arm. She seemed surprised to see him there.

"Jessica," he shouted over the furor of the rising storm, "we've got to find shelter."

He stood up in his stirrups, scanning the countryside with anxious eyes, his blond hair whipping around his face. An overseer's shack stood not far ahead. He pointed in the direction of the shack.

"Hurry, before the rain starts in earnest!"

Nodding dully, Jessica made her way to the shack with Theo close behind. They dismounted quickly, removed the saddles and pads from the horses, and tied the animals close against the structure.

Theo undid the latch on the door and thrust Jessica into the shed, securely closing the door a second before the skies opened up and sent a deluge upon the land. He leaned against the door, sighing in relief as Jessica stared around her. The small shack contained a rough-hewn desk and stool and a cot upon which lay a neatly folded blanket. A single window afforded the only source of light.

Jessica laid the saddle pommel down on the table, and took off her damp cloak, then walked wearily to the cot and sat down, completely ignoring Theo. He sat next to her and took her cold hands into his.

"Jessica. I'm sorry. I shouldn't have told you. It was hardly the sort of thing a gentleman would tell a lady, but you are my cousin and I feel a certain responsibility to look out for you. Surely my father would do no less if he knew that Nicholas was an utter blackguard." He slipped an arm around her. "But the deed is done, and in one respect, I'm not sorry that you know about your husband because it's a damned shame that he has the right to claim what has always rightfully belonged to the Montagus. If there was only a way to change that."

Jessica turned dull green eyes to him, the rain sparkling

in her lashes, the smell of damp velvet and lilacs surrounding her. She leaned her head against his shoulder.

"It's not your fault, Theo. I guess I knew about Nicholas and Charlotte all along but was unwilling to see the truth. It's all clear to me now why Nicholas married me. But I have already done something to disrupt his intentions."

"Nicholas is a fool to prefer Charlotte to you, but tell me, Jessica, how have you thwarted him?"

She smiled sadly. "He'll never be able to hurt me again." Her eyes caught his, and she hoped he couldn't see the agony in their depths. Still he moved closer and held her shivering body tightly.

"Go ahead, Jess, cry if you want. I'll be here for you. Cry as long as you like."

Jessica pressed her face more closely against his shoulder. The smell of wet wool, horses, and sweat were somehow comforting, and she gave herself up to her grief, sobbing long and hard.

She didn't know how long she sat there with Theo rocking her gently, but after a while she sighed, feeling comforted, and resolutely pushed herself away. The time for crying was past. It was time to stand on her own now.

Strength—healthy, beautiful strength—flowed into her body, and for the first time since her marriage to Nicholas, she felt in control of her life and emotions. Never again would she allow herself to become a weepy-eyed, weak, silly mouse of a female. Damn! No one had the right to do that to her.

These past weeks when she had thought herself in love with Nicholas must have been a dream. How could she love a man like him? An image came to mind of the way he had tenderly cared for her after her near accident with the horses, and the night he had rescued her from the rat under her bed. It was followed by the stirring sight of him standing naked before the window, the sun bathing the magnificence of his tall, tanned, lean body in sharp detail. She remembered the exhilarating feelings his body had brought to life within her—and the way his arms had held her possessively afterward. She thought about all she knew of him, and it finally came to her befuddled mind that it little mattered what a bastard he was.

She still loved him.

She clenched her teeth, accepting the truth. All right, so she still loved with him. She could live with that fact, but at least it hadn't totally blinded her: she had written a will. Now she needed Theo's help.

"Listen, Theo, for I am going to trust you, and I shall need your assistance."

Quickly she told him of her suspicions regarding her husband. Theodore's eyes became wider as her story continued. Once she had finished, she clutched his arm in a desperate grip. "I want you to leave Providence tomorrow and take something to Mr. Darby. I'll give you the parcel before you leave."

"Darby? Nicholas's solicitor? What parcel? What are you talking about?"

"I'm talking about my will."

"Your *what*?" Theo's heart leaped within his chest. Unbelievably, this was precisely the direction in which he wanted Jessica's thoughts to drift.

"That land in England, and the money, everything was left to me," she explained. "It's mine. While I was convalescing in my room I made up a will leaving half my holdings to the Montagus and half to the Blackwells in the event of my death. That way at least Nicholas will have no reason to . . . to get me out of the way. But I can't live with him any longer. I intend to leave."

"Leave, Jessica! You're speaking in a rush. Calm down. None of this makes sense, my dear."

"Oh, yes it does, Theo. For the first time since I learned of my heritage things are finally making sense." She looked down at Jeremy Montagu's ring on her right index finger. "I'm going to go to England to live on the Montagu estate. I must get far away from here. I'm sure

Nicholas won't miss me. I'll be safe there. Theo, you must book me passage to London as soon as possible."

"Be reasonable, Jessica." He stood up restlessly. "Please think carefully about what you are about to do. Are you sure it was a good idea to make a will? And why would you want to involve the Blackwells in all of this? If, as you believe, Nicholas is a dangerous man, he could hurt you or your family if he finds out about the will."

"I don't see how he can hurt me any more than he already has, but yes, I know, Theo—I'm taking a chance. That's why you must help me. Please. If you deliver the will to the lawyer, then I can keep it a secret from Nicholas. After I've left, I don't think he'll care enough about me to wonder where I've gone, especially once Mr. Darby informs him of the changes in my will. It's the only way. Won't you help me?"

Jessica gripped Theo's hands tightly, pleading earnestly into his blue eyes, and Theo could hardly keep from showing the triumph in his gaze. Everything was going better than they had planned. That Jessica would give her will so easily into his hands amazed him. It would be a small matter to change the will to eliminate the Blackwells and leave everything to the Montagus—which meant him. He put his arms around her so he need not look into her eyes, and nodded.

"Yes, Jessica, I'll take the will for you and book your passage to England. And God help me."

Jessica had reached up to embrace Theo gratefully when suddenly the door to the shack burst open and slammed loudly against the wall. Startled, Jessica and Theo jumped apart, and Jessica couldn't help the small gasp that escaped her lips. Nicholas's tall form stood clearly silhouetted in the gray light of the doorway.

Chapter 16

Jessica thought she had seen Nicholas angry before, but those previous incidents were nothing compared to the suppressed rage she felt emanating in almost tangible waves from him now. Controlling himself with what seemed an incredible effort, he took a giant step into the shack and placed a viselike hand around Jessica's wrist. He stared at Theo, his eyes livid in the darkened interior, and spoke softly through clenched teeth.

"And now it seems that I am interrupting."

Jessica tried without success to release her arm from his brutal grasp while Theo drew himself up, as if prepared to come to blows.

"Jessica and I were simply caught together in the storm," he said. "I caution you to think upon that carefully, Nicholas. There was absolutely nothing tawdry going on here. Or do you intend to call me out?"

Nicholas spoke with cold politeness. "Mr. Montagu, please leave us now. Titus is outside, and I'm sure he'll be more than happy to escort you back to the house. I expect you to be gone by the time I return there."

Theo's mouth tightened, and he looked at Jessica to

receive her small nod of approval. How would he get her will now? Nevertheless he had no choice but to reluctantly take his leave, confident that the seed of suspicion he had planted in Jessica's mind would keep her away from Nicholas until her will was safely in his own hands. Just to be certain he might prepare a surprise for Jessica. Perhaps Charlotte could be of use again. Smiling inwardly, he snatched the saddle and pad from the rough desk and made a quick exit.

Nicholas viciously kicked the door closed behind him and, catching Jessica by the elbow, marched her the short distance to the cot and pushed her roughly onto it. He stood staring down at her with a cold, murderous expression until he heard Titus and Theodore gallop away. The storm renewed its fury, the rain pounding with a vengeance over their heads, but Nicholas made no move to leave the shack. Jessica defiantly stared up into his face, refusing to be intimidated.

Surprisingly she felt no fear of him. How dare he act the wronged husband after all he had done to hurt her? She sat calmly against the wall, gathered her feet under her, and waited.

Her calm manner further infuriated him. He jerked her to her feet. She lifted an indolent eyebrow. "What's next, Nicholas? Are you going to foolishly act the cuckolded husband, or do you intend to beat me instead and save your breath?"

He spoke harshly and as if he hadn't even heard her words. "What a fool I was to worry when Aaron told me you had been caught in this storm. You and Montagu planned it all, didn't you? As for beating you, I'd dearly love to, Jessica—beat you within an inch of your life."

Instead he grabbed her by the shoulders and shook her until her braids tumbled down from the top of her head, sending pins flying wildly in all directions. He released her suddenly and, losing her balance, she stumbled against the cot. She stared up at his furious face, wanting perversely to push him further beyond his frayed control.

"Well, that was exciting. Do you feel better now? Perhaps it would help if you threw me against the wall a few times until your male ego is appeased."

Nicholas couldn't believe she had spoken so flippantly. His eyes blazed in the darkening gloom, and he took a deep breath to keep himself from committing violence. Finally he spoke very softly.

"You will give me an explanation. I want to know what you were doing in here with him. My God, Jessica, aren't you intelligent enough to realize what he wants from you?"

"I suppose not. But then, if he wants to take me to bed I don't see why you would care, since you reserve that pleasure only for women other than your wife."

"Indeed? And since my wife doesn't condescend to make herself available to me, I would consider my actions justified. Especially considering that you, dear wife, seem to make yourself available to anyone except your husband."

Jessica sucked in her breath sharply. "You base, disgusting— How dare you accuse me when you have been the one to— Oh . . . damn you!"

"We're back to that again, are we?" he said in a bored tone.

"So it would seem." Jessica jumped to her feet, unable to bear being in the same room alone with him. As she swept past him, he once more grabbed her wrist.

"You're not going anywhere until I say you are dismissed."

She tugged futilely at her arm, incensed at his autocratic attitude. "I don't have to answer to anyone, and especially not to you. Let me go!"

Her eyes glowed with hate, and for a brief, despairing moment Nicholas feared he had lost her forever. He knew he had lost all control, but still he reacted instinctively, unable to let her go, using the only weapon he thought powerful enough to force her surrender.

His plundering kiss sent her pulse pounding . . . and her anger soaring. Keeping her wits, she forced herself to relax in his arms, and as soon as his kiss became less demanding, she pushed away from him, breathing deeply. The triumphant look on his face filled her with hatred. She intended to erase it at all costs, her femininity be damned.

Before Nicholas could suspect her action, she doubled up her fist and punched him in the gut with every ounce of pain, rage, and humiliation in her body lending her strength. He doubled over, and she swung her leg hard against his shin for good measure before throwing open the door.

Heedless of the cold, harsh wind and rain that assaulted her, she ran out into the storm, escape her only goal. Almost tripping over her habit, she raised the hem high and streaked out into the muddy field, the rain instantly soaking her, the air smelling of wet earth. Runnels of water poured into her open mouth as she gasped for breath, her progress impeded by her heavy skirt and the clinging mud, which sucked at her ankles and booted feet. Still she struggled on, stumbling now over the uneven, soggy ground.

It came to her slowly that her flight was futile. Soon he would catch her. Why did it seem that she was forever running away from him? When would it stop?

She glanced over her shoulder just as Nicholas reached her, and she tripped, exhausted, and fell into the earth's welcoming softness. Instantly the fight went out of her, and she lay on her stomach, sobbing for breath. Nicholas knelt down next to her, his head bowed, hands on his thighs, also gasping for breath.

Heedless of Nicholas, the mud, the cold, and her defeat, Jessica turned onto her back, letting the stinging winter rain wash over her body. She closed her eyes and breathed in the smell of the mud as the downpour continued. At last she stared up into the damp, enraged face of her husband.

His gray eyes held hers angrily as he lowered his body atop hers and held her wrists firmly on either side of her head. Once again she found herself gazing into the face of a stranger. Her eyes roamed wonderingly over his features. There were so many varied facets to his character. Who was he now?

The rain drummed unheeded on Nicholas's back as he stared down into her wide, searching eyes with their long lashes made spiky by the rain. Beads of moisture dampened the faint blush of her cheeks. Her full lips parted slightly, and a sharp pain struck Nicholas's chest at the thought of another man claiming her sweet mouth. His angry expression softened to one of confused longing, and hesitantly his head dipped down. He released her wrists to hold her face in his hands, heedless of the mud.

Jessica watched in fascination as conflicting emotions played across his expressive features. Rain dripped into her face from his sleek black hair, and she blinked, trying to clear her thoughts, but she could only see the need in his eyes, could only respond instantly to that need. Hesitantly she touched his lips. Her mouth was trembling when he finally kissed her—a soft, tentative, gentle kiss that made her sigh in contentment.

His lips retreated a few inches above her own, and she stared up into puzzled gray eyes that mirrored her own confusion. They continued to gaze searchingly at each other while rain washed down over them. Again he lowered cold, wet lips to her mouth, just as tenderly as before, giving in to the sensations that had once been tightly contained and were now breaking free.

Jessica hugged him tightly to her, returning his kiss most willingly. Groaning, Nicholas crushed her against him as his kisses became more demanding. She closed her eyes and gave herself up to feeling, brutally silencing a protesting inner voice, concentrating only on the feel and taste of Nicholas's open mouth as he kissed her endlessly, his lips moving ever so slowly over hers.

When at last she felt his mouth retreat from her own, her eyes fluttered open. Her breath came in short gasps, and she was surprised to note that Nicholas seemed similarly affected. Standing up, he pushed a lock of wet hair from his face and reached down to help her to her feet. Continuing to hold her hand, he stared intently down into her puzzled face. He seemed to be waiting for her to say something. And then as the rain fell, she knew what he wanted. Yet she couldn't quite bring herself to give it to him.

"Nicholas . . . I . . . let's go back to the shack. I'm cold."

Disappointment dulled his eyes. "Of course. It will do you no good to stand out here in the rain so soon after your fever."

He placed a solicitous arm about her shoulders and led her back to the overseer's hut, attentively helping her over the rough and muddy terrain. Rain drenched them with renewed force, washing away the mud. When Nicholas finally shut the door, he turned to stare at her, a tight smile on his face.

"I'm afraid we'll have to stay until the rain abates somewhat. It seems you are trapped here with me."

Jessica spoke the first words that came into her head. "I don't mind at all. I've missed you."

His brows drew down sharply. "I hadn't noticed."

The familiar hard expression returned to his eyes, and Jessica's heart constricted in pain. She hated that look and longed for the return of the tender, curiously vulnerable man he had been in the field.

"Don't . . . ." She swallowed with difficulty. "Please don't feel that way about me."

"Oh? And how should I feel after finding you in the arms of another man?"

She knew his words were meant to goad her, but despite the hammering in her head that begged caution, she was determined to discover Nicholas's true feelings for her. She stepped confidently up to him and slid her arms around his neck.

"How should you feel?" She rose onto her toes and

arched her body into him, pleased at his quick indrawn breath. "You should feel like this," she whispered huskily.

She pulled his head down and pressed parted lips against his surprised mouth. His lips remained stiff and unyielding for a moment, but Jessica licked them lightly until, to her immense relief, she felt him return her kiss. His arms went tightly around her, pulling her even more closely to him, and she moved her hips against him, amazed at the need that exploded within her. It might be a grave error to feel such overwhelming desire for her husband, especially after what she had learned from Theo, but, perversely, that knowledge only added to her desire to satisfy him. As his hands slid up her narrow rib cage to her breasts, she finally murmured the words she knew he wanted to hear.

"Make love to me, Nicholas. I want you . . . now."

He groaned and released her suddenly. His heavy-lidded eyes assessed her slowly, then widened slightly, the dilated pupils making them appear black.

"Then take off your clothes for me," he said. Slowly he slid the black satin muffler from around her throat. The material slipped softly against her neck. "Take off all of them, and quickly, or I'll rip them off myself."

Slowly, teasingly, and with a seductive smile, Jessica removed her boots and stockings, then undid the buttons down the front of her bodice, her fingers lingering as her husband's impatience grew. Finally the habit fell in a damp, muddy heap around her feet. She kicked it away casually and stood boldly in front of him in corset and white muslin petticoat. Nicholas stepped closer, an appreciative smile on his face, and trailed a finger over the swell of her breasts and slowly down the front of her corset.

"I see you are set on playing games . . . very well." He tugged at the lace over her bosom. "Now this."

"Of course."

Arching her back until her breasts pressed more tightly against her corset, she struggled with the ties, sighing as the whalebone fell away, leaving her torso and breasts free. With a careless hand she deliberately dropped the garment at his feet. The breath caught in Nicholas's throat as her breasts pressed fully against the damp material of her chemise, and she smiled with feminine satisfaction.

"Now the petticoat, Jessica."

"Help me," she murmured seductively.

He smiled slowly. "Witch. Even with your wet hair and dirty face, you're beautiful. And that body is perfect."

Gently he peeled the straps of the petticoat down over her shoulders. He pushed the garment down to her hips and quickly undid the tabs, forcing her limp skirts to her knees. Jessica began to shiver both from the cold and from the warm, deliberate look in her husband's eyes. He moved closer and took her in his arms.

"Are you cold? Let me warm you."

His hands wandered up and down her back, finally moving to cup her buttocks and press her against the full, swelling hardness between his thighs. Jessica closed her eyes, and her breath caught in her throat. His warm breath caressed her as he whispered close against her ear.

"Is that better?"

"Yes . . . much." Jessica sighed. "But I feel I'm at a definite disadvantage as you are the only one clothed." She ran a teasing finger down the front of his shirt. "Don't you think the situation should be remedied?"

"Help me," he said.

She slid her hands under the lapels of his frock coat and slipped it off his shoulders. His hands moved over her back once more, softly kneading her flesh. She fingered the buttons on his linen shirt and slowly unfastened them, then undid the intricate folds of his cravat and let both garments flutter to the floor. Deliberately she pressed her breasts against his naked chest, her arms coming up to hug him close against her.

Nicholas gasped as he felt those soft mounds pressed so tightly against him. Picking her up, he laid her tenderly on the cot. His eyes burned with promise as he stepped out of the rest of his clothes.

Jessica stared fascinated at her husband's body. He's beautiful, she thought. If he doesn't reach out and touch me soon, I'm going to scream. She spoke teasingly. "Nicholas, don't tell me its been so long that you've forgotten how it's done."

He chuckled softly and took her in his arms. Jessica sighed in contentment as he pressed warmly against her, his lips hot on her throat. She closed her eyes and leaned her head back, arching her slender body, delighting in the feel of the velvety smooth firmness of his manhood against her stomach.

In the dusky light filtering through the window, his features were indistinct. The cot felt coarse and grainy against her soft skin, and suddenly, as she gazed into her husband's eyes, Jessica felt a strange, melancholy longing rise slowly into her, a sweet ache that threatened to consume her with overwhelming sadness. All at once she realized the source of that ache: she wanted something she could never possess—his love.

"No," she whispered.

Nicholas tenderly stroked her hair, moved by the poignant expression in her eyes.

"Jessica, was is it? What's wrong?"

She shook her head, unable to explain. Tired of her hopeless thoughts, tired of thinking, she pulled his head down and fastened her lips on his. Nicholas groaned and slanted his mouth hard against hers, tangling his hands in braids that quickly came undone. Jessica moved to lock her arms around his warm, smooth back and gave herself up to emotion, forgetting everything but the feel of his lips moving slowly over hers, the texture of his tongue, the coarse hair rubbing against her breasts, the long legs tangled with hers.

As before, the world began to recede, her inner feelings taking the place of reality as her movements became more frenzied, demanding release. She was hardly aware of his caresses, of his hands moving lightly over her body, his mouth leaving hers to travel slowly down her throat and lower to her breasts, teasing the nipples into fuller erectness. Dazed, Jessica concentrated on feeling, holding his head to her bosom, and finally his lips moved lower, over her taut stomach, and lower still to the mound of silky brown hair.

It didn't enter her mind to protest. Nothing mattered but these feelings, once tightly contained, now bursting free. She arched uncontrollably against him as his lips found her, his fingers torturing her achingly sensitive nipples. She gasped as his tongue explored her, pushing her further, higher; she was completely caught up in the exploding sensations that unbelievably intensified with every languid stroke of his tongue. Yet still he tortured her, moving so slowly, lazily, refusing to give her the release she desperately sought. She grabbed his wet hair in great handfuls.

"Let me, Nicholas. Let me." Her whisper was practically incoherent.

He raised his head and Jessica cried out in disappointment and desire. Through the buzzing in her ears she heard his soft chuckle, and suddenly his mouth was moving insistently upon her again, his thumbs stroking her nipples purposefully. Jessica sank limply back against the cot, the waves of emotion gathering themselves together higher and higher, the crest reaching the limit and going beyond. Unable to stop herself, she cried out as the sensations exploded with bright shards of color, and then came the lulling descent, the colors fading slowly.

Through the soft haze, she became aware of Nicholas's body moving up and over hers. She wrapped her arms around him, and unbelievably, incredibly, the sensations rose again as he slid surely into her. She gasped, holding him tightly as he moved slowly against her, the colors becoming sharper again as he drove into her deeper, deeper.

She strained against him with all the strength left in her depleted body, wanting to forge him into her, wanting to give him as much pleasure as he had given her, as he was giving her now. There came an instant when they seemed to hang together, then the colors showered over them both in streaming, fiery trails, before softly fading into glowing embers.

Gradually the tension left their bodies; their tangled limbs relaxed. Jessica stroked the sleek, damp hair from Nicholas's neck, feeling ever so content. Nicholas lifted his head from the curve of her neck and gazed warmly into her darkened eyes.

"Jessica . . ."

She put her fingers to his lips, then tweaked his nose, an impish look in her eyes. "Tell me, Nicholas, how do you feel now?"

He chuckled and shook his head. "Need you ask? But I must admit, I've never been seduced so thoroughly"—he bent to kiss her lingeringly—"or so pleasurably. I can see that your talents vary widely—from stableboy to temptress."

"And at which do I excel?"

She stretched lazily under him, waiting for his favorable response, but he pondered her question a bit too long for her state of mind. She sniffed and huffily pushed him off her, and none too gently at that.

"I can see that I'll not be able to wheedle any praise from you. You're a stingy man."

She ignored his laughter, and almost immediately realized her error in pushing him away, for without his body to keep her warm, the chill of the shack sent goose bumps over her skin. As another cold draft of air swept in through the rough timber, Nicholas spread a blanket over them both. The worn cotton felt soft against her skin, and she reveled in the intimacy of the moment. Nicholas lightly stroked her cheek and spoke hesitantly, all playfulness gone.

"Jessica—earlier I shouldn't have said those things to you. It was most unfair of me. It's just that when I saw you with Theo, I realized anew how much I—.'' He cut himself short and took a heavy breath.

Jessica looked up into his sincere expression in shock. What was he trying to say? He had actually apologized, but there was more to it than that. To cover her surprise, she made light of the incident.

''It is of no consequence, Nicholas. I seem to have imprinted your shin with my boot on more than one occasion, for which I, too, much apologize.'' She noticed the light was getting dimmer. ''Don't you think we should be getting back to the house? The rain seems to have stopped for now, and I fear if we don't leave soon, I'll have no energy left to climb into the saddle.''

Nicholas's eyes were dark as he rolled over to take her in his arms. ''I seem to have discovered a wealth of energy.''

As he pressed boldly up against her, Jessica became immediately aware of the source of that energy. Her eyes widened in surprise. ''You're surely not serious, are you?''

His smile was wicked.

''Sweet Jesus,'' she whispered before his lips claimed hers.

Chapter 17

Although the rain had stopped and the storm seemed to be breaking up, the ride back to the plantation was most uncomfortable for Jessica. Her clothing was wet, filthy, and cold, and her face was streaked with dirt. She had hastily and painfully fashioned her matted hair into a thick, untidy braid. Fortunately her cloak, although damp, was still clean. No doubt something crawling out of the grave would have more allure than she. She sighed deeply. How was she ever going to face Alcey and Ella Mae in this condition?

Nicholas heard her sigh, and the corners of his mouth turned upward in a smile as he saw her pick distractedly at clumps of dried mud on the skirt of her habit. He reached across the horse's neck and squeezed Jessica's fingers consolingly, then leaned closer to kiss Jessica's lips lingeringly, slipping a hand to the nape of her neck. She sighed helplessly and answered his kiss, softly parting her lips. His mouth retreated from hers, and he wiped a smudge of dirt from her cheek.

Jessica ran a finger over the bump on Nicholas's nose. "We're a fine pair, are we not, Nicholas? The wealthy planter and his gracious wife. I'm sure Alcey and Titus will be surprised when they see us.''

"Don't worry, I've already thought how to circumvent that uncomfortable meeting. I know a way we can sneak in through the back of the house, and no one will be the wiser.'' Her response was less than enthusiastic, and he went on comfortingly. "You'll feel much better after a hot bath. So will I.''

Jessica breathed a sigh of relief as the stable came into view. Nicholas motioned her back behind the trees that formed a dense cover around the main house. Leaning forward, he whispered in a conspiratorial voice. "There's a path that leads to the back of the house. We will be well hidden. Come, follow me.''

Jessica would gladly have followed him into hell if it meant she could get to her room unnoticed. The horses wound down the meandering path, and when they came to the back of the mansion, Jessica and Nicholas, slid like two criminals from their horses. After tethering the animals, they crept stealthily toward the house.

The back door squeaked loudly on its hinges, and they both jumped at the sound. Nicholas put a finger to his lips, his eyes flashing with a boyish look of suppressed excitement, and Jessica gritted her teeth against an urge to laugh. She gratefully drew off the heavy cloak, spread it quietly on the floor, unlaced her muddy boots, then left them atop the cloak. The hallway loomed long and ominous in front of them. No one was in sight. Nicholas took her hand and, stepping carefully in their stocking feet, they reached the bottom of the stairs undetected. They smiled at each other in triumph and began to climb the stairs.

"Oh, there you are, Nick,'' a female voice seemed to boom out. "I thought I heard someone creeping about in the hallway. I've been waiting to see you.''

Jessica and Nicholas froze like two guilty children caught in an act of mischief. Jessica stiffened at the smooth, cultured tones. Charlotte. What the devil was she doing at Providence?

Charlotte stood in the foyer, disapproval on her face as she surveyed their unsightly condition. She was magnificently and immaculately dressed in an extremely low-cut powder-blue gown of poplin printed with tiny cream-colored flowers. Jessica frowned at the woman's obvious display, thinking it more than a bit inappropriate, but she couldn't help noticing that, suitable or not, the gown showed off Charlotte's shapely figure to perfection. Jessica turned to stare accusingly at her husband, and in that instant reality rushed in in cold stark waves, and with it all her distrust and suspicion. Nicholas seemed taken aback by her hard expression though he smiled reassuringly.

"Good heavens, Nick, Jessica," Charlotte exclaimed. "What in the world have you been doing? Can it be that you have been out playing in the dirt?"

Nicholas's mouth twitched, but Jessica was not in the least amused. She damned Charlotte for her uncanny ability to come upon Jessica at her very worst, and she wondered distantly if this scene had been purposely arranged to humiliate her. Nevertheless, she refused to be either embarrassed or humiliated, and she managed to bring a tight smile to her face. She moved away from her husband, suddenly unable to bear his proximity. What a fool she was for wondering if her true feelings for him had shown on her face while they had made love this afternoon. She glanced at his tall figure. How amusing he must think her blatant naivete. And to think she had almost believed his sincerity! She stared up into her husband's face and spoke rather coldly.

"As a matter of fact, Miss Rosemond, Nicholas and I *were* playing in the mud, but you must have Nicholas tell you all about it. I'm sure he would be delighted to oblige."

A puzzled look came over Charlotte's patrician features. Clearing her throat awkwardly, she held forth an envelope pinched tightly between her thumb and forefinger.

"Yes, I see. However, as to the reason for this call. I came personally to deliver this. Due to some terrible oversight, your invitation to my Christmas ball was not delivered with the others. I know this is short notice—the other invitations were sent out nearly three weeks ago, but the ball is this Saturday. I do hope you haven't any other plans." She gestured to Jessica's attire. "I'm sure Jessica will be able to . . . find an appropriate dress for such an occasion. Perhaps the servants can lend you something suitable, my dear."

Jessica eyebrows shot up at the woman's barb. "Oh, you don't think this outfit will do? It *is* an original."

"And how well it suits you, my dear."

"Why, thank you, Charlotte, and may I say—"

Nicholas held up a hand to halt further comments. "As you can see, Charlotte, Jessica and I were caught out in the storm. If you have anything further to discuss, please wait in the drawing room until we can repair our appearance. Otherwise—"

"Very well, Nick. I've waited this long, I suppose I can wait a little longer until you are presentable." Nodding curtly to Jessica, she swept back into the drawing room.

Jessica stared after Charlotte's retreating back, wondering at the woman's audacity to calmly walk into her lover's home, and with his wife in attendance. Nicholas's voice interrupted her thoughts.

"Come along, Jessica. I'm anxious to get clean, and then we can see what she wants."

"Oh, but I already know exactly what she wants, Nicholas, don't you?"

"And what might that be, my love?"

You, thought Jessica. Or did Charlotte already possess his heart? The couple certainly didn't behave like lovers, but then what did she know about it? Nicholas was waiting for an answer, but Jessica just shrugged and turned to quickly climb the stairs.

To her surprise, in her room Ella Mae was laying out

fresh clothing and towels. A bath filled with lilac-scented water was set temptingly before the crackling fire. Jessica drew her fingers through the water and breathed in the heady aroma.

"Ella Mae, how did you know I would want a bath, or even that I was here?"

The girl shrugged. "Pa was worried when yo' an' Marse Nick didn't come on home. He waited a spell till dat Mr. Theo skedaddled, an' den he went back out lookin' fo' ya'll. Well, we was keepin' de bathwater hot anyways, and den Pa come back lookin' real funny, an' tol' Mammy dat when y'all come back yo'd be wantin' to bathe."

Jessica almost gasped in embarrassment. Titus must have seen the muddy footprints leading from the field into the shanty, but had he heard anything through the thin walls? She shrugged, dismissing the incident. Propriety was the least of her worries right now.

" 'Scuse me fo' askin', Miz Jessie, but why is yo' purty clothes all covered with mud? Lawsy, but yo' look bad as de br'ers after dey comes back from coon huntin'."

Jessica's voice was flat. "I slipped in the mud."

Ella Mae raised a dubious eyebrow. "If dat's what yo' ses, dat's what yo' means, but Ah can't say Ah believes yo'." She shook her head as she walked toward the door, reminding Jessica in that instant of a younger Alcey. "Ah'll be back to help yo' change into yo' gown."

Jessica nodded in distraction and began to peel off her sodden, filthy garments. Sighing in relief, she eased her chilled body into the deliciously warm water. It felt like soft satin against her skin, and for a moment she forgot her problems and reveled in the delicate aroma that rose with the soft whiffs of steam. She picked up the scented bar of soap, thinking about what Theo and Amanda had told her about Nicholas and Charlotte's relationship. Somehow she must discover for herself how he truly felt about the woman.

Just as Jessica was lathering her hair for the second

time, Ella Mae returned to help her rinse out the soap and dry herself with fluffy towels. But as she accepted the girl's ministrations, a vague sadness filled her.

Unlike Jessica, Nicholas had a soft smile on his face as he toweled himself dry. The ugly day had turned into something quite beautiful. He thought of Jessica's naked body gleaming in the dull, dusty light of the shack, her strong arms reaching up to hold him, her darkened green eyes fired with passion. Very beautiful indeed.

He had no desire to talk to Charlotte and was annoyed at the woman's inability to accept his marriage and leave him alone. He detested the way she constantly sought to embarrass his wife. Jessica was just now becoming accustomed to her new life, and he didn't want anyone upsetting her, especially not Charlotte.

He dressed quickly, anxious to send Charlotte on her was so that Jessica need not confront the woman again.

Jessica was sitting at her dressing table in her shift. Ella Mae applied a last few strokes to the slightly damp hair and began to style it into an elaborate coiffure. She spoke almost too casually.

"Marse already done gone down to de drawin' room. Ah picked out one o' yo' nicest dresses so's we can show dat Miz Rosemond dat yo' is purtier dan she'll evah hope to be."

Jessica met her own startled green gaze in the mirror. "You mean he's already downstairs with her?"

"Yes'm, he be down dere fo' near to a quarter hour. Ah seen him go down dere while Ah was waitin' fo' yo' to finish with yo' bathin'."

"Well, why didn't you say something?" Jessica reached up and quickly began to pull the pins from her half-styled coiffure. "Forget about my hair. The style is much too pretentious for me anyway. Hurry up, Ella Mae. Help me into my dress."

Scarcely five minutes later, Jessica was flying out the door and down the stairs, her hair waving silkily behind her. The doors to the drawing room were closed. Feeling not the slightest bit of guilt, she crept forward silently to intentionally eavesdrop on the conversation within. If only she could see as well as hear what was going on, but there were no keyholes through which to look. She heard someone approach behind her and straightened quickly, trying for all the world to look nonchalant as she brushed some creases from her full skirt and ran her fingers through her hair, fluffing it over her shoulders.

"Miz Jessica, what yo' doin' hangin' on de door like dat?"

Alcey tucked a feather duster in her apron and came forward. With an expression of alarm, Jessica clapped a hand over the woman's mouth. Alcey lowered her voice.

"Lawsy, chile, yo' don't know a thing 'bout eavesdroppin', does yo'?" She crooked a finger. "Follow me."

Jessica looked on in bemusement as the black woman grabbed her hand and led her down the long hallway toward the back of the house. They turned left into the kitchen, where the servants prepared some foods and beverages and kept the meals from the cookhouse well warmed before serving. They passed into the elegant dining room. The French doors that separated the dining area from the drawing room were closed and the curtains were drawn across the length of the wall. They could hear the soft murmur of conversation in the next room very clearly. Alcey spoke barely above a whisper.

"Now dis here is where Ah does my serious listenin'." Jessica stared at the woman in wonder as Alcey went on. "Ah'm on yo' side, missus. Dat Charlotte Rosemond don't like us black folk no way, no how, an' we all was plumb sceered to dyin' dat Marse Nick was gonna up an' marry dat woman. An'm sho' yo' is gonna enjoy listenin' to marse give her a good dressin' down."

Jessica humphed to herself, but only gave Alcey a forced

half smile. She leaned forward, hugging the black woman to her, and whispered close in her ear.

"Thank you. I'm so glad I can depend on you."

Alcey stepped back, looking with sudden concern at Jessica's flushed cheeks and overly bright eyes. "Yo' sho' yo' feelin' all right, honey chile? Yo' feels awful warm to me, an' yo, was out in dat storm fo' quite a spell. It was powerful foolishness fo' yo' to go out ridin' so soon after yo' snakebite."

Jessica grabbed the woman's hand. "I'm fine, Alcey. Really."

Alcey didn't look convinced, but she bowed formally, straightening her apron. "Well, den, Ah'll leave yo' to it, an' Ah'll be sho' to see dis room is left alone fo' a while."

Jessica stood demurely until the woman disappeared into the kitchen, then she quickly crouched down next to the doors and moved a corner of the curtain aside so she could clearly see the action in the next room.

Nicholas was standing near the oak bar pouring himself a brandy. Charlotte sat prettily on the settee before the fireplace, sipping daintily from a glass of sherry. Jessica made a face, suppressing an urge to rush out of hiding and pull the woman's oh-so-perfectly arranged hair. Nicholas turned from the bar and approached Miss Rosemond.

"Charlotte, we've been engaged in pointless conversation for some time now. What are you really doing here?"

"Why, Nick, I told you. I've come to deliver the invitation."

"Your father has servants, if I'm not mistaken?" he took a sip from his drink. "Surely you could have had one of them deliver the envelope just as well."

"Yes, well, I wanted to apologize for the late delivery. It wouldn't have been proper to . . ."

Charlotte's voice died to a whisper as Nicholas turned to stand before the settee with his back to Jessica. Charlotte leaned forward, and he reached out a long arm and very gently pushed her back into the seat, his hand pressing lightly on her shoulder. He squeezed it and muttered something unintelligible.

Jessica dropped the curtain and clapped a hand over her mouth to keep from gasping aloud. From her vantage point, Nicholas's gesture seemed caressing. She could plainly see that the intimacy she and her husband had shared that afternoon had certainly been effective in moving him to immediate fidelity, she thought with burning sarcasm. Charlotte was truly receiving quite a dressing down from her faithful husband. Damn him straight to hell!

She tightened her hands into fists. At this moment she wasn't sure which one of them she hated more. Gritting her teeth, she lifted the curtain once more to stare at the scene being played before her fever-bright eyes.

Nicholas and set his snifter down and now sat next to Charlotte on the settee. She tried to turn away, but he put his hands to her shoulders and turned her back to face him. He regarded her intently and spoke so softly that Jessica was unable to hear him. Charlotte tried to turn away from him again, this time twisting to gaze over her shoulder, but Nicholas gently took her delicate chin in his hand and forced her to meet his determined gaze. Again he spoke too softly for Jessica to hear.

Charlotte reached up to tightly clasp Nicholas's hand. Her voice floated to Jessica's straining ears.

"But I could never blame you, Nicholas. And I'd hate to have you angry with me. We've known each other for so long." Her voice was pleading.

Jessica's chest constricted with pain when she saw the soft, loving look in Charlotte's eyes, and their clasped hands were enough to convince her anew of her stupidity in lowering her defenses against her husband. She fumed silently, her mind furiously aswirl with the various methods of torture she would like to employ on both of them.

Now Nicholas stood up and, picking up his drink, again moved to stand in front of Charlotte, this time blocking Jessica's view of the woman. She strained to hear what he was saying, but could not. He swung his glass in an elaborate motion, intending, it seemed, to convince Charlotte of something—probably his undying devotion, Jessica thought in disgust. Charlotte suddenly leaped to her feet and threw her arms around him, pressing her body tightly against him. Apparently he had convinced her.

The throbbing in Jessica's head became more intense as she saw Nicholas very gently disengage Charlotte's clinging limbs. He held her hands tightly in his and shook his head, murmuring soft, incomprehensible words. Maybe it had finally occurred to him that his wife might step into the drawing room at any moment! How smoothly he went about his business of infidelity!

Charlotte leaned close to him, running her fine white hand down the gilt buttons of his waistcoat, and spoke in a husky whisper.

Nicholas stepped away from her and shook his head, in bemusement, it seemed. He sighed and spoke loud enough for Jessica to hear him.

"I don't know whether I should be relieved or wary. At any rate, I hope to see you on your best behavior this Saturday at your Christmas ball."

"Of course." Charlotte pouted again and spoke clearly. "But it would be easier if you could somehow prevent Jessica from attending."

He raised an eyebrow. "Really, Charlotte, I hardly think that's necessary."

She shrugged gracefully. "It was just a thought, darling."

Behind the curtain, Jessica raised a free hand to her forehead, feeling the heat there. Of a sudden she began to feel flushed, hot, and shaky. A tight knot was forming just behind her eyes, throbbing dully. Perhaps Alcey was right, and she was getting sick.

What a bargain, she thought despairingly. Charlotte gets my husband, and I get a fever. She was no doubt ill from running out in the rain—among other things.

Could it have been just this afternoon that Nicholas had

loved her so well? How could he think of another woman in the same way? Pushing aside her discomfort, she focused once more upon the scene in the drawing room.

Nicholas had taken Charlotte's hand and was leading her toward the double doors of the drawing room.

"There is no reason why you should wait for Jessica, is there?"

"Not a one, darling. You know how I hate to upset the child." She smiled innocently, and Nicholas shook his head as she took him by the arm, and together they left the room.

Jessica let the curtain fall back over the door, blotting out the scene. She raised her hands to her heated face. Was it possible to be physically ill from heartache? For if that were true, it was surely the only way to describe her condition now. She climbed slowly to her feet and moved to the mahogany table, gripping the edge for support, her hair falling around her face in thick waves. Please, Lord, don't let my suspicions about Nicholas be true, she prayed—more fervently than she had prayed for anything before.

And yet she was certain of his feelings for Charlotte, and she felt filthy and used. How could he have made love to her, Jessica, with so much warmth and feeling, so tenderly, so lovingly, pouring sunshine over her body in golden waves, when it meant nothing? Nothing.

She bit down hard on the flesh of her forefinger to drive away the agony of her heart's defeat. She was determined not to cry for him. He wasn't worthy of her heartfelt tears.

In the hallway, she was almost relieved to find herself alone. Nicholas was most assuredly still at Charlotte's carriage receiving more stolen kisses. The bastard. Her numbness began to drain away to be replaced by anger. What had she ever done to deserve this kind of treatment? Nothing. Blast! She shouldn't have been eavesdropping. It was a stupidly childish thing to have done, and she almost wished she hadn't heard or seen their disgusting exhibition. Then perhaps she could have gone on living in her fantasy world for just a little while longer.

If nothing else, however, what she had seen confirmed her decision to leave him. She must make certain that he never suspected her intentions, however. She didn't want to find another snake in her room!

At the ball on Saturday, she would slip the will to Theodore—for surely he would be there—and have done with the whole mess. Until then, she would give the performance of her life. Would it be difficult to play the sweet, trusting wife?

Her head throbbed in renewed pain. Perhaps she should give in to the temptation and sign herself into the local madhouse, for she felt certain she was heading in that direction. Lord, what a nightmare this marriage had become! What a monstrous mistake! She shook her head, trying to clear it, but she felt so hot and dizzy. She really was coming down with a fine case of ague.

At the sound of the door opening she looked up, blinking. Nicholas entered the house, a pleased and determined look on his face. When he saw Jessica, dressed in low-cut gown of lavender silk, with her hair streaming in natural waves around her face and below her waist, a delighted smile illuminated his face.

"Jessica, what kept you so long, my love? I was becoming concerned over your lengthy delay."

She couldn't believe the claptrap that tumbled so easily from his lips! She started to shiver, as much from a sudden chill as from anger. How dare he refer to her as his love? Painfully she suppressed her feelings.

"I'm . . . I'm not feeling well, Nicholas."

He walked quickly to her and raised a hand to her forehead. "My God, Jessica, you're burning with fever. I knew it was too soon for you to go out after your illness. Damn me for not bringing you home immediately."

Her head spinning, Jessica prayed for enough strength to

reach her room. "Where has Charlotte gone?" she asked weakly.

"The devil take her," he said carelessly. Bending over, he swung Jessica up in his arms. "I'm taking you up to bed."

Bed? Jessica blanched at the thought, her mind whirling giddily. "Haven't you had enough of that for one day?"

Nicholas smiled down into her flushed face. "I don't think I'll ever have enough of you."

The temptation to laugh in disbelief was overwhelming, but instead she smiled shyly at him. "How sweet. But I really do think that I'd like to rest. I'm thoroughly exhausted, and it's all your fault."

"My apologies, madam." He reached the top of the stairs and shouldered open the door to her room. Swiftly he strode to the bed and deposited her gently on its downy surface, breathing a bit heavily.

"My dear wife, thin though you may be, there is your height to consider, and I think I shall have to increase my strength before I insist on again playing the gallant."

Jessica bit back a sharp retort regarding the ease with which he was sure to carry Charlotte's runty body.

"Aren't you glad now that I haven't been stuffing myself with those rich desserts you've been pushing on me?" she asked instead. He nodded in agreement. "Now, if you will excuse me, I'm really not feeling well. I believe my head must weigh twenty pounds."

"Do you need any help undressing?"

"No, I can manage myself, thank you." She hoped the panic did not show on her face.

"Pity you aren't feeling well, for I did have something for you."

Not another rat, Jessica thought to herself. Aloud she said, "Can it wait, Nicholas? I must regain my strength for Charlotte's ball, mustn't I?"

He looked doubtful. "This time, Jessica, I won't allow

you to hasten your recovery, and if I don't think you're well enough to attend, you will not go.''

How convenient, she thought. "I insist, Nicholas. I have never been to a Christmas ball, and I intend to go. I shall be well recovered in ample time, I assure you.''

He bowed crisply. "Very well, madam. However, you are aware that the ball is only six days hence. You shall have to keep to your bed and follow mine and Alcey's instructions without quarrel.''

She stifled her mutinous feelings and forced herself to let out a resigned sigh. "Very well, Nicholas. But during my enforced recovery, do have Alcey select something from her wardrobe for me to wear. I shouldn't want to disappoint Charlotte.'' She lay back on the pillows, and the throbbing in her head diminished a small degree. "Now if you have no objections, Nicholas, I'd really rather forgo this conversation.''

She felt him staring down at her. Wouldn't he ever go away? She felt the light touch of his lips on hers and his hand sliding through her hair. He slipped her shoes from her feet and drew a light quilt over her.

By the time he left the room, Jessica was asleep.

Chapter 18

With a bored sigh, Jessica drifted to the long windows in her bedroom. She saw Aaron exercising Diana in the small paddock in front of the stable and wondered at her chance of escaping both Alcey's and Nicholas's sharp eyes to take a short ride. She had been confined to her room for three days now and she was bored, bored, bored. She felt perfectly fine, but Alcey and Nicholas were not convinced of her miraculous recovery and insisted that she keep to her room.

No doubt Nicholas planned to drive her insane with enforced inactivity. Well, it wasn't going to work; never again would he have such power over her emotions. But try as she might to lend credence to that promise, it was proving increasingly difficult to guard herself against him. How could anyone be so underhanded, yet act so kind and concerned? Nicholas had made it a habit to come and sit with her every day, and he always was on his most charming behavior. So charming, in fact, that Jessica felt her role of trusting wife merging too easily into reality.

Her quick laughter and warm smiles were all too authentic for her peace of mind, while the marriage itself remained a painful sham. At night, Ella Mae slept in Jessica's room on a cot. She told Nicholas she would feel more secure if Ella Mae were there should she suffer a relapse in her convalescence. Amazingly enough, he had agreed with her, although she'd thought briefly that disappointment had clouded his silvery-gray eyes.

He wasn't the only one who was disappointed, thought Jessica time and time again. It was torture to be so close to him, yet know the truth. He was so kind, so considerate of her health, so handsome, so very desirable. She loved him . . . and hated him. At night she turned restlessly in her bed for hours while Ella Mae snored softly nearby.

Perversely, the knowledge that she could not have Nicholas made her want him even more. It was easy to villify him as an evil rogue when she was alone, but when confronted with his actual presence, she was lost in the depths of eyes that mirrored her own unfulfilled need. How could she survive life either with him or without him, for, whether for good or ill, he was in her blood.

Jessica turned sharply away from the window. She had had enough of wandering aimlessly about her room. A short ride on horseback would do wonders for her dragging spirits. Now, how to escape undetected . . . ?

She practically tore her flowered morning dress from her back and ripped the underclothes from her body. She was digging in a drawer, finally locating the split-skirt petticoat for her riding habit, when she heard a soft gasp coming from the connecting door to Nicholas's room. She whirled around, holding the muslin garment in front of her. Nicholas stood on the threshold, his eyes taking in the tempting scene before him.

"Trying to escape me again, I see," he said.

Jessica backed toward the armoire and fumbled around inside, not taking her eyes from him. She finally located her robe strictly by feel and pulled it out of the wardrobe. Nicholas crossed leisurely to the bed, a pile of packages filling his arms, and dropped the boxes untidily to the counterpane. Under his amused, ravenous look, Jessica shifted uncomfortably.

Using the door of the armoire as a temporary shield, she ducked behind it, dropped the petticoat, and hastily slipped into her robe. But Nicholas seemed to stare right through the flimsy fabric, and she squirmed anxiously under his hot gaze, her traitorous body ignoring the mandates of her brain. She lifted her chin and spoke softly, her voice remarkably even.

"I know what you're going to say, so spare yourself the bother and save your breath. But, Nicholas, if I stay one more day in this room, I fear I shall go mad."

He sauntered across the room, stopping not six inches in front of her slippered feet. Again she became aware of the seductive aroma of his cologne mingled with the natural musk of his body. He lifted a burnished curl from over her breast and twirled the reddish-brown lock about his finger.

"Dare I take this to mean that you're feeling better, and that you no longer require Ella Mae's comforting presence at night?" he asked huskily.

Jessica frowned down at her feet. Playing the role of loving wife certainly required her presence in his bedroom, but she was unsure of how much more her ravaged emotions could withstand, and it dismayed her to see how easily he rattled her composure.

Staring into her almost fearful gaze, Nicholas frowned in confusion. "It seems we are back where we started, and you are afraid of me again." He released her hair and moved his hand up to caress her face, running his thumb over the full curve of her lower lip. "What a pity."

Jessica's eyes widened even more as he leaned forward, and she moved away toward the boxes on the bed. "Are those for me?" Her tone of voice suggested that she doubted the possibility.

"And who else do you think I would buy presents for?"

Jessica could very easily think of another woman, but

instead she said, "It is not yet Christmas. Isn't it a bit early to be giving gifts?"

Nicholas shook his head. "You'll find the gifts useful before then, I would imagine."

Her gaze traveled eagerly over the boxes with ill-disguised pleasure, and Nicholas laughed aloud. "Why don't you open them?"

Giving a small, uninhibited chuckle of delight, she climbed onto the bed, tucked her legs under herself, and spread her arms wide. "Which one shall I open first?"

Nicholas pointed to a rather large box. "That one with the gold ribbon, and then the one with the blue."

She quickly began to rip the ribbons, flinging them away in glee. Nicholas moved closer to view the charmingly feminine scene. She lifted the lid, impatiently pushed aside the layers of paper, and gasped at the beautiful material that seemed to shimmer in the morning light. She grasped the gown by the shoulders and, sitting back on her heels, drew it out of the box, holding her arms straight out and upward.

The beautiful material was of the palest creamy yellow silk shot liberally with swirling threads of gold. She put her hand under the delicately laced and beaded bodice, marveling at the fine workmanship. The neckline appeared to be quite low and off the shoulders. The sleeves were short and puffed, the bodice dipping down to a point with three huge, creamy teardrop pearls at the tip. The skirt fell in smooth, fluid lines, the thin gold thread swirling throughout. Jessica closed her gaping mouth and swallowed heavily.

"Do you like it?"

She started at the sound of his voice and lowered the gown slowly and carefully back into the box.

"It is truly the most beautiful gown I've ever seen."

"I would be pleased if you would wear it on Saturday."

Her eyes widened in disbelief.

"You bought this for me, for the ball?"

"Yes, of course. I reasoned that you had little time to

worry about what you would wear. Since Alcey's wardrobe was sadly lacking in the appropriate attire, I took the responsibility of ordering you a gown.''

''I can't believe that it was finished so quickly. It's impossible. I've never heard of such a thing. Surely you must have paid handsomely to see it done on such short notice.''

He shrugged. ''I had Ella Mae fetch me one of your gowns to use as a measurement. But come, there's more. Open the rest.''

Jessica eagerly complied, with an exuberance that delighted him, and he made a mental note to buy her presents more often.

The second box contained a matching petticoat with gauzy skirts of the finest, softest batiste. Jessica rubbed the cloth sensually against her cheek.

Another box contained a golden swansdown pelisse lined with creamy yellow velvet, and yet another box held dainty slippers, frilly garters, and the sheerest silk stockings. The last, smallest box contained a pair of elbow-length fingerless lace gloves.

Jessica turned toward Nicholas, wishing desperately that she could throw herself in his arms and kiss him endlessly in thanks for the lovely gifts, but with bitter suspicion and betrayal always her companions, she could do nothing but grip the gloves and stutter her thanks. He observed her with a mock frown.

''What, not even a kiss for all this feminine frippery? Come now, Jessica, it's a sorry day when a man must bribe and cajole his wife with all this finery for a single kiss.''

She made a show of covering the gloves with the hastily discarded paper. Nicholas's voice interrupted her again.

''Perhaps this will encourage you. You were not in the mood to accept it a few days ago.'' He slipped a black velvet-covered box from the pocket of his frock coat.

"Please, Nicholas, you've done enough," she protested. "No more gifts, I beg you."

"Surely you wouldn't refuse to accept this small token."

He held the box out to her, and reluctantly she drew it from him. She lifted the lid slowly and stared down at the contents in dismay.

"Small token indeed, Nicholas." She closed the lid with a smack and thrust the box back at him. "I simply cannot accept such an extravagant gift."

Nicholas crossed his arms, refusing to take the box. "Jessica, you are my wife. If I choose to buy you such a gift, I would be deeply injured should you not accept it." She looked up at him in absolute hopelessness. "That is, unless, of course, you do not like pearls."

"But I like them fine. I just . . ." She clutched the box close to her breast and turned away from him, showing a lovely profile with trembling lips.

Nicholas was frustrated by her strange reticence. It was obvious that whenever he intended any physical display, she shrank away from him, and he was at a total loss to explain her reaction. Suddenly he remembered her once saying that she could never willingly be intimate with a man she didn't love. He frowned, thinking back to the times they had made love. He knew that she had enjoyed it as much as he had. Her response had been obvious. The answer struck him forcefully as he stared at her tense features. She felt guilty because she could enjoy passion without love. She didn't love him! A sharp ache caught in his chest.

He turned away abruptly, speaking in a tight voice. "Very well, Jessica. That you enjoyed the gifts is reward enough for me. I have no doubt that you shall be the loveliest woman to grace the dance floor on Saturday evening."

For a moment Jessica almost believed he was sincere, but the reality intruded. She lifted the lid of the velvet-covered box once more and stared down at the necklace, earrings, and bracelet of smooth, perfectly matched, creamy pearls. She looked up at her husband's broad back, exceptionally clothed in a bottle-green frock coat. She was so tired of fighting her feelings. Soon she would be leaving him. The pain of that thought was unendurable. She breathed in deeply and slid from the bed, moving to stand just behind him.

"Thank you for all the lovely gifts, Nicholas. I look forward to wearing them."

He turned around, keeping his hands clasped tightly, almost painfully, behind his back and stared down into her pristine features, losing himself in the depths of her spring-green eyes. The soft fragrance of lilacs enfolded him. With a look halfway between pain and pleasure, he tilted her face upward and slowly lowered his lips to hers, barely brushing their sweetness. "Jessica, Jessica," he whispered caressingly. His hand slipped beneath the fabric of her parted robe and over her breast, then fleetingly skimmed her stomach. Then his touch was gone. Her eyes tightly closed, Jessica, beginning to feel faint, waited for him to take her in his arms. But when she opened her eyes, she was alone in the room.

Jessica was enjoying one of the novels by Sir Walter Scott, *The Bride of Lammermoor*, which she'd been pleased to find tucked away in Nicholas's collection, when she heard a knock on the door. Josh interrupted her solitude.

"Yo' pardon, missus, but Ah have a guest here to see yo' "

"How wonderful," Jessica said in relief, delighted to have someone to keep company with her. "I don't care who it is, Josh. Please show them in at once."

Jessica rose from her seat and brushed the creases out of her gown. She was glancing at her reflection in the mirror to see if her hair was tidy when a gentle voice spoke behind her.

"Hello, my dove." Jessica turned sharply and stared at her guest in disbelief.

"Aunt Lucy? Am I dreaming? What . . . what are you doing here? Is Richard with you?" Jessica's eyes skimmed the room for the tall, distinguished figure as she moved forward to embrace Lucy's slight frame.

"No, my dear. He . . . well, never you mind. I only just arrived yesterday to visit Theodore, and I can tell you, I was thoroughly horrified to hear of your accident with the snake. My dear child, are you feeling well now?" Jessica smiled up into her aunt's concerned features and reached out to grasp both her hands.

"I feel much better now that you are here. But, tell me, did you come alone?" Aunt Lucy turned away, and the hands in Jessica's clasp twitched almost spasmatically. "Aunt? What is wrong?"

Lucy composed herself with what looked like an enormous effort. "Now, Jessica, you have just recovered from a serious ailment. Please do not excite yourself over an old woman's worries. There is absolutely nothing the matter."

"If that's so, why are you here alone? Have you and Richard had a falling out?"

Lucy looked stunned and began to laugh. "At our age? Surely you can't be serious. Don't give it another thought, my dear." She tried to turn away, but Jessica grasped the old woman's hand more tightly, certain that there was something Lucy was not telling her.

"Aunt, where is Richard?" She gasped. "Something hasn't happened to him, has it? Please, you must tell me. I swear I am well enough to bear the news, if it be ill."

Lucy glanced around the room in agitation, then almost furtively she leaned closer to Jessica. "Jessica, please keep your voice down. If you only knew how worried I was for you . . ." Lucy sighed. "Jessica, I've come to warn you. Only a few weeks after your wedding, Richard left Kentucky to come after you. He told me he had discovered some evidence regarding Nicholas that frightened him."

"Evidence? What kind of evidence?"

Lucy shook her head, her gray hair shining silver in the sunshine streaming through the tall windows. "I have no idea, my dove. I barely ascertained his true intentions in leaving, and he always considered me too frail to become involved in anything the least bit dangerous. All I know is that he soon left to come to you. After a few days of tortured waiting, I followed, strictly against his instructions, I might add. I was hoping I would find him visiting with Theodore, but he is not there, and neither is he here. Now I am terrified that Nicholas has somehow found him out and hurt him in some way." Lucy pulled her hands from Jessica's suddenly stiff fingers.

"I know it was foolish of me to come, but I was concerned for your welfare. Theo told me Nicholas practically threw him out of the house, after making a point to invite him. Now with Dick missing, I am even more worried." She raised blue-veined hands to her flushed cheeks.

"Richard is a fine, healthy man for all his sixty-five years," she continued, "but Nicholas is so much younger and stronger." She looked up to Jessica's pale face and began to wring her hands together. "I did not want to burden you with my fears, and especially so soon after your illness, but Jessica, I am terrified that some horrible fate has befallen Richard."

Jessica came out of her daze and regarded the older woman with compassion, her mind working furiously. What had Richard discovered in Lexington regarding her husband? Had he journeyed here to warn her and then somehow met with an accident . . . accidents such as she had been having of late? She was suddenly very concerned for Richard Montagu. She couldn't believe that Nicholas would murder an old friend—she still could hardly believe Nicholas could murder anyone—but neither could she continue to ignore the mounting evidence against him. She turned back to Lucy.

"Tell me, aunt, might uncle have received another letter from my parents that upset him?"

Lucy looked startled at Jessica's suggestion. "Why, I have no idea, my dear. I'm just so very sorry that after Richard received the first letter from your father, I coaxed you into this marriage. Can you ever forgive me?"

Despite the dull ache in her heart, Jessica hugged the frail body close to her. "Think no more of it, aunt. You did not know of Nicholas's treachery. I wish you had not left your safe home to come to me. You see, I am already aware of Nicholas's perfidy. Please, do not worry about me, for I have thought of way to ruin his plans. He'll not find me as gullible a victim as he hoped."

"Good heavens, Jessica, you're not to think of any dangerous schemes. We simply must get you away from here."

"No, aunt, I have played my part well, and Nicholas has no idea that I suspect him of treachery. He watches me too closely, and I must play my role to the end so as not to alarm him. But do not despair, I have a plan."

Lucy grasped Jessica's hand, her faded blue eyes darkening with concern. "How can I help you?"

Jessica chuckled. "I had no idea you were such an adventuress at heart, Aunt Lucy. Shall I embroil you in my deep, dark secret? I think not."

"My dear, how can you be so flippant about a matter that concerns your very life?"

Jessica laughed aloud. If her aunt only knew what she had lived through in the past month! Taking Lucy's hand, she moved to a comfortable sofa and pulled Lucy down next to her before she continued.

"Aunt Lucy, if I had not retained my sense of humor, I'm afraid I would have gone screaming to the madhouse weeks ago. Please don't concern yourself with my problems, especially when you have ample ones of your own to worry about."

Lucy shook her head vehemently. "Your problems are

partially of my making, my dove. I could kill myself for allowing you to marry Nicholas, but it seemed such a perfect match. I suppose you know now that your uncle had planned it all along. He wanted you to marry Nicholas, and now the poor man is consumed with guilt over his deed.'' Lucy stared helplessly into the leaping flames. ''Nicholas agreed so quickly to Richard's proposal that I thought he had become smitten with you.''

Jessica sighed deeply. Her poor aunt looked so agitated, Jessica's heart went out to her. Perhaps she would tell someone else of her plan. It might serve to strengthen her resolve and at the same time ease her aunt's distress.

''Aunt, please don't worry for me. Nicholas will not be able to harm me, for I have written a will.'' At Lucy's gasp, Jessica held up her hand. ''Let me explain. There is a Christmas ball being held at the home of one of Nicholas's . . . acquaintances. The next time you see Theodore, I want you to tell him to be prepared to receive my will at the ball, and to take it to Mr. Darby. He knows Mr. Darby. Henceforth, Nicholas will be unable to obtain my wealth, should anything fatal befall me. I have asked Theo to book me passage to England. After I am gone, my problems will be solved, for Nicholas will then have no interest in me and will hopefully leave me in peace. All very simple, no?''

Lucy's eyes had grown very wide as Jessica detailed the plan. ''Good Lord, Jessica, how is Theo involved? He told me nothing of your plans. I know he is trustworthy, but do you think it wise to take such open action against Nicholas? How sure are you of his guilt? And this plan of sailing off to England—why it's preposterous! Why not simply go to the sheriff and have Nicholas incarcerated?''

Jessica gave a short laugh. ''Do you think the law in this town would lift a finger to help me? Aunt Lucy, Nicholas is a well-respected citizen in Charleston, and I am his wife, hence his responsibility.'' Jessica shook her head. ''No, the law would not help me, and I really have no factual evidence against Nicholas, only strong conjecture—and aside from that very inescapable fact, I simply must get away from him. Far away.''

Lucy's gaze grew thoughtful.

"You've fallen in love with him, haven't you?"

Jessica's heart hammered. How easily her aunt had discerned her deepest secret. She saw no derision in her eyes, only compassion.

"Yes, isn't that the strangest tangle? Yes, aunt, despite everything . . . I know it's utter foolishness, but it's something over which I haven't any control. It frightens me, and I am slow to learn how to manage these emotions.

"Paradoxically, I feel so alive when he is near me.'' She put a shaking hand to her face. "So alive.'' She shook her head sharply, staring with a furrowed brow into her aunt's kind gaze. "What is the matter with me? Perhaps I have truly lost my mind after all, for to fall in love with that maniac, I must be quite mad.''

"Jessica . . .''

"No, aunt, I hardly expect an answer. I am just wondering now what we should tell Nicholas when he asks after Richard.''

Aunt Lucy thought for a moment. "Why not tell him what Richard tried to fool me with—that he left Kentucky on business and will be gone for at least several months. Gone to Scotland to look over some breeding stock. Richard was foolish to think he could keep a secret from me. I'll tell Nicholas that I became lonely and decided to visit both you and my son.'' She sighed shakily. "I had the most horrible journey, and I was in constant fear that I would be too late to warn you. It seems that I almost was.''

Jessica patted the older woman's hand. "Have no fear, aunt. As you can plainly see, I am here before your eyes, and I'm sure nothing ill has befallen Richard. He seems most capable of protecting himself. Perhaps he decided that his journey was futile, and so abandoned his quest. He is probably back in Lexington, concerned for your safety.''

Jessica deliberately grasped on to any hope to spare her aunt any more anguish. The poor woman looked ready to drop from exhaustion and worry.

''Oh dear, I hadn't thought of that. Perhaps I should write home immediately.''

''Yes, that seems a wise course to me.'' Jessica stifled an ill-timed yawn.

''Jessica, how rude of me. Here you are, still weak from your illness, and I have prattled on of my problems. Is there anything I can do for you?''

Jessica laughed shortly. ''It is I who am mistress here, no matter what the circumstances, and I who should be inquiring after your needs. I assume that you are staying with Theodore in the city?''

''Yes, that was my original thought, but now I'd like very much to stay here—to keep an eye on things. Surely Nicholas won't attempt anything if I am here, and aside from that,'' she added before Jessica could argue, ''Theodore's establishment is in a state of chaos with workers everywhere. I fear I'd only be in the boy's way.''

Jessica threw up her hands in resignation. ''Very well, I am convinced, and I will feel better if I too can keep my eye on you. I'll have Alcey settle you into one of the guest chambers.''

''Thank you, my dear.'' Lucy took in her elegant surroundings. ''This is quite a lovely home Nicholas has made for himself. I can hardly believe he could be such a contemptible rapscallion.''

''I myself suffer from much the same misgivings. However, in view of the evidence, I am determined to keep alert and wary of him at all times. I'll need your help, aunt. If you stay near me, then, as you say, he will have little opportunity to do me further ill.''

Jessica and Lucy rose from the sofa, and Lucy reached

up to place a soft kiss upon Jessica's cheek. "You're very brave, child, and I shall do anything I can to help you."

Jessica grasped her aunt's hands. "Thank you."

After she had seen to her aunt's comfort, Jessica went to her own room with the intention of taking a short nap. Sleep seemed to be the only way she could briefly escape her problems. She sat up against the pillows, fingering the lace on the sleeve of her nightgown in distraction. Against her will, her mind drifted back to her conversation with Lucy.

Richard's whereabouts were uppermost in her mind. More importantly, had Nicholas injured him in some way? The more she learned, the more damning the evidence against her husband looked.

What did she really know about her new husband? Nothing, except that he was adroit at hiding his true feelings.

"Damned fool me for letting myself so easily fall into his hands," she grumbled to herself.

Yet she remembered every minute detail of their love-making: his tender caresses; the smooth, hard feel of his muscled body gliding under her curious fingers; the strength of him pressed deep within her; his warm breath against her ear as he whispered endearments; and those beautiful silvery eyes.

Tears pricked her eyes. No, she would not cry. Her clenched fist swung out in frustration and knocked a porcelain figure off the bedside table, sending it crashing to the floor.

A moment later the door between the two suites burst open to reveal Nicholas, his face freshly shaven and a towel wrapped carelessly about his wet hips. His hair was matted with soapy lather.

"Good God, Jessica! Are you all right?"

Jessica stared at him with wide eyes, torn between a desire to laugh at his comic appearance and a painful awareness of the towel that kept slipping down over his lean hips. The fabric gaped away from his muscled thigh and showed the full long line of his leg. Tiny drops of water clung to his broad chest, captured like jewels in the crisp hair that narrowed to a thin line down his abdomen.

How beautiful a man's body could be! A familiar, unwanted sensation crept up from between her thighs. She was suddenly, overwhelmingly jealous that an undeserving, wanton creature such as Charlotte could possess both his body and his love.

"Jessica? Are you all right? You look pale. Is your head hurting you again?"

As Nicholas stepped forward, negligently holding the two corners of the towel over his hip, his round, firm buttocks came enticingly into view under the linen. Jessica backed up further against the carved headboard in fear that he might touch her and she would prove herself little more than a lustful strumpet by throwing herself against that gleaming chest.

Already she could imagine his arms around her and his hard, muscled frame pressed tightly to her, his manhood warm and throbbing against her stomach, his lips at her throat. She made a sound that was almost a whimper as he advanced toward her, and she spoke quickly and breathlessly.

"Oh, I forgot to tell you. Lucy Montagu has come for a visit."

Nicholas halted his stride abruptly. "Lucy? Here?" Soap was beginning to seep down into his eyes, and he brushed away the stinging lather. "Has Richard come with her?"

"No, he's in Scotland buying horses, and . . ." Her eyes drifted again to his naked chest. "And Lucy became lonely and decided to visit Theo." She watched his eyes stray to where the lace of her nightgown revealed the agitated beating of her heart and the firm flesh of her breasts. The longing in his eyes was unmistakable, and she was certain that he wasn't listening to a word she said.

"And since Theo's home is in confusion with workmen, I thought she would be more comfortable here."

She saw his eyes darken with passion and swallowed deeply, clutching her gown tightly to her neck. Her green eyes were huge in her thin, pale face, and they stared pleadingly and fearfully into eyes of silvery gray. Her whisper was strained.

"Is that all right with you? Nicholas . . . ?"

He took a step toward her, and the muscles in his lean jaw jumped under the smooth line of his cheek. Then he turned abruptly and spoke in a harsh voice.

"Yes, it's fine, just fine." With a muttered curse, he quickly left the room, slamming the door behind him.

Chapter 19

Jessica regarded her reflection in the mirror with awe. No one who had seen the dirty-faced girl in cap, shirt, and britches that she had once been would believe that she and the elegantly dressed woman with the creamy pearls at her throat were one and the same. She reached up to touch one of the pale yellow silk roses that lavishly adorned the intricate braids and perfect ringlets of her upswept coiffure.

Her thoughts turned back to her visit the day before with Amanda. They had been chatting amiably when Amanda had deftly steered the conversation to what she planned to wear to Charlotte's ball. Jessica was thinking of the dress Nicholas had given her when Amanda had suddenly grasped her hand.

"I can bear it no longer, Jessica. Please, may I see that golden gown that Nicholas bought for you?"

Jessica smiled in puzzlement. "Do you have spies everywhere? How do you know of my dress?"

"You should know by now that I am very devious, and I'm bursting with curiosity. Tell me, what did you do when he gave you the gown and told you about the material?"

Jessica again looked confused. Of late, she thought in frustration, confusion seemed to be a perpetual state with her. "What . . . I don't think I understand."

Amanda looked shocked. "You mean you don't know? Jessica, that material cost a small fortune, let me tell you."

"Well, of course I realized that, but—"

"But did you also realize that Nicholas bought the entire bolt to be certain that no other woman would have a dress like yours?"

"He did what?"

"You mean he didn't tell you? How like a man! Yes, I happened to be at Madame Claudette's shop for a fitting when I saw the material that had just arrived that day. I was tempted to buy some for another occasion but when I asked about the price—well, Thaddeus is generous but not that generous. Anyway, madame told me that it was not for sale since Mr. Carlyle had bought her entire stock."

Jessica hadn't remembered much more of their visit after that. Her thoughts returned to the present now, and she looked down at her skirt, admiring the swirling strands of gold. Why had Nicholas given her the dress? If it was intended to lull her into a false sense of complacency, it was an elaborate and costly gesture.

Jessica moved to the tallboy and searched through her handkerchiefs until she located a long brown envelope. She hesitated only a moment, clutching it tightly, then folded it in half and quickly stuffed it into the small beaded purse hanging from her wrist. She took a deep breath, strengthening her resolve, and quickly left the room.

At the bottom of the stairs, Joshua stepped forward, a wide grin on his face, to open the doors to the drawing room. "Yo' looks beautiful, missus."

"Thank you, Josh."

As the doors shut behind her, she lifted her gaze to her

husband, and the look that came into his eyes set the blood pounding in her head.

His attire was every bit as regal as hers, and her heart beat a little faster, despite her efforts to still it. He wore a black cloth evening frock coat with a black velvet collar. The tails of the coat were long and narrow, reaching to just below the knee. The lapels were cut low and wide, showing the white pleated skirt and intricately tied cravat. His white satin waistcoat with diamond studs gleamed beneath the frock coat. The Beau Brummell trousers were exceptionally form-fitting to his muscular legs, extending to his ankles. Black pumps and a black silk top hat held negligently in his right hand completed the outfit, and Jessica stared with a strangled mixture of pride and wariness at the masculine picture he presented.

Nicholas had envisioned how Jessica would look in the gown, but his imagination proved inadequate to the actual picture. The beaded, lacy bodice clung temptingly to her full bosom and narrow rib cage, with no frills or ruffles to cover the swell of her breasts and her smooth, gracefully sloping shoulders. Her long arms were slender below the puffed sleeves, and her waist seemed amazingly tiny above the full, fluid skirt that rustled softly, the gold thread glittering as she shifted uncomfortably before his unwavering stare. The upswept coiffure accented the hollows of her high cheekbones, and her face glowed with vibrant beauty, her green eyes sparkling, her lips full and pink.

Nicholas collected himself, realizing that he must appear the untried innocent gaping at his ladylove.

"Jessica . . ." He stepped forward to take her cold hands in his.

The contact was immediately electric, and Jessica closed her eyes, fighting to quell the tremors that raced through her body, but her uncertainty and suspicion were like a cloud that dulled her sparkle. Nicholas dropped her hands and moved away to the bar, clenching his own hands into tight fists.

"Where is Lucy? I assumed she would come down with you."

Jessica breathed shakily, flustered that he could rattle her composure with a simple touch of his hand. She was always so confused around him.

"I'm sure Lucy will be down shortly."

Silence descended. Jessica sat down on the settee, tapping her foot restlessly. It seemed that lately they were either making polite, ridiculous conversation or no conversation at all. Her musings were interrupted as Lucy entered the room.

"I'm so sorry I'm late, my dears, but I just couldn't decide what to wear. There was a lovely dark blue gown of velvet and lace, but it just didn't seem appropriate. Then there was another that I was interested in—well, I knew it just wouldn't do . . ."

Nicholas's amused gray eyes met Jessica's over the woman's head, and Jessica resisted an impulse to laugh for Lucy had been very kind to her the past few days, practically never letting Jessica out of her sight.. Finally Nicholas interrupted the woman's chatter.

"Lucy, you look lovely."

"Thank you, Nicholas." She turned nervously away. "But Jessica will surely be the belle of the ball tonight, wouldn't you say?" She watched with a worried expression as Nicholas's eyes fell tenderly on the girl. "But I'm sure I've delayed us already. Shall we go?"

She moved purposefully to swing open the doors, calling for Josh in a loud voice, breaking the spell that had momentarily fell over Jessica and Nicholas, their gazes locked in a mesmerizing grip.

Nicholas donned his hat and, gritting his teeth, followed the ladies into the foyer. He took the swansdown pelisse from the butler and helped Jessica into the sumptuous garment himself, his hands gliding caressingly to her shoulders. Her soft ringlets brushed his fingers, and he leaned forward, unable to tear his gaze from her liquid green eyes.

"Well, I'm ready." Lucy's voice was shrill. "I see that Isaac has brought the carriage around."

Nicholas jerked upright, and Jessica moved quickly to the door. He was dismayed that he could so easily forget himself in the presence of others. For a brief second, it had seemed as though he and Jessica were the only ones in the room. He shook his head and snatched his cloak from Josh. The black man's eyes sparkled with suppressed amusement, and Nicholas glared at the man. Josh grinned even more widely, and Nicholas wondered how he had managed to lose that edge of fear he could once so easily inspire.

"I'm getting soft," he mumbled to himself as he strode down the wide steps to the waiting carriage.

The ride seemed interminable to Jessica. Lucy chattered continuously; Jessica and Nicholas said almost nothing. Finally they arrived at the Rosemonds' plantation house. Jessica was amazed at the press of carriages and people crowding the entrance to the manor. Slowly Isaac made his way through the throng, waiting while other carriages unloaded their passengers.

Jessica closed her eyes and nervously prayed that she would remember everything she had been taught both by her tutors and by Lucy. Tonight she would be entering into a genteel world that was still foreign to her, and she fervently blessed her mother for her foresight in forcing her to undertake the tedious studies. She vowed not to disgrace herself in front of any of Charleston's citizenry.

She took a deep breath as Isaac stopped the carriage in front of the mansion. He hopped from his post, swung the door wide, and folded down the step, all with an impeccably businesslike manner. He offered his hand to Lucy and helped her down, then looked up at Jessica.

"I'll help Mrs. Carlyle, Isaac."

Isaac moved out of the way as Nicholas stepped down

and with a raised eyebrow held out his hand. Jessica extended her own hand gracefully and smiled dazzlingly at her husband. A number of people standing nearby—both men and women—smiled warmly as she came into view.

An elderly gentleman had already offered to show Lucy up to the house, thus freeing Nicholas to escort his wife. Jessica took his elbow in the correct manner, and he led her up the stairs. After the majordomo, a rather harried black man whom Nicholas warmly greeted as Malcolm, had taken their cloaks, he ushered Lucy, Nicholas, and Jessica toward the ballroom.

"Oh, there is Theodore," cried Lucy in delight. "Please pardon me, I am so anxious to see him." Nicholas stiffened as he glanced in Theo's direction, but he nodded politely.

Jessica's breath left her in a rush as she saw the huge, brightly lit ballroom. A thousand candles shining through the crystal teardrops of glittering chandeliers reflected rainbows of color on every surface. Scores of couples spun and swayed to the lovely rhythms of a waltz, the women's colorful dresses barely sweeping the marble floors. Long tables set against the walls, were filled with platters of tempting food and silver bowls of eggnog and punch. Without thinking, Jessica reached for Nicholas's hand, for the moment forgetting the sophisticated image she meant to present, and her eyes sparkled with the unabashed, vibrant enthusiasm of a child.

"Oh, Nicholas, this is so beautiful. Look at the lovely dresses. The women look like graceful flowers, and I can't wait to taste all of the food, and the music is so enchanting. Why, it's just like a fairy tale."

Nicholas was smiling at her ingenuous expression when he saw Charlotte deliberately making her way toward them. "And here is the wicked witch," he murmured softly, frowning.

Jessica's lighthearted mood fell. Charlotte did, indeed, look very wicked in her gorgeous burgundy dress. But before she could reach them, Nicholas swept Jessica away and began the lengthy process of introducing her around.

Jessica struggled to remember the distinguished names that matched the sometimes austere and arrogant faces. She searched the crowd for Amanda, desperate to see a familiar face, but could not locate her. Nicholas squeezed her arm, and she looked up inquiringly.

"I asked if you would care to dance."

He was looking in Charlotte's direction, his brows slightly creased, but Jessica nodded brightly, and he led her out onto the dance floor. They fell easily into the first of the five movements of a quadrille. Jessica couldn't help the delighted smile that came to her face, for she loved to dance. Though she was out of breath by the time the dance ended, Nicholas gave her no respite when the musicians immediately began to play a sedate waltz.

She closed her eyes, letting the melody and Nicholas's strong arm lead her. It was so easy to let fantasy merge with reality on a night like this. Her gown glittered and swirled as they glided around the floor. Finally she smiled softly.

"Thank you for the dance."

He shook his head, his gray eyes warm. "I assure you, the pleasure was all mine, my love."

"I had no idea you were such a fine dancer."

"There is still much you do not know about me, Jessica."

He tightened his hold around her slender waist, whirling her around. Jessica breathed deeply of his clean, spicy scent, intensely aware of his body pressed warmly against her, and it seemed that the dance finished far too quickly. They applauded the musicians, then Nicholas led her to where James Rosemond was standing, a beaming smile on his fleshy face. They spoke politely for a few minutes.

"May I also say that you look absolutely ravishing, my dear," he told Jessica. "It's no wonder Nicholas journeyed all the way to Kentucky to find you."

Jessica's eyes darkened as he mentioned Kentucky, and reality once more intruded into her dreamworld. "Yes, I have often wondered how we found each other so quickly. Why, if I didn't know better, I would have thought he planned this marriage from the start."

She looked up at Nicholas, her expression shuttered. "Now, if you will pardon me, I must see what has become of Lucy. She's no doubt thinking that Nicholas and I have thoroughly deserted her." Her glance caught the powder blue of Lucy's gown, and as she wandered over, she felt her husband's penetrating gaze upon her back as distinctly as if he had touched her.

"Jessica, how lovely you look!"

Jessica's head jerked upright as she recognized Charlotte's honeyed voice, and she steeled herself to meet the woman. Again she was painfully reminded of Charlotte's stunning beauty. The dark shade of burgundy she wore complimented her pale complexion perfectly, and the gown curved almost indecently around her delicate figure. Damn! Jessica could almost see why Nicholas was so enamored of her.

"I'm afraid lovely is more a word to describe you, Charlotte," Jessica said. "Your gown is beautiful." Hidden beneath the polite, pointless conversation seethed a hatred she longed to express.

Charlotte patted her smooth blond hair smugly. "Yes, I suppose that with your coloring this shade would never do, but I find it so elegant and sophisticated; however, I'm sure you wouldn't know anything about that."

"No, I suppose not. I'm certainly not sophisticated enough to find my way into another woman's home and throw myself at her husband. But I suppose it has taken you many years and many husbands to perfect your elegant technique."

Charlotte gasped and took a step back at the sudden brutal barb, but remarkably recovered her poise. "Why,

Jessica, I have no idea what you're talking about, unless, of course, you haven't been able to keep your husband's interest. Perhaps he grew tired of the stench of the barnyard. I am not surprised about that, merely astounded at how low Nick's standards have fallen. He used to be so discriminating in his tastes.''

"Don't you mean tastelessness? But then Nicholas is a man, and I suppose he's not one to refuse anything, especially when it is so everlastingly accommodating.''

Charlotte's eyes hardened into chips of blue stone. She opened her mouth to vent her spleen, but just then she saw Theo coming toward them. She flashed him her most charming smile and held out her hands.

"Theo, where have you been hiding? I've been waiting for our dance.''

Theodore squeezed Charlotte's outstretched fingers briefly, then turned to Jessica. "I heard of your illness last week. I would have come to see you, but as you know, the situation at Providence was not amicable. You look absolutely breathtaking this evening.''

"As you can see, dear cousin, I am very durable.'' She spoke more seriously. "I'm terribly sorry about the way Nicholas treated you, especially as we were only discussing business.'' She held up her arm and glanced meaningfully at the beaded purse hanging from her wrist. "Perhaps later we can conclude our discussion.''

Theo nodded as Charlotte's voice ended any further conversation on the subject.

"Theo, you know how I hate to be ignored, so do be a dear and fetch us some champagne.''

"But, Charlotte, I believe it is time for our dance. Come and humor me.''

Jessica stared after the couple as they walked onto the dance floor, thankful that Theo had taken Charlotte away. Her gaze swept around the brightly lit room, and she caught sight of Nicholas staring with ill-concealed anger at

Theodore Montagu. His look was so venomously murderous that Jessica felt a cold shiver course through her. Her
heart felt like stone when she realized that Nicholas was
probably jealous because Theo was dancing with the woman
he loved.

She saw Aunt Lucy in a far corner chatting merrily with
a distressed-looking older woman. Jessica smiled despite
herself, and wisely decided to leave them alone. A servant
carrying a silver tray laden with icy goblets of champagne
offered her a drink. Jessica had never tasted champagne
before but, shrugging, she accepted and took a sip. How
wonderful, she thought. She stood holding her glass, feeling a bit lost since she couldn't locate anyone she knew.

She was setting the empty glass down when she heard a
light cough behind her. Turning, she was delighted to see
Daniel Cookes. He offered his arm and asked for a dance.
Jessica nodded, and he swept her out onto the dance floor.
After Daniel another gentleman took his place, and more
after him, all posturing and smiling and pushing glasses of
champagne into her protesting hands. Jessica began to feel
the need for fresh air, and a sudden image of herself as she
must appear—a mindless, vacantly smiling woman—made
her feel almost faint. Her emotions were stretched taut,
and her mind was constantly on Theo and her will, but she
forced herself to smile brightly over the rim of her glass
into the eyes of her latest partner, a Mr. Stephen Wainsright,
and tried desperately to concentrate on what he was saying.
Why were her thoughts so thick and dull? She put down
the champagne and kneaded the sudden throbbing at her
brow. Perhaps she had had enough. Mr. Wainsright looked
at her in concern.

"Are you feeling well, Jessica? Perhaps you would like
to find a quiet place to sit?"

Another voice interrupted them. "Why, I think that is a
marvelous idea, Stephen old boy." Jessica was surprised
to see Theodore swaying before her. "Come with me,
cousin. I know a place where you can rest for a moment."

Gratefully Jessica let Theodore draw her away from the protesting Stephen. "Oh, thank you, Theo. I must admit I've had a bit too much champagne."

"No harm done, though you're sure to have a headache later on. But come, I have something for you." Theo drew her down a long hallway to a closed door. "I checked to see if there was anyone in here. It's empty." They slipped into the room.

Now that the moment was at hand to give him the will, Jessica began to feel the faint stirrings of apprehension and doubt. Once it was in his possession there would be no turning back. Theodore seemed to sense her distress and spoke softly.

"Jessica, you need not take those drastic steps, but after what has happened to you so far, I am more than convinced that your intentions are wise."

"I know, Theo, I know, but there is something . . . something not quite right about all of this." She sighed heavily. "I'm sick to death of intrigue, Theo. I'm sick to death of feeling scared and tired and lonely." She fumbled with the catch on the purse, pulled out the envelope containing the will, and thrust it into his hands. "Here then, take the blasted thing. I wish to God I had stayed a poor, ignorant farm girl. Then I would have been sure of a husband who wanted me for myself!"

Theo moved closer and put a consoling hand on her shoulder. "You still have your family, Jessica. You must know how we all feel about you."

"Yes, yes, I know. I don't mean to sound ungrateful, really I don't. You and Richard and Lucy *have* been like family to me. I should be thankful for your support, but instead I'm filled with self-pity. You mustn't think ill of me, Theo."

He squeezed her shoulder softly, then searched in the pocket of his frock coat. "Jessica, I do apologize, but we must be brief. Here is your ticket for passage to England."

She looked down at the plain brown envelope in dismay.

"For God's sake take it, Jessica. It is your only hope now. The ship sails tomorrow morning at eleven o'clock, and I had to pay handsomely to get you a stateroom on such short notice."

"Tomorrow?" Jessica blanched. "So soon?"

"Yes, I'm afraid if not tomorrow then you might have to wait as long as another month."

"Tomorrow." Jessica hung her head, and unconsciously her fingers strayed to her wedding band.

"Listen, Jessica, there isn't much time. I don't want Nicholas to come looking for you. He's been watching me all evening. I will meet you on the road just beyond the drive to Providence tomorrow morning at five o'clock. I'll take you to the ship myself." He shook her limp arm. "Jessica, are you listening to me?"

"Five o'clock on the road beyond the drive."

"Good girl. Make certain no one sees you leave."

"I'll be careful."

"Jessica, my dear, I hate to leave you this way, but I must go or all our plans will go for naught."

"Very well. Please go, and thank you. When I get to England, I plan to repay you for the ticket." She stuffed the envelope into her bag and closed it carefully.

"Good God, Jessica, don't insult me like that. My only concern is that you arrive safely. Now I must go."

He gave her a quick, tight hug and slipped into the hallway.

Jessica slumped wearily to an overstuffed chair, her head in her hands. The future loomed frighteningly uncertain before her. Where would she find the strength to simply walk away from everything she knew and into the unknown? Tension and too much champagne made her eyes droop wearily. She snuggled more deeply into the chair. Just for a few moments she would rest . . .

It seemed as though barely a minute had passed when she heard the door open and sat up slowly.

* * *

Nicholas was less than delighted with the attention his wife was receiving from the overzealous gentlemen at the ball. Despite his efforts to the contrary, a part of his mind was constantly aware of his wife's location, partly out of concern for her health and partly because he wanted to make sure Theodore Montagu was nowhere near her.

When he saw Jessica talking to Charlotte, he almost moved to interrupt the pair, but then decided his wife was fully capable of matching wits with the lovely yet callous Miss Rosemond. After continuing his conversation with Charlotte's father, he turned back to his wife's direction and saw Theodore talking companionably with her. The impulse to spring across the room and tear the man away from Jessica was strong, but Nicholas took firm hold of his emotions. He fought down his rising temper, cautioning himself that Jessica must come to him willingly or it would mean nothing. His angry gaze followed Theodore as he danced with Charlotte.

Finally Jessica was standing alone. He excused himself from James's company and moved to join her, but he was interrupted by several gentleman who wanted to congratulate him on his marriage. With an irritation he was quick to conceal, he noticed Daniel Cookes offering his arm to Jessica for a dance. He gritted his teeth every time her lithesome figure brushed against his friend.

Nicholas lost sight of the couple as they went to a refreshment table, but he was all too aware of fleeting glimpses of his wife's glittering gown as she swirled gracefully in the arms of one man after another. A part of him was pleased that she was enjoying herself, yet another more selfish part was upset that she could so relish the evening without his company. His jaw tightening, he gulped down another shot of brandy.

Charlotte finally insisted on a dance, and Nicholas had no choice but to agree. His frustration knew no bounds when, during the lengthy dance, he lost sight of his wife, who had been speaking with Stephen Wainsright. When he made a movement to end the dance, Charlotte jerked his attention back to her.

"Don't concern yourself with her, darling. I'm sure Stephen will be quite able to occupy her time. He's very adept at it, you know."

Nicholas's shoulders tightened at her words.

"But enough of her," Charlotte went on. "Why, you haven't made one comment on my gown."

She stared up into his chiseled features, painfully feeling his pull on her. He was so handsome, so unconsciously masculine. Nicholas stared down at her with an almost mocking expression.

"My dear Charlotte, I'm sure my insignificant comments would only increase the inflated image you already hold of yourself."

"Oh, Nick, you can be so utterly boorish! I admit that I'm a vain creature at times, but can you doubt that I've reason to be?"

They danced on in silence for a while. Charlotte knew that his thoughts were elsewhere, that his eyes continually searched the room. At last something seemed to catch his attention, and she looked up to see what it was. Theodore Montagu was sauntering leisurely back into the ballroom. She felt Nicholas relax when he saw that Theo was alone.

Her chest tightened painfully as a sudden insight gripped her. Nicholas didn't care about her in the least. His only interest was in that auburn-haired girl he had married. It hurt to admit it. She had always been the pretty one, the special one, the one to whom all attentions were given. If there was one thing that made her lose her temper, it was to be ignored.

As she looked up into Nicholas's face, Charlotte's thoughts were filled with confusion, pain, and an overpowering need for revenge. Revenge *would* come swiftly.

The final act would be played, and she and Theo would emerge victorious.

Soon Theo would signal to her, and their plan would be set in motion. But for the moment there was no sign of him. As the dance came to an end, she could sense Nicholas's restlessness. She started to chat of inconsequential matters, and finally she caught Theo's gaze. He nodded ever so slightly.

"Nicholas, I'm feeling a bit faint with all of these people crushing around us. Do you think you could escort me someplace quiet so that I might rest?"

He appeared reluctant to follow her suggestion, but then nodded curtly. "Very well. Come along. I think there are some things that must be set right between us."

Charlotte looked at him inquiringly, all the while thinking that soon he wouldn't be wearing that superior expression. They passed through the press of people, absently smiling greetings to various friends and acquaintances, and eventually arrived at the closed door to the library.

"I don't think anyone will be in here," she said.

Nicholas was caught off guard when Charlotte quickly shut the library door and flung herself into his arms, pressing her body intimately against him and reaching up to kiss his lips. He had grabbed her wrists from around his neck to pull her away when a quick indrawn breath from the vicinity of a large overstuffed chair drew his attention. Somehow he knew who it was even before she spoke.

"Don't you two ever look to see who's about before carrying on with your disgusting exhibitions? You should at least show that much decorum."

Jessica sprang to her feet, the light from the blazing hearth reflecting fire in her hair and making the gold threads in her gown glow redly. Charlotte turned with her arms still around Nicholas's neck, despite his attempts to free himself. Jessica whipped around a chair, intent upon leaving the room.

"Jessica . . . listen here . . ."

Ignoring Nicholas's words and the commanding tone in which they were spoken, she practically stalked toward the door, barely able to stand the sight of them standing together so cozily. At that moment she was overjoyed that she would be leaving on the next ship to England.

Thinking herself victorious, Charlotte was not above adding to Jessica's humiliation. As she whisked past the entwined couple, Charlotte's dainty foot snaked out from beneath her gown and purposely tangled with Jessica's slippers, then stepped on the hem of her gown. Caught unawares, Jessica cried out as she lost her balance and tumbled to the carpet, ripping her gown as she fell.

Nicholas had leaned forward to try to catch his wife, but Charlotte's body had been in the way. With an infuriated groan, Jessica sprang to her feet, inadvertently compounding the damage done by Charlotte's anchored foot. She was incensed that a woman she had taken to be a sophisticated lady had stooped to such a callow ploy. From somewhere beyond the red haze of her rage she heard Nicholas speaking softly and reasonably.

"Jessica, I don't think that—"

She pointed a trembling finger at him. "You! Get out of my sight! Now! I never want to see you again!"

He was set on arguing with her, but could see from the pain and loathing on her face that any words he might speak would have no effect. With a heavy heart he reached out his hand, but she backed away from him. He nodded ever so slightly, a tightness in his throat, and threw a murderous look at Charlotte. The woman deserved whatever Jessica dished out to her. He bowed crisply in Charlotte's direction and quickly exited the room, but stayed near to the door so he could rush to Jessica's aid if necessary. Seeing the majordomo standing at the end of the hall, he requested that Isaac bring the carriage around and fetch Lucy for a quick departure.

*   *   *

"Charlotte, I want an apology."

"Whatever for? I'm sure I have no idea what you're talking about. What a pity though. Your lovely dress is certainly ruined."

Jessica spoke softly and clearly. "My dear Miss Rosemond, I don't give a damn about the dress." Charlotte gave a small gasp at Jessica's language, but Jessica ignored her. "It is your persistence in pursuing my husband that has me incensed, although I must admit, you two do deserve each other. I do insist, however, that while I am in the vicinity you keep your wanton body away from him."

"It is hardly my fault that Nicholas prefers a woman to a childish hoyden, but considering that your parents must have been born and bred to wallow with swine, I suppose your conduct is to be expected."

Jessica carefully adjusted her necklace, hiding her fury. What right had this woman, who had been born to everything she could ever want in life, to spill her contempt upon people who had proudly sweated and toiled for everything they had ever built? Although it had been badly abused of late, Jessica did have her pride, and a new sense of self-respect and confidence. She would not be made the butt of this woman's callousness a moment longer.

"Miss Rosemond," she began, "if I were you, I should listen very closely to this warning, for you've no idea how close I am to doing violence." Jessica's eyes hardened, and her voice grew tight. "I never want to see you alone with my husband again, or I will find it much too easy to give in to my baser instincts and box your ears."

Charlotte's eyes widened, and she drew herself up regally. "I should expect such crass recourse from one of your ilk."

Jessica smiled with feigned politeness. "Quite right, I've been told that my ilk can be very crass indeed. However, I do mean what I say, for you're a bloody fool if you think that I shall ever let you have him."

"He does not love you."

Jessica flinched. "I know."

"Then why would you ruin his happiness? Why would you have him bound to a woman he loathes?"

"I don't think anyone as void of human compassion as yourself could ever understand my reasons."

"Void of—? How dare you!?"

"Good evening, Miss Rosemond. Remember my warning."

"How dare you leave, you brown-faced cow. Don't you turn your back to me! I'm not finished with you!"

"I think you are. Now, if you will pardon me, it's been an interesting evening."

Jessica drifted gracefully to the door, ignoring the insults that Charlotte flung at her head.

"Come back here, slut. No one ignores me. I won't have it!"

Jessica shut the door quietly behind her and continued toward the front door, completely ignoring Nicholas. Suddenly the door was flung open again, and Charlotte stormed out into the foyer.

"You bitch! We'll see who has the last word . . ."

The silence was deafening, and Nicholas watched in admiration as Jessica quietly accepted her pelisse from the frozen Malcolm. She turned toward Charlotte, whose face was nearly the shade of her gown.

"Good day, Miss Rosemond. Thank you for a lovely evening." Jessica heard a tittering in the corner and noticed Amanda, her face bright with suppressed laughter. "Are you coming, Lucy?"

Regaining his poise at last, Malcolm helped Jessica into her pelisse, and together she and Lucy strode from the quiet house with a queenly air.

Nicholas bowed in Charlotte's direction. "Good evening Charlotte." He nodded to James Rosemond, who was staring at his daughter in disgust, then strolled down the stairs. To Isaac's surprise, he hopped up onto the long driver's seat of the carriage.

''What yo' doin', Marse?''

''I feel the need for some fresh air this evening, Isaac, if you would be so kind as to indulge me.''

Isaac shook his head and climbed up next to Nicholas. He glanced askance at his employer's stoic face and grunted softly. It looked like it was going to be a long ride home.

Chapter 20

Jessica leaned back against the leather seat of the coach, shakily pulling the swansdown pelisse tightly around her. She had no idea how she had summoned enough strength to calmly walk away from Charlotte when she had dearly wanted to throttle her. But she had exacted retribution in her own way, and it had been very satisfying to see Charlotte disgrace herself before the assembled guests. Jessica was pleased that she had remained true to her vow and comported herself as a lady, despite her desires to the contrary.

Lucy was staring wonderingly at her and, perhaps sensing her distress, remained strangely quiet for most of the long ride back to Providence. Finally her aunt said, "Jessica dear, I know it is none of my concern; however, what happened between you and Charlotte?"

"Oh, nothing of consequence."

Lucy grunted. "Ha! That is precisely the sort of answer your uncle would have given me, and I suppose I'll get no more from you on the subject." Her eyes darted sideways, in a manner that struck Jessica as being strangely furtive. "Did you manage to settle your business with Theodore?"

"Yes."

"Well, I hope you know what you're doing. I had a nice long chat with Theo, and I have the oddest feeling he is keeping something from me."

"I doubt that, but he has held true to his part of our bargain admirably." Jessica opened her beaded purse and pulled out an envelope. "I have here a ticket for passage to England tomorrow."

"Tomorrow!"

She clasped a hand over Lucy's mouth. "Please refrain from any loud speech. I should be very hard put to explain this ticket to Nicholas, should he have heard your remark."

Lucy nodded vigorously, and Jessica let her hand drop, regretting her decision to tell her aunt of her plans.

"Tomorrow is so soon." Lucy exclaimed. "How are you going to get away from Nicholas undetected?" A mutinous silence answered her question. "If you don't tell me, I'll go to Nicholas with everything I know. I'm still not certain he is to blame for all that has happened to you."

"I, however, am sure enough."

"What happened to you while you were in the library? I was talking to your friend Amanda, and the next thing I knew, the majordomo was handing me my wrap and I was being escorted to the door. You swept past me with the most serene expression on your face and murder in your eyes, and Charlotte was screaming insults in a most shrill voice. What went on between you?"

Jessica placed her fingers over Lucy's wrist, halting her aunt's wild hand movements. "What went on in that room is not your concern. It is between my husband and me, and I shall say no more on the subject. The scene was embarrassing enough, and I should like nothing more than to forget the whole nasty business."

"Very well." Lucy sat in tight-lipped disapproval for a moment, then spoke softly. "When does your ship depart?'' Jessica sighed. ''Please, Jessica, I am dreadfully worried about you, and I don't like the idea of your going at all. Isn't there some other way?''

''Unless I discover that Nicholas is innocent, there is no other way. Tomorrow morning at five o'clock I am meeting Theo about a mile away from Providence. He will take me to the docks himself. The ship is leaving at eleven o'clock.''

Lucy blanched. ''Theodore is going to take you? Why, he never mentioned any of this to me.''

Again Jessica sighed, wishing she could have bitten her tongue off rather than cause Lucy any more distress.

''There is nothing to fear. I know—''

''You know nothing. I insist on accompanying you. At least that way I can assure myself that you will be safely away on your journey.''

Jessica rolled her eyes. ''Aunt Lucy, I would rather that you not—''

''I don't care a fig for what you want, miss. I am going with you.''

Jessica turned to plead with Lucy in earnest. ''I must meet Theo at exactly five o'clock, and I'll be walking quickly to be at the appointed spot. How are you going to keep pace with me?''

''I'm still young enough to walk one mile, missy, and I'll not let you out of my sight.''

Jessica was set to argue the point, but the carriage came to an abrupt halt. ''Now, Aunt Lucy, not another word about this. I'm leaving tomorrow and alone. Understood?''

Lucy's lips tightened in a mutinous line. Jessica swung open the carriage door herself, quickly sprang from the coach without assistance, and ran into the house. Lucy followed more sedately with Isaac's help and shot a withering stare at Nicholas, making him feel a callow youth of fifteen.

Nicholas sighed deeply, the heaviness in his heart unrelieved after the long, cold journey home. Had he lost Jessica forever?

He dismissed Isaac and walked into the drawing room to pour himself a brandy. He sipped it slowly, thoughtfully, wondering how he could approach his stubborn wife. He set the snifter down with determination. Quickly mounting the stairs, he decided on a direct approach. Whether she liked it or not, there would be complete honesty between them tonight. Not bothering to knock, he strode into Jessica's room.

"What do you want?" She leaped up from where she had been lying on the bed still dressed in her ripped gown, her eyes wet with tears.

"Jessica . . ." Nicholas moved forward, determined to speak his mind.

"Get out of here! I told you I never wanted to see you again, and I meant it!"

The disgust and hatred in her eyes forced the breath from his lungs as if he'd been struck. Still, he did not move.

"What are you waiting for? Are you deaf? Get out!"

He moved forward, intent on making her see reason, but she backed away from him, the loathing in her eyes quickly replaced by fear.

They were alone, thought Jessica, and no one would save her if he decided to kill her now. She was shaking uncontrollably as Nicholas stalked her, a determined look in his eyes. What could she do? How could she defend herself? She searched the room frantically for a weapon.

When he saw the blatant fear and distrust in her wild green eyes, Nicholas's expression hardened. How easily Charlotte had manipulated her into feeling this way! He stopped short and held his hands out, slowly lowering them to his sides.

"Jessica, please listen to me."

She raised her chin away from him, her lower lip

trembling. "I don't believe there is anything we have to stay to one another, Nicholas. Please leave."

"No."

With that simple word her control cracked. "What do you want from me? Lord above, what is it that you want?" She spoke softly, intensely, wanting him to feel her frustration. "Since marrying you, my life has been a continued series of bizarre brushes with death. I've had my brains nearly blown from my head. I've barely escaped being trampled. I've been attacked and feverish. And between those amusements, just for a little spice should I find my life becoming too pedestrian, I've had to witness on three separate occasions my husband in the arms of another woman—once, shortly after he had made love to me!

"I've reached the end of my tether, Nicholas. I'm truly frightened that if one more 'accident' occurs, I shall go tottering off the edge into insanity. I'm sure that would please you, but I for one do not find the idea of spending the rest of my life in a sanitarium very appealing." She stepped toward him in her dismay. "Do you know, can you imagine what it is like to wake up every morning and wonder what new horror the day might bring?" Suddenly her shoulders slumped in defeat. "Then sometimes I don't care anymore. All that I know is that I want you out of my life—now."

Nicholas closed his eyes against the pain. "I'm afraid it isn't as easy as all that, Jessica."

Their gazes met and held.

"Why?" Her whisper was hoarse and strained. "Why?"

His quiet reply sounded loud in the silence of the room. "Because I'm afraid I have fallen in love with you."

Jessica regarded him for a moment in stunned disbelief, then her eyes went wide with her hysteria. "Brilliant! That was brilliant, Nicholas! Spoken with just the right amount of conviction and sincerity! Bravo!" She placed a hand over her heart, the other over her forehead, adopting a love-smitten stance, and lowered her voice to mimic him. "'I'm afraid I have fallen in love with you.' Ha!" She dropped her hands to her hips and faced him.

"Love! What kind of braying jackass do you take me for? Even a simpleton as obviously idiotic as I wouldn't believe your confession." She stepped forward, her eyes crackling in rage. "Is there nothing sacred to you? How can you stand there and lie so boldly to my face? You've even shown your disregard for Charlotte in your contempt-ible declaration to me."

Nicholas had expected disbelief, but he was stung by her ridicule. "Damnation, Jessica, no one speaks to me in such a manner!"

"Oh? A thousand pardons, m'lord, for my gross imper-tinence. Perhaps I should have approached you on my hands and knees, begging forgiveness for having witnessed your loving devotion in the library this very evening."

"Oh, Christ!" Nicholas's voice was harsh and strained. He took a deep breath, humbling himself before a woman for the first time in his life. "Charlotte means nothing. Nothing."

"Indeed? I must say you have a strange way of express-ing your devotion. But then, I suppose your ardent kiss in the library tonight was only an act intended to prove how very much in love you are with your wife. Why, I remem-ber that afternoon in the overseer's shack . . . ."

Unable to continue, Jessica turned away, pain twisting in her heart like a knife as she recalled the passion between them that day, and his betrayal afterward. She felt tears determinedly slipping past her tightly closed eyelids. She squeezed her eyes tighter, damning him and damning her stupid female tears.

Suddenly she felt his arms come around her. She tried to jerk away, but he relentlessly turned her until she was facing him. His hands were gripping her shoulders too tightly to escape. He shook her sharply, and she raised distrustful, watery eyes to him.

"Jessica, why does it concern you if, as you insist, I have taken Charlotte for a mistress? If you carry only hatred in your heart for me, it should not upset you in the least."

His calm, rational question surprised her, and her mind whirled frantically in search of an appropriate response. Finally she shrugged her shoulders, feigning indifference. "I simply don't relish the thought of my husband taking a mistress. It's humiliating."

"Is that the only reason, Jessica?"

"What other reason could there be?"

"You tell me."

He raised her reluctant chin so her eyes met his gaze. "Why are you so upset?"

Why? thought Jessica frantically. Her mind screamed silently at him, though her lips were still. *Isn't it obvious, even to you? Because I love you! Despite everything you've done to me, I admit it, I'm insane, but I love you.*

Aloud she said, "Charlotte was cruel and said some horrible things about my family, defaming my parents' character. I took what I considered appropriate action."

Nicholas seemed disappointed with her reply. Once again she tried to wrench free, but he held her fast. His thoughts cleared with her movement, and he realized belatedly how close he was to her body and how long he had wanted to be there, how sweet she smelled, how much he desired her.

Jessica stiffened at the answering chord his closeness struck in her body. No, she thought. Did she no longer have a will of her own? Had he murdered that as well? His pale eyes stared down into hers, searchingly now, assessing her features with slow deliberation.

"I think you are lying to me, Jessica." Her name sounded like a longing caress on his lips.

Her tongue flicked out to wet her dry lips. "What do you mean?"

"I think there are other reasons for your hatred of Charlotte."

"What other reasons?"

"You tell me, or I shall somehow find the answers myself in my own way."

She struggled now to escape in earnest, knowing what he had in mind, but he continued to hold her fast against the hardness of his body. He leaned forward to kiss her neck, murmuring against her ear. "I love the way you feel against me. You fit me so perfectly, and I you. There's never been another in my heart, I swear it."

She shuddered, catching her breath when she felt his warm, moist tongue slide slowly around her ear and down her neck. The pulling sensations began to intensify. He nuzzled against her lips, his whisper soft. "Even if you lie, say you love me."

She clamped her lips together, frightened that they might speak the forbidden words without her conscious volition. "I will not," he squeaked in a small voice before clamping her lips shut once more.

"Try to kiss me back, then." He smiled wickedly and bent to coax her tight lips into pliancy.

With a muted groan of frustration, Jessica realized she was too easily giving up the struggle as her supple lips parted under his persuasive nibbling and pulling. His tongue slid slowly into her mouth, searching out the hollows, and her breathing merged with his. He kissed her endlessly, not touching her anywhere else except her sensitive lips, his hands now at his sides, his body leaning away from hers. She took a step closer to him, wanting more than just the feel of his mouth, and he backed away, still kissing her. She reached out to hold him, but felt his long fingers twining with hers and holding her hands between their bodies. Her lips parted wider as he continued to kiss her . . . until her senses were dazed with mindless yearning.

Finally he raised his lips from hers and stared into the darkened depths of her half-closed green eyes. She was breathless with the dismaying thought that he might walk away, walk away when every nerve in her body vibrated with the need and love he had aroused in her. She tried to grasp on to his coat, but he still held her hands fast between them. She hated the sound of her pleading voice.

"Please, Nicholas, don't go . . ."

He shook his head, his eyes promising pleasure, and led her hand to the proof of his eagerness straining hotly against the tight cloth of his trousers.

"The price is high, Jessica." As one hypnotized, she watched his lips carefully forming the simple words. "Say you love me."

He released her hand, and his fingers moved lightly along her bare arm to her waist and up to her breast. Her nipple hardened as he caressed her through the thin silk of her gown.

With all his heart Nicholas wanted nothing more than to rip the glittering gown from her body and make love to her long into the night. But, although he realized he was once again coercing a response, he knew the final decision would still be hers.

Jessica felt she would die if he didn't make love to her, but the price *was* high. She closed her eyes. She would be leaving him tomorrow, and the pain of the thought almost overwhelmed her. It would be better to leave without the memories of this last night in his arms. Or would it?

Her eyelids fluttered open. His gaze was steady, yet filled with need. Her hands dropped limply to her sides.

"Say it," he said. His mouth moved slowly over her lips, his hands leisurely caressing her back. "Say it, or I shall leave."

Her eyes lingered on his full firm lips, rich dark hair, and thickly lashed eyes. "Blackmail," she whispered.

He gave a slow, sensual smile, and Jessica trembled

with the force of her emotions. He made a movement away from her, and almost of their own accord, her hands moved up to clutch the lapels of his frock coat. One more night, she thought forlornly, one more night . . .

"Nicholas . . . I . . . God help me, but I love you. I love you."

Jessica expected to feel defeated with her admission, but the blaze of triumph in her husband's eyes warmed her very soul. He pressed her hard against him, his mouth moving softly over her closed eyes, cheeks, forehead, and finally to her lips. Her gown fell to the floor with a soft rustle. She stooped to pick it up, but Nicholas held her fast.

"Leave it, my love. I'll buy you another just like it."

He lifted her up, leaving the gown in a glittering heap, and shouldered open the door to his room. For a moment as he placed her on her feet next to the bed, and she felt his hands moving over her back to undo the ribbons of her corset, Jessica felt a fleeting touch of panic. What was she doing? This man was trying to murder her. What could she be thinking? But the thought evaporated quickly when she turned and felt him undoing the drawstring on her chemise, his fingers straying so gently over her arms. It didn't matter now. Nothing mattered but these feelings churning unbearably with the desire for release.

"Hurry," she whispered, and heard his husky laugh.

"Hurry? There is no need, my love. We have all night— countless nights to come."

Her last token defenses slid with her petticoats to the carpet at her feet. Slowly he lowered himself to his knees, kissing her shoulders, a breast, her stomach. Jessica sucked in her breath when his breath stirred the silky hair between her thighs, and he slid the garters and stockings from her thighs and calves.

He pushed her onto the bed, her legs trailing down over the side, his lips traveling up to the juncture of her parted thighs. She grabbed handfuls of his dark hair at the soft exploration of his fingers and tongue. The instant surge of intense pleasure was overwhelming, and still she wanted to be closer to him, to hold him in her arms this one last time.

"Please, Nicholas, please don't . . ."

He smiled slightly. "No? Your words say one thing and your body something entirely different." His fingers persuasively caressed her, finding her most sensitive places, and Jessica's head dropped back between her shoulders. "You're ready, so beautifully wet and ready."

Jessica was breathing hard, but she forced herself to close her legs and sit up on the bed, pushing her long legs under her. Still on his knees, Nicholas stared in admiration at her naked body.

"Take the pins from your hair, my love."

Slowly she complied, pulling the pins from her elaborate coiffure one by one until her hair fell in a thick auburn cloud around her shoulders and down to her buttocks. Nicholas was a rapt audience, and when the last pin had been removed, he took a moment to disrobe and picked up his hairbrush. He climbed onto the huge bed behind her, and Jessica felt the brush slide through her long strands in firm, even strokes, long and leisurely, deliberately taking his time. He tossed the brush carelessly to the carpet when he was finished and leaned close to inhale deeply of her fresh fragrance and busy his hands in the silky strands.

"Such beautiful hair, full of subtle fire. That night in Lexington in the stables—I wanted to pull it free from its braids. You looked into my eyes with such a sad, longing expression. I wanted to kiss you, like this." He lowered his mouth hungrily to hers. Jessica moaned at the deep pressure. "Now, you're mine."

Suddenly they were tumbling on the sheets, and Nicholas pulled her body on top of his. "You've boasted of your riding prowess," he murmured. "Would you be interested in a more challenging mount?"

She laughed. "I think I can easily accept your challenge."

As she moved tantalizingly over him, the amusement fled from his eyes. He ran his fingers through her hair, drawing it around their faces and Jessica kissed him with all the love and passion that filled her soul. Nicholas crushed her in his embrace.

"Ah, Jess, I love you so much."

At his words the last stubborn vestige of resistance melted from Jessica. She felt herself receding giddily from reality, whirling away into a land of enchantment. All that remained was the damp, seductive musk of his body; the pressure of his mouth moving slowly under her. The intensely concentrated desire expanded, spreading rapidly along her limbs. His taut manhood strained against her thigh.

"Now, Jessica, now," he cried urgently.

A thrill spiraled through her and she moved to impale herself on the firm, long length of him. A startled cry of pleasure broke from her lips; her every movement brought her closer to the peak. Waves of exquisite pleasure broke over her. Higher and higher she soared, riding the winds, straining ever upward. She leaned back, pushing herself against him, trembling in her eagerness, and a cry broke from her lips.

Nicholas stared up at her body, her hair rippling in shining waves over her tall, slender form. She threw her head back, her hair flowing over his legs, and he almost lost control at the expression of ecstasy that suffused her face. When the cry broke from her lips, he gasped and spoke her name as the release came.

Jessica buried her face against his neck. Feeling the wetness of tears, he tried to lift her chin to look into her eyes, but she only tightened her grip and snuggled closer against him. Nicholas sighed and moved her to his side. She smiled with an effort.

"That was the most wonderful ride I've ever experienced."

He smoothed a heavy lock of hair from her face. "The steed is here at your disposal whenever you feel so inclined, m'lady."

A flicker of something like pain flashed in her eyes, but her lips still smiled. "And does my steed require any special care?"

He chuckled and drew her closer against him. "Yes, you must tell me that you love me, willingly and often. I think you should start now."

"But have I not already provided you with enough cosseting tonight?"

His shoulders shook with laughter. "I see that you are stingy with your words. Very well, but since I am so eager to hear those sacred words from your lips . . ." Suddenly her wrists were imprisoned and the weight of his body rolled onto her. She found herself staring up into amused gray eyes. "I am once again at your disposal."

"You, sir, are insatiable."

"Only for you, my darling."

She lowered her eyes shyly, prompting his laughter.

"Just moments ago you made love to me with wild abandon, now you look away in modesty. Madam, you truly have captured my heart, and I am impatient for our future to begin. We've all the time in the world."

His innocent words twisted her heart and brought an aching lump to her throat. Confusion swamped her. How could he be guilty while appearing so sincere? How could he hate her while speaking such tender words of love?

Gazing at her, his expression darkened.

"Jessica, love, what is wrong? Tell me."

"Nothing. It is nothing. Please, just love me."

"I do, Jessica. I swear it and someday, God willing, there will be proof of my devotion. Perhaps a little smiling daughter with wild auburn hair and wicked green eyes."

Despair gripped her. There would never be a child, nothing more of love between them. But her sad thoughts fled when he moved suddenly against her. Once more the tingling in her loins grew to an overwhelming need. His mouth dipped down to capture hers, and she eagerly parted her lips, her tongue meeting his in fiery play. She moved invitingly under him.

The price has not yet been paid, my love," he whispered. "Must I seduce you once more?" He waggled his eyebrows furiously, and Jessica laughed.

"Very well, Nicholas. I love you."

He looked affronted. "That was spoken with as much enthusiasm as if you were considering your needlework. I promise to make you suffer should you not reply with more feeling."

His hand reached down between her thighs. She squirmed under his determined attack and lost the battle completely when his head dipped down and his hot, moist mouth teased her nipple into fullness. The answering jolt of pleasure drew her breath sharply inward. He moved to the other breast nibbling and teasing until her rational thoughts were all obliterated.

"Tell me," he demanded, and she surrendered everything.

"Oh, Nicholas. I love you."

Jessica gazed up at the darkness over her head and listened to the sounds of her husband's even breathing. The clock had just chimed half past four. Soon she must leave her warm bed and travel into the cold and an uncertain future. She turned to stare at her husband's face, relaxed in peaceful slumber, a slight smile curving his lips. She reached out a finger and lightly touched his mouth. He grunted in his sleep and, pulling the blankets with him, turned on his side away from her.

She admired the long, strong line of his back and almost reached out to run her hands down its firm length. But no, she did not want to rouse him. She hoped he would continue sleeping until she was safely aboard the ship bound for England.

Last night he had made love to her as passionately and as lovingly as the day they had been stranded in the shack, and yet he had betrayed her then. There was no guarantee he would not do the same again, and Jessica knew she would be unable to endure his continued infidelity. It would eat at her until she was no more than empty shell.

Sighing softly, she gathered her inner resources for the task ahead, then very quietly slipped from the bed. Abruptly Nicholas threw out a long arm, and she, froze, holding her breath. She let her eyes caress him once more, memorizing every beloved detail, then turned sharply, gliding softly to her room.

Soon she was out of the house and running down the gracefully curving drive, tears coursing down her cheeks. This time she made no effort to stop them.

"Jessica!" She gasped and whirled around, dropping the valise she had quickly packed, a hand over her pounding heart.

"So you thought you could leave without me."

"Aunt Lucy! You almost scared me into an early grave."

"I've been waiting nearly an hour out here for you. I was afraid you might have slipped by me."

"Go back to the house at once. I won't be dragging you into this as well."

Lucy stooped to pick up Jessica's single bag. "I won't hear any more arguments. Let's be on our way."

Jessica opened her mouth to protest, then shut it grimly, for she was actually glad to have her aunt's company. They continued briskly down the drive in silence. Finally the gloom of the oppressive morning was broken by the glimmer of lights on the road ahead. Theo appeared through the fog, seeming to materialize out of thin air.

"Jessica, my dear. I was worried about you. It's already half past five. I thought that something had happened." He glanced aside, surprised to see his mother, and Jessica lowered her gaze from Theo's anxious one.

"I was unavoidably detained." She took a deep breath, unwilling to think of Nicholas slumbering peacefully in his bed, despite her fear and suspicions. "I'm here now, so let's be on our way." She nodded toward Lucy. "Your mother insisted on accompanying me, despite my protestations to the contrary."

Theo looked very angry for a moment, then laughed. "Surely you know by now that mother can be very stubborn when she wants to be." He nodded in Lucy's direction. "There is really no reason why you should come along with us, Mama. I am quite capable of seeing to my cousin's welfare."

"I've my doubts about that, but I'll not be swayed, Theo, so you may as well resign yourself to my company."

Theo quirked a strange grin at Jessica and, shaking his head, leaned forward to grab her valise. He threw it into the boot and opened the door of the carriage with a flourish. Jessica looked up to see the driver huddled on the seat in an uncomfortable ball. She glanced at Theo inquiringly.

"Oh, don't worry about Jacob. He won't utter a word of this to anyone. Come on, let's get out of this damp cold, shall we?"

Lucy climbed into the carriage with Theo's assistance, and Jessica followed. Lucy pulled Jessica down next to her, and Theo swung the door closed. He tapped his knuckles on the carriage roof, and with a jingle of their harnesses the horses started off at a lively trot.

"I must offer my congratulations to you, Jessica," said Theo, "for your unique approach to effectively disgracing Miss Rosemond last evening."

Jessica hid her suddenly scarlet face in her hands and raised frightened eyes to Theo. "Was it bad?"

He chuckled. "It was marvelous. Charlotte's father excused himself to the assembled guests and hauled Charlotte up the staircase. As he climbed out of sight with the mortified Miss Rosemond, I heard him mutter something

about apologizing to the Carlyles, and then he was yelling
to Malcolm to fetch a bar of soap for his daughter's filthy
mouth.''

"Well, that's a relief, but it surely doesn't matter for I
won't be able to thwart her designs much longer, will I?''
Jessica moved aside the leather curtains and stared dis-
mally out the window. It was still quite dark, and there
was nothing to see. She sat further back against the coach
seat and wrapped her pelisse more warmly around her,
determined to fall asleep. The motion of the carriage lulled
her, and her head fell against her aunt's shoulder. Lucy
patted her, smiling softly.

Jessica was brought awake suddenly as the carriage
careened crazily around a sharp bend in the road. Over the
colorful language of the driver as he fought to control his
team, she was thrown against the window and, curious as
to what had caused the rough ride, she plucked aside the
curtain. The sky had lightened considerably, and she was
clearly able to see a large, canvas-covered wagon pulled
by two mules galloping madly down the road. A familiar
buckskin was tied to the back. Good Lord, she'd know
that horse anywhere!

"Theo, stop the carriage,'' she ordered. "Stop it please!
You must turn around.''

Theo exchanged a worried glance with Lucy. "Whatever is the matter Jessica?''

"My parents are in that carriage. I saw my horse tied to
the back. I'm certain of it.'' She turned to grab Lucy's
sleeve. "Please, Aunt Lucy. I know what I saw!''

"I'm sure you did, Jessica, but the fact remains that this
carriage is bound for Charleston.''

Jessica sat back, puzzled. "It won't take but a moment
to catch up to them. I just want to say good-bye.''

She looked at Theo, but he shook his head and stared at
her with an openly malevolent grin. She turned to her aunt
and was stunned by the unconcealed malice in the woman's hard blue eyes. A prickling of fear crawled up her

spine, and she made a movement toward the door, but Lucy's hand reached out like a claw and held her fast.

"I'm afraid you won't be going anywhere, my dear girl."

Jessica's eyes grew wide as Lucy calmly opened her reticule and pulled out a pistol. All of a sudden the pieces of the puzzle fell neatly into place. "You!" She turned accusingly at Theo, but he only shrugged and looked away in disinterest. "Oh, my God, you're the ones. You!" Jessica was almost in shock, her mind reeling with the many implications of her discovery. "Why?"

Lucy laughed gruffly, an unpleasant sound that grated on Jessica's already raw nerves. "Isn't it obvious? I waited eighteen years for Richard to claim his fortune. Eighteen long years, and then when it would have been ours, your stepparents sent for him. I couldn't believe you were alive. I thought you dead, hoped you were dead, despite Richard's foolish dreams to hand you his fortune. The sentimental, old fool. I sent a man ahead of him to ensure you would come back to Kentucky."

Jessica stared at her heretofore gentle aunt in complete horror. She gathered herself together with an effort. "Did your man have bushy red hair?" Lucy nodded maliciously and, despite her fear, Jessica felt her anger boil.

"And did you know that my youngest brother was almost killed in the fire that man deliberately set in my room?"

Lucy dismissed the fate of Joseph with a contemptuous wave of her hand. "It was no great concern of mine that the brat was where he should not have been, but he did help to serve my purpose in luring you to Lexington."

Jessica's eyes glittered with suppressed rage. "And is Richard innocent of your plan, or is this a family affair?"

"The righteous Richard Montagu involved in anything murderous? Don't be absurd. He is completely ignorant, I assure you. But despite what you may be thinking, Jessica,

I do have tender feelings for Richard. He's just a bit too softhearted, in my view. Did you know that his ranch is nearly ruined?'' Jessica started in surprise. ''Yes, raising horses is not as lucrative a venture as you might think. We needed the inheritance to clear our debts, but again he would have willingly put the money into your hands.''

''Where is he now?''

''Oh, he's safe—safe in Scotland looking over some new breeding stock, just as I'm sure you told Nicholas. Clever of me to trick you into believing that Nick might have done away with Richard, wouldn't you say?''

''Oh yes, madam, I can see that you've been very clever, manipulating me, turning me away from my family, my home, even my husband. But I'm curious now. Why Nicholas?''

''Why not? When you came to Lexington, I was appalled at your conduct. I realized that there would be little chance of finding you a husband if you continued with your hoydenish ways. Thus the lessons—the tedious lessons of deportment so you could snare a fine husband. You were a very apt pupil, I must say. You see, I needed to get you married quickly so that your inheritance would not be left in the hands of the orphans, as the will stipulated.''

''Why didn't you simply marry me off to your son? We're third cousins. The blood bond is not strong.'' Jessica cast anger-bright eyes in Theo's direction, and he bowed to her.

''I thought of that,'' Lucy said. ''It would have been much simpler that way, I agree, but I knew Richard would never have condoned the match, for he was set on marrying you off to Nicholas from the beginning.'' She laughed harshly. ''It actually worked to my advantage, for Nicholas was a perfect scapegoat, the one I would use to force you to change your will in our favor.''

''And Theo? I suppose he was a willing participant in your plans?''

Theo looked not the least bit repentant, and Lucy laughed

with genuine amusement. "Why, of course, Jessica dear. Theo and Miss Rosemond have been very helpful in convincing you of your husband's guilt. A pity you'll never be able to save your marriage now."

Through her fear and confusion, Jessica focused on just one thought. Would she ever get the chance to make amends for doubting Nicholas?

Chapter 21

Nicholas woke up abruptly at the sound of a loud commotion coming from the first floor. He glanced aside, irritated at the interruption, and was surprised to see the place beside him empty and cold. The noises downstairs were growing in intensity. Had Charlotte appeared to further condemn his wife? He glanced at the clock. Seven o'clock. Too early even for Charlotte. He jumped from the bed and was just fastening his trousers when a knock sounded at the door, and Alcey burst through the doorway.

"Dere is some large fambly downstairs hollerin' to see Miz Jessie. Dey ses dey is her parents, and dat you is a no-'count cradle-robbin' so-an'-so."

Nicholas lifted his gaze to the heavens and suppressed a smile. Since Jessica's impromptu entrance into his life, he had certainly never lacked for excitement.

"Very well, Alcey. Show them into the dining room and offer them some breakfast. I assume Jessica already heard the ruckus and is in her room changing. I'll be down directly." The woman turned to leave. "And, Alcey, please be polite."

Alcey lifted her nose in the air. "Ah knows darn well

how to behave mahself, marse, an' Ah already tol' 'em dey was welcome to some hot vittles. Don't need no uppity gent tellin' me how to do mah job."

Nicholas grinned as she left in a huff, closing the door a little more forcefully than decorum required. He dressed quickly, denying an urge to see to Jessica's progress dressing. Already he could almost feel her soft, warm body nestled closely against him. He went down the stairs feeling very light of spirit, and actually looked forward to meeting Jessica's family. He had heard quite a bit about them and was curious to see if they matched his mental image.

Whistling gaily, he stepped into the drawing room and was surprised to see the rather tattered group bunched closely together near the hearth. They eyed him with hostility, and though Nicholas was not the kind of man to give in easily to fear, he felt himself growing very uncomfortable. He cleared his throat sharply.

"How do you do? I am Nicholas Carlyle, and you must be—"

A high-pitched scream of rage interrupted him, and a small, dirty form catapulted from the group and attached itself to Nicholas's leg. He cried out as the bite of sharp teeth penetrated the material of his trousers, and he shook his leg forcefully in an attempt to shake the demon loose. It clung with the tenacity of an angry watchdog.

"Joseph! Joseph! Stop that this instant."

Through the haze of his uncomfortable situation Nicholas saw a small, delicate woman stepping hastily forward, and he backed away in some alarm, tripping over a low table, sending the delicate vase upon it flying, and sprawling onto the floor a moment before Alcey, with Titus in tow, threw open the doors to the drawing room. The room erupted in an uproar as Nicholas tried to pull the angry Joseph from his leg while the Blackwells began loudly arguing with Alcey. Titus stood in the center of the room shaking his head. Josh's wide eyes could be seen from just behind the screen of the double doors.

"Quiet!"

The deep voice thundered in commanding tones, and everyone, including Nicholas, turned to stare at Titus with openmouthed awe. Titus leaned forward and plucked the struggling Joseph from Nicholas's rather rumpled form with one gigantic hand. He held the squirming boy out to Sarah.

"Ah believes dat dis here belongs to y'all."

Sarah nodded and accepted the bundle, staring in fear at the black man's big body. Titus bent to offer Nick a hand up, which he gratefully accepted. Trying to retain some dignity, no matter how ill used, he rearranged his mussed clothing and cleared his throat again.

"Yes, well, I assume you now know who I am." He settled a baleful glare on Joseph, who glared right back, and Nicholas was secretly disturbed that both his blackest scowl and most baleful glare failed to inspire fear in the boy.

"You," he said, indicating Joseph, "must be Jessica's youngest brother. How do you do? You've already met Alcey, the housekeeper." The black woman bobbed her head. "This is her husband, Titus, the overseer, and that gentleman lurking in the foyer is Joshua, the butler. Now that that is all settled, who are you?"

Sarah stepped forward timidly and shot a quick glance at her husband, her face flushed in embarrassment. "I am Sarah Blackwell. This is my husband, Andrew, and our boys, Andrew, Edward, the twins Robert and Alexander, Timothy, and of course," she added with a sheepish grin, "you've already met Joseph."

Nicholas rubbed the sore spot on his thigh. "Yes, quite."

Sarah dropped Joseph to his feet and stood with feet braced and arms akimbo. Andrew drew up beside his wife.

"We've come to see our daughter," he said. "We have reason to believe you married her under false pretenses, and we will not be satisfied until we have seen her ourselves.''

Nicholas shook his head. He certainly had been the unfortunate recipient of a most unsavory reputation of late.

''Rest assured, Mr. Blackwell, that your daughter is in safe hands. She should be joining us shortly. Until then, perhaps I can interest you and your family in some breakfast.''

Although Andrew shook his head, Nicholas noticed how the boys cast longing glances toward the dining room and the savory aromas drifting from that direction.

''We'll not be moving until we see our daughter.''

''Very well, sir. I'll have Alcey fetch her down directly.''

He inclined his head toward the black woman, who quickly left the room. The occupants of the drawing room could hear her feet quickly pounding on the stairs. Silence fell thick and awkward in the room. Finally, after an inordinately long period of time, Alcey burst back into the room, fearful and out of breath.

''Ah, can't find her, marse. Ah done looked everywhere, but she ain't in her room, o' yo's. She ain't in Miz Lucy's room, an' Miz Lucy ain't nowhere neither.''

Nicholas began to feel the uncomfortable prick of fear, and his voice betrayed his concern. ''Are you certain?''

''Yes suh! She ain't anywheres. Mebbe she went out on dat gray hoss o' hers.''

Nicholas turned to Titus, but the black man was already moving out the door. Nicholas paced the confines of the room, oblivious to those around him.

Despite her fear for her daughter, Sarah regarded Nicholas with interest, noting the intensity of his worried frown. She was certain he was not acting. A handsome man, she thought, and he seemed to care a great deal about Jessica. For the first time since leaving Virginia, she breathed a little easier. Andrew moved forward, his fists clenched, but Sarah detained him with a gentle hand on his arm and a negative shake of her head.

Titus rushed back into the house. "All de hosses is in de stable. Aaron ses dat no one been down dere today to git one fo' ridin'." Titus shook his head sadly, seeing Nicholas's earnest gaze. "Ah'se sorry, marse, but Ah don't know where she done gone. Ah set some o' de br'ers out 'round de grounds to look fo' her an' Miz Lucy, an' Ah had Aaron saddle some hosses fo' us if dere comes a need." Nicholas's worried eyes locked with Sarah's.

"I believe you are telling the truth, Mr. Carlyle," she said, "however, that doesn't help us find our daughter."

"Damn!" Andrew exploded. "I should have followed your instincts sooner, Sarah."

"Instincts?" asked Nicholas, startled out of his thoughts.

"Yes. The letters that we received from our daughter had my wife very concerned. She is much better than I in reading Jessica's feelings, and she felt that something was wrong. Fool that I am, I denied Sarah's intuition and wanted to give Jess more time to adjust to her new life before we thrust ourselves into it. After Sarah read that Jessica intended to wed you, she was very upset, but again I denied her feelings." Andrew spoke quickly and carelessly, his concern for his daughter causing him to forget discretion. "It was only after she started to write about some small, strange incidents that I too became concerned. For all we knew, Jessica's husband would have been a fortune hunter, and we were afraid for our daughter."

Nicholas was fighting to keep calm, knowing full well that Jessica, and possibly Lucy, could be in dire circumstances. Because his composure was wearing thin, he was getting angry at the constant implied slurs against his character. No one seemed to trust him. He spoke curtly.

"Why did you feel you had to journey here so quickly to see to your daughter's welfare? I assure you I have not murdered her and stuffed her away in some dark hole on the grounds."

Andrew looked a bit uncomfortable but defended himself valiantly. "We are like any other concerned parents, sir, and we did not know you. You could have married our girl for the inheritance. She knew how we felt about arranged marriages, and we found it difficult to believe she would marry a man simply to gain some wealth."

Nicholas snorted, his mind working fast. "As far as I can tell, Jessica didn't care in the least about her inheritance. Every time I informed her about the proceedings regarding the settlement of the estate, she sought to move the conversation onto a different subject. The only reason she married me at all, and she does not know that I know this, was because she was afraid for your lives. Richard told her you would come to Lexington to fetch her back to Virginia, and she did not want to place any of you in danger again." He glanced sternly at Joseph, who had the good grace to look away. "So I'm afraid she chose to marry me, the lesser of two evils, so to speak." His face softened in pleased remembrance. "I must admit that I do not regret her decision, or mine for that matter."

But Andrew looked puzzled. "Yes, she mentioned in one of her letters that because she was getting married I need not journey to Kentucky. But I never wrote to either her or Richard Montagu to say that I would go to Lexington. And what's all this about our lives being in danger?"

"Jessica thought that the fire in her room had been set deliberately. She blamed herself for Joseph's injury, so she decided to go away."

Sarah gasped. "Is that why she left? Oh my God, she told you all of this?"

Nicholas shook his head. "No, no she didn't . . ." He paused, and then reluctantly went on, his desire to know the truth overshadowing his concern for Sarah's feeling. "She was ill and spoke quite a bit in her delirium. I gathered from her fragmented speech that she only married me to assure your safety."

"Ill? What happened to her? Is she well now?"

"Yes, she is fine, fully recovered."

"Thank God." Then a thought occurred to Sarah, and

she gripped her husband's wrist. "But that must mean that Richard Montagu told Jessica a lie to force her into a premature wedding. Why?"

Nicholas was at a loss, but he was becoming more and more concerned by the moment. Again he spoke reluctantly. "That is not all. Since our marriage, there have been three separate attempts on Jessica's life. Though I have sought to find an answer, I am clearly puzzled regarding the identity of the assailant."

The family gasped, and Sarah couldn't help the tears that sprang to her eyes. An icy hand clutched at her heart as she vividly remembered her daughter's wide, fear-glazed eyes and soot-blackened face on the night of the fire. Why hadn't she paid more attention to the girl?

"The incidents looked quite accidental," Nicholas went on. "I believe they were purposely staged to look that way, and I'm frustrated beyond belief at my inability to discover why anyone would want Jessica dead." His dark brows lowered, and an angry scowl pulled at the corners of his mouth. The line of tension along his broad shoulders was clearly apparent. He slammed his fist into his open palm. "I don't know who is behind all of this, but by God, I'm determined to find out."

The group stood in a frozen tableau, each absorbed in thought. The boys still stood huddled by the fire but hardly felt its warmth. Andrew and Sarah stood close together, their fingers entwined. Joseph was holding tightly on to his mother's skirt, his face white. Nicholas stood uncomfortably by the settee, feeling overwhelming frustration and impotent rage. His thoughts flew in a thousand directions, searching for a clue, anything she might have said to him the night before or in her delirium to hint where she might have gone. Titus stood with an arm around his wife's shoulders near the open doors. Suddenly Josh's voice broke the quiet.

"Marse, yo' lawyer, Mistah Darby, is come to see yo'."

"Tell him to go away! I've no time for business now!"

"Marse, de man looks fit to be tied, an' he say it very important."

Nicholas released a disgusted sigh and spoke shortly. "Very well, show him in."

Lawrence Darby was a small, wiry man, his posture and stylish apparel hinting at his immaculate care for detail. When something didn't settle neatly into one of the categorized pigeonholes in his head, he was determined to fix it until it did. When he had been rousted out of his bed in the middle of the night and the will delivered into his hands, along with the accompanying dire warning, he had been rightfully suspicious. Wanting no pall of misdoing cast upon his sterling name, he had risen early and sought out Nicholas at first light. He eyed the strangely subdued group before him and spoke quietly.

"Mr. Carlyle, excuse me if I have come at an inconvenient time, but I have a matter of much urgency to discuss with you regarding your wife's holdings."

Heads snapped up, and twelve pairs of eyes were trained on the little man's head. Mr. Darby looked around uncomfortably, shuffling his beaver hat in his hands. "Perhaps we can discuss this in the privacy of your study, sir."

Nicholas waved away the man's suggestion, and Mr. Darby found himself grabbed by the lapels of his frock coat and unceremoniously dumped onto the settee. The rest of the crowd gathered close around him. The lawyer swallowed heavily, first adjusting the heavy muffler around his neck and then fumbling with his spectacles.

"Out with it, man," barked Nicholas in an impatient voice, and Andrew Blackwell shot his son-in-law an approving glance.

"Well, er, I, uh . . . I assume you are aware of the changes to Mrs. Carlyle's will."

"Will? What will?"

Lawrence Darby groaned. How he hated these unexpected contingencies. "Last night, quite late, another client of mine, Mr. Theodore Montagu, delivered a will to my residence over the office.''

''Montagu? And what did that swine want from you?''

''He came to deliver a will that the lady had given into his care. Her signature matched those on the other documents you gave me, and I am reasonably sure that it was no forgery. The document was also duly witnessed. However . . .''

Nicholas's brows lowered dangerously, and his eyes bored into the man's face. ''Will? Why on earth would Jessica write a will? Well, what did it say? Speak up!''

Mr. Darby cleared his throat again. ''It stated quite clearly that if anything was to happen to Mrs. Carlyle, in the event of her death her properties would be given completely into the care of Mr. and Mrs. Richard Montagu. But as I was saying, the will is not valid. I suspect that someone has tampered with the original. Also, Theodore insisted I not mention any of this to you, as it could prove to be very dangerous to your wife if you discovered the will's existence. But, as I've unfortunately had dealings with the young man, I felt that—''

''Why in heaven's name would Jessica leave all her wealth to Richard and Lucy?'' Nicholas demanded. ''And how could the will prove dangerous to Jessica? Unless . . .'' A dark heaviness grew within him, and the answer burst into his mind with frightful clarity.

''Mother of God! She thought it was me, that I was the one!''

Andrew Blackwell stepped forward and grabbed Nicholas by the shoulder, for he looked ready to fall. ''What is it?''

Nicholas's eyes slowly filled with a murderous light. Andrew backed away, thankful that the hatred and anger he saw was not directed at himself.

''It's all so obvious now. It explains so many things about Jessica's behavior. What a fool I've been! A damned bloody fool.'' With a groan he clapped a hand to his forehead. "Richard . . . I should have known. And I thought he was an old friend. It all makes sense now."

Andrew spoke quietly. "Sir, I'm afraid I don't follow your reasoning. Please elaborate."

With effort Nicholas reined in his feelings enough to explain. "It's all very devilishly clear now. I was such an imbecile to have fallen into the trap so easily. Good God!" He ran a hand through his tousled hair. "You see, Richard was the one who suggested that I marry your daughter. I must admit I was frightened that she might not agree to the marriage, but she did, and quickly. I know now that Richard used the threat of her family's danger to force her decision. You see, with Jessica safely wed, the Montagus were assured that she would retain the family estate and it would not go to charity. The task remained, however, to somehow force her into signing her holdings over to them, and the only way they could do that was to convince Jessica that I was trying to kill her in order to get her wealth."

Sarah mopped at her tears with a handkerchief. "Mr. Carlyle . . ."

"Nicholas, I know my daughter, and I know also that she is a very intelligent young woman. I have trouble believing she would immediately suspect you without just cause. What was the nature of these accidents?"

Nicholas had no desire to upset the woman further. He spoke abruptly. "That really isn't important. The real reason I believe that she suspected me was because—damn!" He thought of Charlotte and remembered the undeniable malice on her face when she had seen Jessica standing in the street before the runaway team. She had worn the same look the previous night when she had purposely thrown herself into his arms at the ball. Was she somehow involved as well? He turned away in mute frustration at his own idiocy.

A cold hand gripped his wrist with amazing force, and

he looked down into Sarah's features and soulful eyes. She spoke softly.

"Why would Jessica suspect you?"

Nicholas sighed heavily. "Jessica had very good reasons for suspecting me." He thought of the gunshot, the horses, the snake, and even the dead rat in her room. "And I admit I was to blame for feeding her doubts, although the circumstances were not as they seemed. Unfortunately, she had no other choice but to believe the repeated evidence before her eyes. I'm sure that had she been in an objective position—had she not fallen in love with me—she would have seen through the charade, but . . . I'll say nothing more on the subject except to my wife."

Suddenly he remembered Mr. Darby's words. The man was still sitting stiffly on the settee.

"Lawrence, you said something about the will being invalid."

"Yes, yes. Why do you think I journeyed out here in such haste? I only looked at the document briefly, but I can only assume that there are parts of it missing. There is one more thing. Mrs. Carlyle is to come to my office this morning at ten o'clock to collect a letter of introduction so that she can prove to the solicitors in England that she is heir to the Montagu estates."

"My God, she intends to journey to England?" Nicholas glanced at his timepiece. "It's eight o'clock now, and it will take at least several hours to ride into the city."

Before anyone could comment further, he was out the door and running toward the stable where his horse was already saddled. He grabbed the reins from the stableboy, and his foot was in the stirrup when he turned to see Titus and Andrew.

"Ah'se afraid dat we is goin' with yo', marse. Yo' almost' done charged off without even gettin' yo' self a weapon." Titus handed him a pistol. "Ah, 'spect yo' gonna need some help."

Gray eyes locked with dark brown, and he nodded. Then Andrew spoke softly.

"She's my daughter, and if anyone lays a hand to my little girl, they'll be answering to me as well." He patted the sturdy, double-barreled shotgun that Titus handed him. "Thank you both. Now let's be off."

Jessica huddled miserably in the corner of the carriage, Lucy's pistol pointed unwaveringly at her heart.

"It was so easy making use of that fool, Charlotte Rosemond," Lucy was saying. "She wanted to wound you so badly, she fell right in with my plans. If it hadn't been for her, we wouldn't have been able to convince you of your husband's guilt nearly so easily."

Jessica glared at the woman with a confidence she was far from feeling. "Yes, I was rather obliging, wasn't I? You certainly must have enjoyed yourself, and at my constant expense."

Lucy disliked the girl's attitude of fearless bravado and sought to twist her spurs deeper. "I did enjoy myself, my dove—almost as much as I enjoyed killing Jeremy and Elizabeth Montagu."

Jessica bolted upright, her shock momentarily wiping out her fear, and her eyes filled with bright tears of anger. "You murdered my parents? You?"

Lucy waved the pistol negligently. "Of course I did. Who else do you think would have done the deed?"

Theo frowned. "Mama, I do believe you should silence your flapping tongue," he said softly.

"What does it matter, Theo?" Her glittering blue eyes turned back to Jessica. "She won't have an opportunity to tell the tale." She continued in a conversational tone. "Shortly after your parents left New Orleans to search for the persons responsible for the attempts on Jeremy's life, they came to Lexington, probably to solicit Richard's help. It was too bad the fire I had set in New Orleans hadn't finished the job, but Jeremy always was a lucky bastard.

Why, that fortune rightfully belonged to Richard. Jeremy's father was a weak, sentimental fool to have left his wealth to the son who deserted him." Her eyes became hard.

"Richard was away on business that day. For secrecy's sake, your parents hired a boy to come to the house with a sealed letter telling Richard to meet them at that little glade you were so fond of frequenting when you stayed with us. I knew well the spot, so I went alone. They were so happy to see me, thinking that I was someone they could trust. Two shots was all that it took. You should have seen the look of surprise on their faces. Why, it was almost comical.

"I buried the bodies myself. Strange how they were never found. If you think of it, Jessica, you may have trampled the ground over their graves many times."

Lucy's eyes seemed to glow with delight in their dark sockets as Jessica backed further away into the corner, terrified by this maddened creature and filled with profound sadness at the thought of her gentle parents. She held her emotions at bay, refusing to think of their deaths. The hurt was too sharp, too overwhelming; it would completely debilitate her if she allowed it free rein. She spoke in a shaking whisper.

"You're insane. No one could live with the knowledge of such an evil deed all of these years and not be driven mad by it."

Lucy laughed. "One presupposes, however, that one must have a conscience to feel remorse. How fortunate that I rid myself of mine long ago. You must admit that I am an admirable actress. Playing the concerned aunt and doting wife is my forte, wouldn't you agree?"

Jessica's whole being was filled with the blackest fear, but she made a valiant effort not to show it. She knew that, should she give in to the terror, she would be undone. Somehow, she thought, I must remain calm and escape from these maniacs.

The image of Nicholas's face swam before her eyes, and she regretted bitterly that she had been so quick to condemn an innocent man. Yet deep within her also lay tremendous relief. Her love was *not* misplaced. Her heart *had* known all along what was right—that her husband was, indeed, worthy of her love.

No doubt Lucy would try to kill her, and she was horrified at the thought, horrified more that she would never see her husband again or tell him of her love. I do love you Nicholas, she thought, and I know now that you love me, too. She took a deep, shaky breath, pushing him out of her mind, determined not to yearn for the impossible.

Yet her spirit cried out in rebellion. No! There must be a way! Think, Jessica, think. She glanced at Theo from under the thick screen of her lashes. He had been very quiet and didn't seem at all pleased about the proceedings. Perhaps he was nervous. Could he possibly be the chink in Lucy's armour? She spoke only to keep herself from screaming aloud.

"Theo, I don't understand you. I know now that you and Lucy staged the runaway horses and the rescue, but I honestly thought that you and I were friends. I suppose you're as convincing an actor as your mother. Tell me, were you the one who fired at me on the trail that day, and did you place the rat and the snake in my room?"

He smiled mockingly into her pale face. "As soon as Nicholas agreed to marry you, Mama sent a fast rider to Charleston to give me a letter detailing her plan. I was shocked to learn of your existence. I, too, thought that the fortune would someday be mine. I was on the trail waiting for you that day, deliberately dressed to resemble Nicholas. We had to work quickly so you would have no time to become well acquainted with your husband's character, and we wanted you to distrust him almost immediately."

He leaned forward, his vivid blue eyes like brilliant, flashing stones. "And yes, I did put the dead rat in your desk. Mama wrote to tell me of your fear of rats. You made the mistake of telling her one day that you had seen one in Richard's stable, and that the creatures terrified you. It was child's play to sneak into Providence and put the rat in your secretaire."

"And the snake?"

"Apparently Titus and Nicholas overlooked one. It was almost too easy to place it in your armoire. I never thought it would strike you. After all, we needed you alive until you could write your will. I thought you would merely find the snake and assume that Nicholas had placed it there. I needed to keep the suspicion running high between you, because it was obvious that, despite all we had done, you were falling in love with him. I couldn't have that."

"Theo, why? It would be years until Richard would leave his wealth to you. Unless . . ." A cold feeling filled her. "Would you actually commit patricide?"

"Patricide? No, dear cuz, of course not." He paused for effect. "You see, my father—my *real* father—is already dead."

Chapter 22

Jessica gasped, raising a hand to her throat, and Theo laughed in delight at her shocked expression.

"Yes, my dear, you can say it. I am a bastard. You've no idea what that's like, do you Jessica? To feel ousted from proper society, always living on the fringes. That's why, I suspect, Richard had me sent away to Charleston at an early age. My eyes are too blue, my hair too blond. Now, only we three know of this family blight. But that number will soon change.

"My mother, though I have not always agreed with her methods, had been good to me—raising me as best she could, seeing that I received the best of everything, the finest education, the finest clothes. But there was something she could not give to me—a father's love. If I cannot have that, at least I shall have wealth."

Jessica spoke sadly, almost pityingly. "Wealth yes, Theo, but what of the blood on your hands? Will you think it worth the price as the years go on? And you, madam"—she turned her wavering gaze to Lucy—"how could you call yourself a mother, yet foster this hatred and evil in your son?"

Lucy smiled, a soft look coming into her eyes, and seemed to speak almost to herself. "It is worth any price. I've had to live with my secret for many years. I was going to leave Richard and go to Theo's father, but the man died, killed in a senseless duel. He was reckless that way, but it only made me love him more." Her eyes became unfocused, and the gun's nozzle dropped an inch. "Theo bares such an uncanny resemblance to him, its almost as though he never really died." Her eyes narrowed as she saw Jessica covertly studying the gun. She jerked it up again as she continued her story.

"I was wild with grief, and when I discovered very early that I was with child, I knew that it could not be Richard's. We had not been intimate in months, so I remedied that situation and hoped that when it came time for me to deliver, Richard would think the birth premature. He did. The birth was very difficult, and I was told that I would never have another child. Richard was desolate, but it only made him dote on Theodore all the more." She sighed shakily, remembering times long past. "As Theo grew older, it was obvious that he resembled neither I nor Richard. Richard's pleasure in the child very quickly declined, and although he has never confronted me regarding Theo's sire, I know he must suspect. I don't think he can bear the thought that his only child is actually another man's, so he keeps his silence." Her eyes focused again.

"Theo has seen the family estate, and he knows of his heritage. Don't believe that you can sway him from his course. We have been living two lives for so very long. Now it will end. Theo will someday have all that he deserves, and I can atone for all that I was never able to do for him." The softness died and the cold blue eyes were turned on Jessica once more. "And you are going to help me, Jessica."

Jessica shivered. "What are you going to do to me?"

Lucy chuckled. "Curious, my dear? Being the fair-minded woman that I am, I will enlighten you, since you seem so eager to know. First we are going to visit the lawyer, a Mr. Lawrence Darby, I believe. There he will give you a letter of introduction to your solicitors in England. I will have use for such a document, and if you do anything to prevent my getting it—do anything to alert Darby's suspicions—we will simply have to kill him, too. Then we will journey to the docks, where your husband has a large number of warehouses. We'll just tuck you into one of them, and then, as is my specialty, we will set it alight. Theo will seemingly rescue me from the flames, and we will both testify that Nicholas was the one who arranged for the fire to be set.

"I made certain to tell anyone who would listen last night how a snake had mysteriously been found in your room, and how Nicholas had dragged you out in a terrible storm. That, combined with your hasty marriage and rather substantial fortune, has gotten many people talking. How they love to gossip! Mr. Darby has even been warned not to tell Nicholas of the will. The lawyer will no doubt wonder about that juicy tidbit. We will collect our inheritances, and you, my dear, can go straight to Hades for all I care."

Jessica stared at Lucy coldly, though tremors gripped her body. "It sounds delightful," she said with feigned indifference as she turned shakily to stare out the window. Her gaze fastened intently on the wide, slow-moving hay wagon in front of their carriage.

This might be her only opportunity. She bunched her muscles, readying them to spring into action. Their driver, Jacob sawed on the reins, unable to pass the large wagon, and as the carriage slowed and jolted from side to side, Jessica leaned toward the door, grasping the handle. It opened easily, and she tumbled out into the muddy road, gasping at the shock of the impact, her arm throbbing painfully where she'd fallen on it. She immediately rolled to her feet, running for fear of her life. The sound of splintering wood came from behind her, followed by tumbling bales of hay and loud cursing as the two vehicles collided. Lifting her skirts high, she sprinted for the cover of the trees.

The warmth of her own blood trickling down her arm did not stop her, nor did the excited voices of Lucy and Theo. Fear filled her as she darted deeper into the woods, her eyes searching desperately for a hiding place. Pounding footsteps, came louder behind her, or perhaps it was only the beating of her heart. Hysterical tears rose to her eyes, and she gritted her teeth to keep from sobbing aloud her anguish. Where? Where could she hide? She ran on, heedless of the branches that whipped at her hair and face.

Her side began to ache with a sharp cramp, but she continued to run, cursing her stupidity in falling so easily into their twisted trap. Her eyes were blind with tears, and she almost didn't see the shattered, fallen tree. The vines clinging loosely to it were grayish-brown but thickly woven. Without a second thought, she scampered over the rotting trunk and wormed her way between it and the vines. She struggled to keep her rasping breath under control as the sounds of pursuit came closer. She closed her eyes tightly and prayed to God that Theo would pass her by. She heard him beating the bushes nearby and almost sighed in relief as his footsteps loudly moved away.

Jessica lay on her side, hugging the moldering tree, determined to stay there all day and all night if necessary. She was grateful that the dark gray velvet of her gown would help to conceal her position. Her heart slowed to a less frantic rhythm, and without her consciously willing it, the image of Nicholas's face floated hazily before her closed eyes. What a fool she had been, so in love with him that she hadn't seen Charlotte's act for what it was, so lacking confidence in herself that she had acted the peevish child. Yet she had loved him through it all—caring when she no longer cared, giving when she had nothing more to give.

Still he had some explaining to do regarding that abominable scene with Charlotte in the drawing room. She almost smiled at the thought. It didn't seem so important now. The only thing that mattered was that she was alive, and somehow, someway, she would get back to him. Somehow she would tell him how much she loved him. Her lips lifted in a soft smile as she remembered the night just past, and she opened her eyes, gazing upward at the clear, blue sky. It was the most beautiful sight she had ever seen.

Suddenly the black bore of a pistol blotted out the light, and she stared up into a different kind of vivid blue—the blue of Theo's eyes.

"Come, cuz, aren't you a bit old for hide-and-seek?"

Nicholas urged the frenzied Lancclot to a faster gait. The horse reveled in this unusual freedom and stretched himself out, his hooves hardly touching the hard-packed road, his lean, muscled flanks glistening with sweat.

"Where. Where would they be?" He was certain that Jessica was with Lucy, and that Lucy was somehow involved in the murderous plan. Perhaps Richard was in Charleston now, waiting for them. If Theo had requested a letter of introduction from Lawrence Darby, it was simple to conclude that Jessica was planning to go to England. Nicholas's hands tightened on the thin leather of the reins. Did she yet realize that they would probably never let her depart from Charleston? He pulled his timepiece from his pocket as Lancelot fairly flew over a large puddle in the road. Nine-thirty, and he still had a good hour and a half ride ahead of him. He'd be too late to intercept them at Darby's office. Even now Jessica could be dead, her beautiful green eyes forever cold and closed.

He wanted to scream his rage to the sky, but only ground his teeth in frustration, willing the miles between him and his wife to disappear. The docks. Surely they would go to the docks and try to escape the country if they meant to murder her. His rage grew over every mile that

Lancelot surged, his fury mounting along with his fear. If anything happened to Jessica, they would pay, and his vengeance would be sweet.

Titus and Andrew had fallen behind Nicholas's fleeing form, and any doubts that Andrew had about the man who had married his daughter evaporated as he followed Nicholas's possessed figure. He and Titus rode side by side in a mile-eating gallop, but they were unable to catch the swifter mount ahead of them.

Titus risked a quick glance at Andrew and shouted over the noise of the pounding hooves. "Marse done fell in love with yo' baby girl, if'n yo' ain't already figured it out."

Andrew stared straight ahead, his brown eyes shining with unshed tears.

"I know," he said.

Jessica was grateful for the respite. The longer it took them to fix the carriage wheel, the better her chances should anyone from Providence set out after her. She settled her gaze on Lucy, who held the pistol barely concealed under her skirt.

"Aren't you getting rather tired of holding that gun?" Jessica asked.

"Shut your mouth, missy. You're in no position to be asking questions."

Jessica was inwardly pleased at Lucy's shortened temper, although she wasn't foolish enough to test it. Lucy was nervous over the lengthy delay in repairing the damage done to the carriage when it had skidded into the side of the large hay wagon. Only now was the dust beginning to settle over the toppled hay bales that littered the road. The black driver of the wagon was vividly upset as he stalked from bale to bale, sometimes jerking them back onto the wagon, sometimes stopping to mutter obscenities at Theo's driver. Taking a deep breath, knowing full well that she was risking her life, Jessica ambled deliberately toward the man.

If Lucy was going to shoot her, she would have to do it in front of a witness, and they were a scant hour from the city. Already the road was becoming busy with morning traffic. Besides, if she was going to die, she thought sadly, better to have it done quickly.

"Sir," Jessica hailed the black man. She could see Lucy gritting her teeth, her hand moving convulsively under her heavy skirts. Lucy motioned to Theo, who moved forward.

"What yo' want now? Yo' gonna throw de rest o' dese bales down from de wagon? Lookit, all busted up all ober de place. Shoot! Mah master gonna have mah hide fo' dis."

"I'm terribly sorry." She saw Theo coming toward her, and spoke quickly and softly. "We'll be traveling to the Carlyle warehouses if you want to be paid for your trouble. Please, you've got to get—"

The black man muttered under his breath, snorted, and turned his back on Jessica as Theo jerked her arm. She winced, rubbing at the bandage she had applied over the slight wound, and yanked away from his grasp.

"What did you say to that man?" he demanded. She shrugged and turned her back on him. He grabbed at her again. "Tell me, or so help me I'll—"

"I apologized for the mess. I didn't notice anyone else doing so. He was rather angry. I doubt he heard a word I said." Her shoulders drooped, for she was sure that the man had ignored her. It had been a small chance at best, but a small chance was better than none at all.

An hour later the wheel was fixed. With the gun at her back, Jessica was prodded rudely into the carriage, and they once again set off, their pace sharply accelerated. Jessica's nerves were dancing as if afire already, and maintaining her composure became a matter of sheer determination. She constantly glanced out of the window, as if willing Nicholas to appear. Lucy seemed amused at her behavior and chuckled.

"I'm afraid it's hopeless, my dear. By now, the household is probably in an uproar wondering where we have gone. They'll not think to go to the docks, I'm quite sure." She leaned toward the cringing young woman, grinning evilly. "You're doomed."

Jessica shut her eyes tightly, yet could not repress a shudder. Silently she prayed.

Although he hadn't seriously done so since Jessica's fever, Nicholas too was praying, and fervently. "Just a little more time, please." He thundered around a bend in the road, and Lancelot barely reacted in time to jump over a bale of hay left carelessly in his path. The horse stumbled as he landed and nearly fell to his knees. Unprepared, his mind on Jessica, Nicholas didn't react to the horse's heaving body and tumbled from the saddle onto the road. He shook the fog from his brain, and automatically leaped up and went straight to his horse. Ascertaining that Lancelot was uninjured, he turned to vent his anger on the first person he saw.

When the black driver saw the fancy gent fall ignominiously to the ground, he couldn't help laughing at the man's predicament. It was marvelous, for once, to see a white man mussing up his fancy duds.

Nicholas heard the man's laughter and his tightly held control snapped. He marched over and grabbed him by his sweaty collar. "You! damned fool! I'd like to know what you find so bloody amusing."

The man stared at Nicholas stupidly, talking slowly to deliberately goad him. "Don't know what yo' talkin' 'bout, Mistah. Ain't mah fault some high-falutin' white folk went an' turned ober mah wagon, Mistah. No, ain't mah fault at all." He shook his head, surveying the damage yet to be rectified.

Nicholas released the man in disgust and turned away. "The name's Carlyle, Nicholas Carlyle."

The black man's head snapped up, and he hurriedly placed his reed-thin body in front of Nicholas, blocking his way to where Lancelot stood with lathered sides.

"Yo' Mistah Carlyle? Shoot! Yo' be owin' mah master some money fo' makin' mah wagon turn ober."

Nicholas stared at the man in puzzlement but did not stop walking. He shoved him out of the way, straightened Lancelot's saddle, and refastened the leather girth. The black man was insistent.

"Dat purty lady say dat Ah was to go to yo' warehouse an' git some money fo' de damages."

Now Nicholas turned his regard on the man, bearly able to hope. The man recognized the intensity of Nicholas's gaze and involuntarily drew back.

"What pretty lady are you talking about?" He shook the man by his bony shoulders.

"Dey was de white folk what hit mah wagon." His lower lip shot out. "Dey didn' say nothin', but dat purty lady with de big green eyes, she say dat if'n Ah comes to de Carlyle warehouse she would pay me fo' mah troubles."

"Good God man, when was this?"

"Lemme see." The man sucked on his teeth for a moment and scratched his head. Nicholas could hardly keep from shaking him again. "Seem to me it were short an hour ago. Dey broke one o' dem wheels on dat fancy coach an' had to fix it."

The men looked up as two galloping horses came around the bend in the road. Nicholas spoke quickly.

"Andrew, Titus. Jessica has been taken to the docks, to my warehouses. This man saw her." He turned back to the now frightened man, who wasn't sure whether he should have opened his mouth. "Was she all right? Unharmed?"

"She looked fine to me. Her clothes was muddied up a bit, an' she had a bloody bandage 'round her arm, but didn't look like nothin' serious . . ."

"Thank God! Listen, man. You go to my warehouses, and I'll gladly repay you for the damage—and thank you."

Nicholas swung up into the saddle and reached down to squeeze the man's shoulder. With a flurry of hooves the three horses charged off down the road, heading for the docks. The men rode grimly now that they knew there was a chance. The horses, sensing their riders' moods, seemed to draw strength from some unknown quarter and surged ahead with powerful muscles.

The warehouse was mostly empty now. The autumn harvest was long past, and spring seemed a long way in coming. Theo had instructed his driver to let them out at the battery. The man and two ladies seemed to stroll casually up and down the boardwalk, then took a sharp turn. Theo took one of Jessica's arms and Lucy the other. Struggle though she might, Jessica was dragged to the damp warehouse. Lucy had triumphantly pulled out the key to unlock the heavy doors, and Jessica was shoved into the damp, musty interior.

"I'm afraid we won't be able to tarry, my dear. It was most disturbing to find out from Mr. Darby's clerk that Mr. Darby had traveled out early to see Nicholas. I really would have liked to have had that letter, but alas, it is a small setback. The haste with which you requested it speaks ill enough for your husband, but I'm wandering off the subject again. We wasted enough valuable time strolling on the boardwalk—much more than I had intended, but we wanted everyone to see you in our friendly company. It will make things look so much more damning for your husband."

She looked about and, spotting a lamp, quickly lit it. "Theo told me you had a wonderful time walking the battery with him the day he toured the city with you. I hope you were satisfied with our choice for your stroll, for it is likely the last thing you will ever see." She swung the lamp around to make her point.

"It's a shame we won't be able to see much more of one another. This is where we say good-bye, my dove. Such a pity you'll never see your lovely estate in England. It is quite beautiful, you know."

Jessica shivered in spite of her grim resolve, and Lucy roughly pushed her down against some moldering bales of cotton. The damp smell filled her quivering nostrils.

"Cold, my dear? It will soon be warm enough, don't you worry."

Jessica raised pleading green eyes to Theo. "Please, Theo, don't do this thing. I can't believe you would go along with the whims of a madwoman."

Theo cupped Jessica's chin gently in his hand. Her eyes overflowed, the tears falling in crystal drops, but it did little to waver his resolve. "Well done, cuz. You have perfected your pitiful act, but my hands are already bloodied, and I must see it through. What's just a little bit more when I have so much to gain? Sometimes I wish it could have been someone else, Jessica. I was in danger of falling in love with you, but . . ." He glanced at Lucy. "I have other obligations. Farewell, cousin."

"It's not too late, Theo! If you'll only—"

Lucy stepped forward and shoved a long length of rope in Theo's hands. "That's enough from you, Mrs. Carlyle. Tie her tightly, son." She held the lamp she carried high in the air. The gun was lowered as she searched the darkness. "I don't see the whale oil. Are you certain you brought it in last night?"

Theo placed Jessica's hands roughly behind her back, and she glared her contempt into his handsome, corrupt face. She felt something hard and heavy behind her and grasped it in her clutching fingers. Without thinking, she raised the hammer up and threw it at the gun in Lucy's hand. Her aim was true, and it painfully connected with Lucy's white knuckles. The gun spun out of the woman's hand and disappeared into a dark corner with a loud, echoing clatter. Lucy spun around, intent on retrieving the pistol, as Theo bent to restrain Jessica more forcefully. Her knee came up, striking him in the groin, with a dull groan of pain he slumped over.

Lucy turned at the sound, swinging the lamp wildly in a wide arc. It hit the side of the wall and the glass shattered, sending the whale oil and flames flying in all directions. In an instant the moldy bales were alight.

Jessica jumped to her feet. For a split second her legs buckled under her, but she quickly regained her balance, to Lucy's roar of rage, and streaked for the door. Theo came staggering after her, his face red and strained. Her hands were on the bolt drawing it back when she felt hard hands catch her around the waist and haul her backward. She fought like a woman possessed, kicking and lashing out with her fists, but Theo was too strong. Her soul cringed with heartrending terror as she heard the sharp click of the pistol hammer being pulled back.

The muzzle was applied painfully to her temple, and Lucy's mad, bright eyes came within inches of her own. The red haze of the fire gave Lucy the appearance of a malignant, twisted fiend from the stygian depths of hell, and Jessica was incapable of stifling the terrified scream that rose to her lips. The macabre mask of Lucy's face split into an even more frightening grin. She prodded Jessica with the gun, laughing into Jessica's horrified face. Then she sobered abruptly, and her gaze took on a penetrating determination.

"You die now," she said.

Jessica whimpered and closed her eyes, tensing. She heard the booming sound as the gun went off and wondered at the lack of pain. Her look of surprise mirrored Lucy's and she saw, almost as if in a dream, the woman reeling back and falling upon the burning bales. The flames licked hungrily at her clothing, but Jessica was certain from the look on Lucy's face that she couldn't feel anything any longer. Theo leaped toward his mother's body, and Jessica turned away from the grisly sight—and right into the arms of her husband. She stared into his face. It must be part of a dream! But the gentle hands that cupped her face were real, and the frantic gray eyes were alive with love and hope.

"Nicholas . . ."

She had barely murmured his name before Theo, charging like a maddened animal, threw his body against Nicholas. Jessica and Nicholas went tumbling to the floor. Nicholas threw the younger man off and pulled Jessica to her feet, placing her behind him. He backed cautiously toward the door and pushed her through. Squinting through the smoke that came billowing out of the open doorway, he saw Theo come staggering out, his head hung low, his eyes glazed with grief and pain. His voice was cracked and raw.

"You killed her! You killed her!"

Jessica gasped as Theo raised his hand, Lucy's discarded pistol clutched shakily in his grasp. His eyes seemed to lose focus for a moment, and Nicholas seized the opportunity to fly forward. Jessica screamed as the pistol discharged, but Nicholas now held Theo's wrist firmly, and the shot had gone off wildly into the air. They struggled for a moment, both intent on claiming the weapon, but Nicholas wrenched the gun away, and Jessica heard a splash as it hit the choppy waters of the bay. A grim smile twisted her husband's features, and she felt a cold shudder crawl up her spine at his murderous expression.

"So, Mr. Montagu, at last we meet honestly face to face."

Theo spun away, ignoring the jeering words, and sent his fist flying into Nicholas's face. Nicholas managed to dodge the blow and sent his own tightly balled fist into Theo's stomach. The man doubled over and staggered back. Nicholas advanced on him, no pity in his eyes, and spoke softly.

"You bloody bastard . . . now we will see how you fight when matched with a man!"

At the word *bastard* Theo's head snapped up, and with a howl of rage he flew at Nicholas, his blue eyes blazing insanely. He buried his fist in Nicholas's stomach and it was Nicholas's turn to double over, but he did not falter. His leg reached out and tripped the man, and Theo landed in the dust at Nicholas's feet. Nicholas picked him up by the cloth of his redingote and smashed him up against the heated wall of the warehouse. Theo cried out in agony as Nicholas continued to batter him against the wall, again and again.

"Stop, Nicholas, stop," Jessica pleaded. "Stop now, or you'll surely kill him. Please, he's suffered enough."

Nicholas released Theodore Montagu, and his limp frame crumpled to the ground as choking and moaning sounds issued from his bruised throat. Nicholas turned, shaking his head, and focused his gaze on the rumpled mud- and soot-stained form of his precious wife.

"Jessica! Thank God."

A moment later she was clutched to his chest, sobbing out her relief and joy. He stared down at her with an expression of such love and tenderness that she knew that she must have been an absolute blind fool not to have recognized the truth of his feelings. Her dirty fingers reached up to lightly touch his lips.

"I wouldn't blame you if you beat me for a runaway wife," she said softly, "but if you must know the truth. I do love you." She closed her eyes for a second. "I love you very much."

Suddenly his mouth was upon hers, telling her everything she had ever wanted to know, and she felt her sense of melancholy disappear from her life forever. A discreet throat-clearing broke them apart, and Jessica lifted her eyes to those of her father. She let out a cry of joy.

"Papa! Oh, Papa. You are here!" She threw herself into his embrace, and his eyes were unashamedly wet as he held her shaking body close to his.

"My daughter. My Jessie."

He rocked her in his arms, smiling into the fond eyes of his new son-in-law, until the sounds of loud voices broke them apart. Titus stepped forward, holding the limp Theo by the shoulders.

"What y'all want me to do with dis here white trash?"

Jessica raised her tearstained face from her father's comforting shoulder and looked about her in confusion. The dock had suddenly become a noisy mass of chaos. Shouting men were swarming over the docks, attempting to put out the fire, and a large crowd had gathered to observe Jessica and Nicholas with much interest. She thought fleetingly of Lucy's body lying forgotten in the inferno, then dismissed the thought with an effort. How would Richard bear the sad news, she wondered. She saw Nicholas motion to a uniformed man standing nearby.

"Cliff!" The man came quickly toward them. Nicholas introduced the sheriff then indicated Theo. "I believe you'll find that this man here set the fire, among his other crimes. I also think he might know something of the murder of Charles MacKensie, the man who stole the horses that nearly ran down my wife. Could you please take care of him?"

Jessica moved away from her father, and Nicholas slipped an arm around her waist. His gaze softened as he looked down at his wife. "I've other much more important matters to attend to."

Chapter 23

Jessica snuggled more closely against her husband's chest and studied the long, lean fingers that held Lancelot's reins loosely in front of her. The past few hours had been full of confessions and revelations for both of them. They were still amazed at how easily they had been manipulated by the seemingly guileless Lucy Montagu. Jessica shook her head, but she knew now that several good things had come out of the tragic affair: she and Nicholas had found each other, and she would be able to help Richard with his failing ranch. She smiled and for the first time in months felt completely at ease with her husband and her life. She was glad she had insisted that Nicholas not hire a coach to take them back to Providence. She pushed herself even more snuggly against his loins, delighted with his body's almost immediate reaction. He leaned forward, tightening his arms around her, his breath soft against her ear.

"You are a wicked woman to tease me so, Jessica."

Her lips curved in a satisfied smile that she was careful to hide. "You don't think that Lancelot is inconvenienced by carrying us both do you?"

"I think he is more than capable, and now that I have

discovered the advantages of such an arrangement, I fear this will not be the last time he bears both our weights.''

Jessica smiled more widely, then leaned back again. The events of the morning and the ''accidents'' of the recent past suddenly sprang to her mind, and the smile flew from her lips. Though they had talked at length about all that had happened to them, there was still one thing that she had not been able to mention. She stared up into her husband's smiling eyes. No shadows lingered in their clear gray depths, and she was hesitant to shatter the comfortable mood. Yet she felt that while the incident was fresh in her mind, she was obligated to speak of it.

''Nicholas . . .''

His grin became teasing as he noted her serious expression. ''Jessica, my love, I am generally called 'Nick' by almost everyone I know. Not even my mother called me Nicholas. Are you still too shy to be so familiar with me?''

She grinned impishly. ''No, not at all, but you simply do not remind me of a 'Nick.' ''

His eyebrows rose sharply in question. ''And what, pray tell, is a 'Nick,' Jessica?''

She feigned a countenance of serious concentration. ''A 'Nick,' my dearest husband, is the sort of fellow who gambles recklessly, who spends his unearned money much too extravagantly on trifles, who scandalizes women with his rakish, leering behavior, and who drinks to excess while regaling his colleagues with his sexual exploits.'' Her eyes grew wide and innocent. ''That hardly seems to describe you, does it?''

Crinkling lines appeared around his eyes as he laughed heartily. ''That sort of fellow does sound rather like a thoroughgoing scoundrel, doesn't he, my dear? I assure you that I have never had the misfortune of meeting anyone remotely fitting such an unsavory description.''

Jessica smiled into his eyes. ''Liar,'' she said.

He squeezed her tightly and, shrugging, gave her the win. ''But seriously, my love, what was it you wanted to ask me?''

She took a deep breath and plunged ahead. "I was wondering why you were so familiar with Charlotte in the drawing room the day of the storm."

"Familiar with Charlotte? What are you talking about?"

"Don't act innocent with me, Nicholas." Jessica's voice was dry with displeasure as she stared straight ahead of her at her father's and Titus's broad backs.

"Honestly, Jessica, although I've found I've a remarkable ability to act stupid lately, I swear I've no idea what you are talking about."

"Is that so, *Nick*? How's this then? I saw you in the drawing room with her, and from the way you two were behaving, it seemed obvious to me that you were much enamored of her."

"You aren't saying that you were crouching in some dark corner of the room spying on me?"

"Of course not," Jessica snapped. "That would have been far too obvious." She threw her head back in a dramatic gesture. "For your information, I was crouched *outside* the drawing room behind the curtains in the dining room."

"I see."

"Now, what do you have to say for yourself?"

"Nothing, except that I shall make it a point to be more wary in the future when I conduct illicit liaisons with my mistresses."

"You—you—"

He laughed and tightened his arms around her stiff form. "That's less than you deserve for being where you should not have been, suspicious baggage. I see that Alcey showed you her favorite spot." He chuckled to himself. "I should have known. It's no wonder you wanted no part of me. Did you hear the conversation between Charlotte and me as well?"

Jessica pouted and answered reluctantly. "Not all of it. You were speaking too softly most of the time."

"Ah, I see. Then you didn't hear me telling Charlotte

that I would have no further dealings with her if she did not cease harassing you, and that I would no longer stand for her insulting behavior toward you?''

''And that is why she flew into your arms?''

''No doubt you also did not see me push her away.''

''Oh yes, you did do that, didn't you?''

''Yes. Now, is there anything else you would like to know while we are on the subject?''

''Yes.'' Jessica heard him sigh with impatience, but she went on anyway. ''If you do not care for Charlotte, as you say, why did you stare so murderously at Theodore when he was dancing with her at the ball?'' She bowed her head contritely. ''I thought you were jealous of the attention Charlotte was receiving.''

''As much as I dislike admitting such an emotion, I was jealous, but not of Charlotte. I wanted to kill Theodore the day I found you two together in the shack, though I know now that it was innocent, and I felt the same way every time I saw you with your heads together having a wonderful time—and especially the night of the ball, when you were so deeply engrossed in conversation.''

''You saw him talking to me?''

''Again, I am forced to admit that I couldn't help myself from watching you all evening, and I was jealous of the attention *you* were receiving, not Charlotte. I—''

''You were jealous?''

He sighed again. ''Yes.''

''How marvelous!'' She smiled in delight before once again becoming serious. ''I thought you took me to the ball only as a convenient excuse for you and Charlotte to more easily carry on your liaison.''

''Now, Jessica, that is the sort of thing *Nick* would do. It never entered *Nicholas's* mind. You were uppermost in his thoughts, as you always are in his heart.''

''Really, Nicholas, you must do something about this tendency toward prevarication. It will be your undoing.'' Then she sobered once more. ''It broke my heart to see you with Charlotte in the drawing room. After what had transpired in the overseer's hut, I honestly thought you had some deep feelings for me, although I felt you would rather die than admit them." She bowed her head dejectedly. "Why didn't you tell me the truth of your feelings for me?"

He leaned down to place a soft kiss at her temple. "It was only when you were delirious from the snakebite that I discovered I had fallen in love with you, and I wanted you to come to me willingly. I realized only then how my father must have suffered with the death of my mother. I think I finally understood and forgave him." He took a deep breath. "I thought you hated me, and I knew you would never believe a declaration of my love. So I was determined to make you fall in love with me. After last night I thought I had succeeded. When I discovered that you had fled from the house this morning, I was frantic with worry."

"It was fortunate that Mr. Darby is so conscientious."

"Yes, I must remember to give him a large bonus. When he came to the house this morning with, of all things, news of your will, I was frankly stunned."

Jessica's face grew uncomfortably hot, and she squirmed in the saddle. Nicholas noted her discomfort.

"You would do well to fidget, little witch. I didn't know whether to beat you for a stubborn, independent, mule-headed fool, or rush out of the house like a wild maniac in search of you." The arms that held her so closely and possessively belied his angry words. "Fortunately for you, I chose the latter, and I was equally fortunate to meet up with that black fellow with the hay wagon."

Jessica jerked in his arms, remembering her fear in talking to the angry man. "I knew I had to attempt something. I never dreamed that he would remember anything I said to him."

"After my abbreviated chat with the man, I'm afraid I

rushed off again, looking like the noble Sir Lancelot in search of his lost Lady Gwenhwyvar.'' His voice grew curt and irritated. ''Damn you, little conniving baggage, for making me look the love-smitten imbecile!''

Jessica's smile became indecently wide as Nicholas continued. ''I've never ridden Lancelot as punishingly, but he was swift, and I made good time into the city, though I had no idea in which warehouse you were being held. When I heard a scream, I didn't stop to think. I swung open the door, and . . . you know the rest.''

Jessica nodded, mentally reliving those terrifying moments. How fragile life was! How quickly it could be ended. ''It's still so difficult to believe Lucy was so very malignant—that she planned to set us against one another from the very beginning. And she would have succeeded sooner if I hadn't fallen in love with you.''

She felt the gentle pressure of his fingers under her chin and lifted her face to his in an unhurried kiss.

Andrew Blackwell turned around in his saddle and stared at the embracing couple. He nudged Titus with his elbow, and the black man smiled broadly, too. The two men shared an indulgent look.

Lancelot continued to plod slowly behind the other horses long after the reins had fallen from his master's usually attentive grasp. Jessica and Nicholas slowly became aware that the horse had come to a stop when they heard a screech of joy and the sound of running feet. Jessica reluctantly drew away from her husband and looked over Lancelot's drooping ears to see her mother and brothers running toward her from the steps of Providence. As she slid from the tired horse, Joey was the first one to reach her.

''Jessie!''

He catapulted into her arms, and with tears streaming down her face, she lifted him high in the air and hugged him tightly to her, delighted to feel his thin arms around her neck and his healthy body in her arms. Then, to his boyish disgust, she proceeded to lavish his face with happy kisses. Finally he squirmed away from her attentions, and Jessica set him carefully on his feet. Straightening up she found herself face to face with her mother. The two women regarded each other warmly for a long moment. Sarah finally broke the silence.

"Well, you're a bit thin and your lovely gown a little worse for wear, but I can see that you've finally grown into a beautiful woman. I must admit that I had my doubts, Dolly."

"Mama . . ." They were suddenly in each other's arms, kissing and hugging, laughing and crying.

Nicholas dismounted from his horse and quietly observed the way Jessica's family gathered eagerly around her. Her brothers were all talking excitedly, each vying for her attention. He felt a sharp pang of envy and the uncomfortable sting of suddenly being an outsider in her life. Then she broke away from them and reached over to draw him into the family's midst, smiling her brilliant, lovely smile. Nicholas lost himself in the deep, green pools, and the uncomfortable feeling receded.

"Mama," Jessica said, "remember what we said about love before I left Virginia?"

"Yes, Dolly."

Jessica raised loving eyes to her husband's face, and he unashamedly returned her stare. "I understand now what you meant."

Sarah Blackwell nodded as she looked into her husband's eyes.

"I know, Jessica."